F. Hodgson Burnett 著

張建平 譯

THE SECRET GARDEN

秘密花園

商務印書館

本書譯文由上海世紀出版股份有限公司譯文出版社授權使用

書　　名：*The Secret Garden* 秘密花園
作　　者：F. Hodgson Burnett
插　　圖：Charles Robinson
譯　　者：張建平
責任編輯：張朗欣　黃家麗
封面設計：楊愛文
出　　版：商務印書館（香港）有限公司
　　　　　香港筲箕灣耀興道 3 號東滙廣場 8 樓
　　　　　http://www.commercialpress.com.hk
發　　行：香港聯合書刊物流有限公司
　　　　　香港新界大埔汀麗路 36 號中華商務印刷大廈 3 字樓
印　　刷：中華商務彩色印刷有限公司
　　　　　香港新界大埔汀麗路 36 號中華商務印刷大廈
版　　次：2019 年 1 月第 1 版第 2 次印刷
　　　　　© 2015 商務印書館（香港）有限公司
　　　　　ISBN 978 962 07 0390 4
　　　　　Printed in Hong Kong

Publisher's Note 出版説明

一個秘密花園，奪去了瑪麗姑母的性命，她姑丈因而對花園心生討厭，將它關閉；這個秘密花園，卻將故事主角連結起來：他們不斷耕耘，使花園重現生機，過程中不僅令驕縱的瑪麗變得溫柔有禮，也令柯林重拾自信，更重要的是他們都獲得了一份難得的友誼。經典故事讀來饒有興味，更啟發讀者對人生的思考。

初、中級英語程度讀者使用本書時，先閱讀英文原文，如遇到理解障礙，則參照中譯作為輔助。在英文原文結束之前或附註解，標註古英語、非現代詞彙拼寫形式及語法；同樣，在譯文結束之前或附註解，以幫助讀者理解原文故事背景。如有餘力，讀者可在閱讀原文部份段落後，查閱相應中譯，觀察同樣詞句在雙語中不同的表達。

《秘密花園》是一個關於友誼、決心和毅力的故事，一讀饒有趣味，再讀更能體會背後的深意。秘密花園重現生機，活在陰霾之下的瑪麗姑丈也獲得了新生，由此可知每個人心中都有個秘密花園，只要打開心房，用愛不斷灌溉，定會開出美麗的花朵。

商務印書館 (香港) 有限公司
編輯出版部

Contents 目錄

1.

There Is No One Left

When Mary Lennox was sent to Misselthwaite Manor to live with her uncle everybody said she was the most disagreeable-looking child ever seen. It was true, too. She had a little thin face and a little thin body, thin light hair and a sour expression. Her hair was yellow, and her face was yellow because she had been born in India and had always been ill in one way or another. Her father had held a position under the English Government and had always been busy and ill himself, and her mother had been a great beauty who cared only to go to parties and amuse herself with gay people. She had not wanted a little girl at all, and when Mary was born she handed her over to the care of an Ayah, who was made to understand that if she wished to please the Mem Sahib she must keep the child out of sight as much as possible. So when she was a sickly, fretful, ugly little baby she was kept out of the way, and when she became a sickly, fretful, toddling thing she was kept out of the way also. She never remembered seeing familiarly anything but the dark faces of her Ayah and the other native servants, and as they always obeyed her and gave her her own way in everything, because the Mem Sahib would be angry if she was disturbed by her crying, by the time she was six years old she was as tyrannical and selfish a little pig as ever lived. The young English governess who came to teach her to read and write disliked her so much that she gave up her place in three months, and when other governesses came to try to fill it they always went away in a shorter time than the first one. So if Mary had not chosen to really want to know how to read books she would never have learned her letters at all.

One frightfully hot morning, when she was about nine years old, she awakened feeling very cross, and she became crosser still when she saw that the servant who stood by her bedside was not her Ayah.

'Why did you come?' she said to the strange woman. 'I will not let you stay. Send my Ayah to me.'

The woman looked frightened, but she only stammered that the Ayah could not come and when Mary threw herself into a passion and beat and kicked her, she looked only more frightened and repeated that it was not possible for the Ayah to come to Missie Sahib.

There was something mysterious in the air that morning. Nothing was done in its regular order and several of the native servants seemed missing, while those whom Mary saw slunk or hurried about with ashy and scared faces. But no one would tell her anything and her Ayah did not come. She was actually left alone as the morning went on, and at last she wandered out into the garden and began to play by herself under a tree near the veranda. She pretended that she was making a flower-bed, and she stuck big scarlet hibiscus blossoms into little heaps of earth, all the time growing more and more angry and muttering to herself the things she would say and the names she would call Saidie when she returned.

'Pig! Pig! Daughter of Pigs!' she said, because to call a native a pig is the worst insult of all.

She was grinding her teeth and saying this over and over again when she heard her mother come out on the veranda with some one[1]. She was with a fair young man and they stood talking together in low strange voices. Mary knew the fair young man who looked like a boy. She had heard that he was a very young officer who had just come from England. The child stared at him, but she stared most at her mother. She always did this when she had a chance to see her, because the Mem Sahib—Mary used to call her that oftener than anything else—was such a tall, slim, pretty person and wore such lovely clothes. Her hair was like curly silk and she had a delicate little nose which seemed to be disdaining things, and she had large laughing eyes. All her clothes were thin and floating, and Mary said they were 'full of lace'. They looked fuller of lace than ever this morning, but her eyes were not laughing at all. They were large and scared and lifted imploringly to the fair boy officer's face.

'Is it so very bad? Oh, is it?' Mary heard her say.

'Awfully,' the young man answered in a trembling voice. 'Awfully, Mrs. Lennox. You ought to have gone to the hills two weeks ago.'

The Mem Sahib wrung her hands.

'Oh, I know I ought!' she cried. 'I only stayed to go to that silly dinner party. What a fool I was!'

At that very moment such a loud sound of wailing broke out from the servants' quarters that she clutched the young man's arm, and Mary stood shivering from head to foot. The wailing grew wilder and wilder.

'What is it? What is it?' Mrs. Lennox gasped.

'some one^2 has died,' answered the boy officer. 'You did not say it had broken out among your servants.'

'I did not know!' the Mem Sahib cried. 'Come with me! Come with me!' and she turned and ran into the house.

After that appalling things happened, and the mysteriousness of the morning was explained to Mary. The cholera had broken out in its most fatal form and people were dying like flies. The Ayah had been taken ill in the night, and it was because she had just died that the servants had wailed in the huts. Before the next day three other servants were dead and others had run away in terror. There was panic on every side, and dying people in all the bungalows.

During the confusion and bewilderment of the second day Mary hid herself in the nursery and was forgotten by everyone. Nobody thought of her, nobody wanted her, and strange things happened of which she knew nothing. Mary alternately cried and slept through the hours. She only knew that people were ill and that she heard mysterious and frightening sounds. Once she crept into the dining-room and found it empty, though a partly finished meal was on the table and chairs and plates looked as if they had been hastily pushed back when the diners rose suddenly for some reason. The child ate some fruit and biscuits, and being thirsty she drank a glass of wine which stood nearly filled. It was sweet, and she did not know how strong it was. Very soon it made her intensely drowsy, and she went back to her nursery and shut herself in again, frightened by cries she heard in the huts and by the hurrying sound of feet. The wine made her so sleepy that she could scarcely keep her eyes open and she lay down on her bed and knew nothing more for a long time.

Many things happened during the hours in which she slept so heavily, but she was not disturbed by the wails and the sound of things being carried in and out of the bungalow.

When she awakened she lay and stared at the wall. The house was perfectly still. She had never known it to be so silent before. She heard neither voices nor footsteps, and wondered if everybody had got well of the cholera and all the trouble was over. She wondered also who would take care of her now her Ayah was dead. There would be a new Ayah, and perhaps she would know some new stories. Mary had been rather tired of the old ones. She did not cry because her nurse had died. She was not an affectionate child and had never cared much for any one[3]. The noise and hurrying about and wailing over the cholera had frightened her, and she had been angry because no one seemed to remember that she was alive. Every one[4] was too panic-stricken to think of a little girl no one was fond of. When people had the cholera it seemed that they remembered nothing but themselves. But if every one had got well again, surely some one would remember and come to look for her.

But no one came, and as she lay waiting the house seemed to grow more and more silent. She heard something rustling on the matting and when she looked down she saw a little snake gliding along and watching her with eyes like jewels. She was not frightened, because he was a harmless little thing who would not hurt her and he seemed in a hurry to get out of the room. He slipped under the door as she watched him.

'How queer and quiet it is,' she said. 'It sounds as if there was no one in the bungalow but me and the snake.'

Almost the next minute she heard footsteps in the compound, and then on the veranda. They were men's footsteps, and the men entered the bungalow and talked in low voices. No one went to meet or speak to them and they seemed to open doors and look into rooms.

'What desolation!' she heard one voice say. 'That pretty, pretty woman! I suppose the child, too. I heard there was a child, though no one ever saw her.'

Mary was standing in the middle of the nursery when they opened the door a few minutes later. She looked an ugly, cross little thing and was frowning because she was beginning to be hungry and feel disgracefully neglected. The first man who came in was a large officer she had once seen talking to her father. He looked tired and troubled, but when he saw her he was so startled that he almost jumped back.

'Barney!' he cried out. 'There is a child here! A child alone! In a place like this! Mercy on us, who is she!'

'I am Mary Lennox,' the little girl said, drawing herself up stiffly. She thought the man was very rude to call her father's bungalow 'A place like this!' 'I fell asleep when every one had the cholera and I have only just wakened up. Why does nobody come?'

'It is the child no one ever saw!' exclaimed the man, turning to his companions. 'She has actually been forgotten!'

'Why was I forgotten?' Mary said, stamping her foot. 'Why does nobody come?'

The young man whose name was Barney looked at her very sadly. Mary even thought she saw him wink his eyes as if to wink tears away.

'Poor little kid!' he said. 'There is nobody left to come.'

It was in that strange and sudden way that Mary found out that she had neither father nor mother left; that they had died and been carried away in the night, and that the few native servants who had not died also had left the house as quickly as they could get out of it, none of them even remembering that there was a Missie Sahib. That was why the place was so quiet. It was true that there was no one in the bungalow but herself and the little rustling snake.

2.

Mistress Mary Quite Contrary

Mary had liked to look at her mother from a distance and she had thought her very pretty, but as she knew very little of her she could scarcely have been expected to love her or to miss her very much when she was gone. She did not miss her at all, in fact, and as she was a self-absorbed child she gave her entire thought to herself, as she had always done. If she had been older she would no doubt have been very anxious at being left alone in the world, but she was very young, and as she had always been taken care of, she supposed she always would be. What she thought was that she would like to know if she was going to nice people, who would be polite to her and give her her own way as her Ayah and the other native servants had done.

She knew that she was not going to stay at the English clergyman's house where she was taken at first. She did not want to stay. The English clergyman was poor and he had five children nearly all the same age and they wore shabby clothes and were always quarreling and snatching toys from each other. Mary hated their untidy bungalow and was so disagreeable to them that after the first day or two nobody would play with her. By the second day they had given her a nickname which made her furious.

It was Basil who thought of it first. Basil was a little boy with impudent blue eyes and a turned-up nose and Mary hated him. She was playing by herself under a tree, just as she had been playing the day the cholera broke out. She was making heaps of earth and paths for a garden and Basil came and stood near to watch her. Presently he got rather interested and suddenly made a suggestion.

'Why don't you put a heap of stones there and pretend it is a rockery?' he said. 'There in the middle,' and he leaned over her to point.

'Go away!' cried Mary. 'I don't want boys. Go away!'

For a moment Basil looked angry, and then he began to tease. He was always teasing his sisters. He danced round and round her and made faces and sang and laughed.

> 'Mistress Mary, quite contrary,
> How does your garden grow?
> With silver bells, and cockle shells,
> And marigolds all in a row.'

He sang it until the other children heard and laughed, too; and the crosser Mary got, the more they sang 'Mistress Mary, quite contrary'; and after that as long as she stayed with them they called her 'Mistress Mary Quite Contrary' when they spoke of her to each other, and often when they spoke to her.

'You are going to be sent home,' Basil said to her, 'at the end of the week. And we're glad of it.'

'I am glad of it, too,' answered Mary. 'Where is home?'

'She doesn't know where home is!' said Basil, with seven-year-old scorn. 'It's England, of course. Our grandmama lives there and our sister Mabel was sent to her last year. You are not going to your grandmama. You have none. You are going to your uncle. His name is Mr. Archibald Craven.'

'I don't know anything about him,' snapped Mary.

'I know you don't,' Basil answered. 'You don't know anything. Girls never do. I heard father and mother talking about him. He lives in a great, big, desolate old house in the country and no one goes near him. He's so cross he won't let them, and they wouldn't come if he would let them. He's a hunchback, and he's horrid.'

'I don't believe you,' said Mary; and she turned her back and stuck her fingers in her ears, because she would not listen any more.

But she thought over it a great deal afterward; and when Mrs. Crawford told her that night that she was going to sail away to England in a few days and go to her uncle, Mr. Archibald Craven, who lived at Misselthwaite Manor, she looked so stony and stubbornly uninterested that they did not know what to think about her. They tried to be kind to her, but she only turned her face away when Mrs. Crawford attempted to kiss her, and held herself stiffly when Mr. Crawford patted her shoulder.

'She is such a plain child,' Mrs. Crawford said pityingly, afterward. 'And her mother was such a pretty creature. She had a very pretty manner, too, and Mary has the most unattractive ways I ever saw in a child. The children call her 'Mistress Mary Quite Contrary,' and though it's naughty of them, one can't help understanding it.'

'Perhaps if her mother had carried her pretty face and her pretty manners oftener into the nursery Mary might have learned some pretty ways too. It is very sad, now the poor beautiful thing is gone, to remember that many people never even knew that she had a child at all.'

'I believe she scarcely ever looked at her,' sighed Mrs. Crawford. 'When her Ayah was dead there was no one to give a thought to the little thing. Think of the servants running away and leaving her all alone in that deserted bungalow. Colonel McGrew said he nearly jumped out of his skin when he opened the door and found her standing by herself in the middle of the room.'

Mary made the long voyage to England under the care of an officer's wife, who was taking her children to leave them in a boarding-school. She was very much absorbed in her own little boy and girl, and was rather glad to hand the child over to the woman Mr. Archibald Craven sent to meet her, in London. The woman was his housekeeper at Misselthwaite Manor, and her name was Mrs. Medlock. She was a stout woman, with very red cheeks and sharp black eyes. She wore a very purple dress, a black silk mantle with jet fringe on it and a black bonnet with purple velvet flowers which stuck up and trembled when she moved her head. Mary did not like her at all, but as she very seldom liked people there was nothing remarkable in that; besides which it was very evident Mrs. Medlock did not think much of her.

'My word! she's[5] a plain little piece of goods!' she said. 'And we'd heard that her mother was a beauty. She hasn't handed much of it down, has she, ma'am[6]?'

'Perhaps she will improve as she grows older,' the officer's wife said good-naturedly. 'If she were not so sallow and had a nicer expression, her features are rather good. Children alter so much.'

'She'll have to alter a good deal,' answered Mrs. Medlock. 'And there's nothing likely to improve children at Misselthwaite—if you ask me!'

They thought Mary was not listening because she was standing a little apart from them at the window of the private hotel they had gone to. She was watching the passing buses and cabs, and people, but she heard quite well and was made very curious about her uncle and the place he lived in. What sort of a place was it, and what would he be like? What was a hunchback? She had never seen one. Perhaps there were none in India.

Since she had been living in other people's houses and had had no Ayah, she had begun to feel lonely and to think queer thoughts which were new to her. She had begun to wonder why she had never seemed to belong to any one even when her father and mother had been alive. Other children seemed to belong to their fathers and mothers, but she had never seemed to really be any one's little girl. She had had servants, and food and clothes, but no one had taken any notice of her. She did not know that this was because she was a disagreeable child; but then, of course, she did not know she was disagreeable. She often thought that other people were, but she did not know that she was so herself.

She thought Mrs. Medlock the most disagreeable person she had ever seen, with her common, highly coloured face and her common fine bonnet. When the next day they set out on their journey to Yorkshire, she walked through the station to the railway carriage with her head up and trying to keep as far away from her as she could, because she did not want to seem to belong to her. It would have made her angry to think people imagined she was her little girl.

But Mrs. Medlock was not in the least disturbed by her and her thoughts. She was the kind of woman who would 'stand no nonsense from young ones.' At least, that is what she would have said if she had been asked. She had not wanted to go to London just when her sister Maria's daughter was going to be married, but she had a comfortable, well paid place as housekeeper at Misselthwaite Manor and the only way in which she could keep it was to do at once what Mr. Archibald Craven told her to do. She never dared even to ask a question.

'Captain Lennox and his wife died of the cholera,' Mr. Craven had said in his short, cold way. 'Captain Lennox was my wife's brother and I am their daughter's guardian. The child is to be brought here. You must go to London and bring her yourself.'

So she packed her small trunk and made the journey.

Mary sat in her corner of the railway carriage and looked plain and fretful. She had nothing to read or to look at, and she had folded her thin little black-gloved hands in her lap. Her black dress made her look yellower than ever, and her limp light hair straggled from under her black crêpe hat.

'A more marred-looking young one I never saw in my life,' Mrs. Medlock thought. (Marred is a Yorkshire word and means spoiled and pettish.) She had never seen a child who sat so still without doing anything; and at last she got tired of watching her and began to talk in a brisk, hard voice.

'I suppose I may as well tell you something about where you are going to,' she said. 'Do you know anything about your uncle?'

'No,' said Mary.

'Never heard your father and mother talk about him?'

'No,' said Mary frowning. She frowned because she remembered that her father and mother had never talked to her about anything in particular. Certainly they had never told her things.

'Humph,' muttered Mrs. Medlock, staring at her queer, unresponsive little face. She did not say any more for a few moments and then she began again.

'I suppose you might as well be told something—to prepare you. You are going to a queer place.'

Mary said nothing at all, and Mrs. Medlock looked rather discomfited by her apparent indifference, but, after taking a breath, she went on.

'Not but that it's a grand big place in a gloomy way, and Mr. Craven's proud of it in his way—and that's gloomy enough, too. The house is six hundred years old and it's on the edge of the moor, and there's[7] near[8] a hundred rooms in it, though most of them's shut up and locked. And there's pictures and fine old furniture and things that's[9] been there for ages, and there's a big park round it and gardens and trees with branches trailing to the ground—some of them.' She paused and took another breath. 'But there's nothing else,' she ended suddenly.

Mary had begun to listen in spite of herself. It all sounded so unlike India, and anything new rather attracted her. But she did not intend to look as if she were interested. That was one of her unhappy, disagreeable ways. So she sat still.

'Well,' said Mrs. Medlock. 'What do you think of it?'

'Nothing,' she answered. 'I know nothing about such places.'

That made Mrs. Medlock laugh a short sort of laugh.

'Eh!' she said, 'but[10] you are like an old woman. Don't you care?'

'It doesn't matter,' said Mary, 'whether I care or not.'

'You are right enough there,' said Mrs. Medlock. 'It doesn't. What you're to be kept at Misselthwaite Manor for I don't know, unless because it's the easiest way. He's not going to trouble himself about you, that's sure and certain. He never troubles himself about no one.'

She stopped herself as if she had just remembered something in time.

'He's got a crooked back,' she said. 'That set him wrong. He was a sour young man and got no good of all his money and big place till he was married.'

Mary's eyes turned towards her in spite of her intention not to seem to care. She had never thought of the hunchback's being married and she was a trifle surprised. Mrs. Medlock saw this, and as she was a talkative woman she continued with more interest. This was one way of passing some of the time, at any rate.

'She was a sweet, pretty thing and he'd have walked the world over to get her a blade o'[11] grass she wanted. Nobody thought she'd marry him, but she did, and people said she married him for his money. But she didn't—she didn't,' positively. 'When she died—'

Mary gave a little involuntary jump.

'Oh! did[12] she die!' she exclaimed, quite without meaning to. She had just remembered a French fairy story she had once read called 'Riquet à la Houppe.' It had been about a poor hunchback and a beautiful princess and it had made her suddenly sorry for Mr. Archibald Craven.

'Yes, she died,' Mrs. Medlock answered. 'And it made him queerer than ever. He cares about nobody. He won't see people. Most of the time he goes away, and when he is at Misselthwaite he shuts himself up in the West Wing and won't let any one but Pitcher see him. Pitcher's an old fellow, but he took care of him when he was a child and he knows his ways.'

It sounded like something in a book and it did not make Mary feel cheerful. A house with a hundred rooms, nearly all shut up and with their doors locked—a house on the edge of a moor—whatsoever a moor was—sounded dreary. A man with a crooked back who shut himself up also! She stared out of the window with her lips pinched together, and it seemed quite natural that the rain should have begun to pour down in gray slanting lines and splash and stream down the window-panes. If the pretty wife had been alive she might have made things cheerful by being something like her own mother and by running in and out and going to parties as she had done in frocks 'full of lace.' But she was not there any more.

'You needn't expect to see him, because ten to one you won't,' said Mrs. Medlock. 'And you mustn't expect that there will be people to talk to you. You'll have to play about and look after yourself. You'll be told what rooms you can go into and what rooms you're to keep out of. There's gardens enough. But when you're in the house don't go wandering and poking about. Mr. Craven won't have it.'

'I shall not want to go poking about,' said sour little Mary; and just as suddenly as she had begun to be rather sorry for Mr.

Archibald Craven she began to cease to be sorry and to think he was unpleasant enough to deserve all that had happened to him.

And she turned her face toward the streaming panes of the window of the railway carriage and gazed out at the gray rainstorm which looked as if it would go on forever and ever. She watched it so long and steadily that the grayness grew heavier and heavier before her eyes and she fell asleep.

3.

Across the Moor

She slept a long time, and when she awakened Mrs. Medlock had bought a lunchbasket[13] at one of the stations and they had some chicken and cold beef and bread and butter and some hot tea. The rain seemed to be streaming down more heavily than ever and everybody in the station wore wet and glistening waterproofs. The guard lighted the lamps in the carriage, and Mrs. Medlock cheered up very much over her tea and chicken and beef. She ate a great deal and afterward fell asleep herself, and Mary sat and stared at her and watched her fine bonnet slip on one side until she herself fell asleep once more in the corner of the carriage, lulled by the splashing of the rain against the windows. It was quite dark when she awakened again. The train had stopped at a station and Mrs. Medlock was shaking her.

'You have had a sleep!' she said. 'It's time to open your eyes! We'rse at Thwaite Station and we've got a long drive before us.'

Mary stood up and tried to keep her eyes open while Mrs.

Medlock collected her parcels. The little girl did not offer to help her, because in India native servants always picked up or carried things and it seemed quite proper that other people should wait on one.

The station was a small one and nobody but themselves seemed to be getting out of the train. The station-master spoke to Mrs. Medlock in a rough good-natured way, pronouncing his words in a queer broad fashion which Mary found out afterward was Yorkshire.

'I see tha's[14] got back,' he said. 'An'[15] tha's browt[16] th'[17] young 'un[18] with thee[19].'

'Aye[20], that's her,' answered Mrs. Medlock, speaking with a Yorkshire accent herself and jerking her head over her shoulder toward Mary. 'How's thy[21] Missus?'

'Well enow[22]. Th' carriage is waitin'[23] outside for thee.'

A brougham stood on the road before the little outside platform. Mary saw that it was a smart carriage and that it was a smart footman who helped her in. His long waterproof coat and the waterproof covering of his hat were shining and dripping with rain as everything was, the burly station-master included.

When he shut the door, mounted the box with the coachman, and they drove off, the little girl found herself seated in a comfortably cushioned corner, but she was not inclined to go to sleep again. She sat and looked out of the window, curious to see something of the road over which she was being driven to the queer place Mrs. Medlock had spoken of. She was not at all a timid child and she was not exactly frightened, but she felt that there was no knowing what might happen in a house with a hundred rooms nearly all shut up—a house standing on the edge of a moor.

'What is a moor?' she said suddenly to Mrs. Medlock.

'Look out of the window in about ten minutes and you'll see,' the woman answered. 'We've got to drive five miles across Missel Moor before we get to the Manor. You won't see much because it's a dark night, but you can see something.'

Mary asked no more questions but waited in the darkness of her corner, keeping her eyes on the window. The carriage lamps cast rays of light a little distance ahead of them and she caught glimpses of the things they passed. After they had left the station they had driven through a tiny village and she had seen whitewashed cottages and the lights of a public house. Then they had passed a church and a vicarage and a little shop-window or so in a cottage with toys and sweets and odd things set out for sale. Then they were on the highroad and she saw hedges and trees. After that there seemed nothing different for a long time—or at least it seemed a long time to her.

At last the horses began to go more slowly, as if they were climbing up-hill[24], and presently there seemed to be no more hedges and no more trees. She could see nothing, in fact, but a dense darkness on either side. She leaned forward and pressed her face against the window just as the carriage gave a big jolt.

'Eh! We're on the moor now sure enough,' said Mrs. Medlock.

The carriage lamps shed a yellow light on a rough-looking road which seemed to be cut through bushes and low growing things which ended in the great expanse of dark apparently spread out before and around them. A wind was rising and making a singular, wild, low, rushing sound.

'It's—it's not the sea, is it?' said Mary, looking round at her companion.

'No, not it,' answered Mrs. Medlock. 'Nor it isn't fields nor mountains, it's just miles and miles and miles of wild land that nothing grows on but heather and gorse and broom, and nothing lives on but wild ponies and sheep.'

'I feel as if it might be the sea, if there were water on it,' said Mary. 'It sounds like the sea just now.'

'That's the wind blowing through the bushes,' Mrs. Medlock said. 'It's a wild, dreary enough place to my mind, though there's plenty that likes[25] it—particularly when the heather's in bloom.'

On and on they drove through the darkness, and though the rain stopped, the wind rushed by and whistled and made strange sounds. The road went up and down, and several times the carriage passed over a little bridge beneath which water rushed very fast with a great deal of noise. Mary felt as if the drive would never come to an end and that the wide, bleak moor was a wide expanse of black ocean through which she was passing on a strip of dry land.

'I don't like it,' she said to herself. 'I don't like it,' and she pinched her thin lips more tightly together.

The horses were climbing up a hilly piece of road when she first caught sight of a light. Mrs. Medlock saw it as soon as she did and drew a long sigh of relief.

'Eh, I am glad to see that bit o' light twinkling,' she exclaimed. 'It's the light in the lodge window. We shall get a good cup of tea after a bit, at all events.'

It was 'after a bit,' as she said, for when the carriage passed through the park gates there was still two miles of avenue to drive through and the trees (which nearly met overhead) made it seem as if they were driving through a long dark vault.

They drove out of the vault into a clear space and stopped before an immensely long but low-built house which seemed to ramble round a stone court. At first Mary thought that there were no lights at all in the windows, but as she got out of the carriage she saw that one room in a corner up-stairs[26] showed a dull glow.

The entrance door was a huge one made of massive, curiously shaped panels of oak studded with big iron nails and bound with great iron bars. It opened into an enormous hall, which was so dimly lighted that the faces in the portraits on the walls and the figures in the suits of armor made Mary feel that she did not want to look at them. As she stood on the stone floor she looked a very small, odd little black figure, and she felt as small and lost and odd as she looked.

A neat, thin old man stood near the manservant who opened the door for them.

'You are to take her to her room,' he said in a husky voice. 'He doesn't want to see her. He's going to London in the morning.'

'Very well, Mr. Pitcher,' Mrs. Medlock answered. 'So long as I know what's expected of me, I can manage.'

'What's expected of you, Mrs. Medlock,' Mr. Pitcher said, 'is that you make sure that he's not disturbed and that he doesn't see what he doesn't want to see.'

And then Mary Lennox was led up a broad staircase and down a long corridor and up a short flight of steps and through another corridor and another, until a door opened in a wall and she found herself in a room with a fire in it and a supper on a table.

Mrs. Medlock said unceremoniously:

'Well, here you are! This room and the next are where you'll live—and you must keep to them. Don't you forget that!'

It was in this way Mistress Mary arrived at Misselthwaite Manor and she had perhaps never felt quite so contrary in all her life.

4.

Martha

When she opened her eyes in the morning it was because a young housemaid had come into her room to light the fire and was kneeling on the hearth-rug raking out the cinders noisily. Mary lay and watched her for a few moments and then began to look about the room. She had never seen a room at all like it and thought it curious and gloomy. The walls were covered with tapestry with a forest scene embroidered on it. There were fantastically dressed people under the trees, and in the distance there was a glimpse of the turrets of a castle. There were hunters and horses and dogs and ladies. Mary felt as if she were in the forest with them. Out of a deep window she could see a great climbing stretch of land which seemed to have no trees on it, and to look rather like an endless, dull, purplish sea.

'What is that?' she said, pointing out of the window.

Martha, the young housemaid, who had just risen to her feet, looked and pointed also.

'That there?' she said.

'Yes.'

'That's th' moor,' with a good-natured grin. 'Does[27] tha'[28] like it?'

'No,' answered Mary. 'I hate it.'

'That's because tha'rt[29] not used to it,' Martha said, going back to her hearth. 'Tha' thinks[30] it's too big an' bare now. But tha' will like it.'

'Do you?' inquired Mary.

'Aye, that I do,' answered Martha, cheerfully polishing away at the grate. 'I just love it. It's none bare. It's covered wi'[31] growin'[32] things as smells sweet. It's fair[33] lovely in spring an' summer when th' gorse an' broom an' heather's in flower. It smells o' honey an' there's such a lot o' fresh air—an' th' sky looks so high an' th' bees an' skylarks makes such a nice noise hummin'[34] an' singin'[35]. Eh! I wouldn't live away from th' moor for anythin'[36].'

Mary listened to her with a grave, puzzled expression. The native servants she had been used to in India were not in the least like this. They were obsequious and servile and did not presume to talk to their masters as if they were their equals. They made salaams and called them 'protector of the poor' and names of that sort. Indian servants were commanded to do things, not asked. It was not the custom to say 'please' and 'thank you' and Mary had always slapped her Ayah in the face when she was angry. She wondered a little what this girl would do if one slapped her in the face. She was a round, rosy, good-natured looking creature, but she had a sturdy way which made Mistress Mary wonder if she might not even slap back—if the person who slapped her was only a little girl.

'You are a strange servant,' she said from her pillows, rather haughtily.

Martha sat up on her heels, with her blacking-brush in her hand, and laughed, without seeming the least out of temper.

'Eh! I know that,' she said. 'If there was a grand Missus at Misselthwaite I should never have been even one of th' under housemaids. I might have been let to be scullery-maid, but I'd never have been let up-stairs. I'm too common an' I talk too much Yorkshire. But this is a funny house for all it's so grand. Seems like there's neither Master nor Mistress except Mr. Pitcher an' Mrs. Medlock. Mr. Craven, he won't be troubled about anythin' when he's here, an' he's nearly always away. Mrs. Medlock gave me th' place out o' kindness. She told me she could never have done it if Misselthwaite had been like other big houses.'

'Are you going to be my servant?' Mary asked, still in her imperious little Indian way.

Martha began to rub her grate again.

'I'm Mrs. Medlock's servant,' she said stoutly. 'An' she's Mr. Craven's—but I'm to do the housemaid's work up here an' wait on you a bit. But you won't need much waitin' on.'

'Who is going to dress me?' demanded Mary.

Martha sat up on her heels again and stared. She spoke in broad Yorkshire in her amazement.

'Canna'³⁷ tha' dress thysen³⁸!' she said.

'What do you mean? I don't understand your language,' said Mary.

'Eh! I forgot,' Martha said. 'Mrs. Medlock told me I'd have to be careful or you wouldn't know what I was sayin'³⁹. I mean can't you put on your own clothes?'

'No,' answered Mary, quite indignantly. 'I never did in my life. My Ayah dressed me, of course.'

'Well,' said Martha, evidently not in the least aware that she was impudent, 'it's time tha' should learn. Tha' cannot begin younger. It'll do thee good to wait on thysen a bit. My mother always said she couldn't see why grand people's children didn't turn out fair fools—what with nurses an' bein'[40] washed an' dressed an' took out to walk as if they was[41] puppies!'

'It is different in India,' said Mistress Mary disdainfully. She could scarcely stand this.

But Martha was not at all crushed.

'Eh! I can see it's different,' she answered almost sympathetically. 'I dare say it's because there's such a lot o' blacks there instead o' respectable white people. When I heard you was comin'[42] from India I thought you was a black too.'

Mary sat up in bed furious.

'What!' she said. 'What! You thought I was a native. You—you daughter of a pig!'

Martha stared and looked hot.

'Who are you callin'[43] names?' she said. 'You needn't be so vexed. That's not th' way for a young lady to talk. I've nothin'[44] against th' blacks. When you read about 'em[45] in tracts they're always very religious. You always read as a black's a man an' a brother. I've never seen a black an' I was fair pleased to think I was goin'[46] to see one close. When I come[47] in to light your fire this mornin'[48] I crep'[49] up to your bed an' pulled th' cover back careful[50] to look at you. An' there you was,' disappointedly, 'no more black than me—for all you're so yeller[51].'

Mary did not even try to control her rage and humiliation.

'You thought I was a native! You dared! You don't know anything about natives! They are not people—they're servants who must salaam to you. You know nothing about India. You know nothing about anything!'

She was in such a rage and felt so helpless before the girl's simple stare, and somehow she suddenly felt so horribly lonely and far away from everything she understood and which understood her, that she threw herself face downward on the pillows and burst into passionate sobbing. She sobbed so unrestrainedly that good-natured Yorkshire Martha was a little frightened and quite sorry for her. She went to the bed and bent over her.

'Eh! you[52] mustn't cry like that there!' she begged. 'You mustn't for sure. I didn't know you'd be vexed. I don't know anythin' about anythin'—just like you said. I beg your pardon, Miss. Do stop cryin'[53].'

There was something comforting and really friendly in her queer Yorkshire speech and sturdy way which had a good effect on Mary. She gradually ceased crying and became quiet. Martha looked relieved.

'It's time for thee to get up now,' she said. 'Mrs. Medlock said I was to carry tha' breakfast an' tea an' dinner into th' room next to this. It's been made into a nursery for thee. I'll help thee on with thy clothes if tha'll get out o' bed. If th' buttons are at th' back tha' cannot button them up tha'self[54].'

When Mary at last decided to get up, the clothes Martha took from the wardrobe were not the ones she had worn when she arrived the night before with Mrs. Medlock.

'Those are not mine,' she said. 'Mine are black.'

She looked the thick white wool coat and dress over, and

added with cool approval:

'Those are nicer than mine.'

'These are th' ones tha' must put on,' Martha answered. 'Mr. Craven ordered Mrs. Medlock to get 'em in London. He said "I won't have a child dressed in black wanderin'[55] about like a lost soul," he said. "It'd make the place sadder than it is. Put colour on her." Mother she said she knew what he meant. Mother always knows what a body means. She doesn't hold with black hersel'[56].'

'I hate black things,' said Mary.

The dressing process was one which taught them both something. Martha had 'buttoned up' her little sisters and brothers but she had never seen a child who stood still and waited for another person to do things for her as if she had neither hands nor feet of her own.

'Why doesn't[57] tha' put on tha' own shoes?' she said when Mary quietly held out her foot.

'My Ayah did it,' answered Mary, staring. 'It was the custom.'

She said that very often—'It was the custom.' The native servants were always saying it. If one told them to do a thing their ancestors had not done for a thousand years they gazed at one mildly and said, 'It is not the custom' and one knew that was the end of the matter.

It had not been the custom that Mistress Mary should do anything but stand and allow herself to be dressed like a doll, but before she was ready for breakfast she began to suspect that her life at Misselthwaite Manor would end by teaching her a number of things quite new to her—things such as putting on her own shoes and stockings, and picking up things she let fall. If Martha had been a well-trained fine young lady's-maid she would have been more subservient and respectful and would have known that it was her business to brush hair, and button boots, and pick things up and lay them away. She was, however, only an untrained Yorkshire rustic who had been brought up in a moorland cottage with a swarm of little brothers and sisters who had never dreamed of doing anything but waiting on themselves and on the younger ones who were either babies in arms or just learning to totter about and tumble over things.

If Mary Lennox had been a child who was ready to be amused she would perhaps have laughed at Martha's readiness to talk, but Mary only listened to her coldly and wondered at her freedom of manner. At first she was not at all interested, but gradually, as the girl rattled on in her good-tempered, homely way, Mary began to notice what she was saying.

'Eh! you should see 'em all,' she said. 'There's twelve of us an' my father only gets sixteen shilling a week. I can tell you my mother's put to it to get porridge for 'em all. They tumble about on th' moor an' play there all day an' mother says th' air of th' moor fattens 'em. She says she believes they eat th' grass same as th' wild ponies do. Our Dickon, he's twelve years old and he's got a young pony he calls his own.'

'Where did he get it?' asked Mary.

'He found it on th' moor with its mother when it was a little one, an' he began to make friends with it an' give it bits o' bread an' pluck young grass for it. And it got to like him so it follows him about an' it lets him get on its back. Dickon's a kind lad an' animals likes him.'

Mary had never possessed an animal pet of her own and had always thought she should like one. So she began to feel a slight interest in Dickon, and as she had never before been interested in any one but herself, it was the dawning of a healthy sentiment. When she went into the room which had been made into a nursery for her, she found that it was rather like the one she had slept in. It was not a child's room, but a grown-up person's room, with gloomy old pictures on the walls and heavy old oak chairs. A table in the center was set with a good substantial breakfast. But she had always had a very small appetite, and she looked with something more than indifference at the first plate Martha set before her.

'I don't want it,' she said.

'Tha' doesn't want thy porridge!' Martha exclaimed incredulously.

'No.'

'Tha' doesn't know how good it is. Put a bit o' treacle on it or a bit o' sugar.'

'I don't want it,' repeated Mary.

'Eh!' said Martha. 'I can't abide to see good victuals go to waste. If our children was at this table they'd clean it bare in five minutes.'

'Why?' said Mary coldly.

'Why!' echoed Martha. 'Because they scarce[58] ever had their stomachs full in their lives. They're as hungry as young hawks an' foxes.'

'I don't know what it is to be hungry,' said Mary, with the indifference of ignorance.

Martha looked indignant.

'Well, it would do thee good to try it. I can see that plain enough,' she said outspokenly. 'I've no patience with folk as sits an' just stares at good bread an' meat. My word! don't[59] I wish Dickon and Phil an' Jane an' th' rest of 'em had what's here under their pinafores.'

'Why don't you take it to them?' suggested Mary.

'It's not mine,' answered Martha stoutly. 'An' this isn't my day out. I get my day out once a month same as th' rest. Then I go home an' clean up for mother an' give her a day's rest.'

Mary drank some tea and ate a little toast and some marmalade.

'You wrap up warm an' run out an' play you,' said Martha. 'It'll do you good and give you some stomach for your meat.'

Mary went to the window. There were gardens and paths and big trees, but everything looked dull and wintry.

'Out? Why should I go out on a day like this?'

'Well, if tha' doesn't go out tha'lt[60] have to stay in, an' what has[61] tha' got to do?'

Mary glanced about her. There was nothing to do. When Mrs. Medlock had prepared the nursery she had not thought of amusement. Perhaps it would be better to go and see what the gardens were like.

'Who will go with me?' she inquired.

Martha stared.

'You'll go by yourself,' she answered. 'You'll have to learn to play like other children does when they haven't got sisters and brothers. Our Dickon goes off on th' moor by himself an' plays for hours. That's how he made friends with th' pony. He's got sheep on th' moor that knows[62] him, an' birds as comes an' eats[63] out of his hand. However little there is to eat, he always saves a bit o' his bread to coax his pets.'

It was really this mention of Dickon which made Mary decide to go out, though she was not aware of it. There would be birds outside though there would not be ponies or sheep. They would be different from the birds in India, and it might amuse her to look at them.

Martha found her coat and hat for her and a pair of stout little boots and she showed her her way down-stairs[64].

'If tha' goes[65] round that way tha'll come to th' gardens,' she said, pointing to a gate in a wall of shrubbery. 'There's lots o' flowers in summer-time, but there's nothin' bloomin'[66] now.' She seemed to hesitate a second before she added, 'One of th' gardens is locked up. No one has been in it for ten years.'

'Why?' asked Mary in spite of herself. Here was another locked door added to the hundred in the strange house.

'Mr. Craven had it shut when his wife died so sudden. He won't let no one go inside. It was her garden. He locked th' door an' dug a hole and buried th' key. There's Mrs. Medlock's bell ringing—I must run.'

After she was gone Mary turned down the walk which led to the door in the shrubbery. She could not help thinking about the garden which no one had been into for ten years. She wondered what it would look like and whether there were any flowers still alive in it. When she had passed through the shrubbery gate she found herself in great gardens, with wide lawns and winding walks with clipped borders. There were trees, and flower-beds, and evergreens clipped into strange shapes, and a large pool with an old gray fountain in its midst. But the flower-beds were bare and wintry and the fountain was not playing. This was not the garden which was shut up. How could a garden be shut up? You could always walk into a garden.

She was just thinking this when she saw that, at the end of the path she was following, there seemed to be a long wall, with ivy growing over it. She was not familiar enough with England to know that she was coming upon the kitchen-gardens where the vegetables and fruit were growing. She went toward the wall and found that there was a green door in the ivy, and that it stood open. This was not the closed garden, evidently, and she could go into it.

She went through the door and found that it was a garden with walls all round it and that it was only one of several walled gardens which seemed to open into one another. She saw another open green door, revealing bushes and pathways between beds containing winter vegetables. Fruit-trees were trained flat against the wall, and over some of the beds there were glass frames. The place was bare and ugly enough, Mary thought, as she stood and stared about her. It might be nicer in summer when things were green, but there was nothing pretty about it now.

Presently an old man with a spade over his shoulder walked through the door leading from the second garden. He looked startled when he saw Mary, and then touched his cap. He had a surly old face, and did not seem at all pleased to see her—but then she was displeased with his garden and wore her 'quite contrary' expression, and certainly did not seem at all pleased to see him.

'What is this place?' she asked.

'One o' th' kitchen-gardens,' he answered.

'What is that?' said Mary, pointing through the other green door.

'Another of 'em,' shortly. 'There's another on t'other[67] side o' th' wall an' there's th' orchard t'other side o' that.'

'Can I go in them?' asked Mary.

'If tha' likes. But there's nowt to see.'

Mary made no response. She went down the path and through the second green door. There she found more walls and winter vegetables and glass frames, but in the second wall there was another green door and it was not open. Perhaps it led into the garden which no one had seen for ten years. As she was not at all a timid child and always did what she wanted to do, Mary went to the green door and turned the handle. She hoped the door would not open because she wanted to be sure she had found the mysterious garden—but it did open quite easily and she walked through it and found herself in an orchard. There were walls all round it also and trees trained against them, and there were bare fruit-trees growing in the winter-browned grass—but there was no green door to be seen anywhere. Mary looked for it, and yet when she had entered the upper end of the garden she had noticed that the wall did not seem to end with the orchard but to extend beyond it as if it enclosed a place at the other side. She could see the tops of trees above the wall, and when she stood still she saw a bird with a bright red breast sitting on the topmost branch of one of them, and suddenly he burst into his winter song—almost as if he had caught sight of her and was calling to her.

She stopped and listened to him and somehow his cheerful, friendly little whistle gave her a pleased feeling—even a disagreeable little girl may be lonely, and the big closed house and big bare moor and big bare gardens had made this one feel as if there was no one left in the world but herself. If she had been an affectionate child, who had been used to being loved, she would have broken her heart, but even though she was 'Mistress Mary Quite Contrary' she was desolate, and the bright-breasted little bird brought a look into her sour little face which was almost a smile. She listened to him until he flew away. He was not like an Indian bird and she liked him and wondered if she should ever see him again. Perhaps he lived in the mysterious garden and knew all about it.

Perhaps it was because she had nothing whatever to do that she thought so much of the deserted garden. She was curious about it and wanted to see what it was like. Why had Mr. Archibald Craven buried the key? If he had liked his wife so much why did he hate her garden? She wondered if she should ever see him, but she knew that if she did she should not like him, and he would not like her, and that she should only stand and stare at him and say nothing, though she should be wanting dreadfully to ask him why he had done such a queer thing.

'People never like me and I never like people,' she thought. 'And I never can talk as the Crawford children could. They were always talking and laughing and making noises.'

She thought of the robin and of the way he seemed to sing his song at her, and as she remembered the tree-top he perched on she stopped rather suddenly on the path.

'I believe that tree was in the secret garden—I feel sure it was,' she said. 'There was a wall round the place and there was no door.'

She walked back into the first kitchen-garden she had entered and found the old man digging there. She went and stood beside him and watched him a few moments in her cold little way. He took no notice of her and so at last she spoke to him.

'I have been into the other gardens,' she said.

'There was nothin' to prevent thee,' he answered crustily.

'I went into the orchard.'

'There was no dog at th' door to bite thee,' he answered.

'There was no door there into the other garden,' said Mary.

'What garden?' he said in a rough voice, stopping his digging for a moment.

'The one on the other side of the wall,' answered Mistress Mary. 'There are trees there—I saw the tops of them. A bird with a red breast was sitting on one of them and he sang.'

To her surprise the surly old weather-beaten face actually changed its expression. A slow smile spread over it and the gardener looked quite different. It made her think that it was curious how much nicer a person looked when he smiled. She had not thought of it before.

He turned about to the orchard side of his garden and began to whistle—a low soft whistle. She could not understand how such a surly man could make such a coaxing sound.

Almost the next moment a wonderful thing happened. She

heard a soft little rushing flight through the air—and it was the bird with the red breast flying to them, and he actually alighted on the big clod of earth quite near to the gardener's foot.

'Here he is,' chuckled the old man, and then he spoke to the bird as if he were speaking to a child.

'Where has tha' been, tha' cheeky little beggar?' he said. 'I've not seen thee before to-day[68]. Has tha begun tha' courtin'[69] this early in th' season? Tha'rt too forrad[70].'

The bird put his tiny head on one side and looked up at him with his soft bright eye which was like a black dewdrop. He seemed quite familiar and not the least afraid. He hopped about and pecked the earth briskly, looking for seeds and insects. It actually gave Mary a queer feeling in her heart, because he was so pretty and cheerful and seemed so like a person. He had a tiny plump body and a delicate beak, and slender delicate legs.

'Will he always come when you call him?' she asked almost in a whisper.

'Aye, that he will. I've knowed[71] him ever since he was a fledgling. He come out of th' nest in th' other garden an' when first he flew over th' wall he was too weak to fly back for a few days an' we got friendly. When he went over th' wall again th' rest of th' brood was gone an' he was lonely an' he come back to me.'

'What kind of a bird is he?' Mary asked.

'Doesn't tha' know? He's a robin redbreast an' they're th' friendliest, curiousest[72] birds alive. They're almost as friendly as dogs—if you know how to get on with 'em. Watch him peckin'[73] about there an' lookin'[74] round at us now an' again. He knows we're talkin'[75] about him.'

It was the queerest thing in the world to see the old fellow. He looked at the plump little scarlet-waistcoated bird as if he were both proud and fond of him.

'He's a conceited one,' he chuckled. 'He likes to hear folk talk about him. An' curious—bless me, there never was his like for curiosity an' meddlin'[76]. He's always comin' to see what I'm plantin'[77]. He knows all th' things Mester Craven never troubles hissel'[78] to find out. He's th' head gardener, he is.'

The robin hopped about busily pecking the soil and now and then stopped and looked at them a little. Mary thought his black dewdrop eyes gazed at her with great curiosity. It really seemed as if he were finding out all about her. The queer feeling in her heart increased.

'Where did the rest of the brood fly to?' she asked.

'There's no knowin'[79]. The old ones turn 'em out o' their nest an' make 'em fly an' they're scattered before you know it. This one was a knowin' one an' he knew he was lonely.'

Mistress Mary went a step nearer to the robin and looked at him very hard.

'I'm lonely,' she said.

She had not known before that this was one of the things which made her feel sour and cross. She seemed to find it out when the robin looked at her and she looked at the robin.

The old gardener pushed his cap back on his bald head and stared at her a minute.

'Art[80] tha' th' little wench from India?' he asked.

Mary nodded.

'Then no wonder tha'rt lonely. Tha'lt be lonelier before tha's done,' he said.

He began to dig again, driving his spade deep into the rich

black garden soil while the robin hopped about very busily employed.

'What is your name?' Mary inquired.

He stood up to answer her.

'Ben Weatherstaff,' he answered, and then he added with a surly chuckle, 'I'm lonely mysel'[81] except when he's with me,' and he jerked his thumb toward the robin. 'He's th' only friend I've got.'

'I have no friends at all,' said Mary. 'I never had. My Ayah didn't like me and I never played with any one.'

It is a Yorkshire habit to say what you think with blunt frankness, and old Ben Weatherstaff was a Yorkshire moor man.

'Tha' an' me are a good bit alike,' he said. 'We was wove out of th' same cloth. We're neither of us good lookin' an' we're both of us as sour as we look. We've got the same nasty tempers, both of us, I'll warrant.'

This was plain speaking, and Mary Lennox had never heard the truth about herself in her life. Native servants always salaamed and submitted to you, whatever you did. She had never thought much about her looks, but she wondered if she was as unattractive as Ben Weatherstaff and she also wondered if she looked as sour as he had looked before the robin came. She actually began to wonder also if she was 'nasty tempered.' She felt uncomfortable.

Suddenly a clear rippling little sound broke out near her and she turned round. She was standing a few feet from a young apple-tree and the robin had flown on to one of its branches and had burst out into a scrap of a song. Ben Weatherstaff laughed outright.

'What did he do that for?' asked Mary.

'He's made up his mind to make friends with thee,' replied

Ben. 'Dang me if he hasn't took a fancy to thee.'

'To me?' said Mary, and she moved toward the little tree softly and looked up.

'Would you make friends with me?' she said to the robin just as if she was speaking to a person. 'Would you?' And she did not say it either in her hard little voice or in her imperious Indian voice, but in a tone so soft and eager and coaxing that Ben Weatherstaff was as surprised as she had been when she heard him whistle.

'Why,' he cried out, 'tha' said that as nice an' human as if tha' was a real child instead of a sharp old woman. Tha' said it almost like Dickon talks to his wild things on th' moor.'

'Do you know Dickon?' Mary asked, turning round rather in a hurry.

'Everybody knows him. Dickon's wanderin' about everywhere. Th' very blackberries an' heather-bells knows him. I warrant th' foxes shows him where their cubs lies an' th' skylarks doesn't hide their nests from him.'

Mary would have liked to ask some more questions. She was almost as curious about Dickon as she was about the deserted garden. But just that moment the robin, who had ended his song, gave a little shake of his wings, spread them and flew away. He had made his visit and had other things to do.

'He has flown over the wall!' Mary cried out, watching him. 'He has flown into the orchard—he has flown across the other wall—into the garden where there is no door!'

'He lives there,' said old Ben. 'He came out o' th' egg there. If he's courtin', he's makin'[82] up to some young madam of a robin that lives among th' old rose-trees there.'

'Rose-trees,' said Mary. 'Are there rose-trees?'

Ben Weatherstaff took up his spade again and began to dig. 'There was ten year'[83] ago,' he mumbled.

'I should like to see them,' said Mary. 'Where is the green door? There must be a door somewhere.'

Ben drove his spade deep and looked as uncompanionable as he had looked when she first saw him.

'There was ten year' ago, but there isn't now,' he said.

'No door!' cried Mary. 'There must be.'

'None as any one can find, an' none as is any one's business. Don't you be a meddlesome wench an' poke your nose where it's no cause to go. Here, I must go on with my work. Get you gone an' play you. I've no more time.'

And he actually stopped digging, threw his spade over his shoulder and walked off, without even glancing at her or saying good-by.

The Cry in the Corridor

At first each day which passed by for Mary Lennox was exactly like the others. Every morning she awoke in her tapestried room and found Martha kneeling upon the hearth building her fire; every morning she ate her breakfast in the nursery which had nothing amusing in it; and after each breakfast she gazed out of the window across to the huge moor which seemed to spread out on all sides and climb up to the sky, and after she had stared for a while she realized that if she did not go out she would have to stay in and do nothing—and so she went out. She did not know that this was the best thing she could have done, and she did not know that, when she began to walk quickly or even run along the paths and down the avenue, she was stirring her slow blood and making herself stronger by fighting with the wind which swept down from the moor. She ran only to make herself warm, and she hated the wind which rushed at her face and roared and held her back as if it were some giant she could not see. But the big breaths of rough fresh air blown over the heather filled her lungs with something which was good for her whole thin body and whipped some red colour into her cheeks and brightened her dull eyes when she did not know anything about it.

But after a few days spent almost entirely out of doors she wakened one morning knowing what it was to be hungry, and when she sat down to her breakfast she did not glance disdainfully at her porridge and push it away, but took up her spoon and began to eat it and went on eating it until her bowl was empty.

'Tha' got on well enough with that this mornin', didn't tha'?' said Martha.

'It tastes nice to-day,' said Mary, feeling a little surprised herself.

'It's th' air of th' moor that's givin'[84] thee stomach for tha' victuals,' answered Martha. 'It's lucky for thee that tha's got victuals as well as appetite. There's been twelve in our cottage as had th' stomach an' nothin' to put in it. You go on playin'[85] you out o' doors every day an' you'll get some flesh on your bones an' you won't be so yeller.'

'I don't play,' said Mary. 'I have nothing to play with.'

'Nothin' to play with!' exclaimed Martha. 'Our children plays with sticks and stones. They just runs[86] about an' shouts[87] an' looks[88] at things.'

Mary did not shout, but she looked at things. There was nothing else to do. She walked round and round the gardens and wandered about the paths in the park. Sometimes she looked for Ben Weatherstaff, but though several times she saw him at work he was too busy to look at her or was too surly. Once when she was walking toward him he picked up his spade and turned away as if he did it on purpose.

One place she went to oftener than to any other. It was the long walk outside the gardens with the walls round them. There were bare flower-beds on either side of it and against the walls ivy grew thickly. There was one part of the wall where the creeping dark green leaves were more bushy[89] than elsewhere. It seemed as if for a long time that part had been neglected. The rest of it had been clipped and made to look neat, but at this lower end of the walk it had not been trimmed at all.

A few days after she had talked to Ben Weatherstaff Mary stopped to notice this and wondered why it was so. She had just paused and was looking up at a long spray of ivy swinging in the wind when she saw a gleam of scarlet and heard a brilliant chirp, and there, on the top of the wall, perched Ben Weatherstaff's robin redbreast, tilting forward to look at her with his small head on one side.

'Oh!' she cried out, 'is[90] it you—is it you?' And it did not seem at all queer to her that she spoke to him as if she was sure that he would understand and answer her.

He did answer. He twittered and chirped and hopped along the wall as if he were telling her all sorts of things. It seemed to Mistress Mary as if she understood him, too, though he was not speaking in words. It was as if he said:

'Good morning! Isn't the wind nice? Isn't the sun nice? Isn't everything nice? Let us both chirp and hop and twitter. Come on! Come on!'

Mary began to laugh, and as he hopped and took little flights along the wall she ran after him. Poor little thin, sallow, ugly Mary—she actually looked almost pretty for a moment.

'I like you! I like you!' she cried out, pattering down the walk;

and she chirped and tried to whistle, which last she did not know how to do in the least. But the robin seemed to be quite satisfied and chirped and whistled back at her. At last he spread his wings and made a darting flight to the top of a tree, where he perched and sang loudly.

That reminded Mary of the first time she had seen him. He had been swinging on a tree-top then and she had been standing in the orchard. Now she was on the other side of the orchard and standing in the path outside a wall—much lower down—and there was the same tree inside.

'It's in the garden no one can go into,' she said to herself. 'It's the garden without a door. He lives in there. How I wish I could see what it is like!'

She ran up the walk to the green door she had entered the first morning. Then she ran down the path through the other door and then into the orchard, and when she stood and looked up there was the tree on the other side of the wall, and there was the robin just finishing his song and beginning to preen his feathers with his beak.

'It is the garden,' she said. 'I am sure it is.'

She walked round and looked closely at that side of the orchard wall, but she only found what she had found before—that there was no door in it. Then she ran through the kitchen-gardens again and out into the walk outside the long ivy-covered wall, and she walked to the end of it and looked at it, but there was no door; and then she walked to the other end, looking again, but there was no door.

'It's very queer,' she said. 'Ben Weatherstaff said there was no door and there is no door. But there must have been one ten years ago, because Mr. Craven buried the key.'

This gave her so much to think of that she began to be quite interested and feel that she was not sorry that she had come to Misselthwaite Manor. In India she had always felt hot and too languid to care much about anything. The fact was that the fresh wind from the moor had begun to blow the cobwebs out of her young brain and to waken her up a little.

She stayed out of doors nearly all day, and when she sat down to her supper at night she felt hungry and drowsy and comfortable. She did not feel cross when Martha chattered away. She felt as if she rather liked to hear her, and at last she thought she would ask her a question. She asked it after she had finished her supper and had sat down on the hearth-rug before the fire.

'Why did Mr. Craven hate the garden?' she said.

She had made Martha stay with her and Martha had not objected at all. She was very young, and used to a crowded cottage full of brothers and sisters, and she found it dull in the great servants' hall down-stairs where the footman and upper-housemaids made fun of her Yorkshire speech and looked upon her as a common little thing, and sat and whispered among themselves. Martha liked to talk, and the strange child who had lived in India, and been waited upon by 'blacks,' was novelty enough to attract her.

She sat down on the hearth herself without waiting to be asked.

'Art tha' thinkin'[91] about that garden yet?' she said. 'I knew tha' would. That was just the way with me when I first heard about it.'

'Why did he hate it?' Mary persisted.

Martha tucked her feet under her and made herself quite comfortable.

'Listen to th' wind wutherin'[92] round the house,' she said. 'You could bare stand up on the moor if you was out on it to-night.'

Mary did not know what 'wutherin' ' meant until she listened, and then she understood. It must mean that hollow shuddering sort of roar which rushed round and round the house as if the giant no one could see were buffeting it and beating at the walls and windows to try to break in. But one knew he could not get in, and somehow it made one feel very safe and warm inside a room with a red coal fire.

'But why did he hate it so?' she asked, after she had listened. She intended to know if Martha did.

Then Martha gave up her store of knowledge.

'Mind,' she said, 'Mrs. Medlock said it's not to be talked about. There's lots o' things in this place that's not to be talked over. That's Mr. Craven's orders. His troubles are none servants' business, he says. But for th' garden he wouldn't be like he is. It was Mrs. Craven's garden that she had made when first they were married an' she just loved it, an' they used to 'tend[93] the flowers themselves. An' none o' th' gardeners was ever let to go in. Him[94] an' her[95] used to go in an' shut th' door an' stay there hours an' hours, readin'[96] and talkin'. An' she was just a bit of a girl an' there was an old tree with a branch bent like a seat on it. An' she made roses grow over it an' she used to sit there. But one day when she was sittin'[97] there th' branch broke an' she fell on th' ground an' was hurt so bad that next day she died. Th' doctors thought he'd go out o' his mind an' die, too. That's why he hates it. No one's never gone in since, an' he won't let any one talk about it.'

Mary did not ask any more questions. She looked at the red fire and listened to the wind 'wutherin'.' It seemed to be 'wutherin' ' louder than ever.

At that moment a very good thing was happening to her. Four good things had happened to her, in fact, since she came to Misselthwaite Manor. She had felt as if she had understood a robin and that he had understood her; she had run in the wind until her blood had grown warm; she had been healthily hungry for the first time in her life; and she had found out what it was to be sorry for some one. She was getting on.

But as she was listening to the wind she began to listen to something else. She did not know what it was, because at first she could scarcely distinguish it from the wind itself. It was a curious sound—it seemed almost as if a child were crying somewhere. Sometimes the wind sounded rather like a child crying, but presently Mistress Mary felt quite sure this sound was inside the house, not outside it. It was far away, but it was inside. She turned round and looked at Martha.

'Do you hear any one crying?' she said.

Martha suddenly looked confused.

'No,' she answered. 'It's th' wind. Sometimes it sounds like as if some one was lost on th' moor an' wailin'[98]. It's got all sorts o' sounds.'

'But listen,' said Mary. 'It's in the house—down one of those long corridors.'

And at that very moment a door must have been opened somewhere down-stairs; for a great rushing draught blew along the passage and the door of the room they sat in was blown open with a crash, and as they both jumped to their feet the light was blown out and the crying sound was swept down the far corridor so that it was to be heard more plainly than ever.

'There!' said Mary. 'I told you so! It is some one crying—and it isn't a grown-up person.'

Martha ran and shut the door and turned the key, but before she did it they both heard the sound of a door in some far passage shutting with a bang, and then everything was quiet, for even the wind ceased 'wutherin'' for a few moments.

'It was th' wind,' said Martha stubbornly. 'An[99] if it wasn't, it was little Betty Butterworth, th' scullery-maid. She's had th' toothache all day.'

But something troubled and awkward in her manner made Mistress Mary stare very hard at her. She did not believe she was speaking the truth.

6.

'There Was Some One Crying—There Was!'

The next day the rain poured down in torrents again, and when Mary looked out of her window the moor was almost hidden by gray mist and cloud. There could be no going out to-day.

'What do you do in your cottage when it rains like this?' she asked Martha.

'Try to keep from under each other's feet mostly,' Martha answered. 'Eh! there[100] does seem a lot of us then. Mother's a good-tempered woman but she gets fair moithered. The biggest ones goes out in th' cow-shed and plays there. Dickon he doesn't mind th' wet. He goes out just th' same as if th' sun was shinin'[101]. He says he sees things on rainy days as doesn't show when it's fair weather. He once found a little fox cub half drowned in its hole and he brought it home in th' bosom of his shirt to keep it warm. Its mother had been killed nearby an' th' hole was swum out an' th' rest o' th' litter was dead. He's got it at home now. He found a half-drowned young crow another time an' he brought it home, too, an' tamed it. It's named Soot because it's so black an' it hops an' flies about with him everywhere.'

The time had come when Mary had forgotten to resent Martha's familiar talk. She had even begun to find it interesting and to be sorry when she stopped or went away. The stories she had been told by her Ayah when she lived in India had been quite unlike those Martha had to tell about the moorland cottage which held fourteen people who lived in four little rooms and never had quite enough to eat. The children seemed to tumble about and amuse themselves like a litter of rough, good-natured collie puppies. Mary was most attracted by the mother and Dickon. When Martha told stories of what 'mother' said or did they always sounded comfortable.

'If I had a raven or a fox cub I could play with it,' said Mary. 'But I have nothing.'

Martha looked perplexed.

'Can tha' knit?' she asked.

'No,' answered Mary.

'Can tha' sew?'

'No.'

'Can tha' read?'

'Yes.'

'Then why doesn't tha read somethin'[102], or learn a bit o' spellin'[103]? Tha'st[104] old enough to be learnin'[105] thy book a good bit now.'

'I haven't any books,' said Mary. 'Those I had were left in India.'

'That's a pity,' said Martha. 'If Mrs. Medlock'd let thee go into th' library, there's thousands o' books there.'

Mary did not ask where the library was, because she was suddenly inspired by a new idea. She made up her mind to go and find it herself. She was not troubled about Mrs. Medlock. Mrs. Medlock seemed always to be in her comfortable housekeeper's sitting-room down-stairs. In this queer place one scarcely ever saw any one at all. In fact, there was no one to see but the servants, and when their master was away they lived a luxurious life below stairs, where there was a huge kitchen hung about with shining brass and pewter, and a large servants' hall where there were four or five abundant meals eaten every day, and where a great deal of lively romping went on when Mrs. Medlock was out of the way.

Mary's meals were served regularly, and Martha waited on her, but no one troubled themselves about her in the least. Mrs. Medlock came and looked at her every day or two, but no one inquired what she did or told her what to do. She supposed that perhaps this was the English way of treating children. In India she had always been attended by her Ayah, who had followed her about and waited on her, hand and foot. She had often been tired of her company. Now she was followed by nobody and was learning to dress herself because Martha looked as though she thought she was silly and stupid when she wanted to have things handed to her and put on.

'Hasn't[106] tha' got good sense?' she said once, when Mary had stood waiting for her to put on her gloves for her. 'Our Susan Ann is twice as sharp as thee an' she's only four year' old. Sometimes tha' looks fair soft in th' head.'

Mary had worn her contrary scowl for an hour after that, but it made her think several entirely new things.

She stood at the window for about ten minutes this morning after Martha had swept up the hearth for the last time and gone down-stairs. She was thinking over the new idea which had come to her when she heard of the library. She did not care very much about the library itself, because she had read very few books; but to hear of it brought back to her mind the hundred rooms with closed doors. She wondered if they were all really locked and what she would find if she could get into any of them. Were there a hundred really? Why shouldn't she go and see how many doors she could count? It would be something to do on this morning when she could not go out. She had never been taught to ask permission to do things, and she knew nothing at all about authority, so she would not have thought it necessary to ask Mrs. Medlock if she might walk about the house, even if she had seen her.

She opened the door of the room and went into the corridor, and then she began her wanderings. It was a long corridor and it branched into other corridors and it led her up short flights of steps which mounted to others again. There were doors and doors, and there were pictures on the walls. Sometimes they were pictures of dark, curious landscapes, but oftenest[107] they were portraits of men and women in queer, grand costumes made of satin and velvet. She found herself in one long gallery whose walls were covered with these portraits. She had never thought there could be so many in any house. She walked slowly down this place and stared at the faces which also seemed to stare at her. She felt as if they were wondering what a little girl from India was doing in their house. Some were pictures of children—little girls in thick satin frocks which reached to their feet and stood out about them, and boys with puffed sleeves and lace collars and long hair, or with big ruffs around their necks. She always stopped to look at the children, and wonder what their names were, and where they had gone, and why they wore such odd clothes. There was a stiff, plain little girl rather like herself. She wore a green brocade dress and held a green parrot on her finger. Her eyes had a sharp, curious look.

'Where do you live now?' said Mary aloud to her. 'I wish you were here.'

Surely no other little girl ever spent such a queer morning. It seemed as if there was no one in all the huge rambling house but her own small self, wandering about up-stairs and down, through narrow passages and wide ones, where it seemed to her that no one but herself had ever walked. Since so many rooms had been built, people must have lived in them, but it all seemed so empty that she could not quite believe it true.

It was not until she climbed to the second floor that she thought of turning the handle of a door. All the doors were shut, as Mrs. Medlock had said they were, but at last she put her hand on the handle of one of them and turned it. She was almost frightened for a moment when she felt that it turned without difficulty and that when she pushed upon the door itself it slowly and heavily opened. It was a massive door and opened into a big bedroom. There were embroidered hangings on the wall, and inlaid furniture such as she had seen in India stood about the room. A broad window with leaded panes looked out upon the moor; and over the mantel was another portrait of the stiff, plain little girl who seemed to stare at her more curiously than ever.

'Perhaps she slept here once,' said Mary. 'She stares at me so that she makes me feel queer.'

After that she opened more doors and more. She saw so many rooms that she became quite tired and began to think that there must be a hundred, though she had not counted them. In all of them there were old pictures or old tapestries with strange scenes worked on them. There were curious pieces of furniture and curious ornaments in nearly all of them.

In one room, which looked like a lady's sitting-room, the hangings were all embroidered velvet, and in a cabinet were about a hundred little elephants made of ivory. They were of different sizes, and some had their mahouts or palanquins on their backs. Some were much bigger than the others and some were so tiny that they seemed only babies. Mary had seen carved ivory in India and she knew all about elephants. She opened the door of the cabinet and stood on a footstool and played with these for quite a long time. When she got tired she set the elephants in order and shut the door of the cabinet.

In all her wanderings through the long corridors and the empty rooms, she had seen nothing alive; but in this room she saw something. Just after she had closed the cabinet door she heard a tiny rustling sound. It made her jump and look around at the sofa by the fireplace, from which it seemed to come. In the corner of the sofa there was a cushion, and in the velvet which covered it there was a hole, and out of the hole peeped a tiny head with a pair of frightened eyes in it.

Mary crept softly across the room to look. The bright eyes belonged to a little gray mouse, and the mouse had eaten a hole into the cushion and made a comfortable nest there. Six baby mice were cuddled up asleep near her. If there was no one else alive in the hundred rooms there were seven mice who did not look lonely at all.

'If they wouldn't be so frightened I would take them back with me,' said Mary.

She had wandered about long enough to feel too tired to wander any farther, and she turned back. Two or three times she lost her way by turning down the wrong corridor and was obliged to ramble up and down until she found the right one; but at last she reached her own floor again, though she was some distance from her own room and did not know exactly where she was.

'I believe I have taken a wrong turning again,' she said, standing still at what seemed the end of a short passage with tapestry on the wall. 'I don't know which way to go. How still everything is!'

It was while she was standing here and just after she had said this that the stillness was broken by a sound. It was another cry, but not quite like the one she had heard last night; it was only a short one, a fretful, childish whine muffled by passing through walls.

'It's nearer than it was,' said Mary, her heart beating rather faster. 'And it is crying.'

She put her hand accidentally upon the tapestry near her, and then sprang back, feeling quite startled. The tapestry was the covering of a door which fell open and showed her that there was another part of the corridor behind it, and Mrs. Medlock was coming up it with her bunch of keys in her hand and a very cross look on her face.

'What are you doing here?' she said, and she took Mary by the arm and pulled her away. 'What did I tell you?'

'I turned round the wrong corner,' explained Mary. 'I didn't know which way to go and I heard some one crying.'

She quite hated Mrs. Medlock at the moment, but she hated her more the next.

'You didn't hear anything of the sort,' said the housekeeper. 'You come along back to your own nursery or I'll box your ears.'

And she took her by the arm and half pushed, half pulled her up one passage and down another until she pushed her in at the door of her own room.

'Now,' she said, 'you stay where you're told to stay or you'll find yourself locked up. The master had better get you a governess, same as he said he would. You're one that needs some one to look sharp after you. I've got enough to do.'

She went out of the room and slammed the door after her, and Mary went and sat on the hearth-rug, pale with rage. She did not cry, but ground her teeth.

'There was some one crying—there was—there was!' she said to herself.

She had heard it twice now, and sometime she would find out. She had found out a great deal this morning. She felt as if she had been on a long journey, and at any rate she had had something to amuse her all the time, and she had played with the ivory elephants and had seen the gray mouse and its babies in their nest in the velvet cushion.

7.

The Key of the Garden

Two days after this, when Mary opened her eyes she sat upright in bed immediately, and called to Martha.

'Look at the moor! Look at the moor!'

The rain-storm had ended and the gray mist and clouds had been swept away in the night by the wind. The wind itself had ceased and a brilliant, deep blue sky arched high over the moorland. Never, never had Mary dreamed of a sky so blue. In India skies were hot and blazing; this was of a deep cool blue which almost seemed to sparkle like the waters of some lovely bottomless lake, and here and there, high, high in the arched blueness floated small clouds of snow-white fleece. The far-reaching world of the moor itself looked softly blue instead of gloomy purple-black or awful dreary gray.

'Aye,' said Martha with a cheerful grin. 'Th' storm's over for a bit. It does like this at this time o' th' year. It goes off in a night like it was pretendin'[108] it had never been here an' never meant to come again. That's because th' spring-time's on its way. It's a long way off yet, but it's comin'.'

'I thought perhaps it always rained or looked dark in England,' Mary said.

'Eh! no[109]!' said Martha, sitting up on her heels among her black lead brushes. 'Nowt o' th' soart!'

'What does that mean?' asked Mary seriously. In India the natives spoke different dialects which only a few people understood, so she was not surprised when Martha used words she did not know.

Martha laughed as she had done the first morning.

'There now,' she said. 'I've talked broad Yorkshire again like Mrs. Medlock said I mustn't. 'Nowt o' th' soart' means "nothin'-of-the-sort," ' slowly and carefully, 'but it takes so long to say it. Yorkshire's th' sunniest place on earth when it is sunny. I told thee tha'd like th' moor after a bit. Just you wait till you see th' gold-coloured gorse blossoms an' th' blossoms o' th' broom, an' th' heather flowerin'[110], all purple bells, an' hundreds o' butterflies flutterin'[111] an' bees hummin' an' skylarks soarin'[112] up an' ingin'. You'll want to get out on it as sunrise an' live out on it all day like Dickon does.'

'Could I ever get there?' asked Mary wistfully, looking through her window at the far-off blue. It was so new and big and wonderful and such a heavenly colour.

'I don't know,' answered Martha. 'Tha's never used tha' legs since tha' was born, it seems to me. Tha' couldn't walk five mile[113]. It's five mile to our cottage.'

'I should like to see your cottage.'

Martha stared at her a moment curiously before she took up

her polishing brush and began to rub the grate again. She was thinking that the small plain face did not look quite as sour at this moment as it had done the first morning she saw it. It looked just a trifle like little Susan Ann's when she wanted something very much.

'I'll ask my mother about it,' she said. 'She's one o' them that nearly always sees a way to do things. It's my day out today an' I'm goin' home. Eh! I am glad. Mrs. Medlock thinks a lot o' mother. Perhaps she could talk to her.'

'I like your mother,' said Mary.

'I should think tha' did,' agreed Martha, polishing away.

'I've never seen her,' said Mary.

'No, tha' hasn't,' replied Martha.

She sat up on her heels again and rubbed the end of her nose with the back of her hand as if puzzled for a moment, but she ended quite positively.

'Well, she's that sensible an' hard workin'[114] an' good-natured an' clean that no one could help likin'[115] her whether they'd seen her or not. When I'm goin' home to her on my day out I just jump for joy when I'm crossin'[116] the moor.'

'I like Dickon,' added Mary. 'And I've never seen him.'

'Well,' said Martha stoutly, 'I've told thee that th' very birds likes him an' th' rabbits an' wild sheep an' ponies, an' th' foxes themselves. I wonder,' staring at her reflectively, 'what Dickon would think of thee?'

'He wouldn't like me,' said Mary in her stiff, cold little way. 'No one does.'

Martha looked reflective again.

'How does tha' like thysel'[117]?' she inquired, really quite as if she were curious to know.

Mary hesitated a moment and thought it over.

'Not at all—really,' she answered. 'But I never thought of that before.'

Martha grinned a little as if at some homely recollection.

'Mother said that to me once,' she said. 'She was at her wash-tub an' I was in a bad temper an' talkin' ill of folk, an' she turns round on me an' says:[118] "Tha' young vixen[119], tha'! There tha' stands[120] sayin' tha' doesn't like this one an' tha' doesn't like that one. How does tha' like thysel'?" It made me laugh an' it brought me to my senses in a minute.'

She went away in high spirits as soon as she had given Mary her breakfast. She was going to walk five miles across the moor to the cottage, and she was going to help her mother with the washing and do the week's baking and enjoy herself thoroughly.

Mary felt lonelier than ever when she knew she was no longer in the house. She went out into the garden as quickly as possible, and the first thing she did was to run round and round the fountain flower garden ten times. She counted the times carefully and when she had finished she felt in better spirits. The sunshine made the whole place look different. The high, deep, blue sky arched over Misselthwaite as well as over the moor, and she kept lifting her face and looking up into it, trying to imagine what it would be like to lie down on one of the little snow-white clouds and float about. She went into the first kitchen-garden and found Ben Weatherstaff working there with two other gardeners. The change in the weather seemed to have done him good. He spoke to her of his own accord.

'Springtime's comin',' he said. 'Cannot tha' smell it?'

Mary sniffed and thought she could.

'I smell something nice and fresh and damp,' she said.

'That's th' good rich earth,' he answered, digging away. 'It's in a good humor makin' ready to grow things. It's glad when plantin' time comes. It's dull in th' winter when it's got nowt to do. In th' flower gardens out there things will be stirrin'[121] down below in th' dark. Th' sun's warmin'[122] 'em. You'll see bits o' green spikes stickin' out o' th' black earth after a bit.'

'What will they be?' asked Mary.

'Crocuses an' snowdrops an' daffydowndillys. Has tha' never seen them?'

'No. Everything is hot, and wet, and green after the rains in India,' said Mary. 'And I think things grow up in a night.'

'These won't grow up in a night,' said Weatherstaff. 'Tha'll have to wait for 'em. They'll poke up a bit higher here, an' push out a spike more there, an' uncurl a leaf this day an' another that. You watch 'em.'

'I am going to,' answered Mary.

Very soon she heard the soft rustling flight of wings again and she knew at once that the robin had come again. He was very pert and lively, and hopped about so close to her feet, and put his head on one side and looked at her so slyly that she asked Ben Weatherstaff a question.

'Do you think he remembers me?' she said.

'remembers thee!' said Weatherstaff indignantly. 'He knows every cabbage stump in th' gardens, let alone th' people. He's never seen a little wench here before, an' he's bent on findin'[123] out all about thee. Tha's no need to try to hide anything from him.'

'Are things stirring down below in the dark in that garden

where he lives?' Mary inquired.

'What garden?' grunted Weatherstaff, becoming surly again.

'The one where the old rose-trees are.' She could not help asking, because she wanted so much to know. 'Are all the flowers dead, or do some of them come again in the summer? Are there ever any roses?'

'Ask him,' said Ben Weatherstaff, hunching his shoulders toward the robin. 'He's the only one as knows. No one else has seen inside it for ten year'.'

Ten years was a long time, Mary thought. She had been born ten years ago.

She walked away, slowly thinking. She had begun to like the garden just as she had begun to like the robin and Dickon and Martha's mother. She was beginning to like Martha, too. That seemed a good many people to like—when you were not used to liking. She thought of the robin as one of the people. She went to her walk outside the long, ivy-covered wall over which she could see the tree-tops; and the second time she walked up and down the most interesting and exciting thing happened to her, and it was all through Ben Weatherstaff's robin.

She heard a chirp and a twitter, and when she looked at the bare flower-bed at her left side there he was hopping about and pretending to peck things out of the earth to persuade her that he had not followed her. But she knew he had followed her and the surprise so filled her with delight that she almost trembled a little.

'You do remember me!' she cried out. 'You do! You are prettier than anything else in the world!'

She chirped, and talked, and coaxed and he hopped, and flirted his tail and twittered. It was as if he were talking. His red waistcoat was like satin and he puffed his tiny breast out and was so fine and so grand and so pretty that it was really as if he were showing her how important and like a human person a robin could be. Mistress Mary forgot that she had ever been contrary in her life when he allowed her to draw closer and closer to him, and bend down and talk and try to make something like robin sounds.

Oh! to[124] think that he should actually let her come as near to him as that! He knew nothing in the world would make her put out her hand toward him or startle him in the least tiniest way. He knew it because he was a real person—only nicer than any other person in the world. She was so happy that she scarcely dared to breathe.

The flower-bed was not quite bare. It was bare of flowers because the perennial plants had been cut down for their winter rest, but there were tall shrubs and low ones which grew together at the back of the bed, and as the robin hopped about under them she saw him hop over a small pile of freshly turned up earth. He stopped on it to look for a worm. The earth had been turned up because a dog had been trying to dig up a mole and he had scratched quite a deep hole.

Mary looked at it, not really knowing why the hole was there, and as she looked she saw something almost buried in the newly-turned soil. It was something like a ring of rusty iron or brass and when the robin flew up into a tree nearby she put out her hand and picked the ring up. It was more than a ring, however; it was an old key which looked as if it had been buried a long time.

Mistress Mary stood up and looked at it with an almost frightened face as it hung from her finger.

'Perhaps it has been buried for ten years,' she said in a whisper. 'Perhaps it is the key to the garden!'

The Robin Who Showed the Way

She looked at the key quite a long time. She turned it over and over, and thought about it. As I have said before, she was not a child who had been trained to ask permission or consult her elders about things. All she thought about the key was that if it was the key to the closed garden, and she could find out where the door was, she could perhaps open it and see what was inside the walls, and what had happened to the old rose-trees. It was because it had been shut up so long that she wanted to see it. It seemed as if it must be different from other places and that something strange must have happened to it during ten years. Besides that, if she liked it she could go into it every day and shut the door behind her, and she could make up some play of her own and play it quite alone, because nobody would ever know where she was, but would think the door was still locked and the key buried in the earth. The thought of that pleased her very much.

Living as it were, all by herself in a house with a hundred mysteriously closed rooms and having nothing whatever to do to amuse herself, had set her inactive brain to working and was actually awakening her imagination. There is no doubt that the fresh, strong, pure air from the moor had a great deal to do with it. Just as it had given her an appetite, and fighting with the wind had stirred her blood, so the same things had stirred her mind. In India she had always been too hot and languid and weak to care much about anything, but in this place she was beginning to care and to want to do new things. Already she felt less 'contrary,' though she did not know why.

She put the key in her pocket and walked up and down her walk. No one but herself ever seemed to come there, so she could walk slowly and look at the wall, or, rather, at the ivy growing on it. The ivy was the baffling thing. Howsoever carefully she looked she could see nothing but thickly-growing, glossy, dark green leaves. She was very much disappointed. Something of her contrariness came back to her as she paced the walk and looked over it at the tree-tops inside. It seemed so silly, she said to herself, to be near it and not be able to get in. She took the key in her pocket when she went back to the house, and she made up her mind that she would always carry it with her when she went out, so that if she ever should find the hidden door she would be ready.

Mrs. Medlock had allowed Martha to sleep all night at the cottage, but she was back at her work in the morning with cheeks redder than ever and in the best of spirits.

'I got up at four o'clock,' she said. 'Eh! it[125] was pretty on th' moor with th' birds gettin'[126] up an' th' rabbits scamperin'[127] about an' th' sun risin'[128]. I didn't walk all th' way. A man gave me a ride in his cart an' I can tell you I did enjoy myself.'

She was full of stories of the delights of her day out. Her mother had been glad to see her and they had got the baking and washing all out of the way. She had even made each of the children a dough-cake with a bit of brown sugar in it.

'I had 'em all pipin'[129] hot when they came in from playin' on th' moor. An' th' cottage all smelt o' nice, clean hot bakin'[130] an' there was a good fire, an' they just shouted for joy. Our Dickon he said our cottage was good enough for a king to live in.'

In the evening they had all sat round the fire, and Martha and her mother had sewed patches on torn clothes and mended stockings and Martha had told them about the little girl who had come from India and who had been waited on all her life by what Martha called 'blacks' until she didn't know how to put on her own stockings.

'Eh! they[131] did like to hear about you,' said Martha. 'They wanted to know all about th' blacks an' about th' ship you came in. I couldn't tell 'em enough.'

Mary reflected a little.

'I'll tell you a great deal more before your next day out,' she said, 'so that you will have more to talk about. I dare say they would like to hear about riding on elephants and camels, and about the officers going to hunt tigers.'

'My word!' cried delighted Martha. 'It would set 'em clean off their heads. Would tha' really do that, Miss? It would be same as a wild beast show like we heard they had in York once.'

'India is quite different from Yorkshire,' Mary said slowly, as she thought the matter over. 'I never thought of that. Did Dickon and your mother like to hear you talk about me?'

'Why, our Dickon's eyes nearly started out o' his head, they got that round,' answered Martha. 'But mother, she was put out about your seemin'[132] to be all by yourself like. She said, "Hasn't Mr. Craven got no governess for her, nor no nurse?" and I said, "No, he hasn't, though Mrs. Medlock says he will when he thinks of it, but she says he mayn't think of it for two or three years." '

'I don't want a governess,' said Mary sharply.

'But mother says you ought to be learnin' your book by this time an' you ought to have a woman to look after you, an' she says: "Now, Martha, you just think how you'd feel yourself, in a big place like that, wanderin' about all alone, an' no mother. You do your best to cheer her up," she says, an' I said I would.'

Mary gave her a long, steady look.

'You do cheer me up,' she said. 'I like to hear you talk.'

Presently Martha went out of the room and came back with something held in her hands under her apron.

'What does tha' think,' she said, with a cheerful grin. 'I've brought thee a present.'

'A present!' exclaimed Mistress Mary. How could a cottage full of fourteen hungry people give any one a present!

'A man was drivin'[133] across the moor peddlin'[134],' Martha explained. 'An' he stopped his cart at our door. He had pots an' pans an' odds an' ends, but mother had no money to buy anythin'. Just as he was goin' away our 'Lizabeth[135] Ellen called out, "Mother, he's got skippin'-ropes[136] with red an' blue handles." An' mother she calls out quite sudden, "Here, stop, mister! How much are they?" An' he says "Tuppence," an' mother she began fumblin'[137] in her pocket an' she says to me, "Martha, tha's brought thee thy wages like a good lass, an' I've got four places to put every penny, but I'm just goin' to take tuppence out of it to buy that child a skippin'-rope," an' she bought one an' here it is.'

She brought it out from under her apron and exhibited it quite proudly. It was a strong, slender rope with a striped red and blue handle at each end, but Mary Lennox had never seen a skipping-rope before. She gazed at it with a mystified expression.

'What is it for?' she asked curiously.

'For!' cried out Martha. 'Does tha' mean that they've not got skippin'-ropes in India, for all they've got elephants and tigers and camels! No wonder most of 'em's black. This is what it's for; just watch me.'

And she ran into the middle of the room and, taking a handle in each hand, began to skip, and skip, and skip, while Mary turned in her chair to stare at her, and the queer faces in the old portraits seemed to stare at her, too, and wonder what on earth this common little cottager had the impudence to be doing under their very noses. But Martha did not even see them. The interest and curiosity in Mistress Mary's face delighted her, and she went on skipping and counted as she skipped until she had reached a hundred.

'I could skip longer than that,' she said when she stopped. 'I've skipped as much as five hundred when I was twelve, but I wasn't as fat then as I am now, an' I was in practice.'

Mary got up from her chair beginning to feel excited herself.

'It looks nice,' she said. 'Your mother is a kind woman. Do you think I could ever skip like that?'

'You just try it,' urged Martha, handing her the skipping-rope. 'You can't skip a hundred at first, but if you practice you'll mount up. That's what mother said. She says, "Nothin' will do her more good than skippin' rope. It's th' sensiblest[138] toy a child can have. Let her play out in th' fresh air skippin' an' it'll stretch her legs an' arms an' give her some strength in 'em." '

It was plain that there was not a great deal of strength in Mistress Mary's arms and legs when she first began to skip. She was not very clever at it, but she liked it so much that she did not want to stop.

'Put on tha' things and run an' skip out o' doors,' said Martha. 'Mother said I must tell you to keep out o' doors as much as you could, even when it rains a bit, so as tha' wrap up warm.'

Mary put on her coat and hat and took her skipping-rope over her arm. She opened the door to go out, and then suddenly thought of something and turned back rather slowly.

'Martha,' she said, 'they were your wages. It was your twopence really. Thank you.' She said it stiffly because she was not used to thanking people or noticing that they did things for her. 'Thank you,' she said, and held out her hand because she did not know what else to do.

Martha gave her hand a clumsy little shake, as if she was not accustomed to this sort of thing either. Then she laughed.

'Eh! tha'[139] art a queer, old-womanish thing,' she said. 'If tha'd been our 'Lizabeth Ellen tha'd have given me a kiss.'

Mary looked stiffer than ever.

'Do you want me to kiss you?'

Martha laughed again.

'Nay, not me,' she answered. 'If tha' was different, p'raps[140] tha'd want to thysel'. But tha' isn't. Run off outside an' play with thy rope.'

Mistress Mary felt a little awkward as she went out of the room. Yorkshire people seemed strange, and Martha was always rather a puzzle to her. At first she had disliked her very much, but now she did not.

The skipping-rope was a wonderful thing. She counted and skipped, and skipped and counted, until her cheeks were quite red, and she was more interested than she had ever been since she was born. The sun was shining and a little wind was blowing—not a rough wind, but one which came in delightful little gusts and brought a fresh scent of newly-turned earth with it. She skipped round the fountain garden, and up one walk and down another. She skipped at last into the kitchen-garden and saw Ben Weatherstaff digging and talking to his robin, which was hopping about him. She skipped down the walk toward him and he lifted his head and looked at her with a curious expression. She had wondered if he would notice her. She wanted him to see her skip.

'Well!' he exclaimed. 'Upon my word! P'raps tha' art a young 'un, after all, an' p'raps tha's got child's blood in thy veins instead of sour buttermilk. Tha's skipped red into thy cheeks as sure as my name's Ben Weatherstaff. I wouldn't have believed tha' could do it.'

'I never skipped before,' Mary said. 'I'm just beginning. I can only go up to twenty.'

'Tha' keep on,' said Ben. 'Tha' shapes[141] well enough at it for a young 'un that's lived with heathen. Just see how he's watchin'[142] thee,' jerking his head toward the robin. 'He followed after thee yesterday. He'll be at it again to-day. He'll be bound to find out what th' skippin'-rope is. He's never seen one. Eh!' shaking his head at the bird, 'tha' curiosity will be th' death of thee sometime if tha' doesn't look sharp.'

Mary skipped round all the gardens and round the orchard, resting every few minutes. At length she went to her own special walk and made up her mind to try if she could skip the whole length of it. It was a good long skip and she began slowly, but before she had gone half-way down the path she was so hot and breathless that she was obliged to stop. She did not mind much, because she had already counted up to thirty. She stopped with a little laugh of pleasure, and there, lo and behold, was the robin swaying on a long branch of ivy. He had followed her and he greeted her with a chirp. As Mary had skipped toward him she felt something heavy in her pocket strike against her at each jump, and when she saw the robin she laughed again.

'You showed me where the key was yesterday,' she said. 'You ought to show me the door to-day; but I don't believe you know!'

The robin flew from his swinging spray of ivy on to the top of the wall and he opened his beak and sang a loud, lovely trill, merely to show off. Nothing in the world is quite as adorably lovely as a robin when he shows off—and they are nearly always doing it.

Mary Lennox had heard a great deal about Magic in her Ayah's stories, and she always said that what happened almost at that moment was Magic.

One of the nice little gusts of wind rushed down the walk, and it was a stronger one than the rest. It was strong enough to wave the branches of the trees, and it was more than strong enough to sway the trailing sprays of untrimmed ivy hanging from the wall. Mary had stepped close to the robin, and suddenly the gust of wind swung aside some loose ivy trails, and more suddenly still she jumped toward it and caught it in her hand. This she did because she had seen something under it—a round knob which had been covered by the leaves hanging over it. It was the knob of a door.

She put her hands under the leaves and began to pull and push them aside. Thick as the ivy hung, it nearly all was a loose and swinging curtain, though some had crept over wood and iron. Mary's heart began to thump and her hands to shake a little in her delight and excitement. The robin kept singing and twittering away and tilting his head on one side, as if he were as excited as she was. What was this under her hands which was square and made of iron and which her fingers found a hole in?

It was the lock of the door which had been closed ten years

and she put her hand in her pocket, drew out the key and found it fitted the keyhole. She put the key in and turned it. It took two hands to do it, but it did turn.

And then she took a long breath and looked behind her up the long walk to see if anyone was coming. No one was coming. No one ever did come, it seemed, and she took another long breath, because she could not help it, and she held back the swinging curtain of ivy and pushed back the door which opened slowly— slowly.

Then she slipped through it, and shut it behind her, and stood with her back against it, looking about her and breathing quite fast with excitement, and wonder, and delight.

She was standing inside the secret garden.

The Strangest House Any One Ever Lived in

It was the sweetest, most mysterious-looking place any one could imagine. The high walls which shut it in were covered with the leafless stems of climbing roses which were so thick that they were matted together. Mary Lennox knew they were roses because she had seen a great many roses in India. All the ground was covered with grass of a wintry brown and out of it grew clumps of bushes which were surely rose-bushes if they were alive. There were numbers of standard roses which had so spread their branches that they were like little trees. There were other trees in the garden, and one of the things which made the place look strangest and loveliest was that climbing roses had run all over them and swung down long tendrils which made light swaying curtains, and here and there they had caught at each other or at a far-reaching branch and had crept from one tree to another and made lovely bridges of themselves. There were neither leaves nor roses on them now and Mary did not know whether they were dead or alive, but their thin gray or brown branches and sprays looked like a sort of hazy mantle spreading over everything, walls, and trees, and even brown grass, where they had fallen from their fastenings and run along the ground. It was this hazy tangle from tree to tree which made it all look so mysterious. Mary had thought it must be different from other gardens which had not been left all by themselves so long; and indeed it was different from any other place she had ever seen in her life.

'How still it is!' she whispered. 'How still!'

Then she waited a moment and listened at the stillness. The robin, who had flown to his tree-top, was still as all the rest. He did not even flutter his wings; he sat without stirring, and looked at Mary.

'No wonder it is still,' she whispered again. 'I am the first person who has spoken in here for ten years.'

She moved away from the door, stepping as softly as if she were afraid of awakening someone. She was glad that there was grass under her feet and that her steps made no sounds. She walked under one of the fairy-like gray arches between the trees and looked up at the sprays and tendrils which formed them.

'I wonder if they are all quite dead,' she said. 'Is it all a quite dead garden? I wish it wasn't.'

If she had been Ben Weatherstaff she could have told whether the wood was alive by looking at it, but she could only see that there were only gray or brown sprays and branches and none showed any signs of even a tiny leaf-bud anywhere.

But she was inside the wonderful garden and she could come

through the door under the ivy any time and she felt as if she had found a world all her own.

The sun was shining inside the four walls and the high arch of blue sky over this particular piece of Misselthwaite seemed even more brilliant and soft than it was over the moor. The robin flew down from his tree-top and hopped about or flew after her from one bush to another. He chirped a good deal and had a very busy air, as if he were showing her things. Everything was strange and silent and she seemed to be hundreds of miles away from any one, but somehow she did not feel lonely at all. All that troubled her was her wish that she knew whether all the roses were dead, or if perhaps some of them had lived and might put out leaves and buds as the weather got warmer. She did not want it to be a quite dead garden. If it were a quite alive garden, how wonderful it would be, and what thousands of roses would grow on every side!

Her skipping-rope had hung over her arm when she came in and after she had walked about for a while she thought she would skip round the whole garden, stopping when she wanted to look at things. There seemed to have been grass paths here and there, and in one or two corners there were alcoves of evergreen with stone seats or tall moss-covered flower urns in them.

As she came near the second of these alcoves she stopped skipping. There had once been a flower-bed in it, and she thought she saw something sticking out of the black earth—some sharp little pale green points. She remembered what Ben Weatherstaff had said and she knelt down to look at them.

'Yes, they are tiny growing things and they might be crocuses or snowdrops or daffodils,' she whispered.

She bent very close to them and sniffed the fresh scent of the damp earth. She liked it very much.

'Perhaps there are some other ones coming up in other places,' she said. 'I will go all over the garden and look.'

She did not skip, but walked. She went slowly and kept her eyes on the ground. She looked in the old border beds and among the grass, and after she had gone round, trying to miss nothing, she had found ever so many more sharp, pale green points, and she had become quite excited again.

'It isn't a quite dead garden,' she cried out softly to herself. 'Even if the roses are dead, there are other things alive.'

She did not know anything about gardening, but the grass seemed so thick in some of the places where the green points were pushing their way through that she thought they did not seem to have room enough to grow. She searched about until she found a rather sharp piece of wood and knelt down and dug and weeded out the weeds and grass until she made nice little clear places around them.

'Now they look as if they could breathe,' she said, after she had finished with the first ones. 'I am going to do ever so many more. I'll do all I can see. If I haven't time to-day I can come to-morrow[143].'

She went from place to place, and dug and weeded, and enjoyed herself so immensely that she was led on from bed to bed and into the grass under the trees. The exercise made her so warm that she first threw her coat off, and then her hat, and without knowing it she was smiling down on to the grass and the pale green points all the time.

The robin was tremendously busy. He was very much pleased to see gardening begun on his own estate. He had often wondered at Ben Weatherstaff. Where gardening is done all sorts of delightful things to eat are turned up with the soil. Now here was this new kind of creature who was not half Ben's size and yet had had the sense to come into his garden and begin at once.

Mistress Mary worked in her garden until it was time to go to her midday dinner. In fact, she was rather late in remembering, and when she put on her coat and hat, and picked up her skipping-rope, she could not believe that she had been working two or three hours. She had been actually happy all the time; and dozens and dozens of the tiny, pale green points were to be seen in cleared places, looking twice as cheerful as they had looked before when the grass and weeds had been smothering them.

'I shall come back this afternoon,' she said, looking all round at her new kingdom, and speaking to the trees and the rose-bushes as if they heard her.

Then she ran lightly across the grass, pushed open the slow old door and slipped through it under the ivy. She had such red cheeks and such bright eyes and ate such a dinner that Martha was delighted.

'Two pieces o' meat an' two helps o' rice puddin'[144]!' she said. 'Eh! mother[145] will be pleased when I tell her what th' skippin'-rope's done for thee.'

In the course of her digging with her pointed stick Mistress Mary had found herself digging up a sort of white root rather like an onion. She had put it back in its place and patted the earth carefully down on it, and just now she wondered if Martha could tell her what it was.

'Martha,' she said, 'what are those white roots that look like onions?'

'They're bulbs,' answered Martha. 'Lots o' spring flowers grow from 'em. Th' very little ones are snowdrops an' crocuses an' th' big ones are narcissusis an' jonquils and daffydowndillys. Th' biggest of all is lilies an' purple flags. Eh! they are nice. Dickon's got a whole lot of 'em planted in our bit o' garden.'

'Does Dickon know all about them?' asked Mary, a new idea taking possession of her.

'Our Dickon can make a flower grow out of a brick walk. Mother says he just whispers things out o' th' ground.'

'Do bulbs live a long time? Would they live years and years if no one helped them?' inquired Mary anxiously.

'They're things as helps[146] themselves,' said Martha. 'That's why poor folk can afford to have 'em. If you don't trouble 'em, most of 'em'll work away underground for a lifetime an' spread out an' have little 'uns. There's a place in th' park woods here where there's snowdrops by thousands. They're the prettiest sight in Yorkshire when th' spring comes. No one knows when they was first planted.'

'I wish the spring was here now,' said Mary. 'I want to see all the things that grow in England.'

She had finished her dinner and gone to her favorite seat on the hearth-rug.

'I wish—I wish I had a little spade,' she said.

'Whatever does tha' want a spade for?' asked Martha, laughing. 'Art tha' goin' to take to diggin'[147]? I must tell mother that, too.'

Mary looked at the fire and pondered a little. She must be careful if she meant to keep her secret kingdom. She wasn't doing any harm, but if Mr. Craven found out about the open door he would be fearfully angry and get a new key and lock it up for-evermore. She really could not bear that.

'This is such a big lonely place,' she said slowly, as if she were turning matters over in her mind. 'The house is lonely, and the park is lonely, and the gardens are lonely. So many places seem shut up. I never did many things in India, but there were more people to look at—natives and soldiers marching by—and sometimes bands playing, and my Ayah told me stories. There is no one to talk to here except you and Ben Weatherstaff. And you have to do your work and Ben Weatherstaff won't speak to me often. I thought if I had a little spade I could dig somewhere as he does, and I might make a little garden if he would give me some seeds.'

Martha's face quite lighted up.

'There now!' she exclaimed, 'if[148] that wasn't one of th' things mother said. She says, "There's such a lot o' room in that big place, why don't they give her a bit for herself, even if she doesn't plant nothin' but parsley an' radishes? She'd dig an' rake away an' be right down happy over it." Them was[149] the very words she said.'

'Were they?' said Mary. 'How many things she knows, doesn't she?'

'Eh!' said Martha. 'It's like she says: "A woman as brings up twelve children learns something besides her A B C. Children's as good as 'rithmetic[150] to set you findin' out things.'

'How much would a spade cost—a little one?' Mary asked.

'Well,' was Martha's reflective answer, 'at Thwaite village there's a shop or so an' I saw little garden sets with a spade an' a rake an' a fork all tied together for two shillings. An' they was stout enough to work with, too.'

'I've got more than that in my purse,' said Mary. 'Mrs. Morrison gave me five shillings and Mrs. Medlock gave me some money from Mr. Craven.'

'Did he remember thee that much?' exclaimed Martha.

'Mrs. Medlock said I was to have a shilling a week to spend. She gives me one every Saturday. I didn't know what to spend it on.'

'My word! that's[151] riches,' said Martha. 'Tha' can buy anything in th' world tha' wants[152]. Th' rent of our cottage is only one an' threepence an' it's like pullin'[153] eye-teeth to get it. Now I've just thought of somethin',' putting her hands on her hips.

'What?' said Mary eagerly.

'In the shop at Thwaite they sell packages o' flower-seeds for a penny each, and our Dickon he knows which is th' prettiest ones an' how to make 'em grow. He walks over to Thwaite many a day just for th' fun of it. Does tha' know how to print letters?' suddenly.

'I know how to write,' Mary answered.

Martha shook her head.

'Our Dickon can only read printin'[154]. If tha' could print we could write a letter to him an' ask him to go an' buy th' garden tools an' th' seeds at th' same time.'

'Oh! you're a good girl!' Mary cried. 'You are, really! I didn't know you were so nice. I know I can print letters if I try. Let's ask Mrs. Medlock for a pen and ink and some paper.'

'I've got some of my own,' said Martha. 'I bought 'em so I could print a bit of a letter to mother of a Sunday. I'll go and get it.'

She ran out of the room, and Mary stood by the fire and twisted her thin little hands together with sheer pleasure.

'If I have a spade,' she whispered, 'I can make the earth nice and soft and dig up weeds. If I have seeds and can make flowers grow the garden won't be dead at all—it will come alive.'

She did not go out again that afternoon because when Martha returned with her pen and ink and paper she was obliged to clear the table and carry the plates and dishes downstairs, and when she got into the kitchen Mrs. Medlock was there and told her to do something, so Mary waited for what seemed to her a long time before she came back. Then it was a serious piece of work to write to Dickon. Mary had been taught very little because her governesses had disliked her too much to stay with her. She could not spell particularly well but she found that she could print letters when she tried. This was the letter Martha dictated to her:

> 'My Dear Dickon:
>
> This comes hoping to find you well as it leaves me at present. Miss Mary has plenty of money and will you go to Thwaite and buy her some flower seeds and a set of garden tools to make a flower-bed. Pick the prettiest ones and easy to grow because[155] she has never done it before and lived in India which is different. Give my love to mother and every one of you. Miss Mary is going to tell me a lot more so that on my next day out you can hear about elephants and camels and gentlemen going hunting lions and tigers.
>
> 'Your loving sister,
> Martha Phoebe Sowerby'

'We'll put the money in th' envelope an' I'll get th' butcher's boy to take it in his cart. He's a great friend o' Dickon's,' said Martha.

'How shall I get the things when Dickon buys them?'

'He'll bring 'em to you himself. He'll like to walk over this way.'

'Oh!' exclaimed Mary, 'then[156] I shall see him! I never thought I should see Dickon.'

'Does tha' want to see him?' asked Martha suddenly, she had looked so pleased.

'Yes, I do. I never saw a boy foxes and crows loved. I want to see him very much.'

Martha gave a little start, as if she suddenly remembered something.

'Now to think,' she broke out, 'to think o' me forgettin'[157] that there; an' I thought I was goin' to tell you first thing this mornin'. I asked mother—and she said she'd ask Mrs. Medlock her own self.'

'Do you mean—' Mary began.

'What I said Tuesday. Ask her if you might be driven over to our cottage some day and have a bit o' mother's hot oat cake, an' butter, an' a glass o' milk.'

It seemed as if all the interesting things were happening in one day. To think of going over the moor in the daylight and when the sky was blue! To think of going into the cottage which held twelve children!

'Does she think Mrs. Medlock would let me go?' she asked, quite anxiously.

'Aye, she thinks she would. She knows what a tidy woman mother is and how clean she keeps the cottage.'

'If I went I should see your mother as well as Dickon,' said Mary, thinking it over and liking the idea very much. 'She doesn't seem to be like the mothers in India.'

Her work in the garden and the excitement of the afternoon ended by making her feel quiet and thoughtful. Martha stayed with her until tea-time, but they sat in comfortable quiet and talked very little. But just before Martha went down-stairs for the tea-tray, Mary asked a question.

'Martha,' she said, 'has the scullery-maid had the toothache again to-day?'

Martha certainly started slightly.

'What makes thee ask that?' she said.

'Because when I waited so long for you to come back I opened the door and walked down the corridor to see if you were coming. And I heard that far-off crying again, just as we heard it the other night. There isn't a wind today, so you see it couldn't have been the wind.'

'Eh!' said Martha restlessly. 'Tha' mustn't go walkin'[158] about in corridors an' listenin'[159]. Mr. Craven would be that there angry there's no knowin' what he'd do.'

'I wasn't listening,' said Mary. 'I was just waiting for you—and I heard it. That's three times.'

'My word! There's Mrs. Medlock's bell,' said Martha, and she almost ran out of the room.

'It's the strangest house any one ever lived in,' said Mary drowsily, as she dropped her head on the cushioned seat of the armchair near her. Fresh air, and digging, and skipping-rope had made her feel so comfortably tired that she fell asleep.

10.

Dickon

The sun shone down for nearly a week on the secret garden. The Secret Garden was what Mary called it when she was thinking of it. She liked the name, and she liked still more the feeling that when its beautiful old walls shut her in no one knew where she was. It seemed almost like being shut out of the world in some fairy place. The few books she had read and liked had been fairy-story books, and she had read of secret gardens in some of the stories. Sometimes people went to sleep in them for a hundred years, which she had thought must be rather stupid. She had no intention of going to sleep, and, in fact, she was becoming wider awake every day which passed at Misselthwaite. She was beginning to like to be out of doors; she no longer hated the wind, but enjoyed it. She could run faster, and longer, and she could skip up to a hundred. The bulbs in the secret garden must have been much astonished. Such nice clear places were made round them that they had all the breathing space they wanted, and really, if Mistress Mary had known it, they began to cheer up under the dark earth and work tremendously. The sun could get at them and warm them, and when the rain came down it could reach them at once, so they began to feel very much alive.

Mary was an odd, determined little person, and now she had something interesting to be determined about, she was very much absorbed, indeed. She worked and dug and pulled up weeds steadily, only becoming more pleased with her work every hour instead of tiring of it. It seemed to her like a fascinating sort of play. She found many more of the sprouting pale green points than she had ever hoped to find. They seemed to be starting up everywhere and each day she was sure she found tiny new ones, some so tiny that they barely peeped above the earth. There were so many that she remembered what Martha had said about the 'snowdrops by the thousands,' and about bulbs spreading and making new ones. These had been left to themselves for ten years and perhaps they had spread, like the snowdrops, into thousands. She wondered how long it would be before they showed that they were flowers. Sometimes she stopped digging to look at the garden and try to imagine what it would be like when it was covered with thousands of lovely things in bloom.

During that week of sunshine, she became more intimate with Ben Weatherstaff. She surprised him several times by seeming to start up beside him as if she sprang out of the earth. The truth was that she was afraid that he would pick up his tools and go away if he saw her coming, so she always walked toward him as silently as possible. But, in fact, he did not object to her as strongly as he had at first. Perhaps he was secretly rather flattered by her evident desire for his elderly company. Then, also, she was more civil than she had been. He did not know that when she first saw him she spoke to him as she would have spoken to a native, and had not known that a cross, sturdy old Yorkshire man was not accustomed to salaam to his masters, and be merely commanded by them to do things.

'Tha'rt like th' robin,' he said to her one morning when he lifted his head and saw her standing by him. 'I never knows when I shall see thee or which side tha'll come from.'

'He's friends with me now,' said Mary.

'That's like him,' snapped Ben Weatherstaff. 'Makin' up to th' women folk just for vanity an' flightiness. There's nothin' he wouldn't do for th' sake o' showin'[160] off an' flirtin'[161] his tail-feathers. He's as full o' pride as an egg's full o' meat.'

He very seldom talked much and sometimes did not even answer Mary's questions except by a grunt, but this morning he said more than usual. He stood up and rested one hobnailed boot on the top of his spade while he looked her over.

'How long has tha' been here?' he jerked out.

'I think it's about a month,' she answered.

'Tha's beginnin'[162] to do Misselthwaite credit,' he said. 'Tha's a bit fatter than tha' was an' tha's not quite so yeller. Tha' looked like a young plucked crow when tha' first came into this garden. Thinks I[163] to myself I never set eyes on an uglier, sourer faced young 'un.'

Mary was not vain and as she had never thought much of her looks she was not greatly disturbed.

'I know I'm fatter,' she said. 'My stockings are getting tighter. They used to make wrinkles. There's the robin, Ben Weatherstaff.'

There, indeed, was the robin, and she thought he looked nicer than ever. His red waistcoat was as glossy as satin and he flirted his wings and tail and tilted his head and hopped about with all sorts of lively graces. He seemed determined to make Ben Weatherstaff admire him. But Ben was sarcastic.

'Aye, there tha' art!' he said. 'Tha' can put up with me for a bit sometimes when tha's got no one better. Tha's been reddenin'[164] up thy waistcoat an' polishin'[165] thy feathers this two weeks. I know what tha's up to. Tha's courtin' some bold young madam somewhere, tellin'[166] thy lies to her about bein' th' finest cock robin on Missel Moor an' ready to fight all th' rest of 'em.'

'Oh! look[167] at him!' exclaimed Mary.

The robin was evidently in a fascinating, bold mood. He hopped closer and closer and looked at Ben Weatherstaff more and more engagingly. He flew on to the nearest currant bush and tilted his head and sang a little song right at him.

'Tha' thinks tha'll get over me by doin' that,' said Ben, wrinkling his face up in such a way that Mary felt sure he was trying not to look pleased. 'Tha' thinks no one can stand out against thee—that's what tha' thinks.'

The robin spread his wings—Mary could scarcely believe her eyes. He flew right up to the handle of Ben Weatherstaff's spade and alighted on the top of it. Then the old man's face wrinkled itself slowly into a new expression. He stood still as if he were afraid to breathe—as if he would not have stirred for the world, lest his robin should start away. He spoke quite in a whisper.

'Well, I'm danged!' he said as softly as if he were saying something quite different. 'Tha' does know how to get at a chap—tha' does! Tha's fair unearthly, tha's so knowin'.'

And he stood without stirring—almost without drawing his

breath—until the robin gave another flirt to his wings and flew away. Then he stood looking at the handle of the spade as if there might be Magic in it, and then he began to dig again and said nothing for several minutes.

But because he kept breaking into a slow grin now and then, Mary was not afraid to talk to him.

'Have you a garden of your own?' she asked.

'No. I'm bachelder an' lodge with Martin at th' gate.'

'If you had one,' said Mary, 'what would you plant?'

'Cabbages an' 'taters[168] an' onions.'

'But if you wanted to make a flower garden,' persisted Mary, 'what would you plant?'

'Bulbs an' sweet-smellin'[169] things—but mostly roses.'

Mary's face lighted up.

'Do you like roses?' she said.

Ben Weatherstaff rooted up a weed and threw it aside before he answered.

'Well, yes, I do. I was[170] learned that by a young lady I was gardener to. She had a lot in a place she was fond of, an' she loved 'em like they was children—or robins. I've seen her bend over an' kiss 'em.' He dragged out another weed and scowled at it. 'That were as much as ten year' ago.'

'Where is she now?' asked Mary, much interested.

'Heaven,' he answered, and drove his spade deep into the soil, ''cording[171] to what parson says.'

'What happened to the roses?' Mary asked again, more interested than ever.

'They was left to themselves.'

Mary was becoming quite excited.

'Did they quite die? Do roses quite die when they are left to themselves?' she ventured.

'Well, I'd got to like 'em—an' I liked her—an' she liked 'em,' Ben Weatherstaff admitted reluctantly. 'Once or twice a year I'd go an' work at 'em a bit—prune 'em an' dig about th' roots. They run wild, but they was in rich soil, so some of 'em lived.'

'When they have no leaves and look gray and brown and dry, how can you tell whether they are dead or alive?' inquired Mary.

'Wait till th' spring gets at 'em—wait till th' sun shines on th' rain and th' rain falls on th' sunshine an' then tha'll find out.'

'How—how?' cried Mary, forgetting to be careful.

'Look along th' twigs an' branches an' if tha' see a bit of a brown lump swelling here an' there, watch it after th' warm rain an' see what happens.' He stopped suddenly and looked curiously at her eager face. 'Why does tha' care so much about roses an' such, all of a sudden?' he demanded.

Mistress Mary felt her face grow red. She was almost afraid to answer.

'I—I want to play that—that I have a garden of my own,' she stammered. 'I—there is nothing for me to do. I have nothing—and no one.'

'Well,' said Ben Weatherstaff slowly, as he watched her, 'that's true. Tha' hasn't.'

He said it in such an odd way that Mary wondered if he was actually a little sorry for her. She had never felt sorry for herself; she had only felt tired and cross, because she disliked people and things so much. But now the world seemed to be changing and getting nicer. If no one found out about the secret garden, she should enjoy herself always.

She stayed with him for ten or fifteen minutes longer and asked him as many questions as she dared. He answered every one of them in his queer grunting way and he did not seem really cross and did not pick up his spade and leave her. He said something about roses just as she was going away and it reminded her of the ones he had said he had been fond of.

'Do you go and see those other roses now?' she asked.

'Not been this year.[172] My rheumatics has made me too stiff in th' joints.'

He said it in his grumbling voice, and then quite suddenly he seemed to get angry with her, though she did not see why he should.

'Now look here!' he said sharply. 'Don't tha' ask so many questions. Tha' rt th' worst wench for askin'[173] questions I've ever come across. Get thee gone an' play thee. I've done talkin' for today.'

And he said it so crossly that she knew there was not the least use in staying another minute. She went skipping slowly down the outside walk, thinking him over and saying to herself that, queer as it was, here was another person whom she liked in spite of his crossness. She liked old Ben Weatherstaff. Yes, she did like him. She always wanted to try to make him talk to her. Also she began to believe that he knew everything in the world about flowers.

There was a laurel-hedged walk which curved round the secret garden and ended at a gate which opened into a wood, in the park. She thought she would slip round this walk and look into the wood and see if there were any rabbits hopping about. She enjoyed the skipping very much and when she reached the little gate she opened it and went through because she heard a low, peculiar whistling sound and wanted to find out what it was.

It was a very strange thing indeed. She quite caught her breath as she stopped to look at it. A boy was sitting under a tree, with his back against it, playing on a rough wooden pipe.

He was a funny looking boy about twelve. He looked very clean and his nose turned up and his cheeks were as red as poppies and never had Mistress Mary seen such round and such blue eyes in any boy's face. And on the trunk of the tree he leaned against, a brown squirrel was clinging and watching him, and from behind a bush nearby a cock pheasant was delicately stretching his neck to peep out, and quite near him were two rabbits sitting up and sniffing with tremulous noses—and actually it appeared as if they were all drawing near to watch him and listen to the strange low little call his pipe seemed to make.

When he saw Mary he held up his hand and spoke to her in a

voice almost as low as and rather like his piping.

'Don't tha' move,' he said. 'It'd flight[174] 'em.'

Mary remained motionless. He stopped playing his pipe and began to rise from the ground. He moved so slowly that it scarcely seemed as though he were moving at all, but at last he stood on his feet and then the squirrel scampered back up into the branches of his tree, the pheasant withdrew his head and the rabbits dropped on all fours and began to hop away, though not at all as if they were frightened.

'I'm Dickon,' the boy said. 'I know tha'rt Miss Mary.'

Then Mary realized that somehow she had known at first that he was Dickon. Who else could have been charming rabbits and pheasants as the natives charm snakes in India? He had a wide, red, curving mouth and his smile spread all over his face.

'I got up slow,' he explained, 'because if tha' makes[175] a quick move it startles 'em. A body 'as[176] to move gentle[177] an' speak low when wild things is[178] about[179].'

He did not speak to her as if they had never seen each other before but as if he knew her quite well. Mary knew nothing about boys and she spoke to him a little stiffly because she felt rather shy.

'Did you get Martha's letter?' she asked.

He nodded his curly, rust-coloured head.

'That's why I come.'

He stooped to pick up something which had been lying on the ground beside him when he piped.

'I've got th' garden tools. There's a little spade an' rake an' a fork an' hoe. Eh! they are good 'uns. There's a trowel, too. An' th' woman in th' shop threw in a packet o' white poppy an' one o' blue larkspur when I bought th' other seeds.'

'Will you show the seeds to me?' Mary said.

She wished she could talk as he did. His speech was so quick and easy. It sounded as if he liked her and was not the least afraid she would not like him, though he was only a common moor boy, in patched clothes and with a funny face and a rough, rusty-red head. As she came closer to him she noticed that there was a clean fresh scent of heather and grass and leaves about him, almost as if he were made of them. She liked it very much and when she looked into his funny face with the red cheeks and round blue eyes she forgot that she had felt shy.

'Let us sit down on this log and look at them,' she said.

They sat down and he took a clumsy little brown paper package out of his coat pocket. He untied the string and inside there were ever so many neater and smaller packages with a picture of a flower on each one.

'There's a lot o' mignonette an' poppies,' he said. 'Mignonette's th' sweetest smellin' thing as grows, an' it'll grow wherever you cast it, same as poppies will. Them[180] as'll come up an' bloom if you just whistle to 'em, them's th' nicest of all.'

He stopped and turned his head quickly, his poppy-cheeked face lighting up.

'Where's that robin as is callin' us?' he said.

The chirp came from a thick holly bush, bright with scarlet berries, and Mary thought she knew whose it was.

'Is it really calling us?' she asked.

'Aye,' said Dickon, as if it was the most natural thing in the world, 'he's callin' some one he's friends with. That's same as sayin' "Here I am. Look at me. I wants a bit of a chat." There he is in the bush. Whose[181] is he?'

'He's Ben Weatherstaff's, but I think he knows me a little,' answered Mary.

'Aye, he knows thee,' said Dickon in his low voice again. 'An' he likes thee. He's took thee on. He'll tell me all about thee in a minute.'

He moved quite close to the bush with the slow movement Mary had noticed before, and then he made a sound almost like the robin's own twitter. The robin listened a few seconds, intently, and then answered quite as if he were replying to a question.

'Aye, he's a friend o' yours,' chuckled Dickon.

'Do you think he is?' cried Mary eagerly. She did so want to know. 'Do you think he really likes me?'

'He wouldn't come near thee if he didn't,' answered Dickon. 'Birds is rare choosers an' a robin can flout a body worse than a man. See, he's making up to thee now. "Cannot[182] tha' see a chap?" he's sayin'.'

And it really seemed as if it must be true. He so sidled and twittered and tilted as he hopped on his bush.

'Do you understand everything birds say?' said Mary.

Dickon's grin spread until he seemed all wide, red, curving mouth, and he rubbed his rough head.

'I think I do, and they think I do,' he said. 'I've lived on th' moor with 'em so long. I've watched 'em break shell an' come out an' fledge an' learn to fly an' begin to sing, till I think I'm one of 'em. Sometimes I think p'raps I'm a bird, or a fox, or a rabbit, or a squirrel, or even a beetle, an' I don't know it.'

He laughed and came back to the log and began to talk about the flower seeds again. He told her what they looked like when they were flowers; he told her how to plant them, and watch them, and feed and water them.

'See here,' he said suddenly, turning round to look at her. 'I'll plant them for thee myself. Where is tha' garden?'

Mary's thin hands clutched each other as they lay on her lap. She did not know what to say, so for a whole minute she said nothing. She had never thought of this. She felt miserable. And she felt as if she went red and then pale.

'Tha's got a bit o' garden, hasn't tha'?' Dickon said.

It was true that she had turned red and then pale. Dickon saw her do it, and as she still said nothing, he began to be puzzled.

'Wouldn't they give thee a bit?' he asked. 'Hasn't tha' got any yet?'

She held her hands tighter and turned her eyes toward him.

'I don't know anything about boys,' she said slowly. 'Could you keep a secret, if I told you one? It's a great secret. I don't know what I should do if any one found it out. I believe I should die!' She said the last sentence quite fiercely.

Dickon looked more puzzled than ever and even rubbed his hand over his rough head again, but he answered quite good-humoredly.

'I'm keepin'[183] secrets all th' time,' he said. 'If I couldn't keep secrets from th' other lads, secrets about foxes' cubs, an' birds' nests, an' wild things' holes, there'd be naught[184] safe on th' moor. Aye, I can keep secrets.'

Mistress Mary did not mean to put out her hand and clutch his sleeve but she did it.

'I've stolen a garden,' she said very fast. 'It isn't mine. It isn't anybody's. Nobody wants it, nobody cares for it, nobody ever goes into it. Perhaps everything is dead in it already. I don't know.'

She began to feel hot and as contrary as she had ever felt in her life.

'I don't care, I don't care! Nobody has any right to take it from me when I care about it and they don't. They're letting it die, all shut in by itself,' she ended passionately, and she threw her arms over her face and burst out crying—poor little Mistress Mary.

Dickon's curious blue eyes grew rounder and rounder.

'Eh-h-h!' he said, drawing his exclamation out slowly, and the way he did it meant both wonder and sympathy.

'I've nothing to do,' said Mary. 'Nothing belongs to me. I found it myself and I got into it myself. I was only just like the robin, and they wouldn't take it from the robin.'

'Where is it?' asked Dickon in a dropped voice.

Mistress Mary got up from the log at once. She knew she felt contrary again, and obstinate, and she did not care at all. She was imperious and Indian, and at the same time hot and sorrowful.

'Come with me and I'll show you,' she said.

She led him round the laurel path and to the walk where the ivy grew so thickly. Dickon followed her with a queer, almost pitying, look on his face. He felt as if he were being led to look at some strange bird's nest and must move softly. When she stepped to the wall and lifted the hanging ivy he started. There was a door and Mary pushed it slowly open and they passed in together, and then Mary stood and waved her hand round defiantly.

'It's this,' she said. 'It's a secret garden, and I'm the only one in the world who wants it to be alive.'

Dickon looked round and round about it, and round and round again.

'Eh!' he almost whispered, 'it is a queer, pretty place! It's like as if a body was in a dream.'

11.

The Nest of the Missel Thrush

For two or three minutes he stood looking round him, while Mary watched him, and then he began to walk about softly, even more lightly than Mary had walked the first time she had found herself inside the four walls. His eyes seemed to be taking in everything—the gray trees with the gray creepers climbing over them and hanging from their branches, the tangle on the walls and among the grass, the evergreen alcoves with the stone seats and tall flower urns standing in them.

'I never thought I'd see this place,' he said at last, in a whisper.

'Did you know about it?' asked Mary.

She had spoken aloud and he made a sign to her.

'We must talk low,' he said, 'or some one'll hear us an' wonder what's to do in here.'

'Oh! I forgot!' said Mary, feeling frightened and putting her hand quickly against her mouth. 'Did you know about the garden?' she asked again when she had recovered herself.

Dickon nodded.

'Martha told me there was one as no one ever went inside,' he answered. 'Us[185] used to wonder what it was like.'

He stopped and looked round at the lovely gray tangle about him, and his round eyes looked queerly happy.

'Eh! the[186] nests as'll be here come springtime,' he said. 'It'd be th' safest nestin'[187] place in England. No one never comin' near an' tangles o' trees an' roses to build in. I wonder all th' birds on th' moor don't build here.'

Mistress Mary put her hand on his arm again without knowing it.

'Will there be roses?' she whispered. 'Can you tell? I thought perhaps they were all dead.'

'Eh! No! Not them—not all of 'em!' he answered. 'Look here!'

He stepped over to the nearest tree—an old, old one with gray lichen all over its bark, but upholding a curtain of tangled sprays and branches. He took a thick knife out of his pocket and opened one of its blades.

'There's lots o' dead wood as ought to be cut out,' he said. 'An' there's a lot o' old wood, but it made some new last year. This here's a new bit,' and he touched a shoot which looked brownish green instead of hard, dry gray.

Mary touched it herself in an eager, reverent way.

'That one?' she said. 'Is that one quite alive—quite?'

Dickon curved his wide smiling mouth.

'It's as wick as you or me,' he said; and Mary remembered that Martha had told her that 'wick' meant 'alive' or 'lively.'

'I'm glad it's wick!' she cried out in her whisper. 'I want them all to be wick. Let us go round the garden and count how many wick ones there are.'

She quite panted with eagerness, and Dickon was as eager as she was. They went from tree to tree and from bush to bush. Dickon carried his knife in his hand and showed her things which she thought wonderful.

'They've run wild,' he said, 'but th' strongest ones has fair thrived on it. The delicatest[188] ones has died out, but th' others has growed[189] an' growed, an' spread an' spread, till they's a wonder. See here!' and he pulled down a thick gray, dry-looking branch. 'A body might think this was dead wood, but I don't believe it is— down to th' root. I'll cut it low down an' see.'

He knelt and with his knife cut the lifeless-looking branch through, not far above the earth.

'There!' he said exultantly. 'I told thee so. There's green in that wood yet. Look at it.'

Mary was down on her knees before he spoke, gazing with all her might.

'When it looks a bit greenish an' juicy like that, it's wick,' he explained. 'When th' inside is dry an' breaks easy, like this here piece I've cut off, it's done for. There's a big root here as all this live wood sprung out of, an' if th' old wood's cut off an' it's dug round, and took care of there'll be—' he stopped and lifted his face to look up at the climbing and hanging sprays above him—'there'll be a fountain o' roses here this summer.'

They went from bush to bush and from tree to tree. He was very strong and clever with his knife and knew how to cut the dry and dead wood away, and could tell when an unpromising bough or twig had still green life in it. In the course of half an hour Mary thought she could tell too, and when he cut through a lifeless-looking branch she would cry out joyfully under her breath when she caught sight of the least shade of moist green. The spade, and hoe, and fork were very useful. He showed her how to use the fork while he dug about roots with the spade and stirred the earth and let the air in.

They were working industriously round one of the biggest standard roses when he caught sight of something which made him utter an exclamation of surprise.

'Why!' he cried, pointing to the grass a few feet away. 'Who did that there?'

It was one of Mary's own little clearings round the pale green points.

'I did it,' said Mary.

'Why, I thought tha' didn't know nothin' about gardenin'[190],' he exclaimed.

'I don't,' she answered, 'but they were so little, and the grass was so thick and strong, and they looked as if they had no room to breathe. So I made a place for them. I don't even know what they are.'

Dickon went and knelt down by them, smiling his wide smile.

'Tha' was right,' he said. 'A gardener couldn't have told thee better. They'll grow now like Jack's bean-stalk. They're crocuses an' snowdrops, an' these here are narcissuses,' turning to another patch, 'an' here's daffydowndillys. Eh! they will be a sight.'

He ran from one clearing to another.

'Tha' has done a lot o' work for such a little wench,' he said, looking her over.

'I'm growing fatter,' said Mary, 'and I'm growing stronger. I used always to be tired. When I dig I'm not tired at all. I like to smell the earth when it's turned up.'

'It's rare good for thee,' he said, nodding his head wisely. 'There's naught as nice as th' smell o' good clean earth, except th' smell o' fresh growin' things when th' rain falls on 'em. I get out on th' moor many a day when it's rainin'[191] an' I lie under a bush an' listen to th' soft swish o' drops on th' heather an' I just sniff an' sniff. My nose end fair quivers like a rabbit's, mother says.'

'Do you never catch cold?' inquired Mary, gazing at him wonderingly. She had never seen such a funny boy, or such a nice one.

'Not me,' he said, grinning. 'I never ketched[192] cold since I was born. I wasn't brought up nesh enough. I've chased about th' moor in all weathers same as th' rabbits does. Mother says I've sniffed up too much fresh air for twelve year' to ever get to sniffin'[193] with cold. I'm as tough as a white-thorn knobstick.'

He was working all the time he was talking and Mary was following him and helping him with her fork or the trowel.

'There's a lot of work to do here!' he said once, looking about quite exultantly.

'Will you come again and help me to do it?' Mary begged. 'I'm sure I can help, too. I can dig and pull up weeds, and do whatever you tell me. Oh! do[194] come, Dickon!'

'I'll come every day if tha' wants me, rain or shine,' he answered stoutly. 'It's th' best fun I ever had in my life—shut in here an' wakenin'[195] up a garden.'

'If you will come,' said Mary, 'if you will help me to make it alive I'll—I don't know what I'll do,' she ended helplessly. What could you do for a boy like that?

'I'll tell thee what tha'll do,' said Dickon, with his happy grin. 'Tha'll get fat an' tha'll get as hungry as a young fox an' tha'll learn how to talk to th' robin same as I do. Eh! we'll[196] have a lot o' fun.'

He began to walk about, looking up in the trees and at the walls and bushes with a thoughtful expression.

'I wouldn't want to make it look like a gardener's garden, all clipped an' spick an' span, would you?' he said. 'It's nicer like this with things runnin'[197] wild, an' swingin'[198] an' catchin'[199] hold of each other.'

'Don't let us make it tidy,' said Mary anxiously. 'It wouldn't seem like a secret garden if it was tidy.'

Dickon stood rubbing his rusty-red head with a rather puzzled look.

'It's a secret garden sure enough,' he said, 'but seems like some one besides th' robin must have been in it since it was shut up ten year' ago.'

'But the door was locked and the key was buried,' said Mary. 'No one could get in.'

'That's true,' he answered. 'It's a queer place. Seems to me as if there'd been a bit o' prunin'[200] done here an' there, later than ten year' ago.'

'But how could it have been done?' said Mary.

He was examining a branch of a standard rose and he shook his head.

'Aye! how[201] could it!' he murmured. 'With th' door locked an' th' key buried.'

Mistress Mary always felt that however many years she lived she should never forget that first morning when her garden began to grow. Of course, it did seem to begin to grow for her that morning. When Dickon began to clear places to plant seeds, she remembered what Basil had sung at her when he wanted to tease her.

'Are there any flowers that look like bells?' she inquired.

'Lilies o' th' valley does,' he answered, digging away with the trowel, 'an' there's Canterbury bells, an' campanulas.'

'Let's plant some,' said Mary.

'There's lilies o' th' valley here already; I saw 'em. They'll have growed too close an' we'll have to separate 'em, but there's plenty. Th' other ones takes two years to bloom from seed, but I can bring you some bits o' plants from our cottage garden. Why does tha' want 'em?'

Then Mary told him about Basil and his brothers and sisters in India and of how she had hated them and of their calling her 'Mistress Mary Quite Contrary.'

'They used to dance round and sing at me. They sang—

> 'Mistress Mary, quite contrary,
> How does your garden grow?
> With silver bells, and cockle shells,
> And marigolds all in a row.'

I just remembered it and it made me wonder if there were really flowers like silver bells.'

She frowned a little and gave her trowel a rather spiteful dig into the earth.

'I wasn't as contrary as they were.'

But Dickon laughed.

'Eh!' he said, and as he crumbled the rich black soil she saw he was sniffing up the scent of it, 'there doesn't seem to be no need for no one to be contrary when there's flowers an' such like, an' such lots o' friendly wild things runnin' about makin' homes for themselves, or buildin'[202] nests an' singin' an' whistlin'[203], does there?'

Mary, kneeling by him holding the seeds, looked at him and stopped frowning.

'Dickon,' she said, 'you are as nice as Martha said you were. I like you, and you make the fifth person. I never thought I should like five people.'

Dickon sat up on his heels as Martha did when she was polishing the grate. He did look funny and delightful, Mary thought, with his round blue eyes and red cheeks and happy looking turned-up nose.

'Only five folk as tha' likes?' he said. 'Who is th' other four?'

'Your mother and Martha,' Mary checked them off on her fingers, 'and the robin and Ben Weatherstaff.'

Dickon laughed so that he was obliged to stifle the sound by putting his arm over his mouth.

'I know tha' thinks I'm a queer lad,' he said, 'but I think tha' art th' queerest little lass I ever saw.'

Then Mary did a strange thing. She leaned forward and asked him a question she had never dreamed of asking any one before. And she tried to ask it in Yorkshire because that was his language, and in India a native was always pleased if you knew his speech.

'Does tha' like me?' she said.

'Eh!' he answered heartily, 'that[204] I does. I likes thee wonderful, an' so does th' robin, I do believe!'

'That's two, then,' said Mary. 'That's two for me.'

And then they began to work harder than ever and more joyfully. Mary was startled and sorry when she heard the big clock in the courtyard strike the hour of her midday dinner.

'I shall have to go,' she said mournfully. 'And you will have to go too, won't you?'

Dickon grinned.

'My dinner's easy to carry about with me,' he said. 'Mother always lets me put a bit o' somethin' in my pocket.'

He picked up his coat from the grass and brought out of a pocket a lumpy little bundle tied up in a quite clean, coarse, blue and white handkerchief. It held two thick pieces of bread with a slice of something laid between them.

'It's oftenest naught but bread,' he said, 'but I've got a fine slice o' fat bacon with it to-day.'

Mary thought it looked a queer dinner, but he seemed ready to enjoy it.

'Run on an' get thy victuals,' he said. 'I'll be done with mine first. I'll get some more work done before I start back home.'

He sat down with his back against a tree.

'I'll call th' robin up,' he said, 'and give him th' rind o' th' bacon to peck at. They likes a bit o' fat wonderful.'

Mary could scarcely bear to leave him. Suddenly it seemed as if he might be a sort of wood fairy who might be gone when she came into the garden again. He seemed too good to be true. She went slowly half-way to the door in the wall and then she stopped and went back.

'Whatever happens, you—you never would tell?' she said.

His poppy-coloured cheeks were distended with his first big

bite of bread and bacon, but he managed to smile encouragingly.

'If tha' was a missel thrush an' showed me where thy nest was, does tha' think I'd tell any one? Not me,' he said. 'Tha' art as safe as a missel thrush.'

And she was quite sure she was.

12.

'Might I Have a Bit of Earth?'

Mary ran so fast that she was rather out of breath when she reached her room. Her hair was ruffled on her forehead and her cheeks were bright pink. Her dinner was waiting on the table, and Martha was waiting near it.

'Tha's a bit late,' she said. 'Where has tha' been?'

'I've seen Dickon!' said Mary. 'I've seen Dickon!'

'I knew he'd come,' said Martha exultantly. 'How does tha' like him?'

'I think—I think he's beautiful!' said Mary in a determined voice.

Martha looked rather taken aback but she looked pleased, too.

'Well,' she said, 'he's th' best lad as ever was born, but us never thought he was handsome. His nose turns up too much.'

'I like it to turn up,' said Mary.

'An' his eyes is so round,' said Martha, a trifle doubtful. 'Though they're a nice colour.'

'I like them round,' said Mary. 'And they are exactly the colour of the sky over the moor.'

Martha beamed with satisfaction.

'Mother says he made 'em that colour with always lookin' up at th' birds an' th' clouds. But he has got a big mouth, hasn't he, now?'

'I love his big mouth,' said Mary obstinately. 'I wish mine were just like it.'

Martha chuckled delightedly.

'It'd look rare an' funny in thy bit of a face,' she said. 'But I knowed it would be that way when tha' saw him. How did tha' like th' seeds an' th' garden tools?'

'How did you know he brought them?' asked Mary.

'Eh! I never thought of him not bringin'[205] 'em. He'd be sure to bring 'em if they was in Yorkshire. He's such a trusty lad.'

Mary was afraid that she might begin to ask difficult questions, but she did not. She was very much interested in the seeds and gardening tools, and there was only one moment when Mary was frightened. This was when she began to ask where the flowers were to be planted.

'Who did tha' ask about it?' she inquired.

'I haven't asked anybody yet,' said Mary, hesitating.

'Well, I wouldn't ask th' head gardener. He's too grand, Mr. Roach is.'

'I've never seen him,' said Mary. 'I've only seen undergardeners and Ben Weatherstaff.'

'If I was you, I'd ask Ben Weatherstaff,' advised Martha. 'He's not half as bad as he looks, for all he's so crabbed. Mr. Craven lets him do what he likes because he was here when Mrs. Craven was alive, an' he used to make her laugh. She liked him. Perhaps he'd find you a corner somewhere out o' the way.'

'If it was out of the way and no one wanted it, no one could mind my having it, could they?' Mary said anxiously.

'There wouldn't be no reason,' answered Martha. 'You wouldn't do no harm.'

Mary ate her dinner as quickly as she could and when she rose from the table she was going to run to her room to put on her hat again, but Martha stopped her.

'I've got somethin' to tell you,' she said. 'I thought I'd let you eat your dinner first. Mr. Craven came back this mornin' and I think he wants to see you.'

Mary turned quite pale.

'Oh!' she said. 'Why! Why! He didn't want to see me when I came. I heard Pitcher say he didn't.'

'Well,' explained Martha, 'Mrs. Medlock says it's because o' mother. She was walkin' to Thwaite village an' she met him. She'd never spoke to him before, but Mrs. Craven had been to our cottage two or three times. He'd forgot, but mother hadn't an' she made bold to stop him. I don't know what she said to him about you but she said somethin' as put him in th' mind to see you before he goes away again, to-morrow.'

'Oh!' cried Mary, 'is he going away tomorrow? I am so glad!'

'He's goin' for a long time. He mayn't come back till autumn or winter. He's goin' to travel in foreign places. He's always doin' it.'

'Oh! I'm so glad—so glad!' said Mary thankfully.

If he did not come back until winter, or even autumn, there would be time to watch the secret garden come alive. Even if he found out then and took it away from her she would have had that much at least.

'When do you think he will want to see—'

She did not finish the sentence, because the door opened, and Mrs. Medlock walked in. She had on her best black dress and cap, and her collar was fastened with a large brooch with a picture of a man's face on it. It was a coloured photograph of Mr. Medlock who had died years ago, and she always wore it when she was dressed up. She looked nervous and excited.

'Your hair's rough,' she said quickly. 'Go and brush it. Martha, help her to slip on her best dress. Mr. Craven sent me to bring her to him in his study.'

All the pink left Mary's cheeks. Her heart began to thump and she felt herself changing into a stiff, plain, silent child again. She did not even answer Mrs. Medlock, but turned and walked into her bedroom, followed by Martha. She said nothing while her dress was changed, and her hair brushed, and after she was quite tidy she followed Mrs. Medlock down the corridors, in silence. What was there for her to say? She was obliged to go and see Mr. Craven and he would not like her, and she would not like him. She knew what he would think of her.

She was taken to a part of the house she had not been into before. At last Mrs. Medlock knocked at a door, and when some one said, 'Come in,' they entered the room together. A man was sitting in an armchair before the fire, and Mrs. Medlock spoke to him.

'This is Miss Mary, sir,' she said.

'You can go and leave her here. I will ring for you when I want you to take her away,' said Mr. Craven.

When she went out and closed the door, Mary could only stand waiting, a plain little thing, twisting her thin hands together. She could see that the man in the chair was not so much a hunchback as a man with high, rather crooked shoulders, and he had black hair streaked with white. He turned his head over his high shoulders and spoke to her.

'Come here!' he said.

Mary went to him.

He was not ugly. His face would have been handsome if it had not been so miserable. He looked as if the sight of her worried and fretted him and as if he did not know what in the world to do with her.

'Are you well?' he asked.

'Yes,' answered Mary.

'Do they take good care of you?'

'Yes.'

He rubbed his forehead fretfully as he looked her over.

'You are very thin,' he said.

'I am getting fatter,' Mary answered in what she knew was her stiffest way.

What an unhappy face he had! His black eyes seemed as if they scarcely saw her, as if they were seeing something else, and he could hardly keep his thoughts upon her.

'I forgot you,' he said. 'How could I remember you? I intended to send you a governess or a nurse, or some one of that sort, but I forgot.'

'Please,' began Mary. 'Please—' and then the lump in her throat choked her.

'What do you want to say?' he inquired.

'I am—I am too big for a nurse,' said Mary. 'And please—please don't make me have a governess yet.'

He rubbed his forehead again and stared at her.

'That was what the Sowerby woman said,' he muttered absent-mindedly.

Then Mary gathered a scrap of courage.

'Is she—is she Martha's mother?' she stammered.

'Yes, I think so,' he replied.

'She knows about children,' said Mary. 'She has twelve. She knows.'

He seemed to rouse himself.

'What do you want to do?'

'I want to play out of doors,' Mary answered, hoping that her voice did not tremble. 'I never liked it in India. It makes me hungry here, and I am getting fatter.'

He was watching her.

'Mrs. Sowerby said it would do you good. Perhaps it will,' he said. 'She thought you had better get stronger before you had a governess.'

'It makes me feel strong when I play and the wind comes over the moor,' argued Mary.

'Where do you play?' he asked next.

'Everywhere,' gasped Mary. 'Martha's mother sent me a skipping-rope. I skip and run—and I look about to see if things are beginning to stick up out of the earth. I don't do any harm.'

'Don't look so frightened,' he said in a worried voice. 'You could not do any harm, a child like you! You may do what you like.'

Mary put her hand up to her throat because she was afraid he might see the excited lump which she felt jump into it. She came a step nearer to him.

'May I?' she said tremulously.

Her anxious little face seemed to worry him more than ever.

'Don't look so frightened,' he exclaimed. 'Of course you may. I am your guardian, though I am a poor one for any child. I cannot give you time or attention. I am too ill, and wretched and distracted; but I wish you to be happy and comfortable. I don't know anything about children, but Mrs. Medlock is to see that you have all you need. I sent for you to-day because Mrs. Sowerby said I ought to see you. Her daughter had talked about you. She thought you needed fresh air and freedom and running about.'

'She knows all about children,' Mary said again in spite of herself.

'She ought to,' said Mr. Craven. 'I thought her rather bold to stop me on the moor, but she said—Mrs. Craven had been kind to her.' It seemed hard for him to speak his dead wife's name. 'She is a respectable woman. Now I have seen you I think she said sensible things. Play out of doors as much as you like. It's a big place and you may go where you like and amuse yourself as you like. Is there anything you want?' as if a sudden thought had struck him. 'Do you want toys, books, dolls?'

'Might I,' quavered Mary, 'might I have a bit of earth?'

In her eagerness she did not realize how queer the words would sound and that they were not the ones she had meant to say. Mr. Craven looked quite startled.

'Earth!' he repeated. 'What do you mean?'

'To plant seeds in—to make things grow—to see them come alive,' Mary faltered.

He gazed at her a moment and then passed his hand quickly over his eyes.

'Do you—care about gardens so much,' he said slowly.

'I didn't know about them in India,' said Mary. 'I was always ill and tired and it was too hot. I sometimes made little beds in the sand and stuck flowers in them. But here it is different.'

Mr. Craven got up and began to walk slowly across the room.

'A bit of earth,' he said to himself, and Mary thought that somehow she must have reminded him of something. When he stopped and spoke to her his dark eyes looked almost soft and kind.

'You can have as much earth as you want,' he said. 'You remind me of some one else who loved the earth and things that grow. When you see a bit of earth you want,' with something like a smile, 'take it, child, and make it come alive.'

'May I take it from anywhere—if it's not wanted?'

'Anywhere,' he answered. 'There! You must go now, I am tired.' He touched the bell to call Mrs. Medlock. 'Good-by. I shall be away all summer.'

Mrs. Medlock came so quickly that Mary thought she must have been waiting in the corridor.

'Mrs. Medlock,' Mr. Craven said to her, 'now I have seen the child I understand what Mrs. Sowerby meant. She must be less delicate before she begins lessons. Give her simple, healthy food. Let her run wild in the garden. Don't look after her too much. She needs liberty and fresh air and romping about. Mrs. Sowerby is to come and see her now and then and she may sometimes go to the cottage.'

Mrs. Medlock looked pleased. She was relieved to hear that she need[206] not 'look after' Mary too much. She had felt her a tiresome charge and had indeed seen as little of her as she dared. In addition to this she was fond of Martha's mother.

'Thank you, sir,' she said. 'Susan Sowerby and me[207] went to school together and she's as sensible and good-hearted a woman as you'd find in a day's walk. I never had any children myself and she's had twelve, and there never was healthier or better ones. Miss Mary can get no harm from them. I'd always take Susan Sowerby's advice about children myself. She's what you might call healthy-minded—if you understand me.'

'I understand,' Mr. Craven answered. 'Take Miss Mary away now and send Pitcher to me.'

When Mrs. Medlock left her at the end of her own corridor Mary flew back to her room. She found Martha waiting there. Martha had, in fact, hurried back after she had removed the dinner service.

'I can have my garden!' cried Mary. 'I may have it where I like! I am not going to have a governess for a long time! Your mother is coming to see me and I may go to your cottage! He says a little girl like me could not do any harm and I may do what I like—anywhere!'

'Eh!' said Martha delightedly, 'that was nice of him wasn't it?'

'Martha,' said Mary solemnly, 'he is really a nice man, only his face is so miserable and his forehead is all drawn together.'

She ran as quickly as she could to the garden. She had been away so much longer than she had thought she should and she knew Dickon would have to set out early on his five-mile walk. When she slipped through the door under the ivy, she saw he was not working where she had left him. The gardening tools were laid together under a tree. She ran to them, looking all round the place, but there was no Dickon to be seen. He had gone away and the secret garden was empty—except for the robin who had just flown across the wall and sat on a standard rose-bush watching her.

'He's gone,' she said woefully. 'Oh! was[208] he—was he—was he only a wood fairy?'

Something white fastened to the standard rose-bush caught her eye. It was a piece of paper, in fact, it was a piece of the letter she had printed for Martha to send to Dickon. It was fastened on the bush with a long thorn, and in a minute she knew Dickon had left it there. There were some roughly printed letters on it and a sort of picture. At first she could not tell what it was. Then she saw it was meant for a nest with a bird sitting on it. Underneath were the printed letters and they said:

'I will cum bak.[209]'

13.

'I Am Colin.'

Mary took the picture back to the house when she went to her supper and she showed it to Martha.

'Eh!' said Martha with great pride. 'I never knew our Dickon was as clever as that. That there's a picture of a missel thrush on her nest, as large as life an' twice as natural.'

Then Mary knew Dickon had meant the picture to be a message. He had meant that she might be sure he would keep her secret. Her garden was her nest and she was like a missel thrush. Oh, how she did like that queer, common boy!

She hoped he would come back the very next day and she fell asleep looking forward to the morning.

But you never know what the weather will do in Yorkshire, particularly in the springtime. She was awakened in the night by the sound of rain beating with heavy drops against her window. It was pouring down in torrents and the wind was 'wuthering' round the corners and in the chimneys of the huge old house. Mary sat up in bed and felt miserable and angry.

'The rain is as contrary as I ever was,' she said. 'It came because it knew I did not want it.'

She threw herself back on her pillow and buried her face. She did not cry, but she lay and hated the sound of the heavily beating rain, she hated the wind and its 'wuthering.' She could not go to sleep again. The mournful sound kept her awake because she felt mournful herself. If she had felt happy it would probably have lulled her to sleep. How it 'wuthered' and how the big raindrops poured down and beat against the pane!

'It sounds just like a person lost on the moor and wandering on and on crying,' she said.

She had been lying awake turning from side to side for about an hour, when suddenly something made her sit up in bed and turn her head toward the door listening. She listened and she listened.

'It isn't the wind now,' she said in a loud whisper. 'That isn't the wind. It is different. It is that crying I heard before.'

The door of her room was ajar and the sound came down the corridor, a far-off faint sound of fretful crying. She listened for a few minutes and each minute she became more and more sure[210]. She felt as if she must find out what it was. It seemed even stranger than the secret garden and the buried key. Perhaps the fact that she was in a rebellious mood made her bold. She put her foot out of bed and stood on the floor.

'I am going to find out what it is,' she said. 'Everybody is in bed and I don't care about Mrs. Medlock—I don't care!'

There was a candle by her bedside and she took it up and went softly out of the room. The corridor looked very long and dark, but she was too excited to mind that. She thought she remembered the corners she must turn to find the short corridor with the door covered with tapestry—the one Mrs. Medlock had come through the day she lost herself. The sound had come up that passage. So she went on with her dim light, almost feeling her way, her heart beating so loud that she fancied she could hear it. The far-off faint crying went on and led her. Sometimes it stopped for a moment or so and then began again. Was this the right corner to turn? She stopped and thought. Yes it was. Down this passage and then to the left, and then up two broad steps, and then to the right again. Yes, there was the tapestry door.

She pushed it open very gently and closed it behind her, and she stood in the corridor and could hear the crying quite plainly, though it was not loud. It was on the other side of the wall at her left and a few yards farther on there was a door. She could see a glimmer of light coming from beneath it. The Someone was crying in that room, and it was quite a young Someone.

So she walked to the door and pushed it open, and there she was standing in the room!

It was a big room with ancient, handsome furniture in it. There was a low fire glowing faintly on the hearth and a night light burning by the side of a carved four-posted bed hung with brocade, and on the bed was lying a boy, crying fretfully.

Mary wondered if she was in a real place or if she had fallen asleep again and was dreaming without knowing it.

The boy had a sharp, delicate face the colour of ivory and he seemed to have eyes too big for it. He had also a lot of hair which tumbled over his forehead in heavy locks and made his thin face seem smaller. He looked like a boy who had been ill, but he was crying more as if he were tired and cross than as if he were in pain.

Mary stood near the door with her candle in her hand, holding her breath. Then she crept across the room, and, as she drew nearer the light attracted the boy's attention and he turned his head on his pillow and stared at her, his gray eyes opening so wide that they seemed immense.

'Who are you?' he said at last in a half-frightened whisper. 'Are you a ghost?'

'No, I am not,' Mary answered, her own whisper sounding half frightened. 'Are you one?'

He stared and stared and stared. Mary could not help noticing what strange eyes he had. They were agate gray and they looked too big for his face because they had black lashes all round them.

'No,' he replied after waiting a moment or so. 'I am Colin.'

'Who is Colin?' she faltered.

'I am Colin Craven. Who are you?'

'I am Mary Lennox. Mr. Craven is my uncle.'

'He is my father,' said the boy.

'Your father!' gasped Mary. 'No one ever told me he had a boy! Why didn't they?'

'Come here,' he said, still keeping his strange eyes fixed on her with an anxious expression.

She came close to the bed and he put out his hand and touched her.

'You are real, aren't you?' he said. 'I have such real dreams very often. You might be one of them.'

Mary had slipped on a woolen wrapper before she left her room and she put a piece of it between his fingers.

'Rub that and see how thick and warm it is,' she said. 'I will pinch you a little if you like, to show you how real I am. For a minute I thought you might be a dream too.'

'Where did you come from?' he asked.

'From my own room. The wind wuthered so I couldn't go to sleep and I heard some one crying and wanted to find out who it was. What were you crying for?'

'Because I couldn't go to sleep either and my head ached. Tell me your name again.'

'Mary Lennox. Did no one ever tell you I had come to live here?'

He was still fingering the fold of her wrapper, but he began to look a little more as if he believed in her reality.

'No,' he answered. 'They daren't.'

'Why?' asked Mary.

'Because I should have been afraid you would see me. I won't let people see me and talk me over.'

'Why?' Mary asked again, feeling more mystified every moment.

'Because I am like this always, ill and having to lie down. My father won't let people talk me over either. The servants are not allowed to speak about me. If I live I may be a hunchback, but I shan't live. My father hates to think I may be like him.'

'Oh, what a queer house this is!' Mary said. 'What a queer house! Everything is a kind of secret. Rooms are locked up and gardens are locked up—and you! Have you been locked up?'

'No. I stay in this room because I don't want to be moved out of it. It tires me too much.'

'Does your father come and see you?' Mary ventured.

'Sometimes. Generally when I am asleep. He doesn't want to see me.'

'Why?' Mary could not help asking again.

A sort of angry shadow passed over the boy's face.

'My mother died when I was born and it makes him wretched to look at me. He thinks I don't know, but I've heard people talking. He almost hates me.'

'He hates the garden, because she died,' said Mary half speaking to herself.

'What garden?' the boy asked.

'Oh! just[211]—just a garden she used to like,' Mary stammered. 'Have you been here always?'

'Nearly always. Sometimes I have been taken to places at the seaside, but I won't stay because people stare at me. I used to wear an iron thing to keep my back straight, but a grand doctor came from London to see me and said it was stupid. He told them to take it off and keep me out in the fresh air. I hate fresh air and I don't want to go out.'

'I didn't when first I came here,' said Mary. 'Why do you keep looking at me like that?'

'Because of the dreams that are so real,' he answered rather fretfully. 'Sometimes when I open my eyes I don't believe I'm awake.'

'We're both awake,' said Mary. She glanced round the room with its high ceiling and shadowy corners and dim firelight. 'It looks quite like a dream, and it's the middle of the night, and everybody in the house is asleep—everybody but us. We are wide awake.'

'I don't want it to be a dream,' the boy said restlessly.

Mary thought of something all at once.

'If you don't like people to see you,' she began, 'do you want me to go away?'

He still held the fold of her wrapper and he gave it a little pull.

'No,' he said. 'I should be sure you were a dream if you went. If you are real, sit down on that big footstool and talk. I want to hear about you.'

Mary put down her candle on the table near the bed and sat down on the cushioned stool. She did not want to go away at all. She wanted to stay in the mysterious hidden-away room and talk to the mysterious boy.

'What do you want me to tell you?' she said.

He wanted to know how long she had been at Misselthwaite; he wanted to know which corridor her room was on; he wanted to know what she had been doing; if she disliked the moor as he disliked it; where she had lived before she came to Yorkshire. She answered all these questions and many more and he lay back on his pillow and listened. He made her tell him a great deal about India and about her voyage across the ocean. She found out that because he had been an invalid he had not learned things as other children had. One of his nurses had taught him to read when he was quite little and he was always reading and looking at pictures in splendid books.

Though his father rarely saw him when he was awake, he was given all sorts of wonderful things to amuse himself with. He never seemed to have been amused, however. He could have anything he asked for and was never made to do anything he did not like to do.

'Every one is obliged to do what pleases me,' he said indifferently. 'It makes me ill to be angry. No one believes I shall live to grow up.'

He said it as if he was so accustomed to the idea that it had ceased to matter to him at all. He seemed to like the sound of Mary's voice. As she went on talking he listened in a drowsy, interested way. Once or twice she wondered if he were not gradually falling into a doze. But at last he asked a question which opened up a new subject.

'How old are you?' he asked.

'I am ten,' answered Mary, forgetting herself for the moment, 'and so are you.'

'How do you know that?' he demanded in a surprised voice.

'Because when you were born the garden door was locked and the key was buried. And it has been locked for ten years.'

Colin half sat up, turning toward her, leaning on his elbows.

'What garden door was locked? Who did it? Where was the key buried?' he exclaimed as if he were suddenly very much interested.

'It—it was the garden Mr. Craven hates,' said Mary nervously. 'He locked the door. No one—no one knew where he buried the key.' 'What sort of a garden is it?' Colin persisted eagerly.

'No one has been allowed to go into it for ten years,' was Mary's careful answer.

But it was too late to be careful. He was too much like herself. He too had had nothing to think about and the idea of a hidden garden attracted him as it had attracted her. He asked question after question. Where was it? Had she never looked for the door? Had she never asked the gardeners?

'They won't talk about it,' said Mary. 'I think they have been told not to answer questions.'

'I would make them,' said Colin.

'Could you?' Mary faltered, beginning to feel frightened. If he could make people answer questions, who knew what might happen!

'Every one is obliged to please me. I told you that,' he said. 'If I were to live, this place would sometime belong to me. They all know that. I would make them tell me.'

Mary had not known that she herself had been spoiled, but she could see quite plainly that this mysterious boy had been. He thought that the whole world belonged to him. How peculiar he was and how coolly he spoke of not living.

'Do you think you won't live?' she asked, partly because she was curious and partly in hope of making him forget the garden.

'I don't suppose I shall,' he answered as indifferently as he had spoken before. 'Ever since I remember anything I have heard people say I shan't. At first they thought I was too little to understand and now they think I don't hear. But I do. My doctor is my father's cousin. He is quite poor and if I die he will have all Misselthwaite when my father is dead. I should think he wouldn't want me to live.'

'Do you want to live?' inquired Mary.

'No,' he answered, in a cross, tired fashion. 'But I don't want to die. When I feel ill I lie here and think about it until I cry and cry.'

'I have heard you crying three times,' Mary said, 'but I did not know who it was. Were you crying about that?' She did so want him to forget the garden.

'I dare say,' he answered. 'Let us talk about something else. Talk about that garden. Don't you want to see it?'

'Yes,' answered Mary, in quite a low voice.

'I do,' he went on persistently. 'I don't think I ever really wanted to see anything before, but I want to see that garden. I want the key dug up. I want the door unlocked. I would let them take me there in my chair. That would be getting fresh air. I am going to make them open the door.'

He had become quite excited and his strange eyes began to shine like stars and looked more immense than ever.

'They have to please me,' he said. 'I will make them take me there and I will let you go, too.'

Mary's hands clutched each other. Everything would be spoiled—everything! Dickon would never come back. She would never again feel like a missel thrush with a safe-hidden nest.

'Oh, don't—don't—don't—don't do that!' she cried out.

He stared as if he thought she had gone crazy!

'Why?' he exclaimed. 'You said you wanted to see it.'

'I do,' she answered almost with a sob in her throat, 'but if you make them open the door and take you in like that it will never be a secret again.'

He leaned still farther forward.

'A secret,' he said. 'What do you mean? Tell me.'

Mary's words almost tumbled over one another.

'You see—you see,' she panted, 'if no one knows but ourselves—if there was a door, hidden somewhere under the ivy—if there was—and we could find it; and if we could slip through it together and shut it behind us, and no one knew any one was inside and we called it our garden and pretended that—that we were missel thrushes and it was our nest, and if we played there almost every day and dug and planted seeds and made it all come alive—'

'Is it dead?' he interrupted her.

'It soon will be if no one cares for it,' she went on. 'The bulbs will live but the roses—'

He stopped her again as excited as she was herself.

'What are bulbs?' he put in quickly.

'They are daffodils and lilies and snowdrops. They are working in the earth now—pushing up pale green points because the spring is coming.'

'Is the spring coming?' he said. 'What is it like? You don't see it in rooms if you are ill.'

'It is the sun shining on the rain and the rain falling on the sunshine, and things pushing up and working under the earth,' said Mary. 'If the garden was a secret and we could get into it we could watch the things grow bigger every day, and see how many roses are alive. Don't you see? Oh, don't you see how much nicer it would be if it was a secret?'

He dropped back on his pillow and lay there with an odd expression on his face.

'I never had a secret,' he said, 'except that one about not living to grow up. They don't know I know that, so it is a sort of secret. But I like this kind better.'

'If you won't make them take you to the garden,' pleaded Mary, 'perhaps—I feel almost sure I can find out how to get in sometime. And then—if the doctor wants you to go out in your chair, and if you can always do what you want to do, perhaps—perhaps we might find some boy who would push you, and we could go alone and it would always be a secret garden.'

'I should—like—that,' he said very slowly, his eyes looking dreamy. 'I should like that. I should not mind fresh air in a secret garden.'

Mary began to recover her breath and feel safer because the idea of keeping the secret seemed to please him. She felt almost sure that if she kept on talking and could make him see the garden in his mind as she had seen it he would like it so much that he could not bear to think that everybody might tramp in to it when they chose.

'I'll tell you what I think it would be like, if we could go into it,' she said. 'It has been shut up so long things have grown into a tangle perhaps.'

He lay quite still and listened while she went on talking about the roses which might have clambered from tree to tree and hung down—about the many birds which might have built their nests there because it was so safe. And then she told him about the robin and Ben Weatherstaff, and there was so much to tell about the robin and it was so easy and safe to talk about it that she ceased to be afraid. The robin pleased him so much that he smiled until he looked almost beautiful, and at first Mary had thought that he was even plainer than herself, with his big eyes and heavy locks of hair.

'I did not know birds could be like that,' he said. 'But if you stay in a room you never see things. What a lot of things you know. I feel as if you had been inside that garden.'

She did not know what to say, so she did not say anything. He evidently did not expect an answer and the next moment he gave her a surprise.

'I am going to let you look at something,' he said. 'Do you see that rose-coloured silk curtain hanging on the wall over the mantel-piece?'

Mary had not noticed it before, but she looked up and saw it. It was a curtain of soft silk hanging over what seemed to be some picture.

'Yes,' she answered.

'There is a cord hanging from it,' said Colin. 'Go and pull it.'

Mary got up, much mystified, and found the cord. When she pulled it the silk curtain ran back on rings and when it ran back it uncovered a picture. It was the picture of a girl with a laughing face. She had bright hair tied up with a blue ribbon and her gay, lovely eyes were exactly like Colin's unhappy ones, agate gray and looking twice as big as they really were because of the black lashes all round them.

'She is my mother,' said Colin complainingly. 'I don't see why she died. Sometimes I hate her for doing it.'

'How queer!' said Mary.

'If she had lived I believe I should not have been ill always,' he grumbled. 'I dare say I should have lived, too. And my father would not have hated to look at me. I dare say I should have had a strong back. Draw the curtain again.'

Mary did as she was told and returned to her footstool.

'She is much prettier than you,' she said, 'but her eyes are just like yours—at least they are the same shape and colour. Why is the curtain drawn over her?'

He moved uncomfortably.

'I made them do it,' he said. 'Sometimes I don't like to see her looking at me. She smiles too much when I am ill and miserable. Besides, she is mine and I don't want everyone to see her.'

There were a few moments of silence and then Mary spoke.

'What would Mrs. Medlock do if she found out that I had been here?' she inquired.

'She would do as I told her to do,' he answered. 'And I should tell her that I wanted you to come here and talk to me every day. I am glad you came.'

'So am I,' said Mary. 'I will come as often as I can, but'—she hesitated—'I shall have to look every day for the garden door.'

'Yes, you must,' said Colin, 'and you can tell me about it afterward.'

He lay thinking a few minutes, as he had done before, and then he spoke again.

'I think you shall be a secret, too,' he said. 'I will not tell them until they find out. I can always send the nurse out of the room and say that I want to be by myself. Do you know Martha?'

'Yes, I know her very well,' said Mary. 'She waits on me.'

He nodded his head toward the outer corridor.

'She is the one who is asleep in the other room. The nurse went away yesterday to stay all night with her sister and she always makes Martha attend to me when she wants to go out. Martha shall tell you when to come here.'

Then Mary understood Martha's troubled look when she had asked questions about the crying.

'Martha knew about you all the time?' she said.

'Yes; she often attends to me. The nurse likes to get away from me and then Martha comes.'

'I have been here a long time,' said Mary. 'Shall I go away now? Your eyes look sleepy.'

'I wish I could go to sleep before you leave me,' he said rather shyly.

'Shut your eyes,' said Mary, drawing her footstool closer, 'and I will do what my Ayah used to do in India. I will pat your hand and stroke it and sing something quite low.'

'I should like that perhaps,' he said drowsily.

Somehow she was sorry for him and did not want him to lie awake, so she leaned against the bed and began to stroke and pat his hand and sing a very low little chanting song in Hindustani.

'That is nice,' he said more drowsily still, and she went on chanting and stroking, but when she looked at him again his black lashes were lying close against his cheeks, for his eyes were shut and he was fast asleep. So she got up softly, took her candle and crept away without making a sound.

14.

A Young Rajah

The moor was hidden in mist when the morning came, and the rain had not stopped pouring down. There could be no going out of doors. Martha was so busy that Mary had no opportunity of talking to her, but in the afternoon she asked her to come and sit with her in the nursery. She came bringing the stocking she was always knitting when she was doing nothing else.

'What's the matter with thee?' she asked as soon as they sat down. 'Tha' looks as if tha'd somethin' to say.'

'I have. I have found out what the crying was,' said Mary.

Martha let her knitting drop on her knee and gazed at her with startled eyes.

'Tha' hasn't!' she exclaimed. 'Never!'

'I heard it in the night,' Mary went on. 'And I got up and went to see where it came from. It was Colin. I found him.'

Martha's face became red with fright.

'Eh! Miss Mary!' she said half crying. 'Tha' shouldn't have

done it—tha' shouldn't! Tha'll get me in trouble. I never told thee nothin' about him—but tha'll get me in trouble. I shall lose my place and what'll mother do!'

'You won't lose your place,' said Mary. 'He was glad I came. We talked and talked and he said he was glad I came.'

'Was he?' cried Martha. 'Art tha' sure? Tha' doesn't know what he's like when anything vexes him. He's a big lad to cry like a baby, but when he's in a passion he'll fair scream just to frighten us. He knows us daren't call our souls our own.'

'He wasn't vexed,' said Mary. 'I asked him if I should go away and he made me stay. He asked me questions and I sat on a big footstool and talked to him about India and about the robin and gardens. He wouldn't let me go. He let me see his mother's picture. Before I left him I sang him to sleep.'

Martha fairly gasped with amazement.

'I can scarcely believe thee!' she protested. 'It's as if tha'd walked straight into a lion's den. If he'd been like he is most times he'd have throwed[212] himself into one of his tantrums and roused th' house. He won't let strangers look at him.'

'He let me look at him. I looked at him all the time and he looked at me. We stared!' said Mary.

'I don't know what to do!' cried agitated Martha. 'If Mrs. Medlock finds out, she'll think I broke orders and told thee and I shall be packed back to mother.'

'He is not going to tell Mrs. Medlock anything about it yet. It's to be a sort of secret just at first,' said Mary firmly. 'And he says everybody is obliged to do as he pleases.'

'Aye, that's true enough—th' bad lad!' sighed Martha, wiping her forehead with her apron.

'He says Mrs. Medlock must. And he wants me to come and talk to him every day. And you are to tell me when he wants me.'

'Me!' said Martha; 'I shall lose my place—I shall for sure!'

'You can't if you are doing what he wants you to do and everybody is ordered to obey him,' Mary argued.

'Does tha' mean to say,' cried Martha with wide open eyes, 'that he was nice to thee!'

'I think he almost liked me,' Mary answered.

'Then tha' must have bewitched him!' decided Martha, drawing a long breath.

'Do you mean Magic?' inquired Mary. 'I've heard about Magic in India, but I can't make it. I just went into his room and I was so surprised to see him I stood and stared. And then he turned round and stared at me. And he thought I was a ghost or a dream and I thought perhaps he was. And it was so queer being there alone together in the middle of the night and not knowing about each other. And we began to ask each other questions. And when I asked him if I must go away he said I must not.'

'Th' world's comin' to a[213] end!' gasped Martha.

'What is the matter with him?' asked Mary.

'Nobody knows for sure and certain,' said Martha. 'Mr. Craven went off his head like when he was born. Th' doctors thought he'd have to be put in a 'sylum[214]. It was because Mrs. Craven died like I told you. He wouldn't set eyes on th' baby. He just raved and said it'd be another hunchback like him and it'd better die.'

'Is Colin a hunchback?' Mary asked. 'He didn't look like one.'

'He isn't yet,' said Martha. 'But he began all wrong. Mother said that there was enough trouble and raging in th' house to set any child wrong. They was afraid his back was weak an' they've always been takin'[215] care of it—keepin' him lyin'[216] down and not lettin'[217] him walk. Once they made him wear a brace but he fretted so he was downright ill. Then a big doctor came to see him an' made them take it off. He talked to th' other doctor quite rough—in a polite way. He said there'd been too much medicine and too much lettin' him have his own way.'

'I think he's a very spoiled boy,' said Mary.

'He's th' worst young nowt as ever was!' said Martha. 'I won't say as he hasn't been ill a good bit. He's had coughs an' colds that's nearly killed him two or three times. Once he had rheumatic fever an' once he had typhoid. Eh! Mrs. Medlock did get a fright then. He'd been out of his head an' she was talkin' to th' nurse, thinkin' he didn't know nothin', an' she said, "He'll die this time sure enough, an' best thing for him an' for everybody." An' she looked at him an' there he was with his big eyes open, starin'[218] at her as sensible as she was herself. She didn't know what'd happen but he just stared at her an' says, "You give me some water an' stop talkin'." '

'Do you think he will die?' asked Mary.

'Mother says there's no reason why any child should live that gets no fresh air an' doesn't do nothin' but lie on his back an' read picture-books an' take medicine. He's weak and hates th' trouble o' bein' taken out o' doors, an' he gets cold so easy[219] he says it makes him ill.'

Mary sat and looked at the fire.

'I wonder,' she said slowly, 'if it would not do him good to go out into a garden and watch things growing. It did me good.'

'One of th' worst fits he ever had,' said Martha, 'was one time they took him out where the roses is by the fountain. He'd been readin' in a paper about people gettin' somethin' he called 'rose cold' an' he began to sneeze an' said he'd got it an' then a new gardener as didn't know th' rules passed by an' looked at him curious. He threw himself into a passion an' he said he'd looked at him because he was going to be a hunchback. He cried himself into a fever an' was ill all night.'

'If he ever gets angry at me, I'll never go and see him again,' said Mary.

'He'll have thee if he wants thee,' said Martha. 'Tha' may as well know that at th' start.'

Very soon afterward a bell rang and she rolled up her knitting.

'I dare say th' nurse wants me to stay with him a bit,' she said. 'I hope he's in a good temper.'

She was out of the room about ten minutes and then she came back with a puzzled expression.

'Well, tha' has bewitched him,' she said. 'He's up on his sofa with his picture-books. He's told the nurse to stay away until six o'clock. I'm to wait in the next room. Th' minute she was gone he called me to him an' says, "I want Mary Lennox to come and talk to me, and remember you're not to tell any one." You'd better go as quick as you can.'

Mary was quite willing to go quickly. She did not want to see Colin as much as she wanted to see Dickon, but she wanted to see him very much.

There was a bright fire on the hearth when she entered his room, and in the daylight she saw it was a very beautiful room indeed. There were rich colours in the rugs and hangings and pictures and books on the walls which made it look glowing and comfortable even in spite of the gray sky and falling rain. Colin looked rather like a picture himself. He was wrapped in a velvet dressing-gown and sat against a big brocaded cushion. He had a red spot on each cheek.

'Come in,' he said. 'I've been thinking about you all morning.'

'I've been thinking about you, too,' answered Mary. 'You don't know how frightened Martha is. She says Mrs. Medlock will think she told me about you and then she will be sent away.'

He frowned.

'Go and tell her to come here,' he said. 'She is in the next room.'

Mary went and brought her back. Poor Martha was shaking in her shoes. Colin was still frowning.

'Have you to do what I please or have you not?' he demanded.

'I have to do what you please, sir,' Martha faltered, turning quite red.

'Has Medlock to do what I please?'

'Everybody has, sir,' said Martha.

'Well, then, if I order you to bring Miss Mary to me, how can Medlock send you away if she finds it out?'

'Please don't let her, sir,' pleaded Martha.

'I'll send her away if she dares to say a word about such a thing,' said Master Craven grandly. 'She wouldn't like that, I can tell you.'

'Thank you, sir,' bobbing a curtsy, 'I want to do my duty, sir.'

'What I want is your duty' said Colin more grandly still. 'I'll take care of you. Now go away.'

When the door closed behind Martha, Colin found Mistress Mary gazing at him as if he had set her wondering.

'Why do you look at me like that?' he asked her. 'What are you thinking about?'

'I am thinking about two things.'

'What are they? Sit down and tell me.'

'This is the first one,' said Mary, seating herself on the big stool. 'Once in India I saw a boy who was a Rajah. He had rubies and emeralds and diamonds stuck all over him. He spoke to his people just as you spoke to Martha. Everybody had to do everything he told them—in a minute. I think they would have been killed if they hadn't.'

'I shall make you tell me about Rajahs presently,' he said, 'but first tell me what the second thing was.'

'I was thinking,' said Mary, 'how different you are from Dickon.'

'Who is Dickon?' he said. 'What a queer name!'

She might as well tell him, she thought she could talk about Dickon without mentioning the secret garden. She had liked to hear Martha talk about him. Besides, she longed to talk about him. It would seem to bring him nearer.

'He is Martha's brother. He is twelve years old,' she explained. 'He is not like any one else in the world. He can charm foxes and squirrels and birds just as the natives in India charm snakes. He plays a very soft tune on a pipe and they come and listen.'

There were some big books on a table at his side and he dragged one suddenly toward him.

'There is a picture of a snake-charmer in this,' he exclaimed. 'Come and look at it.'

The book was a beautiful one with superb coloured illustrations and he turned to one of them.

'Can he do that?' he asked eagerly.

'He played on his pipe and they listened,' Mary explained. 'But he doesn't call it Magic. He says it's because he lives on the moor so much and he knows their ways. He says he feels sometimes as if he was a bird or a rabbit himself, he likes them so. I think he asked the robin questions. It seemed as if they talked to each other in soft chirps.'

Colin lay back on his cushion and his eyes grew larger and larger and the spots on his cheeks burned.

'Tell me some more about him,' he said.

'He knows all about eggs and nests,' Mary went on. 'And he knows where foxes and badgers and otters live. He keeps them secret so that other boys won't find their holes and frighten them. He knows about everything that grows or lives on the moor.'

'Does he like the moor?' said Colin. 'How can he when it's such a great, bare, dreary place?'

'It's the most beautiful place,' protested Mary. 'Thousands of lovely things grow on it and there are thousands of little creatures all busy building nests and making holes and burrows and chippering or singing or squeaking to each other. They are so busy and having such fun under the earth or in the trees or heather. It's their world.'

'How do you know all that?' said Colin, turning on his elbow to look at her.

'I have never been there once, really,' said Mary suddenly remembering. 'I only drove over it in the dark. I thought it was hideous. Martha told me about it first and then Dickon. When Dickon talks about it you feel as if you saw things and heard them and as if you were standing in the heather with the sun shining and the gorse smelling like honey—and all full of bees and butterflies.'

'You never see anything if you are ill,' said Colin restlessly. He looked like a person listening to a new sound in the distance and wondering what it was.

'You can't if you stay in a room,' said Mary.

'I couldn't go on the moor,' he said in a resentful tone.

Mary was silent for a minute and then she said something bold.

'You might—sometime.'

He moved as if he were startled.

'Go on the moor! How could I? I am going to die.'

'How do you know?' said Mary unsympathetically. She didn't like the way he had of talking about dying. She did not feel very sympathetic. She felt rather as if he almost boasted about it.

'Oh, I've heard it ever since I remember,' he answered crossly. 'They are always whispering about it and thinking I don't notice. They wish I would, too.'

Mistress Mary felt quite contrary. She pinched her lips together.

'If they wished I would,' she said, 'I wouldn't. Who wishes you would?'

'The servants—and of course Dr. Craven because he would get Misselthwaite and be rich instead of poor. He daren't say so, but he always looks cheerful when I am worse. When I had typhoid fever his face got quite fat. I think my father wishes it, too.'

'I don't believe he does,' said Mary quite obstinately.

That made Colin turn and look at her again.

'Don't you?' he said.

And then he lay back on his cushion and was still, as if he were thinking. And there was quite a long silence. Perhaps they were both of them thinking strange things children do not usually think of.

'I like the grand doctor from London, because he made them take the iron thing off,' said Mary at last. 'Did he say you were going to die?'

'No.'

'What did he say?'

'He didn't whisper,' Colin answered. 'Perhaps he knew I hated whispering. I heard him say one thing quite aloud. He said, "The lad might live if he would make up his mind to it. Put him in the humor." It sounded as if he was in a temper.'

'I'll tell you who would put you in the humor, perhaps,' said Mary reflecting. She felt as if she would like this thing to be settled one way or the other. 'I believe Dickon would. He's always talking about live things. He never talks about dead things or things that are ill. He's always looking up in the sky to watch birds flying—or looking down at the earth to see something growing. He has such round blue eyes and they are so wide open with looking about. And he laughs such a big laugh with his wide mouth—and his cheeks are as red—as red as cherries.'

She pulled her stool nearer to the sofa and her expression quite changed at the remembrance of the wide curving mouth and wide open eyes.

'See here,' she said. 'Don't let us talk about dying; I don't like it. Let us talk about living. Let us talk and talk about Dickon. And then we will look at your pictures.'

It was the best thing she could have said. To talk about Dickon meant to talk about the moor and about the cottage and the fourteen people who lived in it on sixteen shillings a week—and the children who got fat on the moor grass like the wild ponies. And about Dickon's mother—and the skipping-rope—and the moor with the sun on it—and about pale green points sticking up out of the black sod. And it was all so alive that Mary talked more than she had ever talked before—and Colin both talked and listened as he had never done either before. And they both began to laugh over nothing as children will when they are happy together. And they laughed so that in the end they were making as much noise as if they had been two ordinary healthy natural ten-year-old creatures—instead of a hard, little, unloving girl and a sickly boy who believed that he was going to die.

They enjoyed themselves so much that they forgot the pictures and they forgot about the time. They had been laughing quite loudly over Ben Weatherstaff and his robin and Colin was actually sitting up as if he had forgotten about his weak back, when he suddenly remembered something.

'Do you know there is one thing we have never once thought of,' he said. 'We are cousins.'

It seemed so queer that they had talked so much and never remembered this simple thing that they laughed more than ever, because they had got into the humor to laugh at anything. And in the midst of the fun the door opened and in walked Dr. Craven and Mrs. Medlock.

Dr. Craven started in actual alarm and Mrs. Medlock almost fell back because he had accidentally bumped against her.

'Good Lord!' exclaimed poor Mrs. Medlock, with her eyes almost starting out of her head. 'Good Lord!'

'What is this?' said Dr. Craven, coming forward. 'What does it mean?'

Then Mary was reminded of the boy Rajah again. Colin answered as if neither the doctor's alarm nor Mrs. Medlock's terror were of the slightest consequence. He was as little disturbed or frightened as if an elderly cat and dog had walked into the room.

'This is my cousin, Mary Lennox,' he said. 'I asked her to come and talk to me. I like her. She must come and talk to me whenever I send for her.'

Dr. Craven turned reproachfully to Mrs. Medlock.

'Oh, sir' she panted. 'I don't know how it's happened. There's not a servant on the place tha'd dare to talk—they all have their orders.'

'Nobody told her anything,' said Colin. 'She heard me crying and found me herself. I am glad she came. Don't be silly, Medlock.'

Mary saw that Dr. Craven did not look pleased, but it was quite plain that he dare not oppose his patient. He sat down by Colin and felt his pulse.

'I am afraid there has been too much excitement. Excitement is not good for you, my boy,' he said.

'I should be excited if she kept away,' answered Colin, his eyes beginning to look dangerously sparkling. 'I am better. She makes me better. The nurse must bring up her tea with mine. We will have tea together.'

Mrs. Medlock and Dr. Craven looked at each other in a troubled way, but there was evidently nothing to be done.

'He does look rather better, sir,' ventured Mrs. Medlock. 'But'—thinking the matter over—'he looked better this morning before she came into the room.'

'She came into the room last night. She stayed with me a long time. She sang a Hindustani song to me and it made me go to sleep,' said Colin. 'I was better when I wakened up. I wanted my breakfast. I want my tea now. Tell nurse, Medlock.'

Dr. Craven did not stay very long. He talked to the nurse for a few minutes when she came into the room and said a few words of warning to Colin. He must not talk too much; he must not forget that he was ill; he must not forget that he was very easily tired. Mary thought that there seemed to be a number of uncomfortable things he was not to forget.

Colin looked fretful and kept his strange black-lashed eyes fixed on Dr. Craven's face.

'I want to forget it,' he said at last. 'She makes me forget it. That is why I want her.'

Dr. Craven did not look happy when he left the room. He gave a puzzled glance at the little girl sitting on the large stool. She had become a stiff, silent child again as soon as he entered and he could not see what the attraction was. The boy actually did look brighter, however—and he sighed rather heavily as he went down the corridor.

'They are always wanting me to eat things when I don't want to,' said Colin, as the nurse brought in the tea and put it on the table by the sofa. 'Now, if you'll eat I will. Those muffins look so nice and hot. Tell me about Rajahs.'

15.

Nest Building

A fter another week of rain the high arch of blue sky appeared again and the sun which poured down was quite hot. Though there had been no chance to see either the secret garden or Dickon, Mistress Mary had enjoyed herself very much. The week had not seemed long. She had spent hours of every day with Colin in his room, talking about Rajahs or gardens or Dickon and the cottage on the moor. They had looked at the splendid books and pictures and sometimes Mary had read things to Colin, and sometimes he had read a little to her. When he was amused and interested she thought he scarcely looked like an invalid at all, except that his face was so colourless and he was always on the sofa.

'You are a sly young one to listen and get out of your bed to go following things up like you did that night,' Mrs. Medlock said once. 'But there's no saying it's not been a sort of blessing to the lot of us. He's not had a tantrum or a whining fit since you made friends. The nurse was just going to give up the case because she was so sick of him, but she says she doesn't mind staying now you've gone on duty with her,' laughing a little.

In her talks with Colin, Mary had tried to be very cautious about the secret garden. There were certain things she wanted to find out from him, but she felt that she must find them out without asking him direct questions. In the first place, as she began to like to be with him, she wanted to discover whether he was the kind of boy you could tell a secret to. He was not in the least like Dickon, but he was evidently so pleased with the idea of a garden no one knew anything about that she thought perhaps he could be trusted. But she had not known him long enough to be sure. The second thing she wanted to find out was this: If he could be trusted—if he really could—wouldn't it be possible to take him to the garden without having any one find it out? The grand doctor had said that he must have fresh air and Colin had said that he would not mind fresh air in a secret garden. Perhaps if he had a great deal of fresh air and knew Dickon and the robin and saw things growing he might not think so much about dying. Mary had seen herself in the glass sometimes lately when she had realized that she looked quite a different creature from the child she had seen when she arrived from India. This child looked nicer. Even Martha had seen a change in her.

'Th' air from th' moor has done thee good already,' she had said. 'Tha'rt not nigh so yeller and tha'rt not nigh so scrawny. Even tha' hair doesn't slamp down on tha' head so flat. It's got some life in it so as it sticks out a bit.'

'It's like me,' said Mary. 'It's growing stronger and fatter. I'm sure there's more of it.'

'It looks it, for sure,' said Martha, ruffling it up a little round her face. 'Tha' rt not half so ugly when it's that way an' there's a bit o' red in tha' cheeks.'

If gardens and fresh air had been good for her perhaps they would be good for Colin. But then, if he hated people to look at him, perhaps he would not like to see Dickon.

'Why does it make you angry when you are looked at?' she inquired one day.

'I always hated it,' he answered, 'even when I was very little. Then when they took me to the seaside and I used to lie in my carriage everybody used to stare and ladies would stop and talk to my nurse and then they would begin to whisper and I knew then they were saying I shouldn't live to grow up. Then sometimes the ladies would pat my cheeks and say "Poor child!" Once when a lady did that I screamed out loud and bit her hand. She was so frightened she ran away.'

'She thought you had gone mad like a dog,' said Mary, not at all admiringly.

'I don't care what she thought,' said Colin, frowning.

'I wonder why you didn't scream and bite me when I came into your room?' said Mary. Then she began to smile slowly.

'I thought you were a ghost or a dream,' he said. 'You can't bite a ghost or a dream, and if you scream they don't care.'

'Would you hate it if—if a boy looked at you?' Mary asked uncertainly.

He lay back on his cushion and paused thoughtfully.

'There's one boy,' he said quite slowly, as if he were thinking over every word, 'there's one boy I believe I shouldn't mind. It's that boy who knows where the foxes live—Dickon.'

'I'm sure you wouldn't mind him,' said Mary.

'The birds don't and other animals,' he said, still thinking it over, 'perhaps that's why I shouldn't. He's a sort of animal charmer and I am a boy animal.'

Then he laughed and she laughed too; in fact it ended in their both laughing a great deal and finding the idea of a boy animal hiding in his hole very funny indeed.

What Mary felt afterward was that she need not fear about Dickon.

On that first morning when the sky was blue again Mary wakened very early. The sun was pouring in slanting rays through the blinds and there was something so joyous in the sight of it that she jumped out of bed and ran to the window. She drew up the blinds and opened the window itself and a great waft of fresh, scented air blew in upon her. The moor was blue and the whole world looked as if something Magic had happened to it. There were tender little fluting sounds here and there and everywhere, as if scores of birds were beginning to tune up for a concert. Mary put her hand out of the window and held it in the sun.

'It's warm—warm!' she said. 'It will make the green points push up and up and up, and it will make the bulbs and roots work and struggle with all their might under the earth.'

She kneeled down and leaned out of the window as far as she could, breathing big breaths and sniffing the air until she laughed because she remembered what Dickon's mother had said about the end of his nose quivering like a rabbit's.

'It must be very early,' she said. 'The little clouds are all pink and I've never seen the sky look like this. No one is up. I don't even hear the stable boys.'

A sudden thought made her scramble to her feet.

'I can't wait! I am going to see the garden!'

She had learned to dress herself by this time and she put on her clothes in five minutes. She knew a small side door which she could unbolt herself and she flew down-stairs in her stocking feet and put on her shoes in the hall. She unchained and unbolted and unlocked and when the door was open she sprang across the step with one bound, and there she was standing on the grass, which seemed to have turned green, and with the sun pouring down on her and warm sweet wafts about her and the fluting and twittering and singing coming from every bush and tree. She clasped her hands for pure joy and looked up in the sky and it was so blue and pink and pearly and white and flooded with springtime light that she felt as if she must flute and sing aloud herself and knew that thrushes and robins and skylarks could not possibly help it. She ran around the shrubs and paths toward the secret garden.

'It is all different already,' she said. 'The grass is greener and things are sticking up everywhere and things are uncurling and green buds of leaves are showing. This afternoon I am sure Dickon will come.'

The long warm rain had done strange things to the herbaceous beds which bordered the walk by the lower wall. There were things sprouting and pushing out from the roots of clumps of plants and there were actually here and there glimpses of royal purple and yellow unfurling among the stems of crocuses. Six months before Mistress Mary would not have seen how the world was waking up, but now she missed nothing.

When she had reached the place where the door hid itself under the ivy, she was startled by a curious loud sound. It was the caw—caw of a crow and it came from the top of the wall, and when she looked up, there sat a big glossy-plumaged blue-black bird, looking down at her very wisely indeed. She had never seen a crow so close before and he made her a little nervous, but the next moment he spread his wings and flapped away across the garden. She hoped he was not going to stay inside and she pushed the door open wondering if he would. When she got fairly into the garden she saw that he probably did intend to stay because he had alighted on a dwarf apple-tree and under the apple-tree was lying a little reddish animal with a bushy tail, and both of them were watching the stooping body and rust-red head of Dickon, who was kneeling on the grass working hard.

Mary flew across the grass to him.

'Oh, Dickon! Dickon!' she cried out. 'How could you get here so early! How could you! The sun has only just got up!'

He got up himself, laughing and glowing, and tousled; his eyes like a bit of the sky.

'Eh!' he said. 'I was up long before him. How could I have stayed abed! Th' world's all fair begun again this mornin', it has. An' it's workin' an' hummin' an' scratchin'[220] an' pipin' an' nest-buildin' an' breathin'[221] out scents, till you've got to be out on it 'stead[222] o' lyin' on your back. When th' sun did jump up, th' moor went mad for joy, an' I was in the midst of th' heather, an' I run like mad myself, shoutin'[223] an' singin'. An' I come straight here. I couldn't have stayed away. Why, th' garden was lyin' here waitin'!'

Mary put her hands on her chest, panting, as if she had been running herself.

'Oh, Dickon! Dickon!' she said. 'I'm so happy I can scarcely breathe!'

Seeing him talking to a stranger, the little bushy-tailed animal rose from its place under the tree and came to him, and the rook, cawing once, flew down from its branch and settled quietly on his shoulder.

'This is th' little fox cub,' he said, rubbing the little reddish animal's head. 'It's named Captain. An' this here's Soot. Soot he flew across th' moor with me an' Captain he run[224] same as if th' hounds had been after him. They both felt same as I did.'

Neither of the creatures looked as if he were the least afraid of Mary. When Dickon began to walk about, Soot stayed on his shoulder and Captain trotted quietly close to his side.

'See here!' said Dickon. 'See how these has pushed up, an' these an' these! An' Eh! look at these here!'

He threw himself upon his knees and Mary went down beside him. They had come upon a whole clump of crocuses burst into purple and orange and gold. Mary bent her face down and kissed and kissed them.

'You never kiss a person in that way,' she said when she lifted her head. 'Flowers are so different.'

He looked puzzled but smiled.

'Eh!' he said, 'I've kissed mother many a time that way when I come in from th' moor after a day's roamin'[225] an' she stood there at th' door in th' sun, lookin' so glad an' comfortable.'

They ran from one part of the garden to another and found so many wonders that they were obliged to remind themselves that they must whisper or speak low. He showed her swelling leaf-buds on rose branches which had seemed dead. He showed her ten thousand new green points pushing through the mould. They put their eager young noses close to the earth and sniffed its warmed springtime breathing; they dug and pulled and laughed low with rapture until Mistress Mary's hair was as tumbled as Dickon's and her cheeks were almost as poppy red as his.

There was every joy on earth in the secret garden that morning, and in the midst of them came a delight more delightful than all, because it was more wonderful. Swiftly something flew across the wall and darted through the trees to a close grown corner, a little flare of red-breasted bird with something hanging from its beak. Dickon stood quite still and put his hand on Mary almost as if they had suddenly found themselves laughing in a church.

'We munnot[226] stir,' he whispered in broad Yorkshire. 'We munnot scarce breathe. I knowed he was mate-huntin'[227] when I seed him last. It's Ben Weatherstaff's robin. He's buildin' his nest. He'll stay here if us don't fight him.'

They settled down softly upon the grass and sat there without moving.

'Us mustn't seem as if us was watchin' him too close,' said Dickon. 'He'd be out with us for good if he got th' notion us was interferin'[228] now. He'll be a good bit different till all this is over. He's settin'[229] up housekeepin'[230]. He'll be shyer an' readier to take things ill. He's got no time for visitin'[231] an' gossipin'[232]. Us must keep still a bit an' try to look as if us was grass an' trees an' bushes. Then when he's got used to seein'[233] us I'll chirp a bit an' he'll know us'll not be in his way.'

Mistress Mary was not at all sure that she knew, as Dickon seemed to, how to try to look like grass and trees and bushes. But he had said the queer thing as if it were the simplest and most natural thing in the world, and she felt it must be quite easy to him, and indeed she watched him for a few minutes carefully, wondering if it was possible for him to quietly turn green and put out branches and leaves. But he only sat wonderfully still, and when he spoke dropped his voice to such a softness that it was curious that she could hear him, but she could.

'It's part o' th' springtime, this nest-buildin' is,' he said. 'I warrant it's been goin' on in th' same way every year since th' world was[234] begun. They've got their way o' thinkin' and doin' things an' a body had better not meddle. You can lose a friend in springtime easier than any other season if you're too curious.'

'If we talk about him I can't help looking at him,' Mary said as softly as possible. 'We must talk of something else. There is something I want to tell you.'

'He'll like it better if us talks[235] o' somethin' else,' said Dickon. 'What is it tha's got to tell me?'

'Well—do you know about Colin?' she whispered.

He turned his head to look at her.

'What does tha' know about him?' he asked.

'I've seen him. I have been to talk to him every day this week. He wants me to come. He says I'm making him forget about being ill and dying,' answered Mary.

Dickon looked actually relieved as soon as the surprise died away from his round face.

'I am glad o' that,' he exclaimed. 'I'm right down glad. It makes me easier. I knowed I must say nothin' about him an' I don't like havin'[236] to hide things.'

'Don't you like hiding the garden?' said Mary.

'I'll never tell about it,' he answered. 'But I says[237] to mother, "Mother," I says, "I got a secret to keep. It's not a bad 'un, tha' knows that. It's no worse than hidin'[238] where a bird's nest is. Tha' doesn't mind it, does tha'?" '

Mary always wanted to hear about mother.

'What did she say?' she asked, not at all afraid to hear.

Dickon grinned sweet-temperedly.

'It was just like her, what she said,' he answered. 'She give my head a bit of a rub an' laughed an' she says, "Eh, lad, tha' can have all th' secrets tha' likes. I've knowed thee twelve year'.'

'How did you know about Colin?' asked Mary.

'Everybody as knowed about Mester Craven knowed there was a little lad as was like to be a cripple, an' they knowed Mester Craven didn't like him to be talked about. Folks is sorry for Mester Craven because Mrs. Craven was such a pretty young lady an' they was so fond of each other. Mrs. Medlock stops in our cottage whenever she goes to Thwaite an' she doesn't mind talkin' to mother before us children, because she knows us has been brought up to be trusty. How did tha' find out about him? Martha was in fine trouble th' last time she came home. She said tha'd heard him frettin'[239] an' tha' was askin' questions an' she didn't know what to say.'

Mary told him her story about the midnight wuthering of the wind which had wakened her and about the faint far-off sounds of the complaining voice which had led her down the dark corridors with her candle and had ended with her opening of the door of the dimly lighted room with the carven four-posted bed in the corner. When she described the small ivory-white face and the strange black-rimmed eyes Dickon shook his head.

'Them's just like his mother's eyes, only hers was always laughin'[240], they say,' he said. 'They say as Mr. Craven can't bear to see him when he's awake an' it's because his eyes is so like his mother's an' yet looks so different in his miserable bit of a face.'

'Do you think he wants to die?' whispered Mary.

'No, but he wishes he'd never been born. Mother she says that's th' worst thing on earth for a child. Them as is not wanted scarce ever thrives.[241] Mester Craven he'd buy anythin' as money could buy for th' poor lad but he'd like to forget as he's on earth. For one thing, he's afraid he'll look at him some day and find he's growed hunchback.'

'Colin's so afraid of it himself that he won't sit up,' said Mary. 'He says he's always thinking that if he should feel a lump coming he should go crazy and scream himself to death.'

'Eh! he[242] oughtn't to lie there thinkin' things like that,' said Dickon. 'No lad could get well as thought them sort o' things.'

The fox was lying on the grass close by him looking up to ask for a pat now and then, and Dickon bent down and rubbed his neck softly and thought a few minutes in silence. Presently he lifted his head and looked round the garden.

'When first we got in here,' he said, 'it seemed like everything was gray. Look round now and tell me if tha' doesn't see a difference.'

Mary looked and caught her breath a little.

'Why!' she cried, 'the gray wall is changing. It is as if a green mist were creeping over it. It's almost like a green gauze veil.'

'Aye,' said Dickon. 'An' it'll be greener and greener till th' gray's all gone. Can tha' guess what I was thinkin'?'

'I know it was something nice,' said Mary eagerly. 'I believe it was something about Colin.'

'I was thinkin' that if he was out here he wouldn't be watchin' for lumps to grow on his back; he'd be watchin' for buds to break on th' rose-bushes, an' he'd likely be healthier,' explained Dickon. 'I was wonderin'[243] if us could ever get him in th' humor to come out here an' lie under th' trees in his carriage.'

'I've been wondering that myself. I've thought of it almost every time I've talked to him,' said Mary. 'I've wondered if he could keep a secret and I've wondered if we could bring him here without any one seeing us. I thought perhaps you could push his carriage. The doctor said he must have fresh air and if he wants us to take him out no one dare disobey him. He won't go out for other people and perhaps they will be glad if he will go out with us. He could order the gardeners to keep away so they wouldn't find out.'

Dickon was thinking very hard as he scratched Captain's back.

'It'd be good for him, I'll warrant,' he said. 'Us'd not be thinkin' he'd better never been born. Us'd be just two children watchin' a garden grow, an' he'd be another. Two lads an' a little lass just lookin' on at th' springtime. I warrant it'd be better than doctor's stuff.'

'He's been lying in his room so long and he's always been so afraid of his back that it has made him queer,' said Mary. 'He knows a good many things out of books but he doesn't know anything else. He says he has been too ill to notice things and he hates going out of doors and hates gardens and gardeners. But he likes to hear about this garden because it is a secret. I daren't tell him much but he said he wanted to see it.'

'Us'll have him out here sometime for sure,' said Dickon. 'I could push his carriage well enough. Has tha' noticed how th' robin an' his mate has been workin' while we've been sittin' here? Look at him perched on that branch wonderin' where it'd be best to put that twig he's got in his beak.'

He made one of his low whistling calls and the robin turned his head and looked at him inquiringly, still holding his twig. Dickon spoke to him as Ben Weatherstaff did, but Dickon's tone was one of friendly advice.

'Wheres'ever[244] tha' puts[245] it,' he said, 'it'll be all right. Tha' knew how to build tha' nest before tha' came out o' th' egg. Get on with thee, lad. Tha'st got no time to lose.'

'Oh, I do like to hear you talk to him!' Mary said, laughing delightedly. 'Ben Weatherstaff scolds him and makes fun of him, and he hops about and looks as if he understood every word, and I know he likes it. Ben Weatherstaff says he is so conceited he would rather have stones thrown at him than not be noticed.'

Dickon laughed too and went on talking.

'Tha' knows us won't trouble thee,' he said to the robin. 'Us is near bein' wild things ourselves. Us is nest-buildin' too, bless thee. Look out tha' doesn't tell on us.'

And though the robin did not answer, because his beak was occupied, Mary knew that when he flew away with his twig to his own corner of the garden the darkness of his dew-bright eye meant that he would not tell their secret for the world.

16.

'I Won't!' Said Mary.

They found a great deal to do that morning and Mary was late in returning to the house and was also in such a hurry to get back to her work that she quite forgot Colin until the last moment.

'Tell Colin that I can't come and see him yet,' she said to Martha. 'I'm very busy in the garden.'

Martha looked rather frightened.

'Eh! Miss Mary,' she said, 'it may put him all out of humor when I tell him that.'

But Mary was not as afraid of him as other people were and she was not a self-sacrificing person.

'I can't stay,' she answered. 'Dickon's waiting for me;' and she ran away.

The afternoon was even lovelier and busier than the morning had been. Already nearly all the weeds were cleared out of the garden and most of the roses and trees had been pruned or dug about. Dickon had brought a spade of his own and he had taught

Mary to use all her tools, so that by this time it was plain that though the lovely wild place was not likely to become a 'gardener's garden' it would be a wilderness of growing things before the springtime was over.

'There'll be apple blossoms an' cherry blossoms overhead,' Dickon said, working away with all his might. 'An' there'll be peach an' plum trees in bloom against th' walls, an' th' grass'll be a carpet o' flowers.'

The little fox and the rook were as happy and busy as they were, and the robin and his mate flew backward and forward like tiny streaks of lightning. Sometimes the rook flapped his black wings and soared away over the tree-tops in the park. Each time he came back and perched near Dickon and cawed several times as if he were relating his adventures, and Dickon talked to him just as he had talked to the robin. Once when Dickon was so busy that he did not answer him at first, Soot flew on to his shoulders and gently tweaked his ear with his large beak. When Mary wanted to rest a little Dickon sat down with her under a tree and once he took his pipe out of his pocket and played the soft strange little notes and two squirrels appeared on the wall and looked and listened.

'Tha's a good bit stronger than tha' was,' Dickon said, looking at her as she was digging. 'Tha's beginning to look different, for sure.'

Mary was glowing with exercise and good spirits.

'I'm getting fatter and fatter every day,' she said quite exultantly. 'Mrs. Medlock will have to get me some bigger dresses. Martha says my hair is growing thicker. It isn't so flat and stringy.'

The sun was beginning to set and sending deep gold-coloured

rays slanting under the trees when they parted.

'It'll be fine tomorrow,' said Dickon. 'I'll be at work by sunrise.'

'So will I,' said Mary.

She ran back to the house as quickly as her feet would carry her. She wanted to tell Colin about Dickon's fox cub and the rook and about what the springtime had been doing. She felt sure he would like to hear. So it was not very pleasant when she opened the door of her room, to see Martha standing waiting for her with a doleful face.

'What is the matter?' she asked. 'What did Colin say when you told him I couldn't come?'

'Eh!' said Martha, 'I wish tha'd gone. He was nigh goin' into one o' his tantrums. There's been a nice to do all afternoon to keep him quiet. He would watch the clock all th' time.'

Mary's lips pinched themselves together. She was no more used to considering other people than Colin was and she saw no reason why an ill-tempered boy should interfere with the thing she liked best. She knew nothing about the pitifulness of people who had been ill and nervous and who did not know that they could control their tempers and need not make other people ill and nervous, too. When she had had a headache in India she had done her best to see that everybody else also had a headache or something quite as bad. And she felt she was quite right; but of course now she felt that Colin was quite wrong.

He was not on his sofa when she went into his room. He was lying flat on his back in bed and he did not turn his head toward her as she came in. This was a bad beginning and Mary marched up to him with her stiff manner.

'Why didn't you get up?' she said.

'I did get up this morning when I thought you were coming,' he answered, without looking at her. 'I made them put me back in bed this afternoon. My back ached and my head ached and I was tired. Why didn't you come?'

'I was working in the garden with Dickon,' said Mary.

Colin frowned and condescended to look at her.

'I won't let that boy come here if you go and stay with him instead of coming to talk to me,' he said.

Mary flew into a fine passion. She could fly into a passion without making a noise. She just grew sour and obstinate and did not care what happened.

'If you send Dickon away, I'll never come into this room again!' she retorted.

'You'll have to if I want you,' said Colin.

'I won't!' said Mary.

'I'll make you,' said Colin. 'They shall drag you in.'

'Shall they, Mr. Rajah!' said Mary fiercely. 'They may drag me in but they can't make me talk when they get me here. I'll sit and clench my teeth and never tell you one thing. I won't even look at you. I'll stare at the floor!'

They were a nice agreeable pair as they glared at each other. If they had been two little street boys they would have sprung at each other and had a rough-and-tumble fight. As it was, they did the next thing to it.

'You are a selfish thing!' cried Colin.

'What are you?' said Mary. 'Selfish people always say that. Any one is selfish who doesn't do what they want. You're more selfish than I am. You're the most selfish boy I ever saw.'

'I'm not!' snapped Colin. 'I'm not as selfish as your fine Dickon is! He keeps you playing in the dirt when he knows I am all by myself. He's selfish, if you like!'

Mary's eyes flashed fire.

'He's nicer than any other boy that ever lived!' she said. 'He's—he's like an angel!' It might sound rather silly to say that but she did not care.

'A nice angel!' Colin sneered ferociously. 'He's a common cottage boy off the moor!'

'He's better than a common Rajah!' retorted Mary. 'He's a thousand times better!'

Because she was the stronger of the two she was beginning to get the better of him. The truth was that he had never had a fight with any one like himself in his life and, upon the whole, it was rather good for him, though neither he nor Mary knew anything about that. He turned his head on his pillow and shut his eyes and a big tear was squeezed out and ran down his cheek. He was beginning to feel pathetic and sorry for himself—not for any one else.

'I'm not as selfish as you, because I'm always ill, and I'm sure there is a lump coming on my back,' he said. 'And I am going to die besides.'

'You're not!' contradicted Mary unsympathetically.

He opened his eyes quite wide with indignation. He had never heard such a thing said before. He was at once furious and slightly pleased, if a person could be both at the same time.

'I'm not?' he cried. 'I am! You know I am! Everybody says so.'

'I don't believe it!' said Mary sourly. 'You just say that to make people sorry. I believe you're proud of it. I don't believe it! If you were a nice boy it might be true—but you're too nasty!'

In spite of his invalid back Colin sat up in bed in quite a healthy rage.

'Get out of the room!' he shouted and he caught hold of his pillow and threw it at her. He was not strong enough to throw it far and it only fell at her feet, but Mary's face looked as pinched as a nutcracker.

'I'm going,' she said. 'And I won't come back!'

She walked to the door and when she reached it she turned round and spoke again.

'I was going to tell you all sorts of nice things,' she said. 'Dickon brought his fox and his rook and I was going to tell you all about them. Now I won't tell you a single thing!'

She marched out of the door and closed it behind her, and there to her great astonishment she found the trained nurse standing as if she had been listening and, more amazing still— she was laughing. She was a big handsome young woman who ought not to have been a trained nurse at all, as she could not bear invalids and she was always making excuses to leave Colin to Martha or any one else who would take her place. Mary had never liked her, and she simply stood and gazed up at her as she stood giggling into her handkerchief.

'What are you laughing at?' she asked her.

'At you two young ones,' said the nurse. 'It's the best thing that could happen to the sickly pampered thing to have some one to stand up to him that's as spoiled as himself;' and she laughed into her handkerchief again. 'If he'd had a young vixen of a sister to fight with it would have been the saving of him.'

'Is he going to die?'

'I don't know and I don't care,' said the nurse. 'Hysterics and temper are half what ails him.'

'What are hysterics?' asked Mary.

'You'll find out if you work him into a tantrum after this—but at any rate you've given him something to have hysterics about, and I'm glad of it.'

Mary went back to her room not feeling at all as she had felt when she had come in from the garden. She was cross and disappointed but not at all sorry for Colin. She had looked forward to telling him a great many things and she had meant to try to make up her mind whether it would be safe to trust him with the great secret. She had been beginning to think it would be, but now she had changed her mind entirely. She would never tell him and he could stay in his room and never get any fresh air and die if he liked! It would serve him right! She felt so sour and unrelenting that for a few minutes she almost forgot about Dickon and the green veil creeping over the world and the soft wind blowing down from the moor.

Martha was waiting for her and the trouble in her face had been temporarily replaced by interest and curiosity. There was a wooden box on the table and its cover had been removed and revealed that it was full of neat packages.

'Mr. Craven sent it to you,' said Martha. 'It looks as if it had picture-books in it.'

Mary remembered what he had asked her the day she had gone to his room. 'Do you want anything—dolls—toys—books?' She opened the package wondering if he had sent a doll, and also wondering what she should do with it if he had. But he had not sent one. There were several beautiful books such as Colin had, and two of them were about gardens and were full of pictures.

There were two or three games and there was a beautiful little writing-case with a gold monogram on it and a gold pen and inkstand.

Everything was so nice that her pleasure began to crowd her anger out of her mind. She had not expected him to remember her at all and her hard little heart grew quite warm.

'I can write better than I can print,' she said, 'and the first thing I shall write with that pen will be a letter to tell him I am much obliged.'

If she had been friends with Colin she would have run to show him her presents at once, and they would have looked at the pictures and read some of the gardening books and perhaps tried playing the games, and he would have enjoyed himself so much he would never once have thought he was going to die or have put his hand on his spine to see if there was a lump coming. He had a way of doing that which she could not bear. It gave her an uncomfortable frightened feeling because he always looked so frightened himself. He said that if he felt even quite a little lump some day he should know his hunch had begun to grow. Something he had heard Mrs. Medlock whispering to the nurse had given him the idea and he had thought over it in secret until it was quite firmly fixed in his mind. Mrs. Medlock had said his father's back had begun to show its crookedness in that way when he was a child. He had never told any one but Mary that most of his 'tantrums' as they called them grew out of his hysterical hidden fear. Mary had been sorry for him when he had told her.

'He always began to think about it when he was cross or tired,' she said to herself. 'And he has been cross to-day. Perhaps—perhaps he has been thinking about it all afternoon.'

She stood still, looking down at the carpet and thinking.

'I said I would never go back again—' she hesitated, knitting her brows—'but perhaps, just perhaps, I will go and see—if he wants me—in the morning. Perhaps he'll try to throw his pillow at me again, but—I think—I'll go.'

17.

A Tantrum

She had got up very early in the morning and had worked hard in the garden and she was tired and sleepy, so as soon as Martha had brought her supper and she had eaten it, she was glad to go to bed. As she laid her head on the pillow she murmured to herself:

'I'll go out before breakfast and work with Dickon and then afterward—I believe—I'll go to see him.'

She thought it was the middle of the night when she was awakened by such dreadful sounds that she jumped out of bed in an instant. What was it—what was it? The next minute she felt quite sure she knew. Doors were opened and shut and there were hurrying feet in the corridors and some one was crying and screaming at the same time, screaming and crying in a horrible way.

'It's Colin,' she said. 'He's having one of those tantrums the nurse called hysterics. How awful it sounds.'

As she listened to the sobbing screams she did not wonder that people were so frightened that they gave him his own way in everything rather than hear them. She put her hands over her ears and felt sick and shivering.

'I don't know what to do. I don't know what to do,' she kept saying. 'I can't bear it.'

Once she wondered if he would stop if she dared go to him and then she remembered how he had driven her out of the room and thought that perhaps the sight of her might make him worse. Even when she pressed her hands more tightly over her ears she could not keep the awful sounds out. She hated them so and was so terrified by them that suddenly they began to make her angry and she felt as if she should like to fly into a tantrum herself and frighten him as he was frightening her. She was not used to any one's tempers but her own. She took her hands from her ears and sprang up and stamped her foot.

'He ought to be stopped! Somebody ought to make him stop! Somebody ought to beat him!' she cried out.

Just then she heard feet almost running down the corridor and her door opened and the nurse came in. She was not laughing now by any means. She even looked rather pale.

'He's worked himself into hysterics,' she said in a great hurry. 'He'll do himself harm. No one can do anything with him. You come and try, like a good child. He likes you.'

'He turned me out of the room this morning,' said Mary, stamping her foot with excitement.

The stamp rather pleased the nurse. The truth was that she had been afraid she might find Mary crying and hiding her head under the bed-clothes.

'That's right,' she said. 'You're in the right humour. You go and scold him. Give him something new to think of. Do go, child, as quick as ever you can.'

It was not until afterward that Mary realized that the thing had been funny as well as dreadful—that it was funny that all the grown-up people were so frightened that they came to a little girl just because they guessed she was almost as bad as Colin himself.

She flew along the corridor and the nearer she got to the screams the higher her temper mounted. She felt quite wicked by the time she reached the door. She slapped it open with her hand and ran across the room to the four-posted bed.

'You stop!' she almost shouted. 'You stop! I hate you! Everybody hates you! I wish everybody would run out of the house and let you scream yourself to death! You will scream yourself to death in a minute, and I wish you would!'

A nice sympathetic child could neither have thought nor said such things, but it just happened that the shock of hearing them was the best possible thing for this hysterical boy whom no one had ever dared to restrain or contradict.

He had been lying on his face beating his pillow with his hands and he actually almost jumped around, he turned so quickly at the sound of the furious little voice. His face looked dreadful, white and red and swollen, and he was gasping and choking; but savage little Mary did not care an atom.

'If you scream another scream,' she said, 'I'll scream too—and I can scream louder than you can and I'll frighten you, I'll frighten you!'

He actually had stopped screaming because she had startled him so. The scream which had been coming almost choked him.

The tears were streaming down his face and he shook all over.

'I can't stop!' he gasped and sobbed. 'I can't—I can't!'

'You can!' shouted Mary. 'Half that ails you is hysterics and temper—just hysterics—hysterics—hysterics!' and she stamped each time she said it.

'I felt the lump—I felt it,' choked out Colin. 'I knew I should. I shall have a hunch on my back and then I shall die,' and he began to writhe again and turned on his face and sobbed and wailed but he didn't scream.

'You didn't feel a lump!' contradicted Mary fiercely. 'If you did it was only a hysterical lump. Hysterics makes lumps. There's nothing the matter with your horrid back—nothing but hysterics! Turn over and let me look at it!'

She liked the word 'hysterics' and felt somehow as if it had an effect on him. He was probably like herself and had never heard it before.

'Nurse,' she commanded, 'come here and show me his back this minute!'

The nurse, Mrs. Medlock and Martha had been standing huddled together near the door staring at her, their mouths half open. All three had gasped with fright more than once. The nurse came forward as if she were half afraid. Colin was heaving with great breathless sobs.

'Perhaps he—he won't let me,' she hesitated in a low voice.

Colin heard her, however, and he gasped out between two sobs:

'Sh-show her! She-she'll see then!'

It was a poor thin back to look at when it was bared. Every rib could be counted and every joint of the spine, though Mistress

Mary did not count them as she bent over and examined them with a solemn savage little face. She looked so sour and old-fashioned that the nurse turned her head aside to hide the twitching of her mouth. There was just a minute's silence, for even Colin tried to hold his breath while Mary looked up and down his spine, and down and up, as intently as if she had been the great doctor from London.

'There's not a single lump there!' she said at last. 'There's not a lump as big as a pin—except backbone lumps, and you can only feel them because you're thin. I've got backbone lumps myself, and they used to stick out as much as yours do, until I began to get fatter, and I am not fat enough yet to hide them. There's not a lump as big as a pin! If you ever say there is again, I shall laugh!'

No one but Colin himself knew what effect those crossly spoken childish words had on him. If he had ever had any one to talk to about his secret terrors—if he had ever dared to let himself ask questions—if he had had childish companions and had not lain on his back in the huge closed house, breathing an atmosphere heavy with the fears of people who were most of them ignorant and tired of him, he would have found out that most of his fright and illness was created by himself. But he had lain and thought of himself and his aches and weariness for hours and days and months and years. And now that an angry unsympathetic little girl insisted obstinately that he was not as ill as he thought he was he actually felt as if she might be speaking the truth.

'I didn't know,' ventured the nurse, 'that he thought he had a lump on his spine. His back is weak because he won't try to sit up. I could have told him there was no lump there.' Colin gulped and turned his face a little to look at her.

'C-could you?' he said pathetically.

'Yes, sir.'

'There!' said Mary, and she gulped too.

Colin turned on his face again and but for his long-drawn broken breaths, which were the dying down of his storm of sobbing, he lay still for a minute, though great tears streamed down his face and wet the pillow. Actually the tears meant that a curious great relief had come to him. Presently he turned and looked at the nurse again and strangely enough he was not like a Rajah at all as he spoke to her.

'Do you think—I could—live to grow up?' he said.

The nurse was neither clever nor soft-hearted but she could repeat some of the London doctor's words.

'You probably will if you will do what you are told to do and not give way to your temper, and stay out a great deal in the fresh air.'

Colin's tantrum had passed and he was weak and worn out with crying and this perhaps made him feel gentle. He put out his hand a little toward Mary, and I am glad to say that, her own tantrum having passed, she was softened too and met him half-way with her hand, so that it was a sort of making up.

'I'll—I'll go out with you, Mary,' he said. 'I shan't hate fresh air if we can find—' He remembered just in time to stop himself from saying 'if we can find the secret garden' and he ended, 'I shall like to go out with you if Dickon will come and push my chair. I do so want to see Dickon and the fox and the crow.'

The nurse remade the tumbled bed and shook and straightened the pillows. Then she made Colin a cup of beef tea and gave a cup to Mary, who really was very glad to get it after her excitement.

Mrs. Medlock and Martha gladly slipped away, and after everything was neat and calm and in order the nurse looked as if she would very gladly slip away also. She was a healthy young woman who resented being robbed of her sleep and she yawned quite openly as she looked at Mary, who had pushed her big footstool close to the four-posted bed and was holding Colin's hand.

'You must go back and get your sleep out,' she said. 'He'll drop off after a while—if he's not too upset. Then I'll lie down myself in the next room.'

'Would you like me to sing you that song I learned from my Ayah?' Mary whispered to Colin.

His hand pulled hers gently and he turned his tired eyes on her appealingly.

'Oh, yes!' he answered. 'It's such a soft song. I shall go to sleep in a minute.'

'I will put him to sleep,' Mary said to the yawning nurse. 'You can go if you like.'

'Well,' said the nurse, with an attempt at reluctance. 'If he doesn't go to sleep in half an hour you must call me.'

'Very well,' answered Mary.

The nurse was out of the room in a minute and as soon as she was gone Colin pulled Mary's hand again.

'I almost told,' he said; 'but I stopped myself in time. I won't talk and I'll go to sleep, but you said you had a whole lot of nice things to tell me. Have you—do you think you have found out anything at all about the way into the secret garden?'

Mary looked at his poor little tired face and swollen eyes and her heart relented.

'Ye-es,' she answered, 'I think I have. And if you will go to sleep I will tell you to-morrow.'

His hand quite trembled.

'Oh, Mary!' he said. 'Oh, Mary! If I could get into it I think I should live to grow up! Do you suppose that instead of singing the Ayah song—you could just tell me softly as you did that first day what you imagine it looks like inside? I am sure it will make me go to sleep.'

'Yes,' answered Mary. 'Shut your eyes.'

He closed his eyes and lay quite still and she held his hand and began to speak very slowly and in a very low voice.

'I think it has been left alone so long—that it has grown all into a lovely tangle. I think the roses have climbed and climbed and climbed until they hang from the branches and walls and creep over the ground—almost like a strange gray mist. Some of them have died but many—are alive and when the summer comes there will be curtains and fountains of roses. I think the ground is full of daffodils and snowdrops and lilies and iris working their way out of the dark. Now the spring has begun—perhaps—perhaps—'

The soft drone of her voice was making him stiller and stiller and she saw it and went on.

'Perhaps they are coming up through the grass—perhaps there are clusters of purple crocuses and gold ones—even now. Perhaps the leaves are beginning to break out and uncurl—and perhaps— the gray is changing and a green gauze veil is creeping—and creeping over—everything. And the birds are coming to look at it—because it is—so safe and still. And perhaps—perhaps— perhaps—' very softly and slowly indeed, 'the robin has found a mate—and is building a nest.'

And Colin was asleep.

18.

'Tha' Munnot Waste No Time.'

Of course Mary did not waken early the next morning. She slept late because she was tired, and when Martha brought her breakfast she told her that though Colin was quite quiet he was ill and feverish as he always was after he had worn himself out with a fit of crying. Mary ate her breakfast slowly as she listened.

'He says he wishes tha' would please go and see him as soon as tha' can,' Martha said. 'It's queer what a fancy he's took to thee. Tha' did give it him last night for sure—didn't tha? Nobody else would have dared to do it. Eh! poor[246] lad! He's been spoiled till salt won't save him. Mother says as th' two worst things as can happen to a child is never to have his own way—or always to have it. She doesn't know which is th' worst. Tha' was in a fine temper tha'self, too. But he says to me when I went into his room, "Please ask Miss Mary if she'll please come an' talk to me?" Think o' him saying please! Will you go, Miss?'

'I'll run and see Dickon first,' said Mary. 'No, I'll go and see Colin first and tell him—I know what I'll tell him,' with a sudden inspiration.

She had her hat on when she appeared in Colin's room and for a second he looked disappointed. He was in bed. His face was pitifully white and there were dark circles round his eyes.

'I'm glad you came,' he said. 'My head aches and I ache all over because I'm so tired. Are you going somewhere?'

Mary went and leaned against his bed.

'I won't be long,' she said. 'I'm going to Dickon, but I'll come back. Colin, it's—it's something about the garden.'

His whole face brightened and a little colour came into it.

'Oh! is it!' he cried out. 'I dreamed about it all night. I heard you say something about gray changing into green, and I dreamed I was standing in a place all filled with trembling little green leaves—and there were birds on nests everywhere and they looked so soft and still. I'll lie and think about it until you come back.'

In five minutes Mary was with Dickon in their garden. The fox and the crow were with him again and this time he had brought two tame squirrels.

'I came over on the pony this mornin',' he said. 'Eh! he is a good little chap—Jump is! I brought these two in my pockets. This here one he's called Nut an' this here other one's called Shell.'

When he said 'Nut' one squirrel leaped on to his right shoulder and when he said 'shell' the other one leaped on to his left shoulder.

When they sat down on the grass with Captain curled at their feet, Soot solemnly listening on a tree and Nut and Shell nosing about close to them, it seemed to Mary that it would be scarcely bearable to leave such delightfulness, but when she began to tell her story somehow the look in Dickon's funny face gradually changed her mind. She could see he felt sorrier for Colin than she did. He looked up at the sky and all about him.

'Just listen to them birds—th' world seems full of 'em—all whistlin' an' pipin',' he said. 'Look at 'em dartin'[247] about, an' hearken at 'em callin' to each other. Come springtime seems like as if all th' world's callin'. The leaves is uncurlin'[248] so you can see 'em—an', my word, th' nice smells there is about!' sniffing with his happy turned-up nose. 'An' that poor lad lyin' shut up an' seein' so little that he gets to thinkin' o' things as sets him screamin'[249]. Eh! my![250] we mun get him out here—we mun get him watchin' an listenin' an' sniffin' up th' air an' get him just soaked through wi' sunshine. An' we munnot lose no time about it.'

When he was very much interested he often spoke quite broad Yorkshire though at other times he tried to modify his dialect so that Mary could better understand. But she loved his broad Yorkshire and had in fact been trying to learn to speak it herself. So she spoke a little now.

'Aye, that we mun,' she said (which meant 'Yes, indeed, we must'). 'I'll tell thee what us'll do first,' she proceeded, and Dickon grinned, because when the little wench tried to twist her tongue into speaking Yorkshire it amused him very much. 'He's took a graidely fancy to thee. He wants to see thee and he wants to see Soot an' Captain. When I go back to the house to talk to him I'll ax him if tha' canna' come an' see him tomorrow mornin'—an' bring tha' creatures wi' thee—an' then—in a bit, when there's more leaves out, an' happen a bud or two, we'll get him to come out an' tha' shall push him in his chair an' we'll bring him here an' show him everything.'

When she stopped she was quite proud of herself. She had never made a long speech in Yorkshire before and she had remembered very well.

'Tha' mun talk a bit o' Yorkshire like that to Mester Colin,' Dickon chuckled. 'Tha'll make him laugh an' there's nowt as good for ill folk as laughin' is. Mother says she believes as half a hour's good laugh every mornin' 'ud[251] cure a chap as was makin' ready for typhus fever.'

'I'm going to talk Yorkshire to him this very day,' said Mary, chuckling herself.

The garden had reached the time when every day and every night it seemed as if Magicians were passing through it drawing loveliness out of the earth and the boughs with wands. It was hard to go away and leave it all, particularly as Nut had actually crept on to her dress and Shell had scrambled down the trunk of the apple-tree they sat under and stayed there looking at her with inquiring eyes. But she went back to the house and when she sat down close to Colin's bed he began to sniff as Dickon did though not in such an experienced way.

'You smell like flowers and—and fresh things,' he cried out quite joyously. 'What is it you smell of? It's cool and warm and sweet all at the same time.'

'It's th' wind from th' moor,' said Mary. 'It comes o' sittin' on th' grass under a tree wi' Dickon an' wi' Captain an' Soot an' Nut an' Shell. It's th' springtime an' out o' doors an' sunshine as smells so graidely.'

She said it as broadly as she could, and you do not know how broadly Yorkshire sounds until you have heard some one speak it. Colin began to laugh.

'What are you doing?' he said. 'I never heard you talk like that before. How funny it sounds.'

'I'm givin' thee a bit o' Yorkshire,' answered Mary triumphantly. 'I canna' talk as graidely as Dickon an' Martha can but tha' sees[252] I can shape a bit. Doesn't tha' understand a bit o' Yorkshire when tha' hears[253] it? An' tha' a Yorkshire lad thysel' bred an' born! Eh! I wonder tha'rt not ashamed o' thy face.'

And then she began to laugh too and they both laughed until they could not stop themselves and they laughed until the room echoed and Mrs. Medlock opening the door to come in drew back into the corridor and stood listening amazed.

'Well, upon my word!' she said, speaking rather broad Yorkshire herself because there was no one to hear her and she was so astonished. 'Whoever heard th' like! Whoever on earth would ha'[254] thought it!'

There was so much to talk about. It seemed as if Colin could never hear enough of Dickon and Captain and Soot and Nut and Shell and the pony whose name was Jump. Mary had run round into the wood with Dickon to see Jump. He was a tiny little shaggy moor pony with thick locks hanging over his eyes and with a pretty face and a nuzzling velvet nose. He was rather thin with living on moor grass but he was as tough and wiry as if the muscle in his little legs had been made of steel springs. He had lifted his head and whinnied softly the moment he saw Dickon and he had trotted up to him and put his head across his shoulder and then Dickon had talked into his ear and Jump had talked back in odd little whinnies and puffs and snorts. Dickon had made him give Mary his small front hoof and kiss her on her cheek with his velvet muzzle.

'Does he really understand everything Dickon says?' Colin asked.

'It seems as if he does,' answered Mary. 'Dickon says anything will understand if you're friends with it for sure, but you have to be friends for sure.'

Colin lay quiet a little while and his strange gray eyes seemed to be staring at the wall, but Mary saw he was thinking.

'I wish I was friends with things,' he said at last, 'but I'm not. I never had anything to be friends with, and I can't bear people.'

'Can't you bear me?' asked Mary.

'Yes, I can,' he answered. 'It's funny but I even like you.'

'Ben Weatherstaff said I was like him,' said Mary. 'He said he'd warrant we'd both got the same nasty tempers. I think you are like him too. We are all three alike—you and I and Ben Weatherstaff. He said we were neither of us much to look at and we were as sour as we looked. But I don't feel as sour as I used to before I knew the robin and Dickon.'

'Did you feel as if you hated people?'

'Yes,' answered Mary without any affectation. 'I should have detested you if I had seen you before I saw the robin and Dickon.'

Colin put out his thin hand and touched her.

'Mary,' he said, 'I wish I hadn't said what I did about sending Dickon away. I hated you when you said he was like an angel and I laughed at you but—but perhaps he is.'

'Well, it was rather funny to say it,' she admitted frankly, 'because his nose does turn up and he has a big mouth and his clothes have patches all over them and he talks broad Yorkshire, but—but if an angel did come to Yorkshire and live on the moor— if there was a Yorkshire angel—I believe he'd understand the green things and know how to make them grow and he would know how to talk to the wild creatures as Dickon does and they'd know he was friends for sure.'

'I shouldn't mind Dickon looking at me,' said Colin; 'I want to see him.'

'I'm glad you said that,' answered Mary, 'because—because—'

Quite suddenly it came into her mind that this was the minute to tell him. Colin knew something new was coming.

'Because what?' he cried eagerly.

Mary was so anxious that she got up from her stool and came to him and caught hold of both his hands.

'Can I trust you? I trusted Dickon because birds trusted him. Can I trust you—for sure—*for sure*?' she implored.

Her face was so solemn that he almost whispered his answer.

'Yes—yes!'

'Well, Dickon will come to see you tomorrow morning, and he'll bring his creatures with him.'

'Oh! Oh!' Colin cried out in delight.

'But that's not all,' Mary went on, almost pale with solemn excitement. 'The rest is better. There is a door into the garden. I found it. It is under the ivy on the wall.'

If he had been a strong healthy boy Colin would probably have shouted 'Hooray! Hooray! Hooray!' but he was weak and rather hysterical; his eyes grew bigger and bigger and he gasped for breath.

'Oh! Mary!' he cried out with a half sob. 'Shall I see it? Shall

I get into it? Shall I *live* to get into it?' and he clutched her hands and dragged her toward him.

'Of course you'll see it!' snapped Mary indignantly. 'Of course you'll live to get into it! Don't be silly!'

And she was so un-hysterical and natural and childish that she brought him to his senses and he began to laugh at himself and a few minutes afterward she was sitting on her stool again telling him not what she imagined the secret garden to be like but what it really was, and Colin's aches and tiredness were forgotten and he was listening enraptured.

'It is just what you thought it would be,' he said at last. 'It sounds just as if you had really seen it. You know I said that when you told me first.'

Mary hesitated about two minutes and then boldly spoke the truth.

'I had seen it—and I had been in,' she said. 'I found the key and got in weeks ago. But I daren't tell you—I daren't because I was so afraid I couldn't trust you—*for sure!*'

19.

'It Has Come!'

Of course Dr. Craven had been sent for the morning after Colin had had his tantrum. He was always sent for at once when such a thing occurred and he always found, when he arrived, a white shaken boy lying on his bed, sulky and still so hysterical that he was ready to break into fresh sobbing at the least word. In fact, Dr. Craven dreaded and detested the difficulties of these visits. On this occasion he was away from Misselthwaite Manor until afternoon.

'How is he?' he asked Mrs. Medlock rather irritably when he arrived. 'He will break a blood-vessel in one of those fits some day. The boy is half insane with hysteria and self-indulgence.'

'Well, sir,' answered Mrs. Medlock, 'you'll scarcely believe your eyes when you see him. That plain sour-faced child that's almost as bad as himself has just bewitched him. How she's done it there's no telling. The Lord knows she's nothing to look at and you scarcely ever hear her speak, but she did what none of us dare do.

She just flew at him like a little cat last night, and stamped her feet and ordered him to stop screaming, and somehow she startled him so that he actually did stop, and this afternoon—well just come up and see, sir. It's past crediting.'

The scene which Dr. Craven beheld when he entered his patient's room was indeed rather astonishing to him. As Mrs. Medlock opened the door he heard laughing and chattering. Colin was on his sofa in his dressing-gown and he was sitting up quite straight looking at a picture in one of the garden books and talking to the plain child who at that moment could scarcely be called plain at all because her face was so glowing with enjoyment.

'Those long spires of blue ones—we'll have a lot of those,' Colin was announcing. 'They're called Del-phin-iums.'

'Dickon says they're larkspurs made big and grand,' cried Mistress Mary. 'There are clumps there already.'

Then they saw Dr. Craven and stopped. Mary became quite still and Colin looked fretful.

'I am sorry to hear you were ill last night, my boy,' Dr. Craven said a trifle nervously. He was rather a nervous man.

'I'm better now—much better,' Colin answered, rather like a Rajah. 'I'm going out in my chair in a day or two if it is fine. I want some fresh air.'

Dr. Craven sat down by him and felt his pulse and looked at him curiously.

'It must be a very fine day,' he said, 'and you must be very careful not to tire yourself.'

'Fresh air won't tire me,' said the young Rajah.

As there had been occasions when this same young gentleman had shrieked aloud with rage and had insisted that fresh air would give him cold and kill him, it is not to be wondered at that his doctor felt somewhat startled.

'I thought you did not like fresh air,' he said.

'I don't when I am by myself,' replied the Rajah; 'but my cousin is going out with me.'

'And the nurse, of course?' suggested Dr. Craven.

'No, I will not have the nurse,' so magnificently that Mary could not help remembering how the young native Prince had looked with his diamonds and emeralds and pearls stuck all over him and the great rubies on the small dark hand he had waved to command his servants to approach with salaams and receive his orders.

'My cousin knows how to take care of me. I am always better when she is with me. She made me better last night. A very strong boy I know will push my carriage.'

Dr. Craven felt rather alarmed. If this tiresome hysterical boy should chance to get well he himself would lose all chance of inheriting Misselthwaite; but he was not an unscrupulous man, though he was a weak one, and he did not intend to let him run into actual danger.

'He must be a strong boy and a steady boy,' he said. 'And I must know something about him. Who is he? What is his name?'

'It's Dickon,' Mary spoke up suddenly. She felt somehow that everybody who knew the moor must know Dickon. And she was right, too. She saw that in a moment Dr. Craven's serious face relaxed into a relieved smile.

'Oh, Dickon,' he said. 'If it is Dickon you will be safe enough. He's as strong as a moor pony, is Dickon.'

'And he's trusty,' said Mary. 'He's th' trustiest lad i'[255] Yorkshire.'

She had been talking Yorkshire to Colin and she forgot herself.

'Did Dickon teach you that?' asked Dr. Craven, laughing outright.

'I'm learning it as if it was French,' said Mary rather coldly. 'It's like a native dialect in India. Very clever people try to learn them. I like it and so does Colin.'

'Well, well,' he said. 'If it amuses you perhaps it won't do you any harm. Did you take your bromide last night, Colin?'

'No,' Colin answered. 'I wouldn't take it at first and after Mary made me quiet she talked me to sleep—in a low voice—about the spring creeping into a garden.'

'That sounds soothing,' said Dr. Craven, more perplexed than ever and glancing sideways at Mistress Mary sitting on her stool and looking down silently at the carpet. 'You are evidently better, but you must remember—'

'I don't want to remember,' interrupted the Rajah, appearing again. 'When I lie by myself and remember I begin to have pains everywhere and I think of things that make me begin to scream because I hate them so. If there was a doctor anywhere who could make you forget you were ill instead of remembering it I would have him brought here.' And he waved a thin hand which ought really to have been covered with royal signet rings made of rubies. 'It is because my cousin makes me forget that she makes me better.'

Dr. Craven had never made such a short stay after a 'tantrum'; usually he was obliged to remain a very long time and do a great many things. This afternoon he did not give any medicine or leave any new orders and he was spared any disagreeable scenes. When he went downstairs he looked very thoughtful and when he talked to Mrs. Medlock in the library she felt that he was a much puzzled man.

'Well, sir,' she ventured, 'could you have believed it?'

'It is certainly a new state of affairs,' said the doctor. 'And there's no denying it is better than the old one.'

'I believe Susan Sowerby's right—I do that,' said Mrs. Medlock. 'I stopped in her cottage on my way to Thwaite yesterday and had a bit of talk with her. And she says to me, "Well, Sarah Ann, she mayn't be a good child, an' she mayn't be a pretty one, but she's a child, an' children needs[256] children." We went to school together, Susan Sowerby and me.'

'She's the best sick nurse I know,' said Dr. Craven. 'When I find her in a cottage I know the chances are that I shall save my patient.'

Mrs. Medlock smiled. She was fond of Susan Sowerby.

'She's got a way with her, has Susan,' she went on quite volubly. 'I've been thinking all morning of one thing she said yesterday. She says, "Once when I was givin' th' children a bit of a preach after they'd been fightin'[257] I ses[258] to 'em all, 'When I was at school my jography[259] told as th' world was shaped like a orange an' I found out before I was ten that th' whole orange doesn't belong to nobody. No one owns more than his bit of a quarter an' there's times it seems like there's not enow quarters to go round. But don't you—none o' you—think as you own th' whole orange or you'll find out you're mistaken, an' you won't find it out without hard knocks.' What children learns[260] from children," she says, "is that there's no sense in grabbin' at th' whole orange—peel an' all. If you do you'll likely not get even th' pips, an' them's too bitter to eat." '

'She's a shrewd woman,' said Dr. Craven, putting on his coat.

'Well, she's got a way of saying things,' ended Mrs. Medlock, much pleased. 'sometimes I've said to her, "Eh! Susan, if you was a different woman an' didn't talk such broad Yorkshire I've seen the times when I should have said you was clever." '

That night Colin slept without once awakening and when he opened his eyes in the morning he lay still and smiled without knowing it—smiled because he felt so curiously comfortable. It was actually nice to be awake, and he turned over and stretched his limbs luxuriously. He felt as if tight strings which had held him had loosened themselves and let him go. He did not know that Dr. Craven would have said that his nerves had relaxed and rested themselves. Instead of lying and staring at the wall and wishing he had not awakened, his mind was full of the plans he and Mary had made yesterday, of pictures of the garden and of Dickon and his wild creatures. It was so nice to have things to think about. And he had not been awake more than ten minutes when he heard feet running along the corridor and Mary was at the door. The next minute she was in the room and had run across to his bed, bringing with her a waft of fresh air full of the scent of the morning.

'You've been out! You've been out! There's that nice smell of leaves!' he cried.

She had been running and her hair was loose and blown and she was bright with the air and pink-cheeked, though he could not see it.

'It's so beautiful!' she said, a little breathless with her speed. 'You never saw anything so beautiful! It has *come*! I thought it had come that other morning, but it was only coming. It is here now! It has come, the Spring! Dickon says so!'

'Has it?' cried Colin, and though he really knew nothing about it he felt his heart beat. He actually sat up in bed.

'Open the window!' he added, laughing half with joyful excitement and half at his own fancy. 'Perhaps we may hear golden trumpets!'

And though he laughed, Mary was at the window in a moment and in a moment more it was opened wide and freshness and softness and scents and birds' songs were pouring through.

'That's fresh air,' she said. 'Lie on your back and draw in long breaths of it.

That's what Dickon does when he's lying on the moor. He says he feels it in his veins and it makes him strong and he feels as if he could live forever and ever. Breathe it and breathe it.'

She was only repeating what Dickon had told her, but she

caught Colin's fancy.

' "Forever and ever"! Does it make him feel like that?' he said, and he did as she told him, drawing in long deep breaths over and over again until he felt that something quite new and delightful was happening to him.

Mary was at his bedside again.

'Things are crowding up out of the earth,' she ran on in a hurry. 'And there are flowers uncurling and buds on everything and the green veil has covered nearly all the gray and the birds are in such a hurry about their nests for fear they may be too late that some of them are even fighting for places in the secret garden. And the rose-bushes look as wick as wick can be, and there are primroses in the lanes and woods, and the seeds we planted are up, and Dickon has brought the fox and the crow and the squirrels and a new-born lamb.'

And then she paused for breath. The new-born lamb Dickon had found three days before lying by its dead mother among the gorse bushes on the moor. It was not the first motherless lamb he had found and he knew what to do with it. He had taken it to the cottage wrapped in his jacket and he had let it lie near the fire and had fed it with warm milk. It was a soft thing with a darling silly baby face and legs rather long for its body. Dickon had carried it over the moor in his arms and its feeding bottle was in his pocket with a squirrel, and when Mary had sat under a tree with its limp warmness huddled on her lap she had felt as if she were too full of strange joy to speak. A lamb—a lamb! A living lamb who lay on your lap like a baby!

She was describing it with great joy and Colin was listening and drawing in long breaths of air when the nurse entered. She started a little at the sight of the open window. She had sat stifling in the room many a warm day because her patient was sure that open windows gave people cold.

'Are you sure you are not chilly, Master Colin?' she inquired.

'No,' was the answer. 'I am breathing long breaths of fresh air. It makes you strong. I am going to get up to the sofa for breakfast and my cousin will have breakfast with me.'

The nurse went away, concealing a smile, to give the order for two breakfasts. She found the servants' hall a more amusing place than the invalid's chamber and just now everybody wanted to hear the news from up-stairs. There was a great deal of joking about the unpopular young recluse who, as the cook said, 'had found his master, and good for him.' The servants' hall had been very tired of the tantrums, and the butler, who was a man with a family, had more than once expressed his opinion that the invalid would be all the better 'for a good hiding.'

When Colin was on his sofa and the breakfast for two was put upon the table he made an announcement to the nurse in his most Rajah-like manner.

'A boy, and a fox, and a crow, and two squirrels, and a new-born lamb, are coming to see me this morning. I want them brought upstairs as soon as they come,' he said. 'You are not to begin playing with the animals in the servants' hall and keep them there. I want them here.'

The nurse gave a slight gasp and tried to conceal it with a cough.

'Yes, sir,' she answered.

'I'll tell you what you can do,' added Colin, waving his hand. 'You can tell Martha to bring them here. The boy is Martha's brother. His name is Dickon and he is an animal charmer.'

'I hope the animals won't bite, Master Colin,' said the nurse.

'I told you he was a charmer,' said Colin austerely. 'Charmers' animals never bite.'

'There are snake-charmers in India,' said Mary; 'and they can put their snakes' heads in their mouths.'

'Goodness!' shuddered the nurse.

They ate their breakfast with the morning air pouring in upon them. Colin's breakfast was a very good one and Mary watched him with serious interest.

'You will begin to get fatter just as I did,' she said. 'I never wanted my breakfast when I was in India and now I always want it.'

'I wanted mine this morning,' said Colin. 'Perhaps it was the fresh air. When do you think Dickon will come?'

He was not long in coming. In about ten minutes Mary held up her hand.

'Listen!' she said. 'Did you hear a caw?'

Colin listened and heard it, the oddest sound in the world to hear inside a house, a hoarse 'caw-caw.'

'Yes,' he answered.

'That's Soot,' said Mary. 'Listen again! Do you hear a bleat—a tiny one?'

'Oh, yes!' cried Colin, quite flushing.

'That's the new-born lamb,' said Mary. 'He's coming.'

Dickon's moorland boots were thick and clumsy and though he tried to walk quietly they made a clumping sound as he walked through the long corridors. Mary and Colin heard him marching— marching, until he passed through the tapestry door on to the soft carpet of Colin's own passage.

'If you please, sir,' announced Martha, opening the door, 'if you please, sir, here's Dickon an' his creatures.'

Dickon came in smiling his nicest wide smile. The new-born lamb was in his arms and the little red fox trotted by his side. Nut sat on his left shoulder and Soot on his right and Shell's head and paws peeped out of his coat pocket.

Colin slowly sat up and stared and stared—as he had stared when he first saw Mary; but this was a stare of wonder and delight. The truth was that in spite of all he had heard he had not in the least understood what this boy would be like and that his fox and his crow and his squirrels and his lamb were so near to him and his friendliness that they seemed almost to be part of himself. Colin had never talked to a boy in his life and he was so overwhelmed by his own pleasure and curiosity that he did not even think of speaking.

But Dickon did not feel the least shy or awkward. He had not felt embarrassed because the crow had not known his language and had only stared and had not spoken to him the first time they met. Creatures were always like that until they found out about you. He walked over to Colin's sofa and put the new-born lamb quietly on his lap, and immediately the little creature turned to the warm velvet dressing-gown and began to nuzzle and nuzzle into its folds and butt its tight-curled head with soft impatience against his side. Of course no boy could have helped speaking then.

'What is it doing?' cried Colin. 'What does it want?'

'It wants its mother,' said Dickon, smiling more and more. 'I brought it to thee a bit hungry because I knowed tha'd like to see it feed.'

He knelt down by the sofa and took a feeding-bottle from his pocket.

'Come on, little 'un,' he said, turning the small woolly white head with a gentle brown hand. 'This is what tha's after. Tha'll get more out o' this than tha' will out o' silk velvet coats. There now,' and he pushed the rubber tip of the bottle into the nuzzling mouth and the lamb began to suck it with ravenous ecstasy.

After that there was no wondering what to say. By the time the lamb fell asleep questions poured forth and Dickon answered them all. He told them how he had found the lamb just as the sun was rising three mornings ago. He had been standing on the moor listening to a skylark and watching him swing higher and higher into the sky until he was only a speck in the heights of blue.

'I'd almost lost him but for his song an' I was wonderin' how a chap could hear it when it seemed as if he'd get out o' th' world in a minute—an' just then I heard somethin' else far off among th' gorse bushes. It was a weak bleatin'[261] an' I knowed it was a new lamb as was hungry an' I knowed it wouldn't be hungry if it hadn't lost its mother somehow, so I set off searchin'[262]. Eh! I did have a look for it. I went in an' out among th' gorse bushes an' round an' round an' I always seemed to take th' wrong turnin'[263]. But at last I seed a bit o' white by a rock on top o' th' moor an' I climbed up an' found th' little 'un half dead wi' cold an' clemmin'[264].'

While he talked, Soot flew solemnly in and out of the open window and cawed remarks about the scenery while Nut and Shell made excursions into the big trees outside and ran up and down trunks and explored branches. Captain curled up near Dickon, who sat on the hearth-rug from preference.

They looked at the pictures in the gardening books and Dickon knew all the flowers by their country names and knew exactly which ones were already growing in the secret garden.

'I couldna'[265] say that there[266] name,' he said, pointing to one under which was written 'Aquilegia,'[267] 'but us calls[268] that a columbine, an' that there one it's a snapdragon and they both grow wild in hedges, but these is garden ones an' they're bigger an' grander. There's some big clumps o' columbine in th' garden. They'll look like a bed o' blue an' white butterflies flutterin' when they're out.'

'I'm going to see them,' cried Colin. 'I am going to see them!'

'Aye, that tha' mun,' said Mary quite seriously. 'An' tha' mun not lose no time about it.'

20

'I Shall Live Forever—
And Ever—And Ever!'

B ut they were obliged to wait more than a week because first there came some very windy days and then Colin was threatened with a cold, which two things happening one after the other would no doubt have thrown him into a rage but that there was so much careful and mysterious planning to do and almost every day Dickon came in, if only for a few minutes, to talk about what was happening on the moor and in the lanes and hedges and on the borders of streams. The things he had to tell about otters' and badgers' and water-rats' houses, not to mention birds' nests and field-mice and their burrows, were enough to make you almost tremble with excitement when you heard all the intimate details from an animal charmer and realized with what thrilling eagerness and anxiety the whole busy underworld was working.

'They're same as us,' said Dickon, 'only they have to build

their homes every year. An' it keeps 'em so busy they fair scuffle to get 'em done.'

The most absorbing thing, however, was the preparations to be made before Colin could be transported with sufficient secrecy to the garden. No one must see the chair-carriage and Dickon and Mary after they turned a certain corner of the shrubbery and entered upon the walk outside the ivied walls. As each day passed, Colin had become more and more fixed in his feeling that the mystery surrounding the garden was one of its greatest charms. Nothing must spoil that. No one must ever suspect that they had a secret. People must think that he was simply going out with Mary and Dickon because he liked them and did not object to their looking at him. They had long and quite delightful talks about their route. They would go up this path and down that one and cross the other and go round among the fountain flower-beds as if they were looking at the 'bedding-out plants' the head gardener, Mr. Roach, had been having arranged. That would seem such a rational thing to do that no one would think it at all mysterious. They would turn into the shrubbery walks and lose themselves until they came to the long walls. It was almost as serious and elaborately thought out as the plans of march made by great generals in time of war.

Rumours of the new and curious things which were occurring in the invalid's apartments had of course filtered through the servants' hall into the stable yards and out among the gardeners, but notwithstanding this, Mr. Roach was startled one day when he received orders from Master Colin's room to the effect that he must report himself in the apartment no outsider had ever seen, as the invalid himself desired to speak to him.

'Well, well,' he said to himself as he hurriedly changed his coat, 'what's to do now? His Royal Highness that wasn't to be looked at calling up a man he's never set eyes on.'

Mr. Roach was not without curiosity. He had never caught even a glimpse of the boy and had heard a dozen exaggerated stories about his uncanny looks and ways and his insane tempers. The thing he had heard oftenest was that he might die at any moment and there had been numerous fanciful descriptions of a humped back and helpless limbs, given by people who had never seen him.

'Things are changing in this house, Mr. Roach,' said Mrs. Medlock, as she led him up the back staircase to the corridor on to which opened the hitherto mysterious chamber.

'Let's hope they're changing for the better, Mrs. Medlock,' he answered.

'They couldn't well change for the worse,' she continued; 'and queer as it all is there's them as finds[269] their duties made a lot easier to stand up under. Don't you be surprised, Mr. Roach, if you find yourself in the middle of a menagerie and Martha Sowerby's Dickon more at home than you or me could ever be.'

There really was a sort of Magic about Dickon, as Mary always privately believed. When Mr. Roach heard his name he smiled quite leniently.

'He'd be at home in Buckingham Palace or at the bottom of a coal mine,' he said. 'And yet it's not impudence, either. He's just fine, is that lad.'

It was perhaps well he had been prepared or he might have been startled. When the bedroom door was opened a large crow, which seemed quite at home perched on the high back of a carven chair, announced the entrance of a visitor by saying 'Caw—Caw' quite loudly. In spite of Mrs. Medlock's warning, Mr. Roach only just escaped being sufficiently undignified to jump backward.

The young Rajah was neither in bed nor on his sofa. He was sitting in an armchair and a young lamb was standing by him shaking its tail in feeding-lamb fashion as Dickon knelt giving it milk from its bottle. A squirrel was perched on Dickon's bent back attentively nibbling a nut. The little girl from India was sitting on a big footstool looking on.

'Here is Mr. Roach, Master Colin,' said Mrs. Medlock.

The young Rajah turned and looked his servitor over—at least that was what the head gardener felt happened.

'Oh, you are Roach, are you?' he said. 'I sent for you to give you some very important orders.'

'Very good, sir,' answered Roach, wondering if he was to receive instructions to fell all the oaks in the park or to transform the orchards into water-gardens.

'I am going out in my chair this afternoon,' said Colin. 'If the fresh air agrees with me I may go out every day. When I go, none of the gardeners are to be anywhere near the Long Walk by the garden walls. No one is to be there. I shall go out about two o'clock and everyone must keep away until I send word that they may go back to their work.'

'Very good, sir,' replied Mr. Roach, much relieved to hear that the oaks might remain and that the orchards were safe.

'Mary,' said Colin, turning to her, 'what is that thing you say in India when you have finished talking and want people to go?'

'You say, "You have my permission to go," ' answered Mary.

The Rajah waved his hand.

'You have my permission to go, Roach,' he said. 'But, remember, this is very important.'

'Caw—Caw!' remarked the crow hoarsely but not impolitely.

'Very good, sir. Thank you, sir,' said Mr. Roach, and Mrs. Medlock took him out of the room.

Outside in the corridor, being a rather good-natured man, he smiled until he almost laughed.

'My word!' he said, 'he's got a fine lordly way with him, hasn't he? You'd think he was a whole Royal Family rolled into one— Prince Consort and all.'

'Eh!' protested Mrs. Medlock, 'we've had to let him trample all over every one of us ever since he had feet and he thinks that's what folks was born for.'

'Perhaps he'll grow out of it, if he lives,' suggested Mr. Roach.

'Well, there's one thing pretty sure,' said Mrs. Medlock. 'If he does live and that Indian child stays here I'll warrant she teaches him that the whole orange does not belong to him, as Susan Sowerby says. And he'll be likely to find out the size of his own quarter.'

Inside the room Colin was leaning back on his cushions.

'It's all safe now,' he said. 'And this afternoon I shall see it— this afternoon I shall be in it!'

Dickon went back to the garden with his creatures and Mary stayed with Colin. She did not think he looked tired but he was very quiet before their lunch came and he was quiet while they were eating it. She wondered why and asked him about it.

'What big eyes you've got, Colin,' she said. 'When you are thinking they get as big as saucers. What are you thinking about now?'

'I can't help thinking about what it will look like,' he answered.

'The garden?' asked Mary.

'The springtime,' he said. 'I was thinking that I've really never seen it before. I scarcely ever went out and when I did go I never looked at it. I didn't even think about it.'

'I never saw it in India because there wasn't any,' said Mary.

Shut in and morbid as his life had been, Colin had more imagination than she had and at least he had spent a good deal of time looking at wonderful books and pictures.

'That morning when you ran in and said "It's come! It's come!", you made me feel quite queer. It sounded as if things were coming with a great procession and big bursts and wafts of music. I've a picture like it in one of my books—crowds of lovely people and children with garlands and branches with blossoms on them, every one laughing and dancing and crowding and playing on pipes. That was why I said, "Perhaps we shall hear golden trumpets" and told you to throw open the window.'

'How funny!' said Mary. 'That's really just what it feels like. And if all the flowers and leaves and green things and birds and wild creatures danced past at once, what a crowd it would be! I'm sure they'd dance and sing and flute and that would be the wafts of music.'

They both laughed but it was not because the idea was laughable but because they both so liked it.

A little later the nurse made Colin ready. She noticed that instead of lying like a log while his clothes were put on he sat up and made some efforts to help himself, and he talked and laughed with Mary all the time.

'This is one of his good days, sir,' she said to Dr. Craven, who dropped in to inspect him. 'He's in such good spirits that it makes him stronger.'

'I'll call in again later in the afternoon, after he has come in,' said Dr. Craven. 'I must see how the going out agrees with him. I wish,' in a very low voice, 'that he would let you go with him.'

'I'd rather give up the case this moment, sir, than even stay here while it's suggested,' answered the nurse with sudden firmness.

'I hadn't really decided to suggest it,' said the doctor, with his slight nervousness. 'We'll try the experiment. Dickon's a lad I'd trust with a new-born child.'

The strongest footman in the house carried Colin down-stairs and put him in his wheeled chair near which Dickon waited outside. After the manservant had arranged his rugs and cushions the Rajah waved his hand to him and to the nurse.

'You have my permission to go,' he said, and they both disappeared quickly and it must be confessed giggled when they were safely inside the house.

Dickon began to push the wheeled chair slowly and steadily. Mistress Mary walked beside it and Colin leaned back and lifted his face to the sky. The arch of it looked very high and the small snowy clouds seemed like white birds floating on outspread wings below its crystal blueness. The wind swept in soft big breaths down from the moor and was strange with a wild clear scented sweetness. Colin kept lifting his thin chest to draw it in, and his big eyes looked as if it were they which were listening—listening, instead of his ears.

'There are so many sounds of singing and humming and calling out,' he said. 'What is that scent the puffs of wind bring?'

'It's gorse on th' moor that's openin'[270] out,' answered Dickon.

'Eh! th' bees are at it wonderful to-day.'

Not a human creature was to be caught sight of in the paths they took. In fact every gardener or gardener's lad had been witched away. But they wound in and out among the shrubbery and out and round the fountain beds, following their carefully planned route for the mere mysterious pleasure of it. But when at last they turned into the Long Walk by the ivied walls the excited sense of an approaching thrill made them, for some curious reason they could not have explained, begin[271] to speak in whispers.

'This is it,' breathed Mary. 'This is where I used to walk up and down and wonder and wonder.'

'Is it?' cried Colin, and his eyes began to search the ivy with eager curiousness. 'But I can see nothing,' he whispered. 'There is no door.'

'That's what I thought,' said Mary.

Then there was a lovely breathless silence and the chair wheeled on.

'That is the garden where Ben Weatherstaff works,' said Mary.

'Is it?' said Colin.

A few yards more and Mary whispered again.

'This is where the robin flew over the wall,' she said.

'Is it?' cried Colin. 'Oh! I wish he'd come again!'

'And that,' said Mary with solemn delight, pointing under a big lilac bush, 'is where he perched on the little heap of earth and showed me the key.'

Then Colin sat up.

'Where? Where? There?' he cried, and his eyes were as big as the wolf's in Red Riding-Hood, when Red Riding-Hood felt called upon to remark on them. Dickon stood still and the wheeled chair stopped.

'And this,' said Mary, stepping on to the bed close to the ivy, 'is where I went to talk to him when he chirped at me from the top of the wall. And this is the ivy the wind blew back,' and she took hold of the hanging green curtain.

'Oh! is it—is it!' gasped Colin.

'And here is the handle, and here is the door. Dickon push him in—push him in quickly!'

And Dickon did it with one strong, steady, splendid push.

But Colin had actually dropped back against his cushions, even though he gasped with delight, and he had covered his eyes with his hands and held them there shutting out everything until they were inside and the chair stopped as if by magic and the door was closed. Not till then did he take them away and look round and round and round as Dickon and Mary had done. And over walls and earth and trees and swinging sprays and tendrils the fair green veil of tender little leaves had crept, and in the grass under the trees and the gray urns in the alcoves and here and there everywhere were touches or splashes of gold and purple and white and the trees were showing pink and snow above his head and there were fluttering of wings and faint sweet pipes and humming and scents and scents. And the sun fell warm upon his face like a hand with a lovely touch. And in wonder Mary and Dickon stood and stared at him. He looked so strange and different because a pink glow of colour had actually crept all over him—ivory face and neck and hands and all.

'I shall get well! I shall get well!' he cried out. 'Mary! Dickon! I shall get well! And I shall live forever and ever and ever!'

Ben Weatherstaff

One of the strange things about living in the world is that it is only now and then one is quite sure one is going to live forever and ever and ever. One knows it sometimes when one gets up at the tender solemn dawn-time and goes out and stands alone and throws one's head far back and looks up and up and watches the pale sky slowly changing and flushing and marvelous unknown things happening until the East almost makes one cry out and one's heart stands still at the strange unchanging majesty of the rising of the sun—which has been happening every morning for thousands and thousands and thousands of years. One knows it then for a moment or so. And one knows it sometimes when one stands by oneself in a wood at sunset and the mysterious deep gold stillness slanting through and under the branches seems to be saying slowly again and again something one cannot quite hear, however much one tries. Then sometimes the immense quiet of the dark blue at night with millions of stars waiting and watching makes one sure; and sometimes a sound of far-off music makes it true; and sometimes a look in some one's eyes.

And it was like that with Colin when he first saw and heard and felt the Springtime inside the four high walls of a hidden garden. That afternoon the whole world seemed to devote itself to being perfect and radiantly beautiful and kind to one boy. Perhaps out of pure heavenly goodness the spring came and crowned everything it possibly could into that one place. More than once Dickon paused in what he was doing and stood still with a sort of growing wonder in his eyes, shaking his head softly.

'Eh! it is graidely,' he said. 'I'm twelve goin' on thirteen an' there's a lot o' afternoons in thirteen years, but seems to me like I never seed one as graidely as this 'ere[272].'

'Aye, it is a graidely one,' said Mary, and she sighed for mere joy. 'I'll warrant it's the graidelest one as ever was in this world.'

'Does tha' think,' said Colin with dreamy carefulness, 'as happen it was made loike[273] this 'ere all o' purpose for me?'

'My word!' cried Mary admiringly, 'that there is a bit o' good Yorkshire. Tha'rt shapin'[274] first-rate—that tha' art.'

And delight reigned.

They drew the chair under the plum-tree, which was snow-white with blossoms and musical with bees. It was like a king's canopy, a fairy king's. There were flowering cherry-trees near and apple-trees whose buds were pink and white, and here and there one had burst open wide. Between the blossoming branches of the canopy bits of blue sky looked down like wonderful eyes.

Mary and Dickon worked a little here and there and Colin watched them. They brought him things to look at—buds which were opening, buds which were tight closed, bits of twig whose leaves were just showing green, the feather of a woodpecker which had dropped on the grass, the empty shell of some bird early hatched. Dickon pushed the chair slowly round and round the garden, stopping every other moment to let him look at wonders springing out of the earth or trailing down from trees. It was like being taken in state round the country of a magic king and queen and shown all the mysterious riches it contained.

'I wonder if we shall see the robin?' said Colin.

'Tha'll see him often enow after a bit,' answered Dickon. 'When th' eggs hatches[275] out th' little chap he'll be kep'[276] so busy it'll make his head swim. Tha'll see him flyin'[277] backward an' for'ard carryin'[278] worms nigh as big as himsel' an' that much noise goin' on in th' nest when he gets there as fair flusters him so as he scarce knows which big mouth to drop th' first piece in. An' gapin'[279] beaks an' squawks on every side. Mother says as when she sees th' work a robin has to keep them gapin' beaks filled, she feels like she was a lady with nothin' to do. She says she's seen th' little chaps when it seemed like th' sweat must be droppin'[280] off 'em, though folk can't see it.'

This made them giggle so delightedly that they were obliged to cover their mouths with their hands, remembering that they must not be heard. Colin had been instructed as to the law of whispers and low voices several days before. He liked the mysteriousness of it and did his best, but in the midst of excited enjoyment it is rather difficult never to laugh above a whisper.

Every moment of the afternoon was full of new things and every hour the sunshine grew more golden. The wheeled chair had been drawn back under the canopy and Dickon had sat down on the grass and had just drawn out his pipe when Colin saw something he had not had time to notice before.

'That's a very old tree over there, isn't it?' he said. Dickon looked across the grass at the tree and Mary looked and there was a brief moment of stillness.

'Yes,' answered Dickon, after it, and his low voice had a very gentle sound.

Mary gazed at the tree and thought.

'The branches are quite gray and there's not a single leaf anywhere,' Colin went on. 'It's quite dead, isn't it?'

'Aye,' admitted Dickon. 'But them roses as has climbed all over it will near hide every bit o' th' dead wood when they're full o' leaves an' flowers. It won't look dead then. It'll be th' prettiest of all.'

Mary still gazed at the tree and thought.

'It looks as if a big branch had been broken off,' said Colin. 'I wonder how it was done.'

'It's been done many a year,' answered Dickon. 'Eh!' with a sudden relieved start and laying his hand on Colin. 'Look at that robin! There he is! He's been foragin'[281] for his mate.'

Colin was almost too late but he just caught sight of him, the flash of red-breasted bird with something in his beak. He darted through the greenness and into the close-grown corner and was out of sight. Colin leaned back on his cushion again, laughing a little.

'He's taking her tea to her. Perhaps it's five o'clock. I think I'd like some tea myself.'

And so they were safe.

'It was Magic which sent the robin,' said Mary secretly to Dickon afterward. 'I know it was Magic.' For both she and Dickon had been afraid Colin might ask something about the tree whose branch had broken off ten years ago and they had talked it over together and Dickon had stood and rubbed his head in a troubled way.

'We mun look as if it wasn't no different from th' other trees,' he had said. 'We couldn't never tell him how it broke, poor lad. If he says anything about it we mun—we mun try to look cheerful.'

'Aye, that we mun,' had answered Mary.

But she had not felt as if she looked cheerful when she gazed at the tree. She wondered and wondered in those few moments if there was any reality in that other thing Dickon had said. He had gone on rubbing his rust-red hair in a puzzled way, but a nice comforted look had begun to grow in his blue eyes.

'Mrs. Craven was a very lovely young lady,' he had gone on rather hesitatingly. 'An' mother she thinks maybe she's about Misselthwaite many a time lookin' after Mester Colin, same as all mothers do when they're took out o' th' world. They have to come back, tha' sees. Happen she's been in the garden an' happen it was her set us to work, an' told us to bring him here.'

Mary had thought he meant something about Magic. She was a great believer in Magic. Secretly she quite believed that Dickon worked Magic, of course good Magic, on everything near him and that was why people liked him so much and wild creatures knew he was their friend. She wondered, indeed, if it were not possible that his gift had brought the robin just at the right moment when Colin asked that dangerous question. She felt that his Magic was working all the afternoon and making Colin look like an entirely different boy. It did not seem possible that he could be the crazy creature who had screamed and beaten and bitten his pillow. Even his ivory whiteness seemed to change. The faint glow of colour which had shown on his face and neck and hands when he first got inside the garden really never quite died away. He looked as if he were made of flesh instead of ivory or wax.

They saw the robin carry food to his mate two or three times, and it was so suggestive of afternoon tea that Colin felt they must have some.

'Go and make one of the men servants bring some in a basket to the rhododendron walk,' he said. 'And then you and Dickon can bring it here.'

It was an agreeable idea, easily carried out, and when the white cloth was spread upon the grass, with hot tea and buttered toast and crumpets, a delightfully hungry meal was eaten, and several birds on domestic errands paused to inquire what was going on and were led into investigating crumbs with great activity. Nut and Shell whisked up trees with pieces of cake and Soot took the entire half of a buttered crumpet into a corner and pecked at and examined and turned it over and made hoarse remarks about it until he decided to swallow it all joyfully in one gulp.

The afternoon was dragging towards its mellow hour. The sun was deepening the gold of its lances, the bees were going home and the birds were flying past less often. Dickon and Mary were sitting on the grass, the tea-basket was repacked ready to be taken back to the house, and Colin was lying against his cushions with his heavy locks pushed back from his forehead and his face looking quite a natural colour.

'I don't want this afternoon to go,' he said; 'but I shall come back to-morrow, and the day after, and the day after, and the day after.'

'You'll get plenty of fresh air, won't you?' said Mary.

'I'm going to get nothing else,' he answered. 'I've seen the spring now and I'm going to see the summer. I'm going to see everything grow here. I'm going to grow here myself.'

'That tha' will,' said Dickon. 'Us'll have thee walkin' about here an' diggin' same as other folk afore long.'

Colin flushed tremendously.

'Walk!' he said. 'Dig! Shall I?'

Dickon's glance at him was delicately cautious. Neither he nor Mary had ever asked if anything was the matter with his legs.

'For sure tha' will,' he said stoutly. 'Tha—tha's got legs o' thine[282] own, same as other folks!'

Mary was rather frightened until she heard Colin's answer.

'Nothing really ails them,' he said, 'but they are so thin and weak. They shake so that I'm afraid to try to stand on them.'

Both Mary and Dickon drew a relieved breath.

'When tha' stops[283] bein' afraid tha'lt stand on 'em,' Dickon said with renewed cheer. 'An' tha'lt stop bein' afraid in a bit.'

'I shall?' said Colin, and he lay still as if he were wondering about things.

They were really very quiet for a little while. The sun was dropping lower. It was that hour when everything stills itself, and they really had had a busy and exciting afternoon. Colin looked as if he were resting luxuriously. Even the creatures had ceased moving about and had drawn together and were resting near them. Soot had perched on a low branch and drawn up one leg and dropped the gray film drowsily over his eyes. Mary privately thought he looked as if he might snore in a minute.

In the midst of this stillness it was rather startling when Colin half lifted his head and exclaimed in a loud suddenly alarmed whisper:

'Who is that man?' Dickon and Mary scrambled to their feet.

'Man!' they both cried in low quick voices.

Colin pointed to the high wall.

'Look!' he whispered excitedly. 'Just look!'

Mary and Dickon wheeled about and looked. There was Ben Weatherstaff's indignant face glaring at them over the wall from the top of a ladder! He actually shook his fist at Mary.

'If I wasn't a bachelder, an' tha' was a wench o' mine,' he cried, 'I'd give thee a hidin'!'

He mounted another step threateningly as if it were his energetic intention to jump down and deal with her; but as she came toward him he evidently thought better of it and stood on the top step of his ladder shaking his fist down at her.

'I never thowt[284] much o' thee!' he harangued. 'I couldna' abide thee th' first time I set eyes on thee. A scrawny buttermilk-faced young besom, allus askin' questions an' pokin'[285] tha' nose where it wasna'[286] wanted. I never knowed how tha' got so thick wi' me. If it hadna'[287] been for th' robin— Drat him—'

'Ben Weatherstaff,' called out Mary, finding her breath. She stood below him and called up to him with a sort of gasp. 'Ben Weatherstaff, it was the robin who showed me the way!'

Then it did seem as if Ben really would scramble down on her side of the wall, he was so outraged.

'Tha' young bad 'un!' he called down at her. 'Layin'[288] tha' badness on a robin,—not but what he's impidint[289] enow for anythin'. Him showin' thee th' way! Him! Eh! tha' young nowt' —she could see his next words burst out because he was overpowered by curiosity—'however i' this world did tha' get in?'

'It was the robin who showed me the way,' she protested obstinately. 'He didn't know he was doing it but he did. And I can't tell you from here while you're shaking your fist at me.'

He stopped shaking his fist very suddenly at that very moment and his jaw actually dropped as he stared over her head at something he saw coming over the grass toward him.

At the first sound of his torrent of words Colin had been so surprised that he had only sat up and listened as if he were spellbound. But in the midst of it he had recovered himself and beckoned imperiously to Dickon.

'Wheel me over there!' he commanded. 'Wheel me quite close and stop right in front of him!'

And this, if you please, this is what Ben Weatherstaff beheld and which made his jaw drop. A wheeled chair with luxurious cushions and robes which came toward him looking rather like some sort of State Coach because a young Rajah leaned back in it with royal command in his great black-rimmed eyes and a thin white hand extended haughtily toward him. And it stopped right under Ben Weatherstaff's nose. It was really no wonder his mouth dropped open.

'Do you know who I am?' demanded the Rajah.

How Ben Weatherstaff stared! His red old eyes fixed themselves on what was before him as if he were seeing a ghost. He gazed and gazed and gulped a lump down his throat and did not say a word.

'Do you know who I am?' demanded Colin still more imperiously. 'Answer!'

Ben Weatherstaff put his gnarled hand up and passed it over his eyes and over his forehead and then he did answer in a queer shaky voice.

'Who tha' art?[290]' he said. 'Aye, that I do—wi' tha' mother's eyes starin' at me out o' tha' face. Lord knows how tha' come here. But tha'rt th' poor cripple.'

Colin forgot that he had ever had a back. His face flushed scarlet and he sat bolt upright.

'I'm not a cripple!' he cried out furiously. 'I'm not!'

'He's not!' cried Mary, almost shouting up the wall in her fierce indignation. 'He's not got a lump as big as a pin! I looked and there was none there—not one!'

Ben Weatherstaff passed his hand over his forehead again and gazed as if he could never gaze enough. His hand shook and his mouth shook and his voice shook. He was an ignorant old man and a tactless old man and he could only remember the things he had heard.

'Tha'—tha' hasn't got a crooked back?' he said hoarsely.

'No!' shouted Colin.

'Tha'—tha' hasn't got crooked legs?' quavered Ben more hoarsely yet.

It was too much. The strength which Colin usually threw into his tantrums rushed through him now in a new way. Never yet had he been accused of crooked legs—even in whispers—and the perfectly simple belief in their existence which was revealed by Ben Weatherstaff's voice was more than Rajah flesh and blood could endure. His anger and insulted pride made him forget everything but this one moment and filled him with a power he had never known before, an almost unnatural strength.

'Come here!' he shouted to Dickon, and he actually began to tear the coverings off his lower limbs and disentangle himself.

'Come here! Come here! This minute!'

Dickon was by his side in a second. Mary caught her breath in a short gasp and felt herself turn pale.

'He can do it! He can do it! He can do it! He can!' she gabbled over to herself under her breath as fast as ever she could.

There was a brief fierce scramble, the rugs were tossed on to the ground, Dickon held Colin's arm, the thin legs were out, the thin feet were on the grass. Colin was standing upright—upright—as straight as an arrow and looking strangely tall—his head thrown back and his strange eyes flashing lightning.

'Look at me!' he flung up at Ben Weatherstaff. 'Just look at me—you! Just look at me!'

'He's as straight as I am!' cried Dickon. 'He's as straight as any lad i' Yorkshire!'

What Ben Weatherstaff did Mary thought queer beyond measure. He choked and gulped and suddenly tears ran down his weather-wrinkled cheeks as he struck his old hands together.

'Eh!' he burst forth, 'th' lies folk tells! Tha'rt as thin as a lath an' as white as a wraith, but there's not a knob on thee. Tha'lt make a mon yet. God bless thee!'

Dickon held Colin's arm strongly but the boy had not begun to falter. He stood straighter and straighter and looked Ben Weatherstaff in the face.

'I'm your master,' he said, 'when my father is away. And you are to obey me. This is my garden. Don't dare to say a word about it! You get down from that ladder and go out to the Long Walk and Miss Mary will meet you and bring you here. I want to talk to you. We did not want you, but now you will have to be in the secret. Be quick!'

Ben Weatherstaff's crabbed old face was still wet with that one queer rush of tears. It seemed as if he could not take his eyes from thin straight Colin standing on his feet with his head thrown back.

'Eh! lad[291],' he almost whispered. 'Eh! my lad!' And then remembering himself he suddenly touched his hat gardener fashion and said, 'Yes, sir! Yes, sir!' and obediently disappeared as he descended the ladder.

22.

When the Sun Went Down

When his head was out of sight Colin turned to Mary.
'Go and meet him,' he said; and Mary flew across the grass
to the door under the ivy.

Dickon was watching him with sharp eyes. There were scarlet
spots on his cheeks and he looked amazing, but he showed no
signs of falling.

'I can stand,' he said, and his head was still held up and he
said it quite grandly.

'I told thee tha' could as soon as tha' stopped bein' afraid,'
answered Dickon. 'An' tha's stopped.'

'Yes, I've stopped,' said Colin.

Then suddenly he remembered something Mary had said.

'Are you making Magic?' he asked sharply.

Dickon's curly mouth spread in a cheerful grin.

'Tha's doin' Magic thysel',' he said. 'It's same Magic as made
these 'ere work out o' th' earth,' and he touched with his thick boot

a clump of crocuses in the grass.

Colin looked down at them.

'Aye,' he said slowly, 'there couldna' be bigger Magic than that there—there couldna' be.'

He drew himself up straighter than ever.

'I'm going to walk to that tree,' he said, pointing to one a few feet away from him. 'I'm going to be standing when Weatherstaff comes here. I can rest against the tree if I like. When I want to sit down I will sit down, but not before. Bring a rug from the chair.'

He walked to the tree and though Dickon held his arm he was wonderfully steady. When he stood against the tree trunk it was not too plain that he supported himself against it, and he still held himself so straight that he looked tall.

When Ben Weatherstaff came through the door in the wall he saw him standing there and he heard Mary muttering something under her breath.

'What art sayin'?[292]' he asked rather testily because he did not want his attention distracted from the long thin straight boy figure and proud face.

But she did not tell him. What she was saying was this:

'You can do it! You can do it! I told you you could! You can do it! You can do it! You can!'

She was saying it to Colin because she wanted to make Magic and keep him on his feet looking like that. She could not bear that he should give in before Ben Weatherstaff. He did not give in. She was uplifted by a sudden feeling that he looked quite beautiful in spite of his thinness. He fixed his eyes on Ben Weatherstaff in his funny imperious way.

'Look at me!' he commanded. 'Look at me all over! Am I a

hunchback? Have I got crooked legs?'

Ben Weatherstaff had not quite got over his emotion, but he had recovered a little and answered almost in his usual way.

'Not tha',' he said. 'Nowt o' th' sort. What's tha' been doin' with thysel'—hidin' out o' sight an' lettin' folk think tha' was cripple an' half-witted?'

'Half-witted!' said Colin angrily. 'Who thought that?'

'Lots o' fools,' said Ben. 'Th' world's full o' jackasses brayin'[293] an' they never bray nowt but lies. What did tha' shut thysel' up for?'

'Everyone thought I was going to die,' said Colin shortly. 'I'm not!'

And he said it with such decision Ben Weatherstaff looked him over, up and down, down and up.

'Tha' die!' he said with dry exultation. 'Nowt o' th' sort! Tha's got too much pluck in thee. When I seed thee put tha' legs on th' ground in such a hurry I knowed tha' was all right. Sit thee down on th' rug a bit young Mester an' give me thy orders.'

There was a queer mixture of crabbed tenderness and shrewd understanding in his manner. Mary had poured out speech as rapidly as she could as they had come down the Long Walk. The chief thing to be remembered, she had told him, was that Colin was getting well—getting well. The garden was doing it. No one must let him remember about having humps and dying.

The Rajah condescended to seat himself on a rug under the tree.

'What work do you do in the gardens, Weatherstaff?' he inquired.

'Anythin' I'm told to do,' answered old Ben. 'I'm kep' on by favor—because she liked me.'

'She?' said Colin.

'Tha' mother,' answered Ben Weatherstaff.

'My mother?' said Colin, and he looked about him quietly. 'This was her garden, wasn't it?'

'Aye, it was that!' and Ben Weatherstaff looked about him too. 'She were main fond of it.'

'It is my garden now. I am fond of it. I shall come here every day,' announced Colin. 'But it is to be a secret. My orders are that no one is to know that we come here. Dickon and my cousin have worked and made it come alive. I shall send for you sometimes to help—but you must come when no one can see you.'

Ben Weatherstaff's face twisted itself in a dry old smile.

'I've come here before when no one saw me,' he said.

'What!' exclaimed Colin. 'When?'

'Th' last time I was here,' rubbing his chin and looking round, 'was about two year' ago.'

'But no one has been in it for ten years!' cried Colin.

'There was no door!'

'I'm no one,' said old Ben dryly. 'An' I didn't come through th' door. I come over th' wall. Th' rheumatics held me back th' last two year'.'

'Tha' come an' did a bit o' prunin'!' cried Dickon. 'I couldn't make out how it had been done.'

'She was so fond of it—she was!' said Ben Weatherstaff slowly. 'An' she was such a pretty young thing. She says to me once, "Ben," says she laughin', "if ever I'm ill or if I go away you must take care of my roses." When she did go away th' orders was no one was ever to come nigh. But I come,' with grumpy obstinacy. 'Over th' wall I come—until th' rheumatics stopped me—an' I did a bit o' work once a year. She'd gave her order first.'

'It wouldn't have been as wick as it is if tha' hadn't done it,' said Dickon. 'I did wonder.'

'I'm glad you did it, Weatherstaff,' said Colin. 'You'll know how to keep the secret.'

'Aye, I'll know, sir,' answered Ben. 'An' it'll be easier for a man wi' rheumatics to come in at th' door.'

On the grass near the tree Mary had dropped her trowel. Colin stretched out his hand and took it up. An odd expression came into his face and he began to scratch at the earth. His thin hand was weak enough but presently as they watched him—Mary with quite breathless interest—he drove the end of the trowel into the soil and turned some over.

'You can do it! You can do it!' said Mary to herself. 'I tell you, you can!'

Dickon's round eyes were full of eager curiousness but he said not a word. Ben Weatherstaff looked on with interested face.

Colin persevered. After he had turned a few trowelfuls of soil he spoke exultantly to Dickon in his best Yorkshire.

'Tha' said as tha'd have me walkin' about here same as other folk—an' tha' said tha'd have me diggin'. I thowt tha' was just leein'²⁹⁴ to please me. This is only th' first day an' I've walked— an' here I am diggin'.'

Ben Weatherstaff's mouth fell open again when he heard him, but he ended by chuckling.

'Eh!' he said, 'that sounds as if tha'd got wits enow. Tha'rt a Yorkshire lad for sure. An' tha'rt diggin', too. How'd tha' like to plant a bit o' somethin'? I can get thee a rose in a pot.'

'Go and get it!' said Colin, digging excitedly. 'Quick! Quick!'

It was done quickly enough indeed. Ben Weatherstaff went his way forgetting rheumatics. Dickon took his spade and dug the hole deeper and wider than a new digger with thin white hands could make it. Mary slipped out to run and bring back a watering-can. When Dickon had deepened the hole Colin went on turning the soft earth over and over. He looked up at the sky, flushed and glowing with the strangely new exercise, slight as it was.

'I want to do it before the sun goes quite—quite down,' he said.

Mary thought that perhaps the sun held back a few minutes just on purpose. Ben Weatherstaff brought the rose in its pot from the greenhouse. He hobbled over the grass as fast as he could. He had begun to be excited, too. He knelt down by the hole and broke the pot from the mould.

'Here, lad,' he said, handing the plant to Colin. 'set it in the earth thysel' same as th' king does when he goes to a new place.'

The thin white hands shook a little and Colin's flush grew deeper as he set the rose in the mould and held it while old Ben made firm the earth. It was filled in and pressed down and made steady. Mary was leaning forward on her hands and knees. Soot had flown down and marched forward to see what was being done. Nut and Shell chattered about it from a cherry-tree.

'It's planted!' said Colin at last. 'And the sun is only slipping over the edge. Help me up, Dickon. I want to be standing when it goes. That's part of the Magic.'

And Dickon helped him, and the Magic—or whatever it was— so gave him strength that when the sun did slip over the edge and end the strange lovely afternoon for them there he actually stood on his two feet—laughing.

23.

Magic

Dr. Craven had been waiting some time at the house when they returned to it. He had indeed begun to wonder if it might not be wise to send some one out to explore the garden paths. When Colin was brought back to his room the poor man looked him over seriously.

'You should not have stayed so long,' he said. 'You must not overexert yourself.'

'I am not tired at all,' said Colin. 'It has made me well. To-morrow I am going out in the morning as well as in the afternoon.'

'I am not sure that I can allow it,' answered Dr. Craven. 'I am afraid it would not be wise.'

'It would not be wise to try to stop me,' said Colin quite seriously. 'I am going.'

Even Mary had found out that one of Colin's chief peculiarities was that he did not know in the least what a rude little brute he was with his way of ordering people about. He had lived on a sort of desert island all his life and as he had been the king of it he had made his own manners and had had no one to compare himself with. Mary had indeed been rather like him herself and since she had been at Misselthwaite had gradually discovered that her own manners had not been of the kind which is usual or popular. Having made this discovery she naturally thought it of enough interest to communicate to Colin. So she sat and looked at him curiously for a few minutes after Dr. Craven had gone. She wanted to make him ask her why she was doing it and of course she did.

'What are you looking at me for?' he said.

'I'm thinking that I am rather sorry for Dr. Craven.'

'So am I,' said Colin calmly, but not without an air of some satisfaction. 'He won't get Misselthwaite at all now I'm not going to die.'

'I'm sorry for him because of that, of course,' said Mary, 'but I was thinking just then that it must have been very horrid to have had to be polite for ten years to a boy who was always rude. I would never have done it.'

'Am I rude?' Colin inquired undisturbedly.

'If you had been his own boy and he had been a slapping sort of man,' said Mary, 'he would have slapped you.'

'But he daren't,' said Colin.

'No, he daren't,' answered Mistress Mary, thinking the thing out quite without prejudice. 'Nobody ever dared to do anything you didn't like—because you were going to die and things like that. You were such a poor thing.'

'But,' announced Colin stubbornly, 'I am not going to be a poor thing. I won't let people think I'm one. I stood on my feet this afternoon.'

'It is always having your own way that has made you so queer,' Mary went on, thinking aloud.

Colin turned his head, frowning.

'Am I queer?' he demanded.

'Yes,' answered Mary, 'very. But you needn't be cross,' she added impartially, 'because so am I queer—and so is Ben Weatherstaff. But I am not as queer as I was before I began to like people and before I found the garden.'

'I don't want to be queer,' said Colin. 'I am not going to be,' and he frowned again with determination.

He was a very proud boy. He lay thinking for a while and then Mary saw his beautiful smile begin and gradually change his whole face.

'I shall stop being queer,' he said, 'if I go every day to the garden. There is Magic in there—good Magic, you know, Mary. I am sure there is.'

'So am I,' said Mary.

'Even if it isn't real Magic,' Colin said, 'we can pretend it is. Something is there—something!'

'It's Magic,' said Mary, 'but not black. It's as white as snow.'

They always called it Magic and indeed it seemed like it in the months that followed—the wonderful months—the radiant months—the amazing ones. Oh! the things which happened in that garden! If you have never had a garden, you cannot understand, and if you have had a garden you will know that it would take a whole book to describe all that came to pass there. At first it seemed that green things would never cease pushing their way through the earth, in the grass, in the beds, even in the crevices of the walls. Then the green things began to show buds and the buds began to unfurl and show colour, every shade of blue, every shade of purple, every tint and hue of crimson. In its happy days flowers had been tucked away into every inch and hole and corner. Ben Weatherstaff had seen it done and had himself scraped out mortar from between the bricks of the wall and made pockets of earth for lovely clinging things to grow on. Iris and white lilies rose out of the grass in sheaves, and the green alcoves filled themselves with amazing armies of the blue and white flower lances of tall delphiniums or columbines or campanulas.

'She was main fond o' them—she was,' Ben Weatherstaff said. 'She liked them things as was allus pointin'[295] up to th' blue sky, she used to tell. Not as she was one o' them as looked down on th' earth—not her. She just loved it but she said as th' blue sky allus looked so joyful.'

The seeds Dickon and Mary had planted grew as if fairies had tended them. Satiny poppies of all tints danced in the breeze by the score, gaily defying flowers which had lived in the garden for years and which it might be confessed seemed rather to wonder how such new people had got there. And the roses—the roses! Rising out of the grass, tangled round the sun-dial[296], wreathing the tree trunks and hanging from their branches, climbing up the walls and spreading over them with long garlands falling in cascades— they came alive day by day, hour by hour. Fair fresh leaves, and buds—and buds—tiny at first but swelling and working Magic until they burst and uncurled into cups of scent delicately spilling themselves over their brims and filling the garden air.

Colin saw it all, watching each change as it took place. Every morning he was brought out and every hour of each day when it didn't rain he spent in the garden. Even gray days pleased him.

He would lie on the grass 'watching things growing,' he said. If

you watched long enough, he declared, you could see buds unsheath themselves. Also you could make the acquaintance of strange busy insect things running about on various unknown but evidently serious errands, sometimes carrying tiny scraps of straw or feather or food, or climbing blades of grass as if they were trees from whose tops one could look out to explore the country. A mole throwing up its mound at the end of its burrow and making its way out at last with the long-nailed paws which looked so like elfish hands, had absorbed him one whole morning. Ants' ways, beetles' ways, bees' ways, frogs' ways, birds' ways, plants' ways, gave him a new world to explore and when Dickon revealed them all and added foxes' ways, otters' ways, ferrets' ways, squirrels' ways, and trout' and water-rats' and badgers' ways, there was no end to the things to talk about and think over.

And this was not the half of the Magic. The fact that he had really once stood on his feet had set Colin thinking tremendously and when Mary told him of the spell she had worked he was excited and approved of it greatly. He talked of it constantly.

'Of course there must be lots of Magic in the world,' he said wisely one day, 'but people don't know what it is like or how to make it. Perhaps the beginning is just to say nice things are going to happen until you make them happen. I am going to try and experiment.'

The next morning when they went to the secret garden he sent at once for Ben Weatherstaff. Ben came as quickly as he could and found the Rajah standing on his feet under a tree and looking very grand but also very beautifully smiling.

'Good morning, Ben Weatherstaff,' he said. 'I want you and Dickon and Miss Mary to stand in a row and listen to me because I am going to tell you something very important.'

'Aye, aye, sir!' answered Ben Weatherstaff, touching his fore-head. (One of the long concealed charms of Ben Weatherstaff was that in his boyhood he had once run away to sea and had made voyages. So he could reply like a sailor.)

'I am going to try a scientific experiment,' explained the Rajah. 'When I grow up I am going to make great scientific discoveries and I am going to begin now with this experiment.'

'Aye, aye, sir!' said Ben Weatherstaff promptly, though this was the first time he had heard of great scientific discoveries.

It was the first time Mary had heard of them, either, but even at this stage she had begun to realize that, queer as he was, Colin had read about a great many singular things and was somehow a very convincing sort of boy. When he held up his head and fixed his strange eyes on you it seemed as if you believed him almost in spite of yourself though he was only ten years old—going on eleven. At this moment he was especially convincing because he suddenly felt the fascination of actually making a sort of speech like a grown-up person.

'The great scientific discoveries I am going to make,' he went on, 'will be about Magic. Magic is a great thing and scarcely any one knows anything about it except a few people in old books— and Mary a little, because she was born in India where there are fakirs. I believe Dickon knows some Magic, but perhaps he doesn't know he knows it. He charms animals and people. I would never have let him come to see me if he had not been an animal charmer—which is a boy charmer, too, because a boy is an animal. I am sure there is Magic in everything, only we have not sense enough to get hold of it and make it do things for us—like electricity and horses and steam.'

This sounded so imposing that Ben Weatherstaff became quite excited and really could not keep still.

'Aye, aye, sir,' he said and he began to stand up quite straight.

'When Mary found this garden it looked quite dead,' the orator proceeded. 'Then something began pushing things up out of the soil and making things out of nothing. One day things weren't there and another they were. I had never watched things before and it made me feel very curious. Scientific people are always curious and I am going to be scientific. I keep saying to myself, "What is it? What is it?" It's something. It can't be nothing! I don't know its name so I call it Magic. I have never seen the sun rise but Mary and Dickon have and from what they tell me I am sure that is Magic too. Something pushes it up and draws it. Sometimes since I've been in the garden I've looked up through the trees at the sky and I have had a strange feeling of being happy as if something were pushing and drawing in my chest and making me breathe fast. Magic is always pushing and drawing and making things out of nothing. Everything is made out of Magic, leaves and trees, flowers and birds, badgers and foxes and squirrels and people. So it must be all around us. In this garden—in all the places. The Magic in this garden has made me stand up and know I am going to live to be a man. I am going to make the scientific experiment of trying to get some and put it in myself and make it push and draw me and make me strong. I don't know how to do it but I think that if you keep thinking about it and calling it perhaps it will come. Perhaps that is the first baby way to get it. When I was going to try to stand that first time Mary kept saying to herself as fast as she could, "You can do it! You can do it!" and I did. I had to try myself at the same time, of course, but her Magic helped me—and so did Dickon's. Every morning and evening and as often in the daytime as I can remember I am going to say, "Magic is in me! Magic is making me well! I am going to be as strong as Dickon, as strong as Dickon!" And you must all do it, too. That is my experiment. Will you help, Ben Weatherstaff?'

'Aye, aye, sir!' said Ben Weatherstaff. 'Aye, aye!'

'If you keep doing it every day as regularly as soldiers go through drill[297] we shall see what will happen and find out if the experiment succeeds. You learn things by saying them over and over and thinking about them until they stay in your mind forever and I think it will be the same with Magic. If you keep calling it to come to you and help you it will get to be part of you and it will stay and do things.'

'I once heard an officer in India tell my mother that there were fakirs who said words over and over thousands of times,' said Mary.

'I've heard Jem Fettleworth's wife say th' same thing over thousands o' times—callin' Jem a drunken brute,' said Ben Weatherstaff dryly. 'Summat allus come o' that, sure enough. He gave her a good hidin' an' went to th' Blue Lion an' got as drunk as a lord.'

Colin drew his brows together and thought a few minutes. Then he cheered up.

'Well,' he said, 'you see something did come of it. She used the wrong Magic until she made him beat her. If she'd used the right Magic and had said something nice perhaps he wouldn't have got as drunk as a lord and perhaps—perhaps he might have bought her a new bonnet.'

Ben Weatherstaff chuckled and there was shrewd admiration in his little old eyes.

'Tha'rt a clever lad as well as a straight-legged one, Mester Colin,' he said. 'Next time I see Bess Fettleworth I'll give her a bit of a hint o' what Magic will do for her. She'd be rare an' pleased if th' sinetifik 'speriment[298] worked—an' so 'ud Jem.'

Dickon had stood listening to the lecture, his round eyes shining with curious delight. Nut and Shell were on his shoulders and he held a long-eared white rabbit in his arm and stroked and stroked it softly while it laid its ears along its back and enjoyed itself.

'Do you think the experiment will work?' Colin asked him, wondering what he was thinking. He so often wondered what

Dickon was thinking when he saw him looking at him or at one of his 'creatures' with his happy wide smile.

He smiled now and his smile was wider than usual.

'Aye,' he answered, 'that I do. It'll work same as th' seeds do when th' sun shines on 'em. It'll work for sure. Shall us begin it now?'

Colin was delighted and so was Mary. Fired by recollections of fakirs and devotees in illustrations Colin suggested that they should all sit cross-legged under the tree which made a canopy.

'It will be like sitting in a sort of temple,' said Colin. 'I'm rather tired and I want to sit down.'

'Eh!' said Dickon, 'tha' mustn't begin by sayin' tha'rt tired. Tha' might spoil th' Magic.'

Colin turned and looked at him—into his innocent round eyes.

'That's true,' he said slowly. 'I must only think of the Magic.'

It all seemed most majestic and mysterious when they sat down in their circle. Ben Weatherstaff felt as if he had somehow been led into appearing at a prayer-meeting. Ordinarily he was very fixed in being what he called 'agen'[299] prayer-meetin's[300]' but this being the Rajah's affair he did not resent it and was indeed inclined to be gratified at being called upon to assist. Mistress Mary felt solemnly enraptured. Dickon held his rabbit in his arm, and perhaps he made some charmer's signal no one heard, for when he sat down, cross-legged like the rest, the crow, the fox, the squirrels and the lamb slowly drew near and made part of the circle, settling each into a place of rest as if of their own desire.

'The 'creatures' have come,' said Colin gravely. 'They want to help us.'

Colin really looked quite beautiful, Mary thought. He held his head high as if he felt like a sort of priest and his strange eyes had a wonderful look in them. The light shone on him through the tree canopy.

'Now we will begin,' he said. 'Shall we sway backward and forward, Mary, as if we were dervishes?'

'I canna' do no swayin'[301] back'ard[302] and for'ard,' said Ben Weatherstaff. 'I've got th' rheumatics.'

'The Magic will take them away,' said Colin in a High Priest tone, 'but we won't sway until it has done it. We will only chant.'

'I canna' do no chantin'[303],' said Ben Weatherstaff a trifle testily. 'They turned me out o' th' church choir th' only time I ever tried it.'

No one smiled. They were all too much in earnest. Colin's face was not even crossed by a shadow. He was thinking only of the Magic.

'Then I will chant,' he said. And he began, looking like a strange boy spirit. 'The sun is shining—the sun is shining. That is the Magic. The flowers are growing—the roots are stirring. That is the Magic. Being alive is the Magic—being strong is the Magic. The Magic is in me—the Magic is in me. It is in me—it is in me. It's in every one of us. It's in Ben Weatherstaff's back. Magic! Magic! Come and help!'

He said it a great many times—not a thousand times but quite a goodly number. Mary listened entranced. She felt as if it were at once queer and beautiful and she wanted him to go on and on. Ben Weatherstaff began to feel soothed into a sort of dream which was quite agreeable. The humming of the bees in the blossoms mingled with the chanting voice and drowsily melted into a doze.

Dickon sat cross-legged with his rabbit asleep on his arm and a hand resting on the lamb's back. Soot had pushed away a squirrel and huddled close to him on his shoulder, the gray film dropped over his eyes. At last Colin stopped.

'Now I am going to walk round the garden,' he announced.

Ben Weatherstaff's head had just dropped forward and he lifted it with a jerk.

'You have been asleep,' said Colin.

'Nowt o' th' sort,' mumbled Ben. 'Th' sermon was good enow—but I'm bound to get out afore th' collection.'

He was not quite awake yet.

'You're not in church,' said Colin.

'Not me,' said Ben, straightening himself. 'Who said I were? I heard every bit of it. You said th' Magic was in my back. Th' doctor calls it rheumatics.'

The Rajah waved his hand.

'That was the wrong Magic,' he said. 'You will get better. You have my permission to go to your work. But come back tomorrow.'

'I'd like to see thee walk round the garden,' grunted Ben.

It was not an unfriendly grunt, but it was a grunt. In fact, being a stubborn old party and not having entire faith in Magic he had made up his mind that if he were sent away he would climb his ladder and look over the wall so that he might be ready to hobble back if there were any stumbling.

The Rajah did not object to his staying and so the procession was formed. It really did look like a procession. Colin was at its head with Dickon on one side and Mary on the other. Ben Weatherstaff walked behind, and the 'creatures' trailed after them, the lamb and the fox cub keeping close to Dickon, the white rabbit hopping along or stopping to nibble and Soot following with the solemnity of a person who felt himself in charge.

It was a procession which moved slowly but with dignity. Every few yards it stopped to rest. Colin leaned on Dickon's arm and privately Ben Weatherstaff kept a sharp lookout, but now and then Colin took his hand from its support and walked a few steps alone. His head was held up all the time and he looked very grand.

'The Magic is in me!' he kept saying. 'The Magic is making me strong! I can feel it! I can feel it!'

It seemed very certain that something was upholding and uplifting him. He sat on the seats in the alcoves, and once or twice he sat down on the grass and several times he paused in the path and leaned on Dickon, but he would not give up until he had gone all round the garden. When he returned to the canopy tree his cheeks were flushed and he looked triumphant.

'I did it! The Magic worked!' he cried. 'That is my first scientific discovery.'

'What will Dr. Craven say?' broke out Mary.

'He won't say anything,' Colin answered, 'because he will not be told. This is to be the biggest secret of all. No one is to know anything about it until I have grown so strong that I can walk and run like any other boy. I shall come here every day in my chair and I shall be taken back in it. I won't have people whispering and asking questions and I won't let my father hear about it until the experiment has quite succeeded. Then sometime when he comes back to Misselthwaite I shall just walk into his study and say "Here I am; I am like any other boy. I am quite well and I shall live to be a man. It has been done by a scientific experiment." '

'He will think he is in a dream,' cried Mary. 'He won't believe his eyes.'

Colin flushed triumphantly. He had made himself believe that he was going to get well, which was really more than half the battle, if he had been aware of it. And the thought which stimulated him more than any other was this imagining what his father would look like when he saw that he had a son who was as straight and strong as other fathers' sons. One of his darkest miseries in the unhealthy morbid past days had been his hatred of being a sickly weak-backed boy whose father was afraid to look at him.

'He'll be obliged to believe them,' he said.

'One of the things I am going to do, after the Magic works and before I begin to make scientific discoveries, is to be an athlete.'

'We shall have thee takin' to boxin'[304] in a week or so,' said Ben Weatherstaff. 'Tha'lt end wi' winnin'[305] th' Belt an' bein' champion prize-fighter of all England.'

Colin fixed his eyes on him sternly.

'Weatherstaff,' he said, 'that is disrespectful. You must not take liberties because you are in the secret. However much the Magic works I shall not be a prize-fighter. I shall be a Scientific Discoverer.'

'Ax pardon—ax pardon, sir' answered Ben, touching his forehead in salute. 'I ought to have seed[306] it wasn't a jokin'[307] matter,' but his eyes twinkled and secretly he was immensely pleased. He really did not mind being snubbed since the snubbing meant that the lad was gaining strength and spirit.

24.

'Let Them Laugh.'

The secret garden was not the only one Dickon worked in. Round the cottage on the moor there was a piece of ground enclosed by a low wall of rough stones. Early in the morning and late in the fading twilight and on all the days Colin and Mary did not see him, Dickon worked there planting or tending potatoes and cabbages, turnips and carrots and herbs for his mother. In the company of his 'creatures' he did wonders there and was never tired of doing them, it seemed. While he dug or weeded he whistled or sang bits of Yorkshire moor songs or talked to Soot or Captain or the brothers and sisters he had taught to help him.

'We'd never get on as comfortable as we do,' Mrs. Sowerby said, 'if it wasn't for Dickon's garden. Anything'll grow for him. His 'taters and cabbages is twice th' size of any one else's an' they've got a flavor with 'em as nobody's has.'

When she found a moment to spare she liked to go out and talk to him. After supper there was still a long clear twilight to work in and that was her quiet time. She could sit upon the low rough wall and look on and hear stories of the day. She loved this time. There were not only vegetables in this garden. Dickon had bought penny packages of flower seeds now and then and sown bright sweet-scented things among gooseberry bushes and even cabbages and he grew borders of mignonette and pinks and pansies and things whose seeds he could save year after year or whose roots would bloom each spring and spread in time into fine clumps. The low wall was one of the prettiest things in Yorkshire because he had tucked moorland foxglove and ferns and rock-cress and hedgerow flowers into every crevice until only here and there glimpses of the stones were to be seen.

'All a chap's got to do to make 'em thrive, mother,' he would say, 'is to be friends with 'em for sure. They're just like th' "creatures."[308] If they're thirsty give 'em a drink and if they're hungry give 'em a bit o' food. They want to live same as we do. If they died I should feel as if I'd been a bad lad and somehow treated them heartless.'

It was in these twilight hours that Mrs. Sowerby heard of all that happened at Misselthwaite Manor. At first she was only told that 'Mester Colin' had taken a fancy to going out into the grounds with Miss Mary and that it was doing him good. But it was not long before it was agreed between the two children that Dickon's mother might 'come into the secret.' Somehow it was not doubted that she was 'safe for sure.'

So one beautiful still evening Dickon told the whole story, with all the thrilling details of the buried key and the robin and the gray haze which had seemed like deadness and the secret Mistress Mary had planned never to reveal. The coming of Dickon and how it had been told to him, the doubt of Mester Colin and the final drama of his introduction to the hidden domain, combined with the incident of Ben Weatherstaff's angry face peering over the wall and Mester Colin's sudden indignant strength, made Mrs. Sowerby's nice-looking face quite change colour several times.

'My word!' she said. 'It was a good thing that little lass came to th' Manor. It's been th' makin' o' her an' th' savin'[309] o' him. Standin'[310] on his feet! An' us all thinkin' he was a poor half-witted lad with not a straight bone in him.'

She asked a great many questions and her blue eyes were full of deep thinking.

'What do they make of it at th' Manor—him being so well an' cheerful an' never complainin'[311]?' she inquired.

'They don't know what to make of it,' answered Dickon. 'Every day as comes round his face looks different. It's fillin'[312] out and doesn't look so sharp an' th' waxy colour is goin'. But he has to do his bit o' complainin','' with a highly entertained grin.

'What for, i' Mercy's name?' asked Mrs. Sowerby.

Dickon chuckled.

'He does it to keep them from guessin'[313] what's happened. If the doctor knew he'd found out he could stand on his feet he'd likely write and tell Mester Craven. Mester Colin's savin' th' secret to tell himself. He's goin' to practise his Magic on his legs every day till his father comes back an' then he's goin' to march into his room an' show him he's as straight as other lads. But him an' Miss Mary thinks it's best plan to do a bit o' groanin'[314] an' frettin' now an' then to throw folk off th' scent.'

Mrs. Sowerby was laughing a low comfortable laugh long before he had finished his last sentence.

'Eh!' she said, 'that pair's enjoyin'[315] theirselves[316], I'll warrant. They'll get a good bit o' play actin'[317] out of it an' there's nothin' children likes as much as play actin'. Let's hear what they do, Dickon lad.'

Dickon stopped weeding and sat up on his heels to tell her. His eyes were twinkling with fun.

'Mester Colin is carried down to his chair every time he goes out,' he explained. 'An' he flies out at John, th' footman, for not carryin' him careful enough. He makes himself as helpless lookin' as he can an' never lifts his head until we're out o' sight o' th' house. An' he grunts an' frets a good bit when he's bein' settled into his chair. Him an' Miss Mary's both got to enjoyin' it an' when he groans an' complains she'll say, "Poor Colin! Does it hurt you so much? Are you so weak as that, poor Colin?"—but th' trouble is that sometimes they can scarce keep from burstin'[318] out laughin'. When we get safe into the garden they laugh till they've no breath left to laugh with. An' they have to stuff their faces into Mester Colin's cushions to keep the gardeners from hearin'[319], if any of 'em's about.'

'Th' more they laugh th' better for 'em!' said Mrs. Sowerby, still laughing herself. 'Good healthy child laughin's[320] better than pills any day o' th' year. That pair'll plump up for sure.'

'They are plumpin'[321] up,' said Dickon. 'They're that hungry they don't know how to get enough to eat without makin' talk. Mester Colin says if he keeps sendin'[322] for more food they won't believe he's an invalid at all. Miss Mary says she'll let him eat her share, but he says that if she goes hungry she'll get thin an' they mun both get fat at once.'

Mrs. Sowerby laughed so heartily at the revelation of this

difficulty, that she quite rocked backward and forward in her blue cloak, and Dickon laughed with her.

'I'll tell thee what, lad,' Mrs. Sowerby said when she could speak. 'I've thought of a way to help 'em. When tha' goes to 'em in th' mornin's tha' shall take a pail o' good new milk an' I'll bake 'em a crusty cottage loaf or some buns wi' currants in 'em, same as you children like. Nothin's[323] so good as fresh milk an' bread. Then they could take off th' edge o' their hunger while they were in their garden an' th' fine food they get indoors 'ud polish off th' corners.'

'Eh! mother!' said Dickon admiringly, 'what a wonder tha' art! Tha' always sees a way out o' things. They was quite in a pother yesterday. They didn't see how they was to manage without orderin'[324] up more food—they felt that empty inside.'

'They're two young 'uns growin' fast, an' health's comin' back to both of 'em. Children like that feels like young wolves an' food's flesh an' blood to 'em,' said Mrs. Sowerby. Then she smiled Dickon's own curving smile. 'Eh! but they're enjoyin' theirselves for sure,' she said.

She was quite right, the comfortable wonderful mother creature—and she had never been more so than when she said their 'play actin'' would be their joy. Colin and Mary found it one of their most thrilling sources of entertainment. The idea of protecting themselves from suspicion had been unconsciously suggested to them first by the puzzled nurse and then by Dr. Craven himself.

'Your appetite is improving very much, Master Colin,' the nurse had said one day. 'You used to eat nothing, and so many things disagreed with you.'

'Nothing disagrees with me now' replied Colin, and then seeing the nurse looking at him curiously he suddenly remembered that perhaps he ought not to appear too well just yet. 'At least things don't so often disagree with me. It's the fresh air.'

'Perhaps it is,' said the nurse, still looking at him with a mystified expression. 'But I must talk to Dr. Craven about it.'

'How she stared at you!' said Mary when she went away. 'As if she thought there must be something to find out.'

'I won't have her finding out things,' said Colin. 'No one must begin to find out yet.'

When Dr. Craven came that morning he seemed puzzled, also. He asked a number of questions, to Colin's great annoyance.

'You stay out in the garden a great deal,' he suggested. 'Where do you go?'

Colin put on his favorite air of dignified indifference to opinion.

'I will not let any one know where I go,' he answered. 'I go to a place I like. Every one has orders to keep out of the way. I won't be watched and stared at. You know that!'

'You seem to be out all day but I do not think it has done you harm—I do not think so. The nurse says that you eat much more than you have ever done before.'

'Perhaps,' said Colin, prompted by a sudden inspiration, 'perhaps it is an unnatural appetite.'

'I do not think so, as your food seems to agree with you,' said Dr. Craven. 'You are gaining flesh rapidly and your colour is better.'

'Perhaps—perhaps I am bloated and feverish,' said Colin, assuming a discouraging air of gloom. 'People who are not going to live are often—different.'

Dr. Craven shook his head. He was holding Colin's wrist and

he pushed up his sleeve and felt his arm.

'You are not feverish,' he said thoughtfully, 'and such flesh as you have gained is healthy. If you can keep this up, my boy, we need not talk of dying. Your father will be happy to hear of this remarkable improvement.'

'I won't have him told!' Colin broke forth fiercely. 'It will only disappoint him if I get worse again—and I may get worse this very night. I might have a raging fever. I feel as if I might be beginning to have one now. I won't have letters written to my father—I won't—I won't! You are making me angry and you know that is bad for me. I feel hot already. I hate being written about and being talked over as much as I hate being stared at!'

'Hush-h! my boy,' Dr. Craven soothed him. 'Nothing shall be written without your permission. You are too sensitive about things. You must not undo the good which has been done.'

He said no more about writing to Mr. Craven and when he saw the nurse he privately warned her that such a possibility must not be mentioned to the patient.

'The boy is extraordinarily better,' he said. 'His advance seems almost abnormal. But of course he is doing now of his own free will what we could not make him do before. Still, he excites himself very easily and nothing must be said to irritate him.'

Mary and Colin were much alarmed and talked together anxiously. From this time dated their plan of 'play actin'.'[325]

'I may be obliged to have a tantrum,' said Colin regretfully. 'I don't want to have one and I'm not miserable enough now to work myself into a big one. Perhaps I couldn't have one at all. That lump doesn't come in my throat now and I keep thinking of nice things instead of horrible ones. But if they talk about writing to my father I shall have to do something.'

He made up his mind to eat less, but unfortunately it was not possible to carry out this brilliant idea when he wakened each morning with an amazing appetite and the table near his sofa was set with a breakfast of home-made bread and fresh butter, snow-white eggs, raspberry jam and clotted cream. Mary always breakfasted with him and when they found themselves at the table—particularly if there were delicate slices of sizzling ham sending forth tempting odors from under a hot silver cover—they would look into each other's eyes in desperation.

'I think we shall have to eat it all this morning, Mary,' Colin always ended by saying. 'We can send away some of the lunch and a great deal of the dinner.'

But they never found they could send away anything and the highly polished condition of the empty plates returned to the pantry awakened much comment.

'I do wish,' Colin would say also, 'I do wish the slices of ham were thicker, and one muffin each is not enough for any one.'

'It's enough for a person who is going to die,' answered Mary when first she heard this, 'but it's not enough for a person who is going to live. I sometimes feel as if I could eat three when those nice fresh heather and gorse smells from the moor come pouring in at the open window.'

The morning that Dickon—after they had been enjoying themselves in the garden for about two hours—went behind a big rose-bush and brought forth two tin pails and revealed that one was full of rich new milk with cream on the top of it, and that the other held cottage-made currant buns folded in a clean blue and white napkin, buns so carefully tucked in that they were still hot, there was a riot of surprised joyfulness. What a wonderful thing for Mrs. Sowerby to think of! What a kind, clever woman she must be! How good the buns were! And what delicious fresh milk!

'Magic is in her just as it is in Dickon,' said Colin. 'It makes her think of ways to do things—nice things. She is a Magic person. Tell her we are grateful, Dickon—extremely grateful.'

He was given to using rather grown-up phrases at times. He enjoyed them. He liked this so much that he improved upon it.

'Tell her she has been most bounteous and our gratitude is extreme.'

And then forgetting his grandeur he fell to and stuffed himself with buns and drank milk out of the pail in copious draughts in the manner of any hungry little boy who had been taking unusual exercise and breathing in moorland air and whose breakfast was more than two hours behind him.

This was the beginning of many agreeable incidents of the same kind. They actually awoke to the fact that as Mrs. Sowerby had fourteen people to provide food for she might not have enough to satisfy two extra appetites every day. So they asked her to let them send some of their shillings to buy things.

Dickon made the stimulating discovery that in the wood in the park outside the garden where Mary had first found him piping to the wild creatures there was a deep little hollow where you could build a sort of tiny oven with stones and roast potatoes and eggs in it. Roasted eggs were a previously unknown luxury and very hot potatoes with salt and fresh butter in them were fit for a woodland king—besides being deliciously satisfying. You could buy both potatoes and eggs and eat as many as you liked without feeling as if you were taking food out of the mouths of fourteen people.

Every beautiful morning the Magic was worked by the mystic circle under the plum-tree which provided a canopy of thickening green leaves after its brief blossom-time was ended. After the ceremony Colin always took his walking exercise and throughout the day he exercised his newly found power at intervals. Each day he grew stronger and could walk more steadily and cover more ground. And each day his belief in the Magic grew stronger— as well it might. He tried one experiment after another as he felt himself gaining strength and it was Dickon who showed him the best things of all.

'Yesterday,' he said one morning after an absence, 'I went to Thwaite for mother an' near th' Blue Cow Inn I seed Bob Haworth. He's the strongest chap on th' moor. He's the champion wrestler an' he can jump higher than any other chap an' throw th' hammer farther. He's gone all th' way to Scotland for th' sports some years. He's knowed me ever since I was a little 'un an' he's a friendly sort an' I axed[326] him some questions. Th' gentry calls him a athlete and I thought o' thee, Mester Colin, and I says, "How did tha' make tha' muscles stick out that way, Bob? Did tha' do anythin' extra to make thysel' so strong?" An' he says "Well, yes, lad, I did. A strong man in a show that came to Thwaite once showed me how to exercise my arms an' legs an' every muscle in my body." An' I says, "Could a delicate chap make himself stronger with 'em, Bob?" an' he laughed an' says, "Art tha' th' delicate chap?" an' I says, "No, but I knows a young gentleman that's gettin' well of a long illness an' I wish I knowed some o' them tricks to tell him about." I didn't say no names an' he didn't ask none. He's friendly same as I said an' he stood up an' showed me good-natured like, an' I imitated what he did till I knowed it by heart.'

Colin had been listening excitedly.

'Can you show me?' he cried. 'Will you?'

'Aye, to be sure,' Dickon answered, getting up. 'But he says tha' mun do 'em gentle at first an' be careful not to tire thysel'. Rest in between times an' take deep breaths an' don't overdo.'

'I'll be careful,' said Colin. 'Show me! Show me! Dickon, you are the most Magic boy in the world!'

Dickon stood up on the grass and slowly went through a carefully practical but simple series of muscle exercises. Colin watched them with widening eyes. He could do a few while he was sitting down. Presently he did a few gently while he stood upon his already steadied feet. Mary began to do them also. Soot, who was watching the performance, became much disturbed and left his branch and hopped about restlessly because he could not do them too.

From that time the exercises were part of the day's duties as much as the Magic was. It became possible for both Colin and Mary to do more of them each time they tried, and such appetites were the results that but for the basket Dickon put down behind the bush each morning when he arrived they would have been lost. But the little oven in the hollow and Mrs. Sowerby's bounties were so satisfying that Mrs. Medlock and the nurse and Dr. Craven became mystified again. You can trifle with your breakfast and seem to disdain your dinner if you are full to the brim with roasted eggs and potatoes and richly frothed new milk and oat-cakes and buns and heather honey and clotted cream.

'They are eating next to nothing,' said the nurse. 'They'll die of starvation if they can't be persuaded to take some nourishment. And yet see how they look.'

'Look!' exclaimed Mrs. Medlock indignantly. 'Eh! I'm moithered to death with them. They're a pair of young Satans. Bursting their jackets one day and the next turning up their noses at the best meals Cook can tempt them with. Not a mouthful of that lovely young fowl and bread sauce did they set a fork into yesterday—and the poor woman fair invented a pudding for them—and back it's sent. She almost cried. She's afraid she'll be blamed if they starve themselves into their graves.'

Dr. Craven came and looked at Colin long and carefully. He wore an extremely worried expression when the nurse talked with him and showed him the almost untouched tray of breakfast she had saved for him to look at—but it was even more worried when he sat down by Colin's sofa and examined him. He had been called to London on business and had not seen the boy for nearly two weeks. When young things begin to gain health they gain it rapidly. The waxen tinge had left Colin's skin and a warm rose showed through it; his beautiful eyes were clear and the hollows under them and in his cheeks and temples had filled out. His once dark, heavy locks had begun to look as if they sprang healthily from his forehead and were soft and warm with life. His lips were fuller and of a normal colour. In fact as an imitation of a boy who was a confirmed invalid he was a disgraceful sight. Dr. Craven held his chin in his hand and thought him over.

'I am sorry to hear that you do not eat anything,' he said. 'That will not do. You will lose all you have gained—and you have gained amazingly. You ate so well a short time ago.'

'I told you it was an unnatural appetite,' answered Colin.

Mary was sitting on her stool nearby and she suddenly made a very queer sound which she tried so violently to repress that she ended by almost choking.

'What is the matter?' said Dr. Craven, turning to look at her.

Mary became quite severe in her manner.

'It was something between a sneeze and a cough,' she replied with reproachful dignity, 'and it got into my throat.'

'But' she said afterward to Colin, 'I couldn't stop myself. It just burst out because all at once I couldn't help remembering that last big potato you ate and the way your mouth stretched when you bit through that thick lovely crust with jam and clotted cream on it.'

'Is there any way in which those children can get food secretly?' Dr. Craven inquired of Mrs. Medlock.

'There's no way unless they dig it out of the earth or pick it off the trees,' Mrs. Medlock answered. 'They stay out in the grounds all day and see no one but each other. And if they want anything different to eat from what's sent up to them they need only ask for it.'

'Well,' said Dr. Craven, 'so long as going without food agrees with them we need not disturb ourselves. The boy is a new creature.'

'So is the girl,' said Mrs. Medlock. 'She's begun to be downright pretty since she's filled out and lost her ugly little sour look. Her hair's grown thick and healthy looking and she's got a bright colour. The glummest, ill-natured little thing she used to be and now her and Master Colin laugh together like a pair of crazy young ones. Perhaps they're growing fat on that.'

'Perhaps they are,' said Dr. Craven. 'Let them laugh.'

25.

The Curtain

And the secret garden bloomed and bloomed and every morning revealed new miracles. In the robin's nest there were Eggs and the robin's mate sat upon them keeping them warm with her feathery little breast and careful wings. At first she was very nervous and the robin himself was indignantly watchful. Even Dickon did not go near the close-grown corner in those days, but waited until by the quiet working of some mysterious spell he seemed to have conveyed to the soul of the little pair that in the garden there was nothing which was not quite like themselves— nothing which did not understand the wonderfulness of what was happening to them—the immense, tender, terrible, heart-breaking beauty and solemnity of Eggs. If there had been one person in that garden who had not known through all his or her innermost being that if an Egg were taken away or hurt the whole world would whirl round and crash through space and come to an end—if there had been even one who did not feel it and act accordingly there could have been no happiness even in that golden springtime air. But they all knew it and felt it and the robin and his mate knew they knew it.

At first the robin watched Mary and Colin with sharp anxiety. For some mysterious reason he knew he need not watch Dickon. The first moment he set his dew-bright black eye on Dickon he knew he was not a stranger but a sort of robin without beak or feathers. He could speak robin (which is a quite distinct language not to be mistaken for any other). To speak robin to a robin is like speaking French to a Frenchman. Dickon always spoke it to the robin himself, so the queer gibberish he used when he spoke to humans did not matter in the least. The robin thought he spoke this gibberish to them because they were not intelligent enough to understand feathered speech. His movements also were robin. They never startled one by being sudden enough to seem dangerous or threatening. Any robin could understand Dickon, so his presence was not even disturbing.

But at the outset it seemed necessary to be on guard against the other two. In the first place the boy creature did not come into the garden on his legs. He was pushed in on a thing with wheels and the skins of wild animals were thrown over him. That in itself was doubtful. Then when he began to stand up and move about he did it in a queer unaccustomed way and the others seemed to have to help him. The robin used to secrete himself in a bush and watch this anxiously, his head tilted first on one side and then on the other. He thought that the slow movements might mean that he was preparing to pounce, as cats do. When cats are preparing to pounce they creep over the ground very slowly. The robin talked this over with his mate a great deal for a few days but after that he decided not to speak of the subject because her terror was so great that he was afraid it might be injurious to the Eggs.

When the boy began to walk by himself and even to move more quickly it was an immense relief. But for a long time—or it seemed a long time to the robin—he was a source of some anxiety. He did not act as the other humans did. He seemed very fond of walking but he had a way of sitting or lying down for a while and then getting up in a disconcerting manner to begin again.

One day the robin remembered that when he himself had been made to learn to fly by his parents he had done much the same sort of thing. He had taken short flights of a few yards and then had been obliged to rest. So it occurred to him that this boy was learning to fly—or rather to walk. He mentioned this to his mate and when he told her that the Eggs would probably conduct themselves in the same way after they were fledged she was quite comforted and even became eagerly interested and derived great pleasure from watching the boy over the edge of her nest—though she always thought that the Eggs would be much cleverer and learn more quickly. But then she said indulgently that humans were always more clumsy and slow than Eggs and most of them never seemed really to learn to fly at all. You never met them in the air or on tree-tops.

After a while the boy began to move about as the others did, but all three of the children at times did unusual things. They would stand under the trees and move their arms and legs and heads about in a way which was neither walking nor running nor sitting down. They went through these movements at intervals every day and the robin was never able to explain to his mate what they were doing or trying to do. He could only say that he was sure that the Eggs would never flap about in such a manner; but as the boy who could speak robin so fluently was doing the thing with them, birds could be quite sure that the actions were not of a dangerous nature. Of course neither the robin nor his mate had ever heard of the champion wrestler, Bob Haworth, and his exercises for making the muscles stand out like lumps. Robins are not like human beings; their muscles are always exercised from the first and so they develop themselves in a natural manner. If you have to fly about to find every meal you eat, your muscles do not become atrophied (atrophied means wasted away through want of use).

When the boy was walking and running about and digging and weeding like the others, the nest in the corner was brooded over by a great peace and content. Fears for the Eggs became things of the past. Knowing that your Eggs were as safe as if they were locked in a bank vault and the fact that you could watch so many curious things going on made setting a most entertaining occupation. On wet days the Eggs' mother sometimes felt even a little dull because the children did not come into the garden.

But even on wet days it could not be said that Mary and Colin were dull. One morning when the rain streamed down unceasingly and Colin was beginning to feel a little restive, as he was obliged to remain on his sofa because it was not safe to get up and walk about, Mary had an inspiration.

'Now that I am a real boy,' Colin had said, 'my legs and arms and all my body are so full of Magic that I can't keep them still. They want to be doing things all the time. Do you know that when I waken in the morning, Mary, when it's quite early and the birds are just shouting outside and everything seems just shouting for joy—even the trees and things we can't really hear—I feel as if I must jump out of bed and shout myself. If I did it, just think what would happen!'

Mary giggled inordinately.

'The nurse would come running and Mrs. Medlock would come running and they would be sure you had gone crazy and they'd send for the doctor,' she said.

Colin giggled himself. He could see how they would all look—how horrified by his outbreak and how amazed to see him standing upright.

'I wish my father would come home,' he said. 'I want to tell him myself. I'm always thinking about it—but we couldn't go on like this much longer. I can't stand lying still and pretending, and besides I look too different. I wish it wasn't raining to-day.'

It was then Mistress Mary had her inspiration.

'Colin,' she began mysteriously, 'do you know how many rooms there are in this house?'

'About a thousand, I suppose,' he answered.

'There's about a hundred no one ever goes into,' said Mary. 'And one rainy day I went and looked into ever so many of them. No one ever knew, though Mrs. Medlock nearly found me out. I lost my way when I was coming back and I stopped at the end of your corridor. That was the second time I heard you crying.'

Colin started up on his sofa.

'A hundred rooms no one goes into,' he said. 'It sounds almost like a secret garden. Suppose we go and look at them. You could wheel me in my chair and nobody would know where we went.'

'That's what I was thinking,' said Mary. 'No one would dare to follow us. There are galleries where you could run. We could do our exercises. There is a little Indian room where there is a cabinet full of ivory elephants. There are all sorts of rooms.'

'Ring the bell,' said Colin.

When the nurse came in he gave his orders.

'I want my chair,' he said. 'Miss Mary and I are going to look at the part of the house which is not used. John can push me as far as the picture-gallery because there are some stairs. Then he must go away and leave us alone until I send for him again.'

Rainy days lost their terrors that morning. When the footman had wheeled the chair into the picture-gallery and left the two together in obedience to orders, Colin and Mary looked at each other delighted. As soon as Mary had made sure that John was really on his way back to his own quarters below stairs, Colin got out of his chair.

'I am going to run from one end of the gallery to the other,' he said, 'and then I am going to jump and then we will do Bob Haworth's exercises.'

And they did all these things and many others. They looked at the portraits and found the plain little girl dressed in green brocade and holding the parrot on her finger.

'All these,' said Colin, 'must be my relations. They lived a long time ago. That parrot one, I believe, is one of my great, great, great, great aunts. She looks rather like you, Mary—not as you look now but as you looked when you came here. Now you are a great deal fatter and better looking.'

'So are you,' said Mary, and they both laughed.

They went to the Indian room and amused themselves with the ivory elephants. They found the rose-coloured brocade boudoir and the hole in the cushion the mouse had left but the mice had grown up and run away and the hole was empty. They saw more rooms and made more discoveries than Mary had made on her first pilgrimage. They found new corridors and corners and flights of steps and new old pictures they liked and weird old things they did not know the use of. It was a curiously entertaining morning and the feeling of wandering about in the same house with other people but at the same time feeling as if one were miles away from them was a fascinating thing.

'I'm glad we came,' Colin said. 'I never knew I lived in such a big queer old place. I like it. We will ramble about every rainy day. We shall always be finding new queer corners and things.'

That morning they had found among other things such good appetites that when they returned to Colin's room it was not possible to send the luncheon away untouched.

When the nurse carried the tray down-stairs she slapped it down on the kitchen dresser so that Mrs. Loomis, the cook, could see the highly polished dishes and plates.

'Look at that!' she said. 'This is a house of mystery, and those two children are the greatest mysteries in it.'

'If they keep that up every day,' said the strong young footman John, 'there'd be small wonder that he weighs twice as much to-day as he did a month ago. I should have to give up my place in time, for fear of doing my muscles an injury.'

That afternoon Mary noticed that something new had happened in Colin's room. She had noticed it the day before but had said nothing because she thought the change might have been made by chance. She said nothing today but she sat and looked fixedly at the picture over the mantel. She could look at it because the curtain had been drawn aside. That was the change she noticed.

'I know what you want me to tell you,' said Colin, after she had stared a few minutes. 'I always know when you want me to tell you something. You are wondering why the curtain is drawn back. I am going to keep it like that.'

'Why?' asked Mary.

'Because it doesn't make me angry any more to see her laughing. I wakened when it was bright moonlight two nights ago and felt as if the Magic was filling the room and making everything so splendid that I couldn't lie still. I got up and looked out of the window. The room was quite light and there was a patch of moonlight on the curtain and somehow that made me go and pull the cord. She looked right down at me as if she were laughing because she was glad I was standing there. It made me like to look at her. I want to see her laughing like that all the time. I think she must have been a sort of Magic person perhaps.'

'You are so like her now,' said Mary, 'that sometimes I think perhaps you are her ghost made into a boy.'

That idea seemed to impress Colin. He thought it over and then answered her slowly.

'If I were her ghost—my father would be fond of me.'

'Do you want him to be fond of you?' inquired Mary.

'I used to hate it because he was not fond of me. If he grew fond of me I think I should tell him about the Magic. It might make him more cheerful.'

26.

'It's Mother!'

Their belief in the Magic was an abiding thing. After the morning's incantations Colin sometimes gave them Magic lectures.

'I like to do it,' he explained, 'because when I grow up and make great scientific discoveries I shall be obliged to lecture about them and so this is practise. I can only give short lectures now because I am very young, and besides Ben Weatherstaff would feel as if he were in church and he would go to sleep.'

'Th' best thing about lecturin'[327],' said Ben, 'is that a chap can get up an' say aught he pleases an' no other chap can answer him back. I wouldn't be agen' lecturin' a bit mysel' sometimes.'

But when Colin held forth under his tree old Ben fixed devouring eyes on him and kept them there. He looked him over with critical affection. It was not so much the lecture which interested him as the legs which looked straighter and stronger each day, the boyish head which held itself up so well, the once sharp chin and hollow cheeks which had filled and rounded out and the eyes which had begun to hold the light he remembered in another pair. Sometimes when Colin felt Ben's earnest gaze meant that he was much impressed he wondered what he was reflecting on and once when he had seemed quite entranced he questioned him.

'What are you thinking about, Ben Weatherstaff?' he asked.

'I was thinkin'' answered Ben, 'as I'd warrant tha's gone up three or four pound[328] this week. I was lookin' at tha' calves an' tha' shoulders. I'd like to get thee on a pair o' scales.'

'It's the Magic and—and Mrs. Sowerby's buns and milk and things,' said Colin. 'You see the scientific experiment has succeeded.'

That morning Dickon was too late to hear the lecture. When he came he was ruddy with running and his funny face looked more twinkling than usual. As they had a good deal of weeding to do after the rains they fell to work. They always had plenty to do after a warm deep sinking rain. The moisture which was good for the flowers was also good for the weeds which thrust up tiny blades of grass and points of leaves which must be pulled up before their roots took too firm hold. Colin was as good at weeding as any one in these days and he could lecture while he was doing it.

'The Magic works best when you work, yourself,' he said this morning. 'You can feel it in your bones and muscles. I am going to read books about bones and muscles, but I am going to write a book about Magic. I am making it up now. I keep finding out things.'

It was not very long after he had said this that he laid down his trowel and stood up on his feet. He had been silent for several minutes and they had seen that he was thinking out lectures, as he often did. When he dropped his trowel and stood upright it seemed to Mary and Dickon as if a sudden strong thought had made him do it. He stretched himself out to his tallest height and he threw out his arms exultantly. Colour glowed in his face and his strange eyes widened with joyfulness. All at once he had realized something to the full.

'Mary! Dickon!' he cried. 'Just look at me!'

They stopped their weeding and looked at him.

'Do you remember that first morning you brought me in here?' he demanded.

Dickon was looking at him very hard. Being an animal charmer he could see more things than most people could and many of them were things he never talked about. He saw some of them now in this boy.

'Aye, that we do,' he answered.

Mary looked hard too, but she said nothing.

'Just this minute,' said Colin, 'all at once I remembered it myself—when I looked at my hand digging with the trowel—and I had to stand up on my feet to see if it was real. And it is real! I'm well—I'm well!'

'Aye, that th' art!' said Dickon.

'I'm well! I'm well!' said Colin again, and his face went quite red all over.

He had known it before in a way, he had hoped it and felt it and thought about it, but just at that minute something had rushed all through him—a sort of rapturous belief and realization and it had been so strong that he could not help calling out.

'I shall live forever and ever and ever!' he cried grandly. 'I shall find out thousands and thousands of things. I shall find out about

people and creatures and everything that grows—like Dickon—
and I shall never stop making Magic. I'm well! I'm well! I feel—
I feel as if I want to shout out something—something thankful,
joyful!'

Ben Weatherstaff, who had been working near a rose-bush,
glanced round at him.

'Tha' might sing th' Doxology,' he suggested in his dryest
grunt. He had no opinion of the Doxology and he did not make
the suggestion with any particular reverence.

But Colin was of an exploring mind and he knew nothing
about the Doxology.

'What is that?' he inquired.

'Dickon can sing it for thee, I'll warrant,' replied Ben Weatherstaff.

Dickon answered with his all-perceiving animal charmer's
smile.

'They sing it i' church,' he said. 'Mother says she believes th'
skylarks sings[329] it when they gets[330] up i' th' mornin'.'

'If she says that, it must be a nice song,' Colin answered. 'I've
never been in a church myself. I was always too ill. Sing it, Dickon.
I want to hear it.'

Dickon was quite simple and unaffected about it. He understood what Colin felt better than Colin did himself. He understood by a sort of instinct so natural that he did not know it
was understanding. He pulled off his cap and looked round still
smiling.

'Tha' must take off tha' cap,' he said to Colin, 'an' so mun tha',
Ben—an' tha' mun stand up, tha' knows.'

Colin took off his cap and the sun shone on and warmed

his thick hair as he watched Dickon intently. Ben Weatherstaff scrambled up from his knees and bared his head too with a sort of puzzled half-resentful look on his old face as if he didn't know exactly why he was doing this remarkable thing.

Dickon stood out among the trees and rose-bushes and began to sing in quite a simple matter-of-fact way and in a nice strong boy voice:

'Praise God from whom all blessings flow,
Praise Him all creatures here below,
Praise Him above ye[331] *Heavenly Host,*
Praise Father, Son, and Holy Ghost.
Amen.'

When he had finished, Ben Weatherstaff was standing quite still with his jaws set obstinately but with a disturbed look in his eyes fixed on Colin. Colin's face was thoughtful and appreciative.

'It is a very nice song,' he said. 'I like it. Perhaps it means just what I mean when I want to shout out that I am thankful to the Magic.' He stopped and thought in a puzzled way. 'Perhaps they are both the same thing. How can we know the exact names of everything? Sing it again, Dickon. Let us try, Mary. I want to sing it, too. It's my song. How does it begin? "Praise God from whom all blessings flow"?'

And they sang it again, and Mary and Colin lifted their voices as musically as they could and Dickon's swelled quite loud and beautiful—and at the second line Ben Weatherstaff raspingly cleared his throat and at the third line he joined in with such vigor that it seemed almost savage and when the 'Amen' came to an end Mary observed that the very same thing had happened to him which had happened when he found out that Colin was not a cripple—his chin was twitching and he was staring and winking and his leathery old cheeks were wet.

'I never seed no sense in th' Doxology afore,' he said hoarsely, 'but I may change my mind i' time. I should say tha'd gone up five pound this week Mester Colin—five on 'em!'

Colin was looking across the garden at something attracting his attention and his expression had become a startled one.

'Who is coming in here?' he said quickly. 'Who is it?'

The door in the ivied wall had been pushed gently open and a woman had entered. She had come in with the last line of their song and she had stood still listening and looking at them. With the ivy behind her, the sunlight drifting through the trees and dappling her long blue cloak, and her nice fresh face smiling across the greenery she was rather like a softly coloured illustration in one of Colin's books. She had wonderful affectionate eyes which seemed to take everything in—all of them, even Ben Weatherstaff and the 'creatures' and every flower that was in bloom. Unexpectedly as she had appeared, not one of them felt that she was an intruder at all. Dickon's eyes lighted like lamps.

'It's Mother—that's who it is!' he cried and went across the grass at a run.

Colin began to move toward her, too, and Mary went with him. They both felt their pulses beat faster.

'It's mother!' Dickon said again when they met half-way. 'I knowed tha' wanted to see her an' I told her where th' door was hid.'

Colin held out his hand with a sort of flushed royal shyness but his eyes quite devoured her face.

'Even when I was ill I wanted to see you,' he said, 'you and Dickon and the secret garden. I'd never wanted to see any one or anything before.'

The sight of his uplifted face brought about a sudden change in her own. She flushed and the corners of her mouth shook and a mist seemed to sweep over her eyes.

'Eh! dear[332] lad!' she broke out tremulously. 'Eh! dear lad!' as if she had not known she were going to say it. She did not say, 'Mester Colin,' but just 'dear lad' quite suddenly. She might have said it to Dickon in the same way if she had seen something in his face which touched her. Colin liked it.

'Are you surprised because I am so well?' he asked.

She put her hand on his shoulder and smiled the mist out of her eyes.

'Aye, that I am!' she said; 'but tha'rt so like thy mother tha' made my heart jump.'

'Do you think,' said Colin a little awkwardly, 'that will make my father like me?'

'Aye, for sure, dear lad,' she answered and she gave his shoulder a soft quick pat. 'He mun come home—he mun come home.'

'Susan Sowerby,' said Ben Weatherstaff, getting close to her. 'Look at th' lad's legs, wilt tha'? They was like drumsticks i' stockin' two month'[333] ago—an' I heard folk tell as they was bandy an' knock-kneed both at th' same time. Look at 'em now!'

Susan Sowerby laughed a comfortable laugh.

'They're goin' to be fine strong lad's legs in a bit,' she said. 'Let him go on playin' an' workin' in the garden an' eatin'[334] hearty an' drinkin'[335] plenty o' good sweet milk an' there'll not be a finer pair i' Yorkshire, thank God for it.'

She put both hands on Mistress Mary's shoulders and looked her little face over in a motherly fashion.

'An' thee, too!' she said. 'Tha'rt grown near as hearty as our 'Lisabeth Ellen. I'll warrant tha'rt like thy mother too. Our Martha told me as Mrs. Medlock heard she was a pretty woman. Tha'lt be like a blush rose when tha' grows[336] up, my little lass, bless thee.'

She did not mention that when Martha came home on her 'day out' and described the plain sallow child she had said that she had no confidence whatever in what Mrs. Medlock had heard. 'It doesn't stand to reason that a pretty woman could be th' mother o' such a fou'[337] little lass,' she had added obstinately.

Mary had not had time to pay much attention to her changing face. She had only known that she looked 'different' and seemed to have a great deal more hair and that it was growing very fast. But remembering her pleasure in looking at the Mem Sahib in the past she was glad to hear that she might some day look like her.

Susan Sowerby went round their garden with them and was told the whole story of it and shown every bush and tree which had come alive. Colin walked on one side of her and Mary on the other. Each of them kept looking up at her comfortable rosy face, secretly curious about the delightful feeling she gave them—a sort of warm, supported feeling. It seemed as if she understood them as Dickon understood his 'creatures.' She stooped over the flowers and talked about them as if they were children. Soot followed her and once or twice cawed at her and flew upon her shoulder as if it were Dickon's. When they told her about the robin and the first flight of the young ones she laughed a motherly little mellow laugh in her throat.

'I suppose learnin' 'em to fly is like learnin' children to walk, but I'm feared I should be all in a worrit[338] if mine[339] had wings instead o' legs,' she said.

It was because she seemed such a wonderful woman in her nice moorland cottage way that at last she was told about the Magic.

'Do you believe in Magic?' asked Colin after he had explained about Indian fakirs. 'I do hope you do.'

'That I do, lad,' she answered. 'I never knowed it by that name but what does th' name matter? I warrant they call it a different name i' France an' a different one i' Germany. Th' same thing as set th' seeds swellin'[340] an' th' sun shinin' made thee a well lad an' it's th' Good Thing. It isn't like us poor fools as think it matters if us is called out of our names. Th' Big Good Thing doesn't stop to worrit, bless thee. It goes on makin' worlds by th' million— worlds like us. Never thee stop believin'[341] in th' Big Good Thing an' knowin' th' world's full of it—an' call it what tha' likes. Tha' wert[342] singin' to it when I come into th' garden.'

'I felt so joyful,' said Colin, opening his beautiful strange eyes at her. 'Suddenly I felt how different I was—how strong my arms and legs were, you know—and how I could dig and stand—and I jumped up and wanted to shout out something to anything that would listen.'

'Th' Magic listened when tha' sung th' Doxology. It would ha' listened to anything tha'd sung. It was th' joy that mattered. Eh! lad, lad—what's names to th' Joy Maker,' and she gave his shoulders a quick soft pat again.

She had packed a basket which held a regular feast this morning, and when the hungry hour came and Dickon brought it out from its hiding place, she sat down with them under their tree and watched them devour their food, laughing and quite gloating over their appetites. She was full of fun and made them laugh at all sorts of odd things. She told them stories in broad Yorkshire and taught them new words. She laughed as if she could not help it when they told her of the increasing difficulty there was in pretending that Colin was still a fretful invalid.

'You see we can't help laughing nearly all the time when we are together,' explained Colin. 'And it doesn't sound ill at all. We try to choke it back but it will burst out and that sounds worse than ever.'

'There's one thing that comes into my mind so often,' said Mary, 'and I can scarcely ever hold in when I think of it suddenly. I keep thinking suppose Colin's face should get to look like a full moon. It isn't like one yet but he gets a tiny bit fatter every day— and suppose some morning it should look like one—what should we do!'

'Bless us all, I can see tha' has a good bit o' play actin' to do,' said Susan Sowerby. 'But tha' won't have to keep it up much longer. Mester Craven'll come home.'

'Do you think he will?' asked Colin. 'Why?'

Susan Sowerby chuckled softly.

'I suppose it 'ud nigh break thy heart if he found out before tha' told him in tha' own way,' she said. 'Tha's laid awake nights plannin'[343] it.'

'I couldn't bear any one else to tell him,' said Colin. 'I think about different ways every day, I think now I just want to run into his room.'

'That'd be a fine start for him,' said Susan Sowerby. 'I'd like to see his face, lad. I would that! He mun come back—that he mun.'

One of the things they talked of was the visit they were to make to her cottage. They planned it all. They were to drive over the moor and lunch out of doors among the heather. They would see all the twelve children and Dickon's garden and would not come back until they were tired.

Susan Sowerby got up at last to return to the house and Mrs. Medlock. It was time for Colin to be wheeled back also. But before he got into his chair he stood quite close to Susan and fixed his eyes on her with a kind of bewildered adoration and he suddenly caught hold of the fold of her blue cloak and held it fast.

'You are just what I—what I wanted,' he said. 'I wish you were my mother—as well as Dickon's!'

All at once Susan Sowerby bent down and drew him with her warm arms close against the bosom under the blue cloak—as if he had been Dickon's brother. The quick mist swept over her eyes.

'Eh! dear lad!' she said. 'Thy own mother's in this 'ere very garden, I do believe. She couldna' keep out of it. Thy father mun come back to thee—he mun!'

In the Garden

In each century since the beginning of the world wonderful things have been discovered. In the last century more amazing things were found out than in any century before. In this new century hundreds of things still more astounding will be brought to light. At first people refuse to believe that a strange new thing can be done, then they begin to hope it can be done, then they see it can be done—then it is done and all the world wonders why it was not done centuries ago. One of the new things people began to find out in the last century was that thoughts—just mere thoughts—are as powerful as electric batteries—as good for one as sunlight is, or as bad for one as poison. To let a sad thought or a bad one get into your mind is as dangerous as letting a scarlet fever germ get into your body. If you let it stay there after it has got in you may never get over it as long as you live.

So long as Mistress Mary's mind was full of disagreeable thoughts about her dislikes and sour opinions of people and her determination not to be pleased by or interested in anything, she was a yellow-faced, sickly, bored and wretched child. Circumstances, however, were very kind to her, though she was not at all aware of it. They began to push her about for her own good. When her mind gradually filled itself with robins, and moorland cottages crowded with children, with queer crabbed old gardeners and common little Yorkshire housemaids, with springtime and with secret gardens coming alive day by day, and also with a moor boy and his 'creatures,' there was no room left for the disagreeable thoughts which affected her liver and her digestion and made her yellow and tired.

So long as Colin shut himself up in his room and thought only of his fears and weakness and his detestation of people who looked at him and reflected hourly on humps and early death, he was a hysterical half-crazy little hypochondriac who knew nothing of the sunshine and the spring and also did not know that he could get well and could stand upon his feet if he tried to do it. When new beautiful thoughts began to push out the old hideous ones, life began to come back to him, his blood ran healthily through his veins and strength poured into him like a flood. His scientific experiment was quite practical and simple and there was nothing weird about it at all. Much more surprising things can happen to any one who, when a disagreeable or discouraged thought comes into his mind, just has the sense to remember in time and push it out by putting in an agreeable determinedly courageous one. Two things cannot be in one place.

'Where you tend a rose, my lad, A thistle cannot grow.'

While the secret garden was coming alive and two children were coming alive with it, there was a man wandering about certain far-away beautiful places in the Norwegian fiords and the valleys and mountains of Switzerland and he was a man who for ten years had kept his mind filled with dark and heart-broken thinking. He had not been courageous; he had never tried to put any other thoughts in the place of the dark ones. He had wandered by blue lakes and thought them; he had lain on mountain-sides with sheets of deep blue gentians blooming all about him and flower breaths filling all the air and he had thought them. A terrible sorrow had fallen upon him when he had been happy and he had let his soul fill itself with blackness and had refused obstinately to allow any rift of light to pierce through. He had forgotten and deserted his home and his duties. When he traveled about, darkness so brooded over him that the sight of him was a wrong done to other people because it was as if he poisoned the air about him with gloom. Most strangers thought he must be either half mad or a man with some hidden crime on his soul. He was a tall man with a drawn face and crooked shoulders and the name he always entered on hotel registers was, 'Archibald Craven, Misselthwaite Manor, Yorkshire, England.'

He had traveled far and wide since the day he saw Mistress Mary in his study and told her she might have her 'bit of earth.' He had been in the most beautiful places in Europe, though he had remained nowhere more than a few days. He had chosen the quietest and remotest spots. He had been on the tops of mountains whose heads were in the clouds and had looked down on other mountains when the sun rose and touched them with such light as made it seem as if the world were just being born.

But the light had never seemed to touch himself until one day when he realized that for the first time in ten years a strange thing had happened. He was in a wonderful valley in the Austrian Tyrol and he had been walking alone through such beauty as might have lifted, any man's soul out of shadow. He had walked a long way and it had not lifted his. But at last he had felt tired and had thrown himself down to rest on a carpet of moss by a stream. It was a clear little stream which ran quite merrily along on its narrow way through the luscious damp greenness. Sometimes it made a sound rather like very low laughter as it bubbled over and round stones. He saw birds come and dip their heads to drink in it and then flick their wings and fly away. It seemed like a thing alive and yet its tiny voice made the stillness seem deeper. The valley was very, very still.

As he sat gazing into the clear running of the water, Archibald Craven gradually felt his mind and body both grow quiet, as quiet as the valley itself. He wondered if he were going to sleep, but he was not. He sat and gazed at the sunlit water and his eyes began to see things growing at its edge. There was one lovely mass of blue forget-me-nots growing so close to the stream that its leaves were wet and at these he found himself looking as he remembered he had looked at such things years ago. He was actually thinking tenderly how lovely it was and what wonders of blue its hundreds of little blossoms were. He did not know that just that simple thought was slowly filling his mind—filling and filling it until other things were softly pushed aside. It was as if a sweet clear spring had begun to rise in a stagnant pool and had risen and risen until at last it swept the dark water away. But of course he did not think of this himself. He only knew that the valley seemed to grow quieter and quieter as he sat and stared at the bright delicate blueness. He did not know how long he sat there or what was happening to him, but at last he moved as if he were awakening and he got up slowly and stood on the moss carpet, drawing a long, deep, soft breath and wondering at himself. Something seemed to have been unbound and released in him, very quietly.

'What is it?' he said, almost in a whisper, and he passed his hand over his forehead. 'I almost feel as if—I were alive!'

I do not know enough about the wonderfulness of undiscovered things to be able to explain how this had happened to him. Neither does any one else yet. He did not understand at all himself—but he remembered this strange hour months afterward when he was at Misselthwaite again and he found out quite by accident that on this very day Colin had cried out as he went into the secret garden:

'I am going to live forever and ever and ever!'

The singular calmness remained with him the rest of the evening and he slept a new reposeful sleep; but it was not with him very long. He did not know that it could be kept. By the next night he had opened the doors wide to his dark thoughts and they had come trooping and rushing back. He left the valley and went on his wandering way again. But, strange as it seemed to him, there were minutes—sometimes half-hours—when, without his knowing why, the black burden seemed to lift itself again and he knew he was a living man and not a dead one. Slowly—slowly— for no reason that he knew of—he was 'coming alive' with the garden.

As the golden summer changed into the deep golden autumn he went to the Lake of Como. There he found the loveliness of a dream. He spent his days upon the crystal blueness of the lake or he walked back into the soft thick verdure of the hills and tramped until he was tired so that he might sleep. But by this time he had begun to sleep better, he knew, and his dreams had ceased to be a terror to him.

'Perhaps,' he thought, 'my body is growing stronger.'

It was growing stronger but—because of the rare peaceful hours when his thoughts were changed—his soul was slowly growing stronger, too. He began to think of Misselthwaite and wonder if he should not go home. Now and then he wondered vaguely about his boy and asked himself what he should feel when he went and stood by the carved four-posted bed again and looked down at the sharply chiseled ivory-white face while it slept and the black lashes rimmed so startlingly the close-shut eyes. He shrank from it.

One marvel of a day he had walked so far that when he returned the moon was high and full and all the world was purple shadow and silver. The stillness of lake and shore and wood was so wonderful that he did not go into the villa he lived in. He walked down to a little bowered terrace at the water's edge and sat upon a seat and breathed in all the heavenly scents of the night. He felt the strange calmness stealing over him and it grew deeper and deeper until he fell asleep.

He did not know when he fell asleep and when he began to dream; his dream was so real that he did not feel as if he were dreaming. He remembered afterward how intensely wide awake and alert he had thought he was. He thought that as he sat and breathed in the scent of the late roses and listened to the lapping of the water at his feet he heard a voice calling. It was sweet and clear and happy and far away. It seemed very far, but he heard it as distinctly as if it had been at his very side.

'Archie! Archie! Archie!' it said, and then again, sweeter and clearer than before, 'Archie! Archie!'

He thought he sprang to his feet not even startled. It was such a real voice and it seemed so natural that he should hear it.

'Lilias! Lilias!' he answered. 'Lilias! where[344] are you?'

'In the garden,' it came back like a sound from a golden flute. 'In the garden!'

And then the dream ended. But he did not awaken. He slept soundly and sweetly all through the lovely night. When he did awake at last it was brilliant morning and a servant was standing staring at him. He was an Italian servant and was accustomed, as all the servants of the villa were, to accepting without question any strange thing his foreign master might do. No one ever knew when he would go out or come in or where he would choose to sleep or if he would roam about the garden or lie in the boat on the lake all night. The man held a salver with some letters on it and he waited quietly until Mr. Craven took them. When he had gone away Mr. Craven sat a few moments holding them in his hand and looking at the lake. His strange calm was still upon him and something more—a lightness as if the cruel thing which had been done had not happened as he thought—as if something had changed. He was remembering the dream—the real—real dream.

'In the garden!' he said, wondering at himself. 'In the garden! But the door is locked and the key is buried deep.'

When he glanced at the letters a few minutes later he saw that the one lying at the top of the rest was an English letter and came from Yorkshire. It was directed in a plain woman's hand but it was not a hand he knew. He opened it, scarcely thinking of the writer, but the first words attracted his attention at once.

Dear Sir:

I am Susan Sowerby that made bold to speak to you once on the moor. It was about Miss Mary I spoke. I will make bold to speak again. Please, sir, I would come home if I was you. I think you would be glad to come and—if you will excuse me, sir—I think your lady would ask you to come if she was here.

Your obedient servant,
Susan Sowerby

Mr. Craven read the letter twice before he put it back in its envelope. He kept thinking about the dream.

'I will go back to Misselthwaite,' he said. 'Yes, I'll go at once.'

And he went through the garden to the villa and ordered Pitcher to prepare for his return to England.

In a few days he was in Yorkshire again, and on his long railroad journey he found himself thinking of his boy as he had never thought in all the ten years past. During those years he had only wished to forget him. Now, though he did not intend to think about him, memories of him constantly drifted into his mind. He remembered the black days when he had raved like a madman because the child was alive and the mother was dead. He had refused to see it, and when he had gone to look at it at last it had been such a weak wretched thing that everyone had been sure it would die in a few days. But to the surprise of those who took care of it the days passed and it lived and then everyone believed it would be a deformed and crippled creature.

He had not meant to be a bad father, but he had not felt like a father at all. He had supplied doctors and nurses and luxuries, but he had shrunk from the mere thought of the boy and had buried himself in his own misery. The first time after a year's absence he returned to Misselthwaite and the small miserable looking thing languidly and indifferently lifted to his face the great gray eyes with black lashes round them, so like and yet so horribly unlike the happy eyes he had adored, he could not bear the sight of them and turned away pale as death. After that he scarcely ever saw him except when he was asleep, and all he knew of him was that he was a confirmed invalid, with a vicious, hysterical, half-insane temper. He could only be kept from furies dangerous to himself by being given his own way in every detail.

All this was not an uplifting thing to recall, but as the train whirled him through mountain passes and golden plains the man who was 'coming alive' began to think in a new way and he thought long and steadily and deeply.

'Perhaps I have been all wrong for ten years,' he said to himself. 'Ten years is a long time. It may be too late to do anything—quite too late. What have I been thinking of!'

Of course this was the wrong Magic—to begin by saying 'too late.' Even Colin could have told him that. But he knew nothing of Magic—either black or white. This he had yet to learn. He wondered if Susan Sowerby had taken courage and written to him only because the motherly creature had realized that the boy was much worse—was fatally ill. If he had not been under the spell of the curious calmness which had taken possession of him he would have been more wretched than ever. But the calm had brought a sort of courage and hope with it. Instead of giving way to thoughts of the worst he actually found he was trying to believe in better things.

'Could it be possible that she sees that I may be able to do him good and control him?' he thought. 'I will go and see her on my way to Misselthwaite.'

But when on his way across the moor he stopped the carriage at the cottage, seven or eight children who were playing about gathered in a group and bobbing seven or eight friendly and polite curtsies told him that their mother had gone to the other side of the moor early in the morning to help a woman who had a new baby. 'Our Dickon,' they volunteered, was over at the Manor working in one of the gardens where he went several days each week.

Mr. Craven looked over the collection of sturdy little bodies and round red-cheeked faces, each one grinning in its own particular way, and he awoke to the fact that they were a healthy likable lot. He smiled at their friendly grins and took a golden sovereign from his pocket and gave it to 'our 'Lizabeth Ellen' who was the oldest.

'If you divide that into eight parts there will be half a crown for each of you,' he said.

Then amid grins and chuckles and bobbing of curtsies he drove away, leaving ecstasy and nudging elbows and little jumps of joy behind.

The drive across the wonderfulness of the moor was a soothing thing. Why did it seem to give him a sense of homecoming which he had been sure he could never feel again—that sense of the beauty of land and sky and purple bloom of distance and a warming of the heart at drawing nearer to the great old house which had held those of his blood for six hundred years? How he had driven away from it the last time, shuddering to think of its closed rooms and the boy lying in the four-posted bed with the brocaded hangings. Was it possible that perhaps he might find him changed a little for the better and that he might overcome his shrinking from him? How real that dream had been—how wonderful and clear the voice which called back to him, 'In the garden—In[345] the garden!'

'I will try to find the key,' he said. 'I will try to open the door. I must—though I don't know why.'

When he arrived at the Manor the servants who received him with the usual ceremony noticed that he looked better and that he did not go to the remote rooms where he usually lived attended by Pitcher. He went into the library and sent for Mrs. Medlock. She came to him somewhat excited and curious and flustered.

'How is Master Colin, Medlock?' he inquired.

'Well, sir,' Mrs. Medlock answered, 'he's—he's different, in a manner of speaking.'

'Worse?' he suggested.

Mrs. Medlock really was flushed.

'Well, you see, sir,' she tried to explain, 'neither Dr. Craven, nor the nurse, nor me can exactly make him out.'

'Why is that?'

'To tell the truth, sir, Master Colin might be better and he might be changing for the worse. His appetite, sir, is past understanding—and his ways—'

'Has he become more—more peculiar?' her master asked, knitting his brows anxiously.

'That's it, sir. He's growing very peculiar—when you compare him with what he used to be. He used to eat nothing and then suddenly he began to eat something enormous—and then he stopped again all at once and the meals were sent back just as they used to be. You never knew, sir, perhaps, that out of doors he never would let himself be taken. The things we've gone through to get him to go out in his chair would leave a body trembling like a leaf. He'd throw himself into such a state that Dr. Craven said he couldn't be responsible for forcing him. Well, sir, just without warning—not long after one of his worst tantrums he suddenly insisted on being taken out every day by Miss Mary and Susan Sowerby's boy Dickon that could push his chair. He took a fancy to both Miss Mary and Dickon, and Dickon brought his tame animals, and, if you'll credit it, sir, out of doors he will stay from morning until night.'

'How does he look?' was the next question.

'If he took his food natural, sir, you'd think he was putting on flesh—but we're afraid it may be a sort of bloat. He laughs sometimes in a queer way when he's alone with Miss Mary. He never used to laugh at all. Dr. Craven is coming to see you at once, if you'll allow him. He never was as puzzled in his life.'

'Where is Master Colin now?' Mr. Craven asked.

'In the garden, sir. He's always in the garden—though not a human creature is allowed to go near for fear they'll look at him.'

Mr. Craven scarcely heard her last words.

'In the garden,' he said, and after he had sent Mrs. Medlock away he stood and repeated it again and again. 'In the garden!'

He had to make an effort to bring himself back to the place he was standing in and when he felt he was on earth again he turned and went out of the room. He took his way, as Mary had done, through the door in the shrubbery and among the laurels and the fountain beds. The fountain was playing now and was encircled by beds of brilliant autumn flowers. He crossed the lawn and turned into the Long Walk by the ivied walls. He did not walk quickly, but slowly, and his eyes were on the path. He felt as if he were being drawn back to the place he had so long forsaken, and he did not know why. As he drew near to it his step became still more slow[346]. He knew where the door was even though the ivy hung thick over it—but he did not know exactly where it lay—that buried key.

So he stopped and stood still, looking about him, and almost the moment after he had paused he started and listened—asking himself if he were walking in a dream.

The ivy hung thick over the door, the key was buried under the shrubs, no human being had passed that portal for ten lonely years—and yet inside the garden there were sounds. They were the sounds of running scuffling feet seeming to chase round and round under the trees, they were strange sounds of lowered suppressed voices—exclamations and smothered joyous cries. It seemed actually like the laughter of young things, the uncontrollable laughter of children who were trying not to be heard but who in a moment or so—as their excitement mounted—would burst forth. What in heaven's name was he dreaming of—what in heaven's name did he hear? Was he losing his reason and thinking he heard things which were not for human ears? Was it that the far clear voice had meant?

And then the moment came, the uncontrollable moment when the sounds forgot to hush themselves. The feet ran faster and faster—they were nearing the garden door—there was quick strong young breathing and a wild outbreak of laughing shows which could not be contained—and the door in the wall was flung wide open, the sheet of ivy swinging back, and a boy burst through it at full speed and, without seeing the outsider, dashed almost into his arms.

Mr. Craven had extended them just in time to save him from falling as a result of his unseeing dash against him, and when he held him away to look at him in amazement at his being there he truly gasped for breath.

He was a tall boy and a handsome one. He was glowing with life and his running had sent splendid colour leaping to his face. He threw the thick hair back from his forehead and lifted a pair of strange gray eyes—eyes full of boyish laughter and rimmed with black lashes like a fringe. It was the eyes which made Mr. Craven gasp for breath.

'Who—What? Who!' he stammered.

This was not what Colin had expected—this was not what he had planned. He had never thought of such a meeting. And yet to come dashing out—winning a race—perhaps it was even better. He drew himself up to his very tallest. Mary, who had been running with him and had dashed through the door too, believed that he managed to make himself look taller than he had ever looked before—inches taller.

'Father,' he said, 'I'm Colin. You can't believe it. I scarcely can myself. I'm Colin.'

Like Mrs. Medlock, he did not understand what his father meant when he said hurriedly:

'In the garden! In the garden!'

'Yes,' hurried on Colin. 'It was the garden that did it—and Mary and Dickon and the creatures—and the Magic. No one knows. We kept it to tell you when you came. I'm well, I can beat Mary in a race. I'm going to be an athlete.'

He said it all so like a healthy boy—his face flushed, his words tumbling over each other in his eagerness—that Mr. Craven's soul shook with unbelieving joy.

Colin put out his hand and laid it on his father's arm.

'Aren't you glad, Father?' he ended. 'Aren't you glad? I'm going to live forever and ever and ever!'

Mr. Craven put his hands on both the boy's shoulders and held him still. He knew he dared not even try to speak for a moment.

'Take me into the garden, my boy,' he said at last. 'And tell me all about it.'

And so they led him in.

The place was a wilderness of autumn gold and purple and violet blue and flaming scarlet and on every side were sheaves of late lilies standing together—lilies which were white or white and ruby. He remembered well when the first of them had been planted that just at this season of the year their late glories should reveal themselves. Late roses climbed and hung and clustered and the sunshine deepening the hue of the yellowing trees made one feel that one stood in an embowered temple of gold. The newcomer stood silent just as the children had done when they came into its grayness. He looked round and round.

'I thought it would be dead,' he said.

'Mary thought so at first,' said Colin. 'But it came alive.'

Then they sat down under their tree—all but Colin, who wanted to stand while he told the story.

It was the strangest thing he had ever heard, Archibald Craven thought, as it was poured forth in headlong boy fashion. Mystery and Magic and wild creatures, the weird midnight meeting—the coming of the spring—the passion of insulted pride which had dragged the young Rajah to his feet to defy old Ben Weatherstaff to his face. The odd companionship, the play acting, the great secret so carefully kept. The listener laughed until tears came into his eyes and sometimes tears came into his eyes when he was not laughing. The Athlete, the Lecturer, the Scientific Discoverer was a laughable, lovable, healthy young human thing.

'Now,' he said at the end of the story, 'it need not be a secret any more. I dare say it will frighten them nearly into fits when they see me—but I am never going to get into the chair again. I shall walk back with you, Father—to the house.'

Ben Weatherstaff's duties rarely took him away from the

gardens, but on this occasion he made an excuse to carry some vegetables to the kitchen and being invited into the servant's hall by Mrs. Medlock to drink a glass of beer he was on the spot—as he had hoped to be—when the most dramatic event Misselthwaite Manor had seen during the present generation actually took place.

One of the windows looking upon the courtyard gave also a glimpse of the lawn. Mrs. Medlock, knowing Ben had come from the gardens, hoped that he might have caught sight of his master and even by chance of his meeting with Master Colin.

'Did you see either of them, Weatherstaff?' she asked.

Ben took his beer-mug from his mouth and wiped his lips with the back of his hand.

'Aye, that I did,' he answered with a shrewdly significant air.

'Both of them?' suggested Mrs. Medlock.

'Both of 'em,' returned Ben Weatherstaff. 'Thank ye kindly, ma'am, I could sup up another mug of it.'

'Together?' said Mrs. Medlock, hastily overfilling his beer-mug in her excitement.

'Together, ma'am,' and Ben gulped down half of his new mug at one gulp.

'Where was Master Colin? How did he look? What did they say to each other?'

'I didna'[347] hear that,' said Ben, 'along o' only bein' on th' stepladder lookin' over th' wall. But I'll tell thee this. There's been things goin' on outside as you house people knows nowt about. An' what tha'll find out tha'll find out soon.'

And it was not two minutes before he swallowed the last of his beer and waved his mug solemnly toward the window which took in through the shrubbery a piece of the lawn.

'Look there,' he said, 'if tha's curious. Look what's comin' across th' grass.'

When Mrs. Medlock looked she threw up her hands and gave a little shriek and every man and woman servant within hearing bolted across the servants' hall and stood looking through the window with their eyes almost starting out of their heads.

Across the lawn came the Master of Misselthwaite and he looked as many of them had never seen him. And by his side with his head up in the air and his eyes full of laughter walked as strongly and steadily as any boy in Yorkshire—Master Colin!

THE END

Notes

1	someone	29	you are	57	don't
2	Someone	30	think	58	scarcely
3	anyone	31	with	59	Don't
4	Everyone	32	growing	60	you will
5	She's	33	fairly	61	have
6	madam	34	humming	62	know
7	there are	35	singing	63	…come and eat
8	nearly	36	anything	64	downstairs
9	that've	37	'Can't	65	go
10	But	38	yourself	66	blooming
11	of	39	saying	67	the other
12	Did	40	being	68	today
13	lunch basket	41	were	69	courting
14	tha've	42	coming	70	forward
15	And	43	calling	71	known
16	brought	44	nothing	72	most curious
17	the	45	them	73	pecking
18	one	46	going	74	looking
19	you	47	came	75	talking
20	yes	48	morning	76	meddling
21	your	49	crept	77	planting
22	enough	50	carefully	78	himself
23	waiting	51	yellow	79	knowing
24	uphill	52	You	80	Are
25	like	53	crying	81	myself
26	upstairs	54	yourself	82	making
27	Do	55	wandering	83	years
28	you	56	herself	84	giving

85 playing
86 run
87 shout
88 look
89 bushier
90 Is
91 thinking
92 wuthering
93 attend
94 He
95 she
96 reading
97 sitting
98 wailing
99 An'
100 There
101 shining
102 something
103 spelling
104 You are
105 learning
106 haven't
107 most often
108 pretending
109 No
110 flowering
111 fluttering
112 soaring
113 miles

114 …hard-working
115 liking
116 crossing
117 yourself
118 ,
119 vixen
120 stand
121 stirring
122 warming
123 finding
124 To
125 It
126 getting
127 scampering
128 rising
129 piping
130 baking
131 They
132 seeming
133 driving
134 peddling
135 Elizabeth
136 skipping
137 fumbling
138 most sensible
139 Tha'
140 perhaps
141 shape
142 watching

143 tomorrow
144 pudding
145 Mother
146 help
147 digging
148 If
149 …These were
150 arithmetic
151 That's
152 want
153 pulling
154 printing
155 …prettiest and
easy-to-grow ones
because…
156 Then
157 forgetting
158 walking
159 listening
160 showing
161 flirting
162 beginning
163 …I think
164 reddening
165 polishing
166 telling
167 Look
168 potatoes
169 sweet-smelling

338 worried
339 I
340 swelling
341 believing
342 were
343 planning
344 Where
345 in
346 slower
347 did not

秘密花園

Preface to the Chinese Translation
中文譯本序

弗朗西絲‧霍奇森‧伯內特一生寫過許多作品，其中最著名的是三部小說：《小爵士》、《小公主》和《秘密花園》。《秘密花園》出版於 1909 年，評論家認為這可能是她最好、最有生命力的作品。

　　無論在翻譯過程中，還是全部譯完之後，這部作品給我的最大體驗就是——感人。故事情節感人，書中的人物也感人。作者用許多感人的細節，敘述了瑪麗、柯林、克拉文先生乃至老花匠本‧威瑟斯塔夫的轉變過程。起初，誠如評論家所說，這些人或多或少都不太正常，這種不正常不但表現在生理上（瑪麗面黃肌瘦，克拉文被當成駝子，柯林被誤認為瘸子），更表現在心理上。在他們眼裏，生活就像瑪麗剛剛踏進秘密花園時所看見的一樣，全是灰濛濛的。但是，狄肯，這個家有 12 個兄弟姐妹、全家 14 人擠住在 4 個小房間裏的男孩，卻從花園裏幾乎枯死的樹枝裏看見了一絲綠色，從樹根下感覺到了生命的萌動。於是，在保密狀態下（因為克拉文先生下過命令，不讓任何人進這個花園），狄肯和瑪麗開始了一場拯救運動；隨着春天的來臨，在陽光雨露的滋潤下，瀕於死亡的花園果然恢復了生機，而瑪麗那顆幼小心靈也像花園一樣得到了復甦。當她用自己的轉變再去影響柯林的時候，我們看到了兩個同樣倔強的孩子之間的衝撞，而衝撞之後則是柯林的慢慢"覺醒"和振奮。說到這裏，我們不得不提一下書中另一個人物，她就是狄肯的媽媽，一個生育了 12 個兒女的約克郡婦女——蘇珊・索爾比太太。可以説，這是作者筆下一個理想化了的人物。美麗、善良，具有人類所有母親的一切良好品質。當得知瑪麗身體虛弱，有厭食症時，她從微薄的收入中拿出錢來，買了一根跳繩，讓給瑪麗做傭人的女兒瑪莎教她到室外去鍛煉。當聽説柯林既厭世，又有嚴重的大少爺脾氣，動不動就發脾氣時，她又通過女管家梅洛太太之口説，"地球像一個橙……這個橙不屬於任何人。……每個人都只能擁有屬於他的一個角落。要想擁有整個橙——連皮帶肉——是荒唐的。要是你想這樣做，很可能連種子都得不到，而種子是很苦的，根本不能吃。"多麼富有哲理，多像是個循循善誘的老師。譯到這裏的時候，我產生了這樣的感覺：這不應該是一部純粹的兒童小説，它的讀者也應該包括為人父母的家長。最後，我要用"亞馬遜網上書店"一個讀者的話來結束我這篇短文："他們對秘密花園的拜訪，事實上會改變他們所有人的生活，而對於造成這些改變的方式，即使最挑剔的讀者也會深受感動。難怪這是一部如此令人愛不釋手的經典著作。"

張建平

第一章
一個也沒剩下

當瑪麗‧倫諾斯被送到米塞爾斯威特莊園跟她姑丈一起生活的時候，人人都說從沒見過長得這麼不討人喜歡的孩子。這倒也是事實。她有一張瘦削的小臉，一個瘦弱的身體，一頭稀疏的淺色頭髮，一臉的苦相。頭髮是黃的，臉色也是黃的，因為她生在印度，一年到頭不是患這個病就是患那個病。她爸爸在英國政府部門任職，一天到晚忙個不停，自己也總是生病；她媽媽是個大美人，一心只顧着參加各種聚會，和一些俊男美女尋歡作樂。夫人本來就沒想要個女孩子，瑪麗一出世，她就把孩子給了一個印度保姆托管，並讓保姆明白，她若要討夫人喜歡，就要盡可能別讓她看見這個孩子。所以，當瑪麗是個愛生病、愛哭鬧、相貌醜陋的嬰兒時，總是見不到媽媽；當她成了個愛生病、愛哭鬧、蹣跚學步的小孩時，同樣總是見不到媽媽。她看來看去只看見保姆和其他當地傭人黑幽幽的臉，傭人們事事順從她，她要怎麼樣就怎麼樣，因為如果讓她的哭鬧聲驚擾了夫人，夫人就會生氣，這麼一來，瑪麗剛滿六歲時，就已經成了最專橫、最自私的小霸王。請了一位年輕的英國家庭女教師前來教她讀書寫字，女教師很不喜歡瑪麗，不到三個月就辭職了，其他女教師來填補空缺，總是比第一個走得更快。因此，如果瑪麗不是真心想要學會讀書識字的話，她一輩子連字母都學不會。

她九歲左右那年，一個酷熱的早晨，她醒來時覺得非常惱火，當她看見站在身邊的傭人不是原來的保姆時，怒火就更大了。

"你來做甚麼？"她對這個陌生的女人說。"我不想你留在這裏。幫我把保姆叫來。"

這女人看來很驚慌，但她只是結結巴巴地說，保姆來不了了。瑪麗耍性子，對着女人又打又踢，女人看來更加驚慌，連續不停地說保姆不可能來伺候小姐了。

這個早晨家裏的氣氛有點神秘。一切都沒照常規進行，有數個當地的傭人好像失蹤了，而瑪麗看見的那數個都偷偷摸摸或匆匆忙忙地走來走去，一個個臉色蒼白、神情驚慌。但是誰也不想告訴她發生了甚麼事，她的保姆也沒來。上午都快過去了，始終沒人來理她，她忍不住了，走到了花園裏，一個人在靠近遊廊的一棵樹下玩了起來。她假裝在做一個花圃，把大株的紅色木槿花插進小堆的泥土裏，怒火越來越大，不停地嘀咕着等塞伊蒂回來後她要說的事和罵她的話。

"豬！豬！豬的女兒！"她說，因為罵一個當地人是豬，對他們是最大的污辱。

她咬着牙齒把這句話說了一遍又一遍，這時她聽見她的媽媽和另一個人來到外面遊廊裏。和她在一起的是個金髮白膚的年輕男人，他們站在那裏説話，聲音很低、很怪。瑪麗認識這個年輕男人，他看來像個男孩子。她聽説他是個很年輕的軍官，剛從英國來。瑪麗盯着他看，但她看得更多的是她的媽媽。每當她有機會看見媽媽的時候，就總是盯着她看，因為夫人——瑪麗就愛這麼叫她——長得高挑苗條，十分美麗，衣服也非常漂亮。她的頭髮像鬈曲的絲綢，她有一個小巧的鼻子，好像鄙視一切，她有一雙會笑的大眼睛。她所有的衣服都是薄如蟬翼、隨風飄曳，瑪麗説它們是"全套了花邊"的。今天早晨，它們的花邊看來比任何時候都多，但是她的眼睛裏一點笑意都沒有。這雙大眼睛裏充滿恐懼，抬起來帶着懇求的神色看着金髮白膚的年輕軍官的臉。

"情況真的這麼壞嗎？哦，是真的嗎？"瑪麗聽見她説。

"可怕極了，"年輕男人回答時聲音都在發抖。"可怕極了，倫諾斯太太。你應該在兩個星期前就到山裏去。"

夫人絞着雙手。

"哦，我知道應該去！"她哭道。"我留下來只是為了去赴那個倒霉的晚宴。我多傻啊！"

就在這時，傭人們住的地方傳來一聲驚天動地的慘叫，夫人一下子抓住年輕男人的手臂，瑪麗站在那裏渾身直哆嗦。叫聲越來越淒厲。

"甚麼事？甚麼事？"倫諾斯夫人呼吸急促地問道。

"有個人死了，"年輕軍官答道。"你沒聽説你的傭人之中已經爆發瘟疫？"

"我不知道！"夫人哭道。"跟我來！跟我來！"她轉身奔進屋裏去。

後來，可怕的事情發生了，瑪麗終於明白了早晨的秘密。霍亂以最致命的方式爆發，人們像蒼蠅似的死去。保姆在夜間被感染上，剛才她死了，所以傭人們在小屋裏痛哭。第二天沒到，又有三個傭人死了，其他傭人在驚恐中逃走。到處都是恐懼，所有的平房裏都有垂死的人。

第二天，家裏一片混亂，瑪麗躲進了兒童室裏，所有人都忘記了她。沒有人想到她，沒有人需要她，發生了許多怪事她一無所知。一連數小時裏，瑪麗不是哭就是睡。她只知道有人病了，她聽到了神秘而可怕的聲音。有一次她悄悄走到餐廳裏，發現那裏空蕩蕩的，桌上放着吃了一半的飯菜，椅和盤子的樣子看來是用餐的人由於某種原因，突然站起來時將它們匆匆推開的。瑪麗吃了一些水果和餅乾，因為口渴，她又喝了幾乎滿滿一杯酒。酒是甜的，她不知道酒性有多強。很快她就覺得暈乎乎的，她回到兒童室裏，又把自己關在裏面，小屋裏的哭聲和匆匆忙忙的腳步聲令她非常害怕。酒力使她昏昏欲睡，她幾乎睜不開眼睛，就躺在自己的牀上，很長時間甚麼都不知道。

在她呼呼大睡的這段時間裏，發生了很多事情，但是慘叫聲和東西在平房裏搬進搬出的聲音都未能把她吵醒。

她醒來時，躺在牀上，眼睛盯着牆壁。屋裏安靜極了。在她的記憶裏，以前家裏從來沒有這麼安靜。她聽不見說話聲，也聽不見腳步聲，她疑惑，不知道人們是否已經從霍亂中康復，瘟疫是否已經過去。她還奇怪，現在她的保姆死了，將由誰來照料她呢。應該有個新的保姆，也許她還會聽到一些新的故事。那些舊的故事瑪麗都聽厭了。她沒有因為保姆死了而哭。她不是個多情的孩子，從來不太關心任何人。由於霍亂而產生的喧鬧、忙亂和慘叫使她害怕，她非常生氣，因為好像沒有人記得她還活着。人人都驚慌失措，誰也顧不得這個沒人喜歡的小女孩了。當霍亂襲來時，所有的人似乎都只顧着自己，別的甚麼都不記得了。但是如果所有的人都康復了的話，肯定會有人記起她並來照料她的。

但是沒有人來，當她躺在牀上等待時，屋裏好像越來越安靜了。她聽見地蓆上有窸窸窣窣的聲音，朝下一看，只見一條小蛇正在爬過來，一雙珠子似的眼睛看着她。她並不害怕，因為這是一條無毒的小蛇，不會傷害她，牠似乎急於逃出這個房間。她看着牠從門底下鑽了出去。

"多奇怪，多安靜啊，"她說。"聽聲音好像屋裏只有我和這條蛇。"

幾乎緊接着，她聽見院子裏傳來腳步聲，隨後腳步聲到了遊廊裏。那是男人的腳步聲，數個男人進了屋，低聲說着話。沒有人來接他們或跟他們說話，他們好像打開了一扇扇門，朝房間裏看。

"多荒涼啊！"她聽見一個聲音說。"那個漂亮的，漂亮的女人！我想那個孩子也挺漂亮的。我聽說有個孩子，雖然從來沒人見過她。"

數分鐘之後，他們打開了兒童室的門，瑪麗正站在兒童室中央。她看來是個醜陋的、愛發脾氣的小女孩，她正在皺眉頭，因為她肚子餓了，而且這樣遭人忽視，很沒面子。第一個進來的男人是個身材高大的軍官，她曾見過他跟她爸爸說話。他一臉的倦容和困惑，但是當他看見瑪麗時大吃一驚，幾乎要往後一跳。

"巴尼！"他叫道。"這裏有個小孩！一個孤零零的小孩！在這樣的地方！天哪，她是誰！"

"我是瑪麗‧倫諾斯，"小女孩說，直挺挺地站着。她認為這個人把她爸爸的平房說成"這樣的地方！"很粗魯。"當所有人都患了霍亂的時候，我睡着了，我剛剛醒來。為甚麼一個人也不來？"

"這就是那個誰也沒見過的孩子！"那個人叫道，轉向他的同伴。"她被徹底忘掉了！"

"我為甚麼被忘掉呢？"瑪麗跺着腳說。"為甚麼一個人也不來？"

那個叫巴尼的年輕人很傷心地看着她。瑪麗甚至覺得自己看見他在眨眼睛，要將眼淚眨掉。

"可憐的小女孩！"他說。"不會有人來了，這裏一個人也沒剩下。"

就是以這種奇怪而突然的方式，瑪麗發現自己的爸爸和媽媽都沒有了；他們在夜裏死去並被拖走了，唯一數個活下來的傭人也都盡快離開這間屋，他們中甚至沒有一個想起家裏還有個小姐。所以這裏才這麼安靜。的確，這座平房裏除了她自己和那條窸窣爬行的小蛇外，一個人也沒有了。

第二章

倔強的瑪麗

瑪麗喜歡在遠處看她媽媽，她認為媽媽很漂亮，但是，由於她不太認識她，所以，要她愛媽媽，媽媽去世之後要她十分懷念媽媽，這簡直是不可能的。事實上，她根本就不懷念她，由於她是個自私的孩子，還是像從前一樣，一心只想着自己。如果她年紀再大一點的話，看見自己被孤零零地留在世界上，無疑是會十分擔心的。但是她很年幼，向來要由人來照顧，所以還以為永遠都會這樣呢。她所考慮的是，她想知道自己是不是會到好家庭去，像她原來的保姆和其他當地傭人一樣對她客氣，讓她為所欲為。

一開始她被送到一個英國牧師的家裏，她知道她不會在那裏留下去。她也不想留下去。這個英國牧師很窮，他有五個幾乎差不多年齡的孩子，他們穿着破衣爛衫，老是吵架，搶奪玩具。瑪麗討厭他們骯髒的平房，跟他們格格不入，剛過了一兩天就沒人願意跟她玩了。第二天他們給她起了個外號，使她勃然大怒。

起初是由巴茲爾想到的。巴茲爾是個小男孩，有一雙不安份的藍眼睛，一個翹鼻，瑪麗恨他。當時她正一個人在一棵樹下玩耍，就像霍亂襲來那天她一個人玩耍一樣。她做了許多土堆和小徑，用來造一個花園，巴茲爾走了過來，站在一邊看她玩。不久他產生了濃厚的興趣，突然提出了一個建議。

"你為甚麼不在那裏堆一堆石頭，把它當成假山呢？"他說。"就在中間那裏，"他身體湊過去，指給她看。

"滾開！"瑪麗叫道。"我不跟男孩子玩。滾開！"

一時間巴茲爾十分惱火，隨後他就作弄她。他經常作弄他的姊姊妹妹。他圍着她跳來跳去，朝她做鬼臉，又唱又笑。

> 瑪麗，瑪麗，真倔強，
>> 你這花園成個甚麼樣？
> 銀鐘花和海扇殼，
>> 還有萬壽菊排成一行。

他不停地唱着，直到其他的孩子都聽見，並且也哈哈大笑；瑪麗越惱火，他們越是有興致地唱"瑪麗，瑪麗，真倔強"；從那以後，在瑪麗住在他們家的日子裏，他們彼此間說起瑪麗或跟瑪麗說話時，就叫她"倔強瑪麗"。

"到這個週末，"巴茲爾對她說，"你就要被送到家裏去了。我們很高興。"

"我也很高興，"瑪麗回答說。"我的家在哪裏呢？"

"她不知道家在哪裏！"巴茲爾以七歲孩子的譏諷口氣說，"當然是在英國了。我們的祖母住在那裏，我們的姐姐梅布爾去年被送到祖母那裏去了。你不會到你祖母那裏去。你沒有祖母。你要到你姑丈那裏去。他的名字叫阿奇博爾德‧克拉文。"

"我根本不認識他，"瑪麗惡聲惡氣地說。

"我知道你不認識，"巴茲爾回答說。"你甚麼都不知道。女孩子就這副德性。我聽爸爸媽媽提過他。他住在鄉下一座巨大、荒蕪的舊宅裏，沒有人接近他。他脾氣很壞，不讓人接近他，他不叫他們，他們就不准到他跟前去。他是個駝子。他的樣子可怕極了。"

"我不相信你，"瑪麗說；她轉過身去，把手指塞進耳朵裏，因為她再也不想聽他說下去了。

但是她後來把這件事考慮了很久；當那天晚上哥羅福太太對她說，過兩三天就要送她乘船去英國，到住在米塞爾斯威特莊園，即她姑丈阿奇博爾德‧克拉文先生的家時，她臉上一點表情都沒有，倔強地顯示她對此毫無興趣，弄得別人不知道該拿她怎麼辦。他們試着對她好，但是當哥羅福太太想要吻她時，她只是把臉轉開去，當哥羅福先生拍拍她肩膀時，她僵硬地站着，毫無反應。

"她是個相貌平庸的孩子，"事後哥羅福太太表示惋惜地說。"而她的媽媽卻是個大美人。舉止也可愛，像瑪麗這樣討人厭的孩子我從沒見過。孩子們叫她'倔強瑪麗'，雖然孩子們這樣做很淘氣，但是你不能不承認他們說得有道理。"

"如果她媽媽常帶着那張漂亮臉蛋和可愛舉止到兒童室去看她，瑪麗也許就會學到一點她可愛的舉止。說起來真令人傷心，這個漂亮的人如今就這麼走了，要知道，許多人完全就不知道她有個孩子呢。"

"我肯定她幾乎從來不去探望這孩子，"哥羅福太太嘆息道。"保姆死了之後，沒有一個人想到過這個小女孩。想想吧，傭人們紛紛逃離，把她孤零零地扔在那座荒蕪的平房裏。麥克格魯上校説他打開門看見她一個人站在房間中央時，簡直大吃一驚。"

瑪麗在一位軍官妻子的照顧下長途跋涉去英國，那位軍官妻子是要把她的孩子們送到寄宿學校去。她一心只顧着自己的孩子，當阿奇博爾德‧克拉文先生派一個女人到倫敦來接瑪麗時，軍官妻子很高興把瑪麗交給了她。這個女人是米塞爾斯威特莊園的管家，叫梅洛太太，是個健壯的女人，她有着通紅的臉頰，敏鋭的黑眼睛。她穿一件很紫的衣服，一件黑色的絲披風，綴着烏黑的流蘇，還戴着一頂黑帽，上面插着紫色天鵝絨花。她的頭一動，那朵花就隨着震動。瑪麗一點也不喜歡她，但是，考慮到她從來不喜歡任何人，所以這件事也沒甚麼好奇怪的；再説，梅洛太太也沒把她當一回事。

"哎呀！她真是個不起眼的小孩！"她説，"我們聽説她媽媽是個大美人。她沒有把她的美貌傳給瑪麗，是嗎，夫人？"

"她長大後也許會變漂亮的，"軍官妻子溫和地説。"如果她的臉色不這麼黃，表情開朗一點……她的五官挺不錯的。女大十八變呢。"

"她是要好好變變，"梅洛太太説。"如果你問我的話，那我要告訴你，在米塞爾斯威特可沒甚麼能令孩子們變好的！"

她們住在一間私人酒店裏，瑪麗站在離他們較遠的窗前，她們以為她沒有在聽她們説話。她正在看着窗外來往的公共汽車、馬車和人群，但是她們的話她聽得一清二楚。她對她姑丈和他住的那個地方充滿了好奇。那是個甚麼樣的地方，他會是個甚麼樣的人呢？駝背是怎麼一回事呢？她從沒見到過駝子。也許印度沒有駝子。

由於是住在別人家裏，又沒有保姆照顧她，她開始感到孤單，腦裏出現了一些奇怪想法，這在她來説是未曾試過的。她開始疑惑，即使在她爸爸媽媽活着的時候，她好像也從來不屬於任何人，這是怎麼一回事呢。別的孩子好像屬於他們的爸爸媽媽，而她這個小女孩似乎從來就不真正屬於任何人。她有保姆，而且不愁吃穿，但是從來沒人注意過她。她不知道這是因為她是個討人厭的孩子；但是，當然了，那時候她的確不知道她討人厭。她常常認為別的孩子討人厭，卻不知道她自己也是這樣。

她認為梅洛太太是她見過的人當中最令人討厭的，她有一張平常的、通紅的臉，戴着普通、漂亮的帽。第二天她們踏上去約克郡的旅程，在進車站上火車的路上，瑪麗把頭抬得高高的，盡量跟梅洛太太保持距離，因為她不想令人認為自己是她的孩子。想到別人認為她是梅洛太太的小孩，她會生氣的。

但是梅洛太太根本沒把她和她的想法放在心上。她是那種"不能容忍小孩子胡鬧"的女人。至少，如果別人問她的話，她是會這麼説的。她姐姐的女兒正要結婚，在這種時候，她根本不想去倫敦，但是她在米塞爾斯威特莊園當管家，位置舒適，報酬高，她要保住這個位置的唯一辦法就是，阿奇博爾德·克拉文先生要她做甚麼，她必須立即照辦。她甚至從來不敢問一句為甚麼。

「倫諾斯上尉和他妻子患霍亂死了，」克拉文先生曾經以他簡捷、冷漠的口氣對她説。「倫諾斯上尉是我妻子的弟弟，我是他們孩子的監護人。這個孩子要帶到這裏來。你必須親自到倫敦去接她。」

於是她就收拾好簡單的行李上路了。

瑪麗坐在火車車廂她自己的角落裏，看來相貌平庸，滿臉悲色。她沒有書讀，沒有東西可看，只好把兩隻戴着黑手套的細小的手交叉抱在胸前，她的一身黑衣服使她的臉色更黃，鬆軟的淺色頭髮從黑色縐布帽裏垂下來。

「我一輩子沒見過看來比她更任性的小孩，」梅洛太太看着瑪麗，暗自思忖。她從沒見過一個孩子這麼一動不動地坐着，甚麼也不做；最後她看厭了，開始用尖刻生硬的聲音説起話來。

「看來我不妨跟你説説你要去的那個地方，」她説。「你了解你的姑丈嗎？」

「不，」瑪麗説。

「從沒聽你爸爸媽媽提起過他？」

「沒有，」瑪麗説着皺起了眉頭。因為她想到她的爸爸媽媽從來沒跟她説過甚麼具體的事情。他們當然從來沒告訴她甚麼事情。

「哼，」梅洛太太嘀咕了一聲，看着她奇怪的、反應冷淡的小臉。她一時沒再説甚麼話，過了一會才又説起話來。

「我看有些事情要告訴你——讓你有點準備。你要去的是一個怪地方。」

瑪麗甚麼也沒説，看着她這種無動於衷的樣子，梅洛太太覺得很尷尬，但是，她吸了一口氣後，繼續往下説。

"不但是因為那是個令人憂傷的大宅，而且克拉文先生以他的方式為此感到驕傲——這也夠令人憂傷的。這間大宅有六百年歷史，它座落在曠野邊緣，屋裏有將近一百個房間，大多數都空關着並且上了鎖。那裏有畫像，上等的老傢具，以及其他上了年紀的東西，周圍有一個大林苑，有花園，樹木——有些樹的樹枝拖曳到地上。"她頓了一下，又吸了一口氣。"但是別的就沒甚麼了，"她的話戛然而止。

瑪麗剛才不由自主地聽了起來。這一切跟印度太不一樣了，任何新鮮的東西對她都很有吸引力。但是她不想露出自己感興趣的樣子。這也是她令人遺憾、不討人喜歡的地方之一。所以她一動不動地坐着。

"喔，"梅洛太太説，"你覺得怎麼樣？"

"沒怎麼樣，"她回答説。"這種地方我一點都不了解。"

這句話讓梅洛太太微微一笑。

"哦！"她説，"但是你像個老太太。你不在意吧？"

"不管我在意與否都沒關係，"瑪麗説。

"你這句話説得太對了，"梅洛太太説。"是沒關係。我不知道為甚麼要讓你住在米塞爾斯威特莊園，除非是因為這是最方便的辦法。他是不會為你費心的，這一點毫無疑問，他從來不為任何人費心。"

她停了下來，似乎正好想起了甚麼事情。

"他是駝子，"她説。"這使他感到自卑。年輕的時候，雖然有錢，有這麼大的地方，他卻總是悶悶不樂，直到結婚以後才有了改變。"

儘管瑪麗想要顯得滿不在乎的樣子，卻還是把眼睛轉向了梅洛太太。她從沒想到這駝背是結了婚的，她稍微感到一點驚訝。梅洛太太看出了這一點，她本來就是個健談的女人，這一來說得更有興致了。好歹這是一種消磨時間的辦法。

"他的妻子可愛、美麗，為了找到她要的一棵草，他願意走遍世界。誰也沒有想到她會嫁給他，但她硬是這麼做了，有人說她是看中了他的錢。但她不是——她不是看中他的錢，"梅洛太太說得很堅決。"她死的時候——"

瑪麗禁不住身體往上跳了一下。

"哦！她死了嗎！"她情不自禁地叫道。她剛剛想起了法國的佩羅童話《利凱小簇》。說的是一個可憐的駝子和一個美麗公主的故事，這使她突然為克拉文先生感到難過起來。

"是的，她死了，"梅洛太太回答說。"這使他比原來更古怪了。他對誰都不關心。他不想見人。大部份日子他都不住在家裏，即使住在米塞爾斯威特時，他也是把自己關在西廂房裏，除了匹契爾之外誰也不能去見他。匹契爾是個老伯伯，克拉文先生小時候匹契爾就開始照顧他，所以知道他的脾氣和習慣。"

這些聽起來像書裏寫的一樣，瑪麗並不高興。一座有一百個房間的大屋，幾乎全都空關着，上了鎖——一座在曠野邊緣的大屋——不管曠野是甚麼玩意——聽起來怪可怕的。一個把自己關起來的駝背男人，聽起來也很可怕！她緊閉着嘴巴凝視窗外，灰濛濛的雨成斜線傾瀉下來，拍打着窗玻璃，順着窗玻璃往下流淌，這是很自然的景象。如果漂亮的姑母還活着的話，她會讓生活變得令人愉快，有點像她自己的媽媽，像她那樣穿着"全套花邊"的衣裙，進進出出，參加各種聚會。但是她永遠不在了。

"你別指望見他，因為你十有八九見不到他，"梅洛太太説。"你也別指望那裏會有人跟你説話。你只好自己一個人玩，自己照顧自己。會有人告訴你甚麼房間你可以進去，甚麼房間不能進去。那裏有很多花園。但是你進了那座屋後，不能走來走去，東摸西摸。克拉文先生不允許這樣做。"

"我才不想東摸西摸呢，"小瑪麗暴躁地説；就像她突然為克拉文先生感到難過一樣，她又突然不為他感到難過了，並且認為他太不可愛，有那麼多倒霉的事情落到他的頭上也是正常的事。

她把臉轉向火車車廂雨水流淌的窗玻璃上，凝視着灰濛濛的暴雨，那雨看起來好像下不停似的。她一動不動地看了很久，那灰色在她眼前越來越深，她睡着了。

第三章

穿越曠野

她睡了很長時間，醒來時只見梅洛太太已經在某個站頭買好了午飯，她們吃了雞，冷肉和牛油麵包，還喝了一點熱茶。雨似乎下得更急，車站裏所有人都穿着濕漉漉、閃閃亮的雨衣。列車員打開了車廂裏的燈，梅洛太太喝着茶，吃着雞肉、牛肉，興致非常高。她吃了很多，然後就呼呼入睡，瑪麗坐在那裏，看着她，看着她滑到一邊去的漂亮的帽，到後來，她自己在車廂角落裏又睡着了，雨水拍打着窗，就像催眠曲一樣。等她再次醒來時，天已黑了。火車停在一個站上，梅洛太太在搖她。

"你睡得很舒服！"她說。"該睜開眼睛了！我們到了斯威特站，我們還要坐馬車走很長的路呢。"

瑪麗費力地睜開惺忪睡眼，梅洛太太忙着收拾行李包裹，她卻習慣性地站在一旁等着。在印度，僕人工作天經地義，主人只需要在一旁等待就可以了。

這是一個小站，好像只有她們兩個下車。站長聲音粗啞、態度和藹地跟梅洛太太說話，發音有明顯的地方口音，聽起來怪怪的，後來瑪麗才知道這是約克話。

"看起來是回來了，"他說。"還帶來個小女孩。"

"是啊，就是這個女孩，"梅洛太太答道，說的也是約克話，並回過頭去看瑪麗。"你夫人好嗎？"

"挺好的。馬車在外面等着你們呢。"

一輛四輪馬車停在小站台外側的大路上。瑪麗看見這是一輛漂亮馬車，扶她上車的男僕樣子也挺好看。他的長雨衣和帽上的防雨套閃閃發亮，像任何東西（包括魁梧的站長）一樣滴着雨水。

他關上車門，登上駕駛座，坐在車夫旁邊，隨後車便走起來了，小女孩發現自己坐在一個有座墊的角落裏，挺舒服的，但是她不想再睡覺。她坐在那裏，看着窗外，看見路上的一些東西，心裏挺好奇，她正是在這條路上前往梅洛太太跟她說過的那個怪地方。她根本不是個膽怯的孩子，她並沒真正感到害怕，但是對於一座有着一百個房間，幾乎全都空關着的屋——一座座落在曠野邊緣的屋會發生甚麼樣的事情，她感到心裏沒底。

"甚麼叫曠野？"她突然問梅洛太太。

"再過大約十分鐘，朝窗外面看，你就會看見了，"梅洛太太回答說。"我們要穿越五英里米塞爾曠野，才能到達莊園。這是個天色很暗的夜晚，所以你看不見多少，但是總能看見一些。"

瑪麗沒有再問甚麼，而是坐在角落裏，在黑暗中等待，眼睛盯在窗上。車燈的光線照出他們前面一點的地方，她不時瞥見一些東西從眼前掠過。他們離開車站後，穿過了一個小村莊，她看見了白中帶青的小屋，小酒店的燈光。隨後他們經過了一座教堂和一座牧師住所，一個小店的小櫥窗，裏面陳列着出售的玩具、糖果和雜貨。然後他們到了大路上，她看見了樹籬和樹。在這之後一段很長時間裏，景色似乎沒有變化——至少對她來說是很長一段時間。

最後馬的速度慢了許多，好像是在爬山，不一會似乎就再也看不見樹籬，也看不見樹了。事實上，她甚麼也看不見，只看見兩邊沉沉的夜色。她向前傾着身體，把臉貼在窗上，就在這時車震盪了一下。

"咦！我們肯定到了曠野上了，"梅洛太太説。

車燈泛黃的燈光灑在看來高低不平的路上，這條路像是從灌木叢和低矮植物裏開出來的，路的盡頭是茫茫一片黑色，它顯然在他們前面和四周鋪展。一陣風平地而起，發出奇特、狂野、低沉、強勁的聲響。

"這——這不是海吧，是嗎？"瑪麗回頭看着她的同伴説。

"不，不是的，"梅洛太太回答説。"也不是田地和山，只不過是一英里又一英里的荒地，除了石楠、荊豆和金雀花之外，甚麼也不生長，除了野馬和綿羊之外，甚麼動物也沒有。"

"如果那上面有水的話，我還以為那是海呢，"瑪麗説。"現在這聲音聽起來就像大海的聲音。"

"這是大風吹過灌木叢的聲音，"梅洛太太説。"在我看來，這是個非常荒蕪、可怕的地方，雖然有很多人喜歡這裏——特別是當石楠開花的時候。"

他們在黑暗中不斷向前，雖然雨已經停了，風還在呼嘯、低鳴，發出奇怪的聲音。道路忽上忽下，有好幾次馬車從橋上經過，橋下是湍急河水，嘩嘩作響。瑪麗只覺得旅程永遠沒有結束的時候，廣袤荒蕪的曠野像無垠的黑色海洋，她在一片乾涸土地上渡過這個海洋。

"我不喜歡這個地方，"她自言自語道。"我不喜歡，"她把瘦小的嘴巴閉得更緊了。

拉車的馬正在往一條上山的路上爬，這時瑪麗才第一次看見了燈光。梅洛太太幾乎與她同時看見，並且長長舒了一口氣。

"哦，看見那點閃爍燈光我真高興，"她叫道。"那是門房裏的燈光。不管怎麼樣，再過一小會，我們就可以好好喝上一杯茶了。"

她所謂的"一小會"，其實是在馬車穿過林苑大門後還要在大道上走兩英里，穿過樹林（這些樹幾乎就在頭頂上），他們就像走在一個有天然拱頂、又長又黑的洞裏。

馬車駛出這個洞，到了一個開闊的地方，停在一排長長的低矮建築物前，一個石頭圍起的院子有條路通向大門，起初瑪麗以為窗裏根本沒有燈光，但是下了馬車後，她看見樓上一個角落的房間裏透出昏暗燈光。

面前是一扇巨大的門，用厚實、形狀奇特的橡木板造成，上面釘着大鐵釘，包着寬鐵條。開門進去是一個大廳，牆上掛着肖像，上面的人全都一身盔甲，由於燈光非常暗，瑪麗不想朝他們看。她站在石頭地板上，看來像一個黑漆漆、怪兮兮的小影子，她的感覺就像她看來那樣又小又怪，不知所措。

一個利落的瘦老伯伯站在給他們開門的男傭人旁邊。

"你帶她到她的房間去，"他用粗啞的聲音説。"他不想見她。他早上要去倫敦。"

"好的，匹契爾先生，"梅洛太太回答説。"只要我知道要我做甚麼，我都會做好的。"

"要你做的事嘛，梅洛太太，"匹契爾先生説，"就是保證不讓他受到打擾，不讓他看見他不想見到的東西。"

於是，瑪麗・倫諾斯被帶上一座寬闊的樓梯，順着一條長走廊向前，往上走了兩三步梯級，又走過一條走廊，又一條走廊，最後看見牆上開着一扇門，她走進了一個房間，裏面生着火，晚飯已經放在桌上。

梅洛太太唐突地説：

"好了，你到了！這個房間和隔壁那房間就歸你住——你必須留在這裏。別忘了！"

瑪麗就這樣來到了米塞爾斯威特莊園，她長這麼大，恐怕從來沒有感到這樣彆扭。

第四章

瑪莎

早上，一個年輕女傭人進房間生火，把她吵醒，她睜開眼睛，只見女傭人跪在壁爐前的地毯上嘩啦嘩啦地往外耙出爐灰。瑪麗躺在牀上看了一會，然後打量起房間來。她從沒見過這樣的房間，覺得它又怪又悶。牆上掛着掛毯，上面繡的是森林景色。樹下是穿着奇裝異服的人們，遠處隱約可見一座城堡的塔樓。畫上有獵人、馬、狗和女士。瑪麗感到自己像他們一樣置身於森林之中。透過一扇厚窗，她看見一片往上延伸的土地，上面好像沒有樹木，很像是一片無邊無際、死氣沉沉、紫色的海。

"那是甚麼？"她指着窗外面問道。

年輕的女傭人瑪莎剛剛站起來，看了一下，也用手一指。

"你是說那兒？"她説。

"是的。"

"那是曠野，"她溫和地一笑。"你喜歡嗎？"

"不，"瑪麗回答說。"我討厭它。"

"這是因為你還不習慣，"瑪莎說，回到壁爐旁邊。"你認為它太大，現在很荒蕪。但是你會喜歡它的。"

"你喜歡嗎？"瑪麗問。

"是的，我喜歡，"瑪莎回答說，高興地擦着爐柵。"我真喜歡它了。它並不荒蕪。它上面長着東西，聞起來好香好香。到了春天和夏天，當荊豆花、金雀花和石楠花開放的時候，那裏真漂亮了。那裏有蜂蜜香味，空氣十分新鮮——天空看來那麼高，蜜蜂嗡嗡，雲雀歌唱，好聽極了。嗨！不管拿甚麼來跟我換，我都不願從曠野上搬走。"

瑪麗一臉嚴肅和困惑地聽她說。她在印度時很熟悉、土生土長的傭人，一點都不是這種樣子的。他們善於奉承，卑躬屈膝，從來不敢這樣不分尊卑地跟主人說話。他們向主人行額手禮，稱他們為"窮人的保護者"甚麼的。讓印度傭人們做事情不用說請，只要命令就行。瑪麗不習慣說"請"和"謝謝"，一生氣就打保姆的耳光。她有點疑惑：如果有人打這個女孩的耳光，不知道她會怎麼樣。她是個圓臉蛋、紅臉龐、相貌溫和的女孩，但是她的一舉一動果斷有力，瑪麗小姐心想，如果打她耳光的人僅僅是個小女孩的話，她甚至會還手。

"你是個奇怪的傭人，"她頭枕着枕頭，相當淘氣地說。

瑪莎蹲坐在腳跟上，手裏握着黑漆刷子，呵呵笑着，一點都沒生氣的樣子。

"哦！這我知道，"她說。"如果米塞爾斯威特裏有個傲慢的女主人，我是連個下房傭人都做不成的。我也許可以做個在廚房裏做粗重工作的傭人，但我絕對不能上樓。我長得太一般，說話約克口音太重。但是這間屋雖然很大，卻很怪。好像除了匹契爾先生和梅洛太太外，既沒有男主人，也沒有女主人。克拉文先生住在這裏的時候，不會為任何事情操心，何況他幾乎從來不住在這裏。好心的梅洛太太給了我這個位子。她對我說，如果米塞爾斯威特像其他大戶家庭一樣的話，她決不會這樣做。"

"你將會是我的傭人嗎？"瑪麗問，依然像在印度時那樣專橫。

瑪莎又擦起爐柵。

"我是梅洛太太的傭人，"她大膽地說，"她是克拉文先生的傭人——但是我到樓上來是做我傭人的工作，稍微伺候你一下。不過你可不能過份依賴我。"

"誰為我穿衣服呢？"瑪麗問。

瑪莎又蹲坐在腳跟上，盯着瑪麗看。她用約克話表示自己的驚異。

"你自己不會穿衣服嗎！"她說。

"你這是甚麼意思？我聽不懂你的話，"瑪麗說。

"哦！我忘了，"瑪莎說。"梅洛太太告訴過我，我一定要注意，否則你會聽不懂我在說甚麼。我的意思是，你就不能給自己穿上衣服嗎？"

"不能，"瑪麗氣呼呼地回答說。"我從來沒有這麼做。當然是我的保姆幫我穿衣服。"

"哦，"瑪莎說，顯然一點都不知道她很沒規矩，"那你現在該學一學了。現在開始已經不算小了。自己動手做一點事情對你有好處。我媽媽常說，她不明白為甚麼大戶家庭的孩子，像木偶似的由保姆們洗臉、穿衣、帶出去散步，他們怎麼會不變成傻子！"

"印度可不是這樣的，"她不屑地說。眼前這種情況實在令她難以忍受。

但是瑪莎絲毫不為所動。

"嗨！我知道是不一樣，"她幾乎帶着同情答道。"我想那是因為那裏有許多黑人，而不是受尊重的白人。當我聽到你是從印度來時，我以為你也是黑人呢。"

瑪麗生氣地從牀上坐了起來。

"甚麼！"她說。"甚麼！你以為我是個當地人。你——你是豬的女兒！"

瑪莎注視着她，看來動怒了。

"你罵誰？"她說。"你不必這樣生氣。年輕小姐不該這樣說話的。我對黑人一點都沒反感。如果你讀過有關他們的小冊子，你會發現他們都是虔誠的教徒。你讀這些小冊子的時候，總是覺得黑人就像是你的男人和兄弟。我從沒見到過黑人，當我想到我將這麼近地見到一個黑人的時候，我很高興。今天早上我來給你生火時，我悄悄走到你的牀邊，小心地把被拉開，想要看看你。而你，"她失望地說，"卻並不比我黑——儘管你這麼黃。"

瑪麗覺得受了污辱，她甚至不想控制自己的怒火。

"你以為我是個當地人！你很大膽！你對當地人一點都不了解！他們不是普通的人——他們是傭人，必須向主人行額手禮。你對印度毫無了解。你甚麼事情都不懂！"

她的怒火大極了，可是瑪莎只是盯着她看，弄得她不知道該怎麼辦，突然間，她覺得自己孤獨得可怕，離開一切她能理解、也能理解她的東西都那麼遙遠，她臉朝下撲在枕頭上，傷心地抽泣起來。她毫無節制地抽泣着，弄得溫和的約克郡女孩瑪莎有點害怕起來，並感到對不起她。她走到牀前，俯身向着她。

"嗨！你可不能這樣哭！"她懇求道。"你千萬別哭。我不知道你會氣成這樣。我甚麼都不懂——就像你説的那樣。我請求你原諒，小姐。別哭了。"

她那種古怪的約克話和堅定的舉動顯得很友好，令人感到舒服，對瑪麗產生了很好的效果。她漸漸停止了哭泣，安靜下來。瑪莎這才鬆了口氣。

"現在你該起牀了，"她説。"梅洛太太説由我領你到隔壁房間去吃早餐、吃點心、吃晚飯。那裏變成了你的兒童室。只要你起了牀，我就幫你穿衣服。如果衣服鈕扣在背後的話，你自己是扣不上的。"

當瑪麗最後決定起牀時，發現瑪莎從衣櫃裏拿來的衣服不是她昨晚跟梅洛太太來這裏時穿的。

"這些衣服不是我的，"她説。"我的衣服是黑色的。"

她打量了一遍這些厚的白色羊毛外衣和連衣裙，冷冷地表示讚賞説："這些衣服比我的好。"

"這些一定要穿上，"瑪莎回答説。"這些是克拉文先生吩咐梅洛太太在倫敦買的。他説，'我不願意讓一個孩子穿一身黑衣服，像個幽靈似的逛來逛去，'他説，'這樣會使這個地方比原來更令人傷心。把她打扮得鮮亮點。'媽媽説她知道克拉文先生的意思。媽媽總是能理解別人的心思。她也看不慣黑色。"

“我討厭黑色的東西，”瑪麗說。

穿衣服的過程給她們兩個都上了一課。瑪莎常給她的弟弟妹妹們“扣鈕扣”，但是她從沒見過一個小孩子一動不動站着，等候別人為她做事，好像她沒有手腳似的。

“你為甚麼不自己穿上鞋呢？”她看見瑪麗悄悄地把腳伸出來，就問道。

“以前都是由我的保姆給我穿的，”瑪麗瞪着眼睛說。“這是習慣。”

她常常這樣說——“這是習慣。”土生土長的傭人也常常這樣說。如果有人要他們做一件他們的祖先一千年來從沒做過的事情，他們會溫和地盯着別人，說，“這不是習慣。”別人就知道這件事算是完了。

要瑪麗小姐動手做事可不是習慣，她只要站在那裏，像個木偶玩具似的讓人幫她穿衣服，但是在她穿好衣服去吃早餐之前，她開始感到她在米塞爾斯威特莊園生活到最後，將學會做一些對她來說十分新奇的事情——比如自己穿鞋和襪，撿起她掉在地上的東西。如果瑪莎原來是個受過良好教育的年輕小姐的傭人，她就應該對主人低聲下氣，必恭必敬，應該知道她的任務就是梳頭髮、撿東西、將東西放開。然而，她只是個未受訓練的約克郡鄉下女孩，在曠野旁的一個小屋裏長大，家裏有一群弟弟妹妹，他們做夢也沒想過由別人伺候他們，而總是自己照顧自己，或者照顧比他們小的弟妹，這些弟妹不是被抱在懷裏，就是剛剛開始學走路，老是被絆倒。

如果瑪麗·倫諾斯是個一逗就樂的孩子，瑪莎的健談或許會使她發笑，但瑪麗只是冷冷地聽她說，為她那種不分尊卑的行為感到不解。起初她絲毫沒有興趣，但漸漸地，隨着瑪莎心平氣和、熟不拘禮的講述，瑪麗開始留心她說的話。

"嗨！你真應該見見他們，"她說。"我們兄弟姐妹有十二個，我爸爸每週只有十六先令的收入。我可以告訴你，我媽媽要費多大的力才能使弟妹們吃到粥。他們跌跌撞撞地在曠野上跑來跑去，整天在那裏玩，媽媽說曠野上的空氣讓他們長肉。她說她相信他們像野馬一樣吃草。我們家的狄肯十二歲，他抓到一匹矮種馬，稱牠是他自己的馬。"

"他在哪裏抓到的？"瑪麗問。

"當時牠還很小，狄肯在曠野上發現牠跟牠媽媽在一起，他開始跟牠交朋友，給牠吃一點麵包，並且拔嫩草給牠吃。牠開始喜歡上他，跟他到處跑，還讓他騎到牠的背上。狄肯是個善良的孩子，動物喜歡他。"

瑪麗從來沒有得到過屬於她自己的寵物，她總是認為自己很想有一隻。所以她對狄肯產生了一點興趣，由於她以前除了對自己外，從沒對任何人產生過興趣，所以說這是一種健康的情感苗子。當她走進被改建成她的兒童室的房間時，發現那裏跟她睡覺的房間很相像。那不是個孩子的房間，而是個成年人的房間，牆上掛着陰森森的舊畫像，放着結實的舊橡木椅。中間有一張桌，上面擺好了豐盛的早餐。但是她向來胃口很小，對於瑪莎放在她面前的第一盤東西，她的反應比冷漠還要冷漠。

"我不想吃，"她說。

"你不想吃粥！"瑪莎驚叫道，簡直不相信自己的耳朵。

"是的。"

"你不知道粥是多好的東西。要是裏面放一點糖漿或蔗糖的話。"

"我不想吃，"瑪麗重複道。

"嗨！"瑪莎說。"我不能看着好端端的糧食被浪費掉。如果我的弟妹們坐在這張桌上，不用五分鐘就能把這些東西吃個清光。"

"為甚麼？"瑪麗冷冷地說。

"為甚麼！"瑪莎應道。"因為他們長這麼大，難得有吃飽肚子的時候。他們餓得就像小鷹和狐狸一樣。"

"我不知道甚麼叫餓，"瑪麗說，無知中透着冷漠。

瑪莎面露惱色。

"嗯，你試着吃吃看，對你有好處的。這一點我看得很清楚，"她坦率地說。"我可沒有耐心陪人坐着，瞪眼看着可口的麵包和肉。說老實話！我真希望狄肯、菲爾、簡和我所有弟妹們都吃掉這些。"

"你為甚麼不帶這些東西給他們呢？"瑪麗提出建議。

"這又不是我的，"瑪莎不客氣地說。"而且今天也不是我休息的日子。我跟其他人一樣，每月休息一天。到時候我就回家去，幫媽媽洗洗刷刷，讓她休息一天。"

瑪麗喝了點茶，吃了兩三口麵包和果醬。

"你把衣服穿暖和點，跑到外面去玩，"瑪莎說。"這樣對你有好處，使你有胃口吃肉。"

瑪麗走到窗前。外面有花園、小徑和大樹，但是一切都毫無生氣，看來冷颼颼的。

"到外面去？這樣的天氣我為甚麼要到外面去呢？"

"好吧，如果你不想出去，那就留在屋裏，你又能做甚麼呢？"

瑪麗打量四周。的確沒有甚麼事情可做。梅洛太太在準備兒童室的時候，可沒想到娛樂這一方面。也許還是到外面去看看花園是甚麼樣子的比較好。

"誰跟我一起去呢？"她問道。

瑪莎瞪大了眼睛。

"你一個人去呀，"她答道。"你必須學會像那些沒有兄弟姐妹的孩子一樣自己去玩。我家狄肯常常一個人到曠野上去，一玩就是兩三個小時。所以他才跟那匹小馬交上了朋友。他讓曠野上的羊認識了他，小鳥從他手上吃東西。儘管他自己沒甚麼東西吃，他總是省下一點麵包甚麼的餵他的寵物。"

正是由於提到了狄肯，瑪麗才決定到外面去，儘管她並沒有意識到這一點。儘管外面不可能有小馬和羊，但是小鳥總歸會有的。那些鳥或許跟印度的鳥不一樣，看着牠們她也許會感到有趣的。

瑪莎給她拿來外衣、帽和一雙厚實的小靴子，並指給她下樓去的路。

"你繞過那條路就能走到花園，"她說，指着一面灌木牆上的一扇門，"夏天那裏有許多花，但是現在甚麼花也沒有。"她似乎遲疑了一下，然後接着說，"有一個花園被鎖起來了。十年來從來沒人進去。"

"為甚麼？"瑪麗情不自禁地問。這間奇怪的屋裏已經有了一百個被鎖住的門，這裏又添了一個。

「當克拉文先生的妻子突然死去後，他就命令把它鎖了起來。他不想讓任何人進去。這是她的花園。他鎖上了門，挖了個坑把鑰匙埋了進去。梅洛太太搖鈴了——我要趕快過去。」

瑪莎走了之後，瑪麗下樓走上那條小路，朝灌木牆上的那扇門走去。她不由自主地想着那個十年從沒人進去的花園，她想知道那是甚麼樣子的，現在那裏面是不是還有活着的花。她穿過灌木門，進入大花園，那裏有寬闊的草坪，彎曲的小路，小路上有經過修剪的花壇。那裏有樹木、花壇、被修剪成奇形怪狀的常綠植物，還有一個大水池，中間是一個灰色的舊噴泉。但是花園裏一片凋零，噴泉也沒噴水。這裏不是那個被鎖上的花園。花園怎麼可以被鎖上呢？人們應該隨時可以走進花園。

她正想到這兒，看見腳下這條小路的盡頭，好像有一面長牆，常春藤爬出了牆頭。她對英國不太熟悉，不知道她走進的是家庭菜園，裏面種着蔬菜和水果。她朝那面牆走去，發現常春藤中有一扇綠色的門，門開着。顯然這不是那座被關閉的花園，她可以進去。

她走進門，發現這個花園四面是牆，這只是數個似乎互相貫通、四面是牆的花園中的一個。她看見另一個打開着的綠色的門，裏面露出灌木叢和花壇之間的小徑，花壇裏種着冬季的蔬菜。果樹被培養得緊貼着牆，一些花壇上面有玻璃罩。瑪麗站在那裏，環顧四周，只覺得這個地方荒禿禿的，很難看。到了夏天，植物返青，那時候或許會好看一點，但是此刻，這裏實在沒有美麗可言。

不一會，一個老伯伯肩扛鑣穿過第二個花園的門走了過來。他看見瑪麗時吃了一驚，然後碰了一下帽。他有一張不友好的老臉，看見她時絲毫不顯得高興——但當時她對他的花園沒有好感，臉上露着那副"倔強"的表情，見到他自然也很不高興。

　　"這是甚麼地方？"她問。

　　"菜園，"他答道。

　　"那是甚麼呀？"瑪麗指着另一扇綠色的門問道。

　　"另一個菜園，"回答很簡單。"在牆的那邊還有一個，那個菜園的另一邊有一個果園。"

　　"我能進去嗎？"瑪麗問。

　　"想去你就去吧。但是那裏沒有甚麼可看的。"

　　瑪麗沒有理他。她順着小徑走進第二扇綠色的門。她在那裏看見更多的牆、冬季蔬菜和玻璃罩，但是第二面牆上又有一扇門，門沒有開着。也許這扇門裏面就是那個十年從沒人進去的花園。她是個從來不懂得甚麼叫膽怯的孩子，向來要做甚麼就做甚麼，她走到那扇綠色的門跟前，轉動門的把手。她希望門不要打開，因為她想確認她發現了那座秘密的花園——但是門很容易就打開了，她走進去，裏面是個果園。四周同樣有牆，果樹被培養得緊貼着牆，冬季枯黃的草地裏種着光禿禿的果樹——但是到處都見不到綠色的門。瑪麗尋找着門，當她走到花園的北端時，注意到這面牆似乎並不是到果園就結束了，而是超越了果園，好像還圍着另一面的一個地方。她靜靜地站在那裏，看見樹梢從牆頭伸出來，一隻胸脯鮮紅的鳥棲息在最高的一根樹枝上，突然，牠發出了牠那冬天的啾鳴，好像看見了瑪麗，正在召喚她。

她停下腳步，聽牠啾鳴，牠那歡樂、友好的低聲啾鳴使她產生一種愉快的心情——就算一個令人討厭的女孩也會感到孤獨，這間封閉的大屋、荒蕪的大曠野和光禿禿的大花園使女孩覺得這個世界上好像只剩下了她一個人。如果她是個感情充沛的孩子，習慣於受到寵愛，她會感到心痛的；但即使她是"倔強瑪麗"，她還是感到孤獨悽涼，這隻胸脯鮮亮的鳥使這個苦着小臉的女孩幾乎露出了一絲笑意。她聽牠啾鳴，直到牠飛走。牠不像印度的鳥，她喜歡牠，不知道自己能不能再見到牠。也許牠住在那個秘密的花園裏，知道花園的一切。

大概她實在沒別的事情可做，就不停地想着那個被遺棄的花園。她對它充滿好奇，想看看它是甚麼樣子的。阿奇博爾德·克拉文為甚麼要把鑰匙埋掉呢？既然他這麼愛他的妻子，為甚麼要恨她的花園呢？她拿不定主意，自己要不要見他，但有一點可以肯定，就算見到他，她不會喜歡他，他也不會喜歡她，她只會站在那裏，眼睛瞪着他，一句話也不說，當然她心癢難熬，要問問他為甚麼做出這樣的怪事。

"從來沒人喜歡我，我也不喜歡任何人，"她心想。"我從來不像哥羅福家的孩子那樣會說話。他們整天說說笑笑，吵吵鬧鬧。"

她想着那隻知更鳥和牠似乎在對她唱歌的那個樣子，正當她想到牠棲息的那棵樹時，突然在小徑上停下了腳步。

"我相信那棵樹是在那個秘密花園裏——我有把握，"她說。"那裏有一圈圍牆，牆上沒有門。"

她回到第一個菜園，看見老伯伯在那裏挖地。她走過去，站在他旁邊，冷冷地看了一會。他沒有理她，因此，最後她跟他說起話來。

"我到別的花園裏去過了，"她說。

"沒甚麼能阻止你，"他堅決地回答說。

"我進了果園。"

"那裏門口沒有狗來咬你，"他答道。

"那裏沒有門通往另一個花園，"瑪麗說。

"甚麼花園？"他粗聲粗氣地說，一時停下了手中的工作。

"牆那邊的那個，"瑪麗小姐答道。"那裏有樹——我看見了樹梢。一隻紅胸脯的鳥停在一棵樹上，牠還唱歌呢。"

沒想到那張被歲月磨蝕的乖戾的老臉表情大變，一絲笑意在那上面慢慢蕩漾開來，這個園丁幾乎換了個人。瑪麗心想，一個人笑的時候竟然會變得這麼可愛，真是件怪事。以前她從沒想過。

他轉身對着果園那裏，吹起了口哨——聲音低緩柔和。她想不到一個如此乖戾的老伯伯居然能發出這樣吸引的聲音。

幾乎緊接着，一件美妙的事情發生了。她聽見空中傳來急速飛行的窸窣聲——原來是那隻紅胸脯的小鳥飛到了他們面前，牠降落在離園丁很近的一個大土塊上。

"牠來了，"老伯伯咯咯地笑着說，然後跟小鳥說起話來，就像跟一個孩子說話一樣。

"你這不要臉的小乞丐，你去哪裏了？"他說。"今天我還沒見過你呢。這麼早的季節你就開始求偶了嗎？你也太超前了。"

鳥把小頭歪在一邊，一隻溫和明亮的眼睛朝上看着老伯伯，那眼睛就像黑色的露珠。牠似乎對這裏很熟，一點都不害怕。牠跳來跳去，快樂地啄着地面，尋找種子和小蟲。看到這種情景，瑪麗的心裏不由得產生了一種奇怪的感覺，因為小鳥這麼美麗、愉快，簡直像個人似的。牠有豐滿的小身體，優美的喙，細長漂亮的腿。

"你每次叫牠，牠都能來嗎？"她幾乎沒聲地問道。

"噢，會的。牠羽毛還沒豐滿的時候我就認識牠了。牠從另外一個花園的鳥巢裏鑽出來；牠第一次從牆那邊飛過來之後，因為太弱小了，好幾天不能飛回去，我們就成了朋友。當牠再飛到牆那邊去的時候，跟牠一窩裏的鳥都飛走了，牠成了孤鳥，就又飛到了我這裏。"

"牠是甚麼鳥？"瑪麗問。

"你不知道嗎？牠是紅胸脯知更鳥，牠們是最友好、最好奇的鳥。牠們幾乎像狗一樣友好——只要你懂得怎樣跟牠們相處。看牠在地上啄來啄去，不時地回過頭來看看我們。牠知道我們正在說牠。"

看見這個老伯伯是世界上最奇怪的事情。他看着這隻豐滿的小鳥，牠猩紅的胸脯就像穿了一件背心，老伯伯似乎既喜歡牠又為牠驕傲。

"牠是隻聰明的鳥，"他咯咯地笑着說。"牠喜歡聽到別人談論牠。牠還很好奇——天哪，從沒見過像牠這樣有好奇心、愛管閒事的東西。牠老是到這裏來看我種東西。克拉文先生不願費心弄個明白的事情牠都知道。牠是這裏的花匠頭，真的。"

知更鳥跳來跳去，用力地啄着泥土，不時地停下來朝他們看上兩三眼。瑪麗感覺到牠那雙黑露珠似的眼睛十分好奇地盯着她。看起來牠真的像是要查明她的來龍去脈。她心裏那種奇怪的感覺越來越強烈。

"牠那窩鳥飛到哪裏去了呢?"她問。

"不知道。鳥爸爸鳥媽媽把小鳥趕出窩去,讓牠們飛,沒等你知道,牠們就飛散了。這隻鳥挺懂事,牠知道牠成了孤兒。"

瑪麗小姐朝知更鳥走近一步,仔細打量牠。

"我是孤兒,我也孤獨一個。"她說。

以前她從不知道,孤獨是她感到彆扭,容易煩躁的原因之一。當知更鳥看着她,她也看着知更鳥的時候,她似乎找到了原因。

老花匠把帽往他的禿頭後面一推,朝她注視了一分鐘。

"你就是從印度來的那個小女孩?"他問。

瑪麗點點頭。

"那就難怪你孤獨了。在你死去之前你會更加孤獨,"他說。

他又挖起地來,把鏟深深地插進花園黑油油的沃土裏,而知更鳥則忙碌地跳來跳去。

"你叫甚麼名字?"瑪麗問。

他站直腰來回答她。

"本‧威瑟斯塔夫,"他答道,然後又乖戾地咯咯笑了一下,"我也很孤獨,只有知更鳥陪着我的時候例外,"他把大拇指朝知更鳥一指。"牠是我唯一的朋友。"

"我一個朋友也沒有,"瑪麗說。"我從來沒有朋友。我的印度保姆不喜歡我,我從來不跟任何人一起玩。"

實話實說是約克郡人的習慣,而老本‧威瑟斯塔夫是約克郡曠野上的人。

"你跟我真是一夥的，"他說。"我們穿一樣的褲，我們都沒有漂亮的臉蛋，我們看來都怪怪的，我敢打賭，我們兩個都有臭脾氣。"

這倒是大實話，瑪麗·倫諾斯從沒聽人這樣實事求是地評論她。土生土長的傭人不管你做甚麼，總是對你行禮、唯命是從。她從沒想過自己長甚麼樣，但是她不知道自己是不是像本·威瑟斯塔夫一樣不討人喜歡，也不知道她是不是像知更鳥到來之前的本·威瑟斯塔夫那樣看來不順眼。她還實實在在地考慮起自己是不是真的有"臭脾氣"。她感到很不舒服。

突然她耳邊響起清晰的潺潺流水般輕柔的聲音，她回頭看去。離她兩三步遠的地方有一棵小蘋果樹，知更鳥飛到了最高的一根樹枝上，發出一陣啾鳴。本·威瑟斯塔夫縱聲大笑。

"牠這是做甚麼？"瑪麗問。

"牠打定主意要跟你交朋友了，"本答道。"我敢說牠已經喜歡上你了。"

"喜歡我？"瑪麗說，輕輕地朝小樹那裏走去，抬頭往上看。

"你會跟我交朋友嗎？"她對知更鳥說，就像跟一個人說話一樣。"你會嗎？"她說話的聲音既不生硬，也不像在印度時那樣專橫，而是溫柔、急切、吸引人，本·威瑟斯塔夫覺得很驚訝，就像瑪麗聽見他吹口哨時感到驚訝一樣。

"真想不到，"他叫了起來，"你剛才說話的樣子真像個地道的女孩，而不是個兇巴巴的老婆婆。你說話的樣子簡直像曠野上的狄肯跟他的動物們說話一樣。"

"你認識狄肯嗎？"瑪麗問，一下子轉過身來。

"人人都認識他。狄肯到處遊蕩。就連黑刺莓和灰色歐石楠也都認識他。我敢打賭，狐狸會領他去看牠們的小孩，雲雀不會把牠們的巢對他藏起來。"

瑪麗還想再問一些問題。她對狄肯的好奇幾乎像對秘密花園的好奇一樣強烈。但是就在這時，知更鳥結束了啾鳴，稍稍揮動了一下翅膀，將翅膀展開，飛走了。牠結束了探訪，做別的事情去了。

"牠飛到牆那邊去了！"瑪麗叫道，注視着牠。"牠飛進了果園裏——牠飛過了另一面牆——飛進了那座沒有門的花園！"

"牠住在那裏，"本說。"牠是從那裏的蛋裏鑽出來的。如果牠要求偶的話，牠會向住在那些老玫瑰樹上的雌知更鳥求。"

"玫瑰樹，"瑪麗說。"那裏有玫瑰樹嗎？"

本·威瑟斯塔夫又拿起鏟準備挖土。

"十年前是有的，"他喃喃地說。

"我想看看它們，"瑪麗說。"綠色的門在哪裏呢？總該有一扇門呀。"

本把鏟深深地插進地裏，看來又像瑪麗第一次見到他時一樣難以相處了。

"十年前是有的，但是現在沒有了，"他說。

"沒有門！"瑪麗叫道。"一定有門的。"

"誰也找不到，也跟任何人都沒關係。你別做個愛管閒事的女孩，毫沒來由地到處都插一手。嗨，我要工作了。你自己去玩吧。我沒時間了。"

他真的停止了挖土，扛起鏟就走，看都沒看她一眼，連再見都沒說一聲。

第五章

走廊裏的哭聲

最初數天，瑪麗・倫諾斯的日子過得很平淡。每天早晨她從掛着壁毯的房間裏醒來，看見瑪莎跪在壁爐前生火；每天早晨她在兒童室裏吃早餐，兒童室一點都不好玩；每天吃過早餐後，她就在窗前看着外面寬闊的曠野，那曠野好像從四面八方向外伸展，一直延伸到天邊。看了一會之後，她便意識到，如果她不到外面去，她就只好留在家裏，無事可做——於是她就到外面去，她不知道，當她順着小徑和林蔭道快步行走，甚至奔跑的時候，她就加速了體內的血液循環，在與從曠野上吹來的大風作鬥爭的過程中使自己強壯起來。她跑的目的只是為了使自己暖和，她討厭風吹在臉上，在耳邊怒吼，把她往後面拽，好像是一個她無法看見的巨人。但是大口大口地吸進了從歐石楠上吹過的清新空氣後，增大了她的肺活量，使她瘦弱的身體健康起來，臉頰上有了血色，呆滯的雙目有了亮光，而這一切她一點都不知道。

她這樣幾乎整天留在外面，沒過兩三天，有一天早晨醒來，她知道甚麼叫餓了，當她坐在早餐桌前時，她沒有再對她的粥皺眉頭並把它推開，而是拿起調羹，吃了起來，直到把粥吃乾淨。

"今天早上你吃得很好，是嗎？"瑪莎問。

"今天粥的味道很好，"瑪麗說，自己都覺得有點驚訝。

"是曠野上的空氣讓你對食物有了胃口，"瑪莎回答說。"你真幸運，又有胃口又有食物。我們家裏有十二個孩子，他們有胃口，但是沒有食物往裏面填。你接着在外面玩，就會在骨頭上長出肉來，你的臉色就不會這麼黃了。"

"我不玩，"瑪麗說，"我沒有甚麼東西玩。"

"沒有東西玩！"瑪莎叫道。"我的弟弟妹妹們用樹枝和石子都能玩。他們只是奔跑，叫喊，看各種各樣的東西。"

瑪麗沒有叫喊，但是她也看了各種各樣的東西。別的實在沒甚麼可做。她在花園裏走了一圈又一圈，在林苑的小徑上繞來繞去。有時候她去找本·威瑟斯塔夫，雖然見到過他數次，但是他不是忙得抬不起頭來，就是十分乖戾。有一次她朝他走去，他卻好像故意扛起鏟，轉身走開。

有一個地方她去得比其他地方要勤。那就是有圍牆圍住的花園外面，那條長長的小路。小路兩邊有凋零的花壇，牆邊長着繁茂的常春藤。牆的一邊，爬藤植物深綠色的葉比其他地方都茂盛。好像那個地方很久以來一直沒有人打理。其他地方的葉都被修剪得整整齊齊，但是小路的南端絲毫都沒人來修剪。

跟本·威瑟斯塔夫談過話的數天之後，瑪麗不再注意這個現象，不去考慮為甚麼會這樣。有一天，她正停下腳步，抬頭看着常春藤的長枝條在風中搖曳，卻見一抹猩紅色在眼前一亮，接着聽見了明亮的啾鳴聲，只見本・威瑟斯塔夫的紅胸脯知更鳥棲息在牆頭，小頭歪在一邊，向前傾着身體看着她。

"哦！"她叫了起來，"是你嗎——是你嗎？"她跟牠説話一點都不覺得奇怪，好像她肯定牠能聽懂並回答她。

牠的確回答了她。牠嘰嘰喳喳，婉轉啾鳴，在牆頭跳來跳去，好像要把所有的事情都告訴她。瑪麗小姐似乎覺得自己也能聽懂牠的意思，儘管牠並沒有説出話來。牠好像在説：

"早上好！風真好，不是嗎？太陽真好，不是嗎？一切都真好，不是嗎？讓我們都來唱歌、跳躍、啾鳴吧。來吧！來吧！"

瑪麗笑了起來，知更鳥在牆上跳躍，順着牆飛上一小段路，瑪麗就跟在牠後面奔跑。面黃肌瘦、相貌難看的瑪麗——一時間她看來幾乎顯得漂亮了。

"我喜歡你！我喜歡你！"她叫道，啪嗒啪嗒地順着牆往前跑；她發出唧唧聲，並且試着吹口哨，其實她一點都不會吹。但是知更鳥好像很滿意，用啾鳴和口哨來回答她。最後牠展開翅膀，箭一般飛到一棵樹的樹梢上，棲息在那裏，嘹亮地歌唱起來。

這使瑪麗想起了她第一次見到牠時的情景。當時牠站在果園裏，而牠在一棵樹梢上搖擺。現在她在果園的另一邊，站在一面牆外面的小徑上——牆高高地聳立在她頭頂上——裏面還是那棵樹。

"那是在沒人能進去的花園裏，"她對自己説。"那是沒有門的花園。牠就住在那裏。嗨，我真想看看花園是甚麼樣子的！"

她順着小路往北朝那扇綠色的門跑去，第一天早上她就是從那裏進去的，然後她順着小徑往南穿過另一扇門，進入果園，站定下來，抬頭看着牆那邊的樹和知更鳥，知更鳥剛唱完歌，正在啄羽毛。

"就是這個花園，"她說。"我肯定就是它。"

她繞了一圈，仔細查看果園牆的這一邊，但是她的發現還是像原來一樣——牆上沒有門。然後她又跑着穿過菜園，來到外面常春藤覆蓋的長牆外的小路上，她走到小路盡頭，看着那面牆，但是牆上沒有門；於是她走到另一頭，又看了看，那裏同樣沒有門。

"真奇怪，"她說。"本·威瑟斯塔夫說這裏沒有門，這裏真的沒有門。但是十年前這裏肯定是有門的，因為克拉文先生把鑰匙埋了起來。"

這件事使她產生了很多想法，她感到了濃厚的興趣，覺得自己到米塞爾斯威特莊園來並不遺憾。在印度的時候她總是覺得太熱，太沒精打采，所以對甚麼都不太關心。而現在，曠野上清新的風已令她稍微清醒了一點。

她幾乎整天留在屋外，晚上當她坐下來吃晚飯時，感到又餓又睏，但很舒服。當瑪莎東拉西扯地閒聊時，她沒有發脾氣。她覺得自己很喜歡聽她閒聊，最後她想到要問她一個問題。吃過晚飯坐在壁爐前的地毯上，她把問題提了出來。

"克拉文先生為甚麼要恨那個花園？"她說。

她讓瑪莎留下來陪她，瑪莎一點也不拒絕。她年紀很輕，長年和一大群兄弟姐妹擠在一間小屋裏，在樓下傭人們集中的大廳裏，男傭人和上房傭人老愛拿她的約克話開玩笑，把她當成個不起眼的小孩，他們坐在一起說悄悄話，對於這些瑪莎覺得很無聊。瑪莎喜歡說話，這個原來生活在印度，由"黑人"照料的陌生孩子在她看來很新奇，對她具有足夠吸引力。

沒等瑪麗開口，她就自己坐到了地毯上。

"你還在想着那個花園？"她說。"我知道你會想的。我第一次聽到的時候也是這樣。"

"他為甚麼要恨它呢？"瑪麗盯着問。

瑪莎把兩腿盤在身體下面，讓自己坐得舒服一點。

"聽風在屋四周呼嘯，"她說。"如果今天晚上你到曠野上去，你會受不了的。"

瑪麗本來不懂呼嘯是甚麼意思，但是聽見外面的風聲之後她就明白了。這一定是指那種令人毛骨悚然的怒吼聲，一遍一遍地在屋四周震響，好像一個無形的巨人拍打着牆和窗，要闖進來。但是人們知道他進不來，而且置身在生着紅通通爐火的屋裏還感到十分安全和暖和。

"但是他為甚麼這麼恨它呢？"她聽過了風聲之後問道。如果瑪莎知道的話，她也想知道。

於是瑪莎把她所知道的都說了出來。

"記住，"她說，"梅洛太太說這事不能傳出去。這裏有許多事情是不能亂說的。這是克拉文先生的命令。他說，他的麻煩事跟傭人們無關。要不是為了那個花園，他才不會像現在這樣呢。那是克拉文太太的花園，是他們剛結婚時她建造的，她非常喜歡它，他們總是親自照料那裏的花，從來不讓任何花匠進去。克拉文先生和克拉文太太常常到裏面去，關上門，在裏面一留就是數小時，讀書、説話。太太當時還像個小女孩，那裏有一棵老樹，上面有一根樹枝彎下來，像個座位。她把玫瑰嫁接到那上面，她常常坐在那裏。但是有一天她坐在那裏時，樹枝斷了，她摔到了地上，摔得很厲害，第二天就死了。醫生們認為克拉文先生神經上出了毛病，也會死掉。所以他恨那個花園。從那以後誰也不准進去，他不准任何人談論那個花園。"

瑪麗沒有再問甚麼問題。她看着紅紅的爐火，聽着風的"呼嘯"。聽起來好像比原來"呼嘯"得更響了。

這時候，一件很好的事情發生在她身上。事實上，自從她來到米塞爾斯威特莊園之後，已經有四件好事發生在她身上了；她感到她好像聽懂了一隻知更鳥的話，知更鳥也好像聽懂了她的話；她在風裏奔跑，直到血變熱；她生平第一次懂得甚麼叫餓，而這正是健康的標誌；她發現了甚麼叫為別人難過。

但是她聽着風聲的同時，還聽見了別的聲音。她不知道是甚麼聲音，因為一開始她很難把它與風聲區別開來。這是一種奇怪的聲音——簡直像是一個孩子在甚麼地方哭。有時候風聲的確像一個孩子的哭聲，但是不一會瑪麗小姐就肯定，這聲音是屋裏面發出來的，不是在屋外面。聲音在很遠的地方，但是在裏面。她轉過身去看着瑪莎。

"你聽見有人在哭嗎？"她説。

瑪莎突然顯得很慌張。

"沒有，"她回答説。"是風聲。有時候風聲聽起來，就像是有人在曠野上迷了路而發出的痛哭聲。風聲會變得像任何東西的聲音。"

"但是你聽，"瑪麗説。"聲音是在屋裏——就在那些長走廊中的一條裏面。"

就在這時候，樓下某個地方肯定有一扇門被打開了；因為一股強風從走廊吹來，她們留在裏面的那個房間的門砰一下被吹開了，她們兩人同時跳了起來。燈被吹滅了，哭聲從遠處的走廊傳來，這回她們聽得很真切。

"聽！"瑪麗説。"我説得不錯吧！是有人在哭——不是個大人。"

瑪莎奔過去關上門，轉動了一下鑰匙，但是在這之前，她們聽見遠處走廊裏有一扇門砰一聲關了起來，一切又都歸於沉寂，就連風聲也停止"呼嘯"了一會。

"是風聲，"瑪莎固執地説。"如果不是風聲，就是廚房裏做粗重工作的傭人小貝蒂・巴特沃斯。她整天喊牙痛。"

但是她的舉止慌張、尷尬，令瑪麗小姐緊緊盯着她看。她不相信瑪莎説的是真話。

"有人在哭——真的！"

第二天，大雨又傾盆而下，瑪麗從窗裏往外看去，只見曠野被籠罩在灰色的迷霧和濃雲之中。今天不可能出去了。

"每逢這樣的大雨天，你們在小屋裏做甚麼呢？"她問瑪莎。

"盡力避免被別人踩到，"瑪莎回答說。"嗨！那時候我們家確實人太多了。媽媽脾氣很好，可是她也很煩惱。大的數個到外面的牛棚去玩。狄肯不怕潮濕。他還像大太陽天氣一樣到外面去。他說他在下雨天裏看見的東西，在好天氣裏是看不見的。有一次他看見一隻小狐狸在洞裏差點被淹死，他用襯衣把牠包起來，給牠取暖，把牠帶回家。狐狸媽媽在附近被人打死了，狐狸洞被淹了，其他小狐狸都死了。現在狄肯就把這隻小狐狸養在家裏。又有一次，他發現一隻被淹得半死的小烏鴉，他把牠也帶回家來，馴養牠。因為牠很黑，所以名字就叫'煤煙'，牠跟着狄肯到處跑，到處飛。"

瑪麗終於不再討厭瑪莎這種不分尊卑地説話的樣子。她甚至覺得很有趣，當瑪莎停下來或離去時，她覺得挺不是滋味。她住在印度時保姆給她説的故事跟瑪莎説的完全不同，瑪莎説她們家曠野上的小屋裏，十四個人住在四個小房間裏，從來都吃不飽肚子。孩子們就像毛皮粗糙的、好脾氣的柯利小牧羊犬到處亂跑，自得其樂。瑪莎的媽媽和狄肯最讓瑪麗感興趣。每當瑪莎説到"媽媽"怎麼説，怎麼做的時候，她都聽得津津有味。

　　"如果我有一隻烏鴉或者一隻小狐狸，我就可以跟牠玩了，"瑪麗説。"可是我甚麼都沒有。"

　　瑪莎一臉的困惑。

　　"你會編織嗎？"她問。

　　"不會，"瑪麗答道。

　　"會用針線嗎？"

　　"不會。"

　　"能讀書嗎？"

　　"能。"

　　"那你為甚麼不讀點甚麼呢，或者學點拼寫？你已經不小了，應該好好用功學習了。"

　　"我沒有書呀，"瑪麗説。"我的書都留在印度了。"

　　"真可惜，"瑪莎説。"要是梅洛太太能讓你進藏書室去就好了，那裏有數千本書呢。"

　　瑪麗沒有問藏書室在哪裏，因為她靈機一動，想到了一個新點子。她打定主意要自己去找到藏書室。她不怕會讓梅洛太太發現。梅洛太太好像整天留在樓下她舒適的管家客廳裏。在這個古怪地方，誰都難得見到誰。事實上，這裏見來見去的都是傭人，當他們的主人不在時，他們在樓下過着很奢華的日子，那裏有一個大廚房，裏面掛滿銅的和白鑞的器皿，閃閃發亮，還有一個傭人大廳，那裏每天都要開四五次飯，菜餚非常豐盛，只要梅洛太太不在，那裏就會大吵大鬧。

瑪麗每頓飯都開得很準時，由瑪莎伺候她，但是此外誰也不費半點心思來照料她。梅洛太太每天或隔天來看看她，但是誰也不問她做些甚麼或告訴她該做甚麼。她以為這大概就是英國人對待孩子的方法。在印度的時候，她總是由保姆來照料，保姆到處跟着她，殷勤地伺候她。她常常討厭保姆作伴。現在沒有人跟着她了，她要自己學着穿衣服，因為，當她要別人把東西遞到她手上，替她把衣服穿上時，瑪莎的神情好像是覺得她又傻又笨。

"你的神經不正常嗎？"有一次當瑪麗站在那裏等着瑪莎給她戴手套時，瑪莎對她說。"我家蘇珊·安只有四歲，可她比你聰明一倍。有時候你看來腦是有問題。"

聽了這些話，瑪麗的倔強脾氣又上來了，一張臉繃了一個小時，但是她因而起了數個新念頭。

今天早晨，瑪莎最後一次掃乾淨壁爐，下樓去之後，她在窗前站了大約十分鐘。她在仔細考慮聽到藏書室之後產生的那個新念頭。她對藏書室本身並不怎麼在乎，因為她沒唸過甚麼書；但是聽到提起它，使她想起了關着門的一百個房間。她很想知道它們是不是真的鎖上了，如果她能進入其中的任何一間，她會在裏面發現甚麼。真的有一百個房間嗎？她為甚麼不去數數看到底有多少呢？今天早上她不能出去，正好可以做這件事。從來沒人教過她做甚麼事情要徵得同意，她也不懂甚麼叫許可，所以即使見到梅洛太太的話，她也不會想到要問一聲她能不能在屋裏走走。

她打開房門，走進走廊，然後就開始漫遊起來。這個走廊很長，並且岔向其他走廊，她順着走廊走上兩三步梯級，又走進其他走廊。走廊裏有一個又一個的門，牆上有畫。有時候是暗淡、奇怪的風景畫，但最多的是男男女女的肖像，身穿奇形怪狀、雍容華貴的緞子和天鵝絨衣服。她發現自己置身於一個長畫廊裏，兩邊牆上都掛着這樣的肖像畫。她從沒想到一座屋裏竟會有這麼多的畫。她在這個地方慢慢地走，注視着畫上的面龐，它們好像也在注視她。她感到它們好像在納悶：這個從印度來的小女孩在它們的屋裏做甚麼。有些是孩子的畫像——小女孩們穿着厚緞子連衣裙，裙子拖到腳跟，很顯眼，男孩子們穿着泡泡袖和花邊領襯衣，留着長髮，或在頸項上圍着大輪狀皺領。她不時停下腳步看那些孩子，猜想着他們的名字，他們到哪裏去了，他們為甚麼穿這樣怪的衣服。其中有一個相貌平庸傻愣愣的小女孩，長得很像她自己。她穿着綠色錦緞連衣裙，手裏拿着一隻綠色鸚鵡。她的眼睛裏有一種尖刻、好奇的神色。

"你現在住在哪裏？"瑪麗大聲對她説。"我希望你住在這裏。"

肯定沒有第二個小女孩像瑪麗這樣度過一個奇怪的早晨。看起來這座大而無當的屋裏好像只有她這個小小的瑪麗，樓上樓下到處逛，穿過寬寬窄窄的走廊，這些地方在她看來只有她一個人走過。既然建造了這麼多的房間，肯定有人曾經住在裏面，但現在似乎到處都空關着，她無法相信這是真的。

直到爬上二樓時她才想到轉動一扇門的把手。梅洛太太說得不錯，所有門都關着，但是最後她握住了其中一扇門把手，轉動了一下。一時間她幾乎嚇了一跳，因為她沒怎麼用力就覺得把手轉動了，她推了一下，門慢慢地、沉重地打開了。這是一扇很結實的門，裏面是個大臥室。牆上有繡花的懸掛物，臥室四周擺放着有嵌飾的傢具，跟她在印度時看見的一樣。裝有鉛框的大玻璃窗開向曠野；壁爐架上方又掛着那個相貌平庸、傻愣愣的小女孩的一幅肖像，好像比剛才更好奇地注視着瑪麗。

　　"也許她以前曾睡在這裏，"瑪麗說。"她這樣盯着我，讓我覺得好奇怪。"

　　隨後她打開了更多門。她看了那麼多的房間，感到厭倦了，雖然沒有數過，卻覺得一定有一百個。所有房間裏都有舊畫像或舊掛毯，上面是奇怪的景色。幾乎所有房間裏都有奇怪的傢具和奇怪的裝飾品。

　　其中有一個房間，像是一位小姐的客廳，懸掛物都是繡花的天鵝絨；在一個陳列櫃裏，放着大約一百隻象牙雕出來的小象。這些小象大小不一，有些背上還有趕象人或象轎。有些很大，有些則很小，只不過是象嬰孩。瑪麗在印度時見過牙雕，她對象也很熟悉。她打開陳列櫃的門，站在一隻擱腳凳上，把這些象拿來玩了很長時間。玩厭了之後，她就把它們一隻隻放好，關上櫃門。

　　在那些長走廊和空房間裏繞來繞去，她始終沒見到一個活的東西；但是在這個房間裏她看到了一些東西。她剛關上櫃門，就聽到一種輕微的窸窸窣窣的聲音。她嚇了一跳，聲音好像是從壁爐旁邊的沙發那裏發出來的，她到那裏去查看。沙發的一角有個軟墊，墊上蓋着一塊天鵝絨布，布上有個洞，一個小頭從洞裏探出來，頭上有一雙受驚的眼睛。

瑪麗悄悄走上前去看。原來長着這雙明亮眼睛的是一隻灰色小鼠，這隻老鼠在墊上咬了一個洞，在那裏做了一個舒適的窩。六隻小老鼠簇擁着睡在牠身邊。如果説這一百個房間裏沒有一個活的東西的話，至少這裏有七隻老鼠，牠們看來一點也不孤獨。

"如果牠們不是這麼害怕的話，我要把牠們抱回去，"瑪麗説。

她逛了很久，實在太累了，再也沒有力氣往前走，就返回來。她有兩三次走錯了走廊，迷了路，只好上下亂竄，直到找到她應該走的走廊；最後她終於找到了她房間所在的那層樓，儘管離她自己的房間還有相當距離，而且她不知道她到底是在甚麼地方。

"看起來我又轉錯了，"她説，呆呆地站着，眼前好像是一個短走廊的盡頭，牆上掛着壁毯。"我不知道該往哪裏走。這兒多安靜啊！"

就在她這麼站着並説了這句話之後，寂靜被一個聲音打破了。這又是一個哭聲，但是跟她昨天晚上聽到的不太一樣；這是一種短促的、苦惱的、孩子般的哀號，聲音雖然被甚麼東西堵住，還是穿過牆壁傳了出來。

"聲音比昨天近，"瑪麗説，她的心跳加快了許多。"這的確是哭聲。"

她不經意地將手放在旁邊的掛毯上，緊接着大吃一驚，往後一跳。這塊掛毯原來是一塊門簾，門正開着，她看見門後面又是一段走廊，梅洛太太手拿一串鑰匙，滿臉怒氣地正從那裏走來。

"你在這裏做甚麼？"她一邊説，一邊抓住瑪麗的手臂就走。

"我怎麼對你説的？"

"我走錯方向了，"瑪麗解釋道。"我不知道該往哪裏走，我聽見有人在哭。"

這時候她很恨梅洛太太，但是接下來她更恨她了。

"你甚麼都沒聽見，"管家婆説。"你回你的兒童室去，要不我就打你一道耳光。"

她抓着瑪麗的手臂，又推又拉地走過一個又一個走廊，最後來到她自己的房門前，把她推了進去。

"聽着，"她説，"讓你在哪裏留着你就在哪裏留着，否則的話就把你鎖起來。主人最好替你找個家庭教師，他説過要替你找的。你這樣的孩子是要有個人好好管教管教。我可是忙不過來。"

她走出房間，砰一聲關上門，瑪麗坐在壁爐毯上，氣得臉發白。她沒有哭，而是咬着牙齒。

"明明有人在哭——有人在哭——真的！"她自言自語道。

她現在已經聽到兩次了，這件事情她一定要查明。今天上午她發現了許多事情。她感到自己好像經歷了一次遠距離的旅行，不管怎麼説，一路上始終都有令她開心的東西，她玩過了牙雕小象，在天鵝絨墊做的窩裏看見了灰老鼠和牠的嬰孩。

第七章

花園的鑰匙

兩天以後，瑪麗一睜開眼睛就在牀上坐起來，叫着瑪莎。

"看那曠野！看那曠野！"

暴雨已經停了，昨夜的風已把灰濛濛的霧和雲吹散。風本身也已停止，明媚、湛藍的天空高懸在曠野之上。瑪麗做夢也沒想到會有這麼藍的天空。印度的天空總是赤日炎炎、酷熱難耐；這裏的天空藍得使人感到陰涼，幾乎像是深不見底、人見人愛的湖裏的湖水那樣閃亮，白羊毛似的小塊雲在天穹的一片藍色裏隨處飄浮。廣袤的曠野本身不再是令人壓抑的紫黑色或可怕的灰色，取而代之的是柔和的藍色。

"啊，"瑪莎愉快地咧了一下嘴說。"暴雨暫時過去了。每年這個時候都是這樣的。暴雨在晚上停下來，好像從沒來過，以後也不會再來了。這是因為春天要來了。春天離這裏還有很遠距離，但是它正在來臨。"

花園的鑰匙 · *355*

"我本來還以為英國一年到頭都會下雨，看來永遠都這麼陰沉沉的呢，"瑪麗說。

"哦，才不呢！"瑪莎說，坐在腳跟上，周圍放着她給壁爐塗石墨用的刷。"才不是那麼一回事呢！"（這句話瑪莎說的是約克郡方言。）

"你說甚麼？"瑪麗一本正經地問。在印度的時候土生土長的人們總是說只有少數人聽得懂的方言，所以當瑪莎說出她聽不懂的話時，她並不覺得驚奇。

瑪莎像第一個早晨那樣哈哈大笑。

"真要命，"她說。"我又說起約克郡土話了，梅洛太太叮囑過我不能說的。我剛才的意思是：'根本就不是這麼一回事'，"她說得又慢又小心，"但說起來話就長了。出太陽的時候，約克是世界上陽光最足的地方。我跟你說過，過一段日子，你就會喜歡上曠野的。你等着吧，等到金色的荊豆、金雀花、石楠都開了花，等你看到了所有的紫色鐘形花冠，看到成百上千隻蝴蝶翻飛、蜜蜂嗡嗡，雲雀翱翔、歌唱，到那時候，你就會像狄肯一樣在太陽升起的時候就到曠野上去，整天留在那裏了。"

"我能到那裏去嗎？"瑪麗渴望地說，透過窗戶看着遠處那一片藍色。那是一個如此嶄新、廣袤、奇妙的天地，如此可愛的顏色。

"我不知道，"瑪莎說。"在我看來，你自從生下來後，還沒好好使用過你的腳。你連五英里的路都走不動。那裏離我家的小屋有五英里地。"

"我真想看看你家的小屋。"

瑪莎好奇地盯着她看了一會，才又拿起刷擦起爐柵。她在想，現在這張平庸的小臉，並不像自己第一天早晨看見時那麼乖戾。它看來有點像小蘇珊·安非常想要某種東西時的樣子。

　　"我要問問我的媽媽，"她說。"她是個甚麼事情都有辦法的人。今天是我休息的日子，我準備回家去。哈！我真高興。梅洛太太很看得起媽媽。或許媽媽能跟她談談。"

　　"我喜歡你的媽媽，"瑪麗說。

　　"我想你是會喜歡的，"瑪莎附和道，繼續擦着。

　　"我從沒見過她，"瑪麗說。

　　"是的，你是沒見過，"瑪莎答道。

　　她又蹲坐在腳跟上，用手背擦着鼻尖，好像一時間為甚麼事情感到了困惑，但最後她還是拿定了主意。

　　"嗯，我媽媽通情達理、賣力工作、心地好，而且整潔，誰都會不由自主地喜歡上她，不管他們是否見到過她。每到我休息回家的日子，在穿過曠野時我總是高興得蹦蹦跳跳。"

　　"我喜歡狄肯，"瑪麗接着說。"我從沒見過他。"

　　"哦，"瑪莎大膽地說，"我跟你說過，就連小鳥也喜歡他，還有兔子、野羊、小馬甚至狐狸。我不知道，"瑪莎沉思地盯着她，"他怎樣看你？"

　　"他不會喜歡我的，"瑪麗說，口氣堅決、冷冰冰。"沒有人會喜歡我。"

　　瑪莎臉上又露出沉思的樣子。

　　"你自己是不是很喜歡自己呢？"她問道，似乎她的確很想知道。

瑪麗遲疑片刻，仔細想了一下。

　　“一點都不喜歡——真的，”她答道。“但是以前我從沒想過這一點。”

　　瑪莎微微咧嘴一笑，好像想起了甚麼熟悉的往事。

　　“媽媽有一次也是這麼對我說的，”她說。“當時她正在水池邊洗東西，我在發脾氣，說別人的壞話，她轉過身來對我說：‘你這小女孩，你！你站在那裏說你不喜歡這個、不喜歡那個。你喜歡你自己嗎？’我笑了起來，脾氣很快就沒有了。”

　　她把早餐端給瑪麗之後就興致勃勃地走了，她要走上五英里地，穿越曠野到自家的小屋去，她要去幫媽媽工作，洗洗刷刷，烤好一週的食物，並且玩個痛快。

　　當瑪麗知道瑪莎不在屋裏時，更感到孤單。她盡快地跑到花園裏，第一件事就是圍着噴泉花園跑上十圈。她仔細地數着，跑完之後感到精神好多了。陽光使所有地方看來都變了樣。湛藍的天穹高懸在曠野上，同樣也高懸在米塞爾斯威特莊園之上，她始終抬着頭，仰望着天穹，想像着如果躺在一朵小小的白雲上面，隨着它飄浮，會是甚麼滋味。她走進第一座菜園，看見本·威瑟斯塔夫跟另外兩個花匠在那裏工作。天氣的變化似乎使他變得精神起來。他主動跟她說話。

　　“春天來了，”他說。“你能聞到嗎？”

　　瑪麗嗅嗅鼻子，覺得自己能夠聞到。

　　“我聞到了新鮮、潮濕、好聞的氣味，”她說。

　　“這是肥沃土地的氣味，”他回答說，一邊繼續挖土。“它現在興致勃勃，做好了在它上面長東西的準備。每當播種的季節來到它就高興。在冬天，因為沒事情可做，它就死氣沉沉。在那邊的花園裏，植物會在地底下的黑暗中甦醒過來，太陽會使它們暖和。過不了多久，你就會看見一些綠色的苗從黑色的泥土中鑽出來。"

"是些甚麼花呢？"瑪麗問道。

"番紅花、雪花蓮和黃水仙。你見過嗎？"

"沒有。在印度，下過雨之後，一切都是熱的、潮濕、發綠，"瑪麗說。"我還以為所有東西都是一個晚上就長出來了呢。"

"這些東西一個晚上可長不出來，"威瑟斯塔夫說。"你要耐心等待。它們會這裏竄高一點，那裏長出更多的小苗，今天一瓣葉舒展開來，明天又有一瓣舒展開來。你看着就是了。"

"我會看的，"瑪麗回答說。

很快她又聽到了翅膀輕輕拍打的聲音，立刻知道知更鳥又來了。牠非常活潑歡快，在她的腳跟前跳躍，頭歪在一邊，那麼害羞地看着她，她向本·威瑟斯塔夫問了一個問題。

"你覺得牠還記得我嗎？"她說。

"記得你！"威瑟斯塔夫大聲喘着氣說。"牠記得菜園裏每一棵捲心菜的菜根，更別說人了。以前牠從沒在這裏見過一個女孩，牠想要了解你的一切。你沒有必要試圖向牠隱瞞一切。"

"在牠住的那個花園裏，植物也在地底下的黑暗中甦醒嗎？"瑪麗問道。

"哪個花園？"威瑟斯塔夫嘀咕道，又變得乖戾起來。

"就是長着老玫瑰樹的那個花園。"瑪麗情不自禁地問，因為她太想知道了。"那裏的花都死了嗎，或者到了夏天有一部份能夠活過來？那裏還有玫瑰嗎？”

“問牠吧，”本·威瑟斯塔夫説，肩膀朝知更鳥那裏一聳。“只有牠才知道。十年來除了牠誰也沒有進去。”

十年時間可真夠長，瑪麗想。她就是十年前出生的。

她慢慢地走開，邊走邊想。她開始喜歡起那個花園，就像她開始喜歡起知更鳥、狄肯和瑪莎的媽媽一樣。她也開始喜歡起瑪莎來。當你還不習慣喜歡別人的時候，喜歡這數個人好像已經夠多的了。她把知更鳥也當成人。她在外面沿着常春藤覆蓋的長牆繼續走着，看見樹梢露出牆頭；當她第二次在那裏走來走去時，一件最有趣、最令人激動的事情發生了，這完全是本·威瑟斯塔夫的知更鳥的功勞。

她聽見一聲啾鳴，就抬起頭來朝她左邊光禿禿的花壇看去，只見牠在那裏跳來跳去，假裝在從泥土裏啄甚麼東西，讓她相信牠沒有跟蹤她。但是她知道牠一直在跟着她，她心裏充滿驚喜，幾乎抖了起來。

“你真的記得我！”她叫道。“你記得我！你比世界上任何東西都漂亮！”

她嘰嘰喳喳地説個不停，聲音很吸引人，牠蹦蹦跳跳，搖擺着尾巴，唧唧啾鳴。好像牠也在説話。牠的紅背心好像是緞子的，牠鼓起瘦小的胸脯，那麼優美，那麼端莊，真的像是在向她炫耀，一隻知更鳥會顯得多麼了不起，多麼像個人。當牠允許她越來越靠近牠，俯下身去跟牠説話，並且試圖發出像知更鳥一樣的聲音時，她忘記了自己曾經是個非常倔強的女孩。

哦！想想吧，牠竟然讓她靠這麼近！牠知道，世界上沒有甚麼能夠讓她向牠伸出手去，或者哪怕是最輕微地驚嚇牠。牠知道，因為她是個真正的人——而且比世界上任何一個人都好。她幸福極了，簡直都不敢喘氣了。

花壇並不完全荒蕪。只不過是花沒有了，因為那些多年生的植物被割了下來歇冬了，但是花壇的背後有高高低低的灌木，當知更鳥在牠們下面蹦跳時，瑪麗看見牠跳過了一小堆新挖出來的泥土。牠停在土堆上面，搜尋一條毛毛蟲。這些土是一隻狗給挖出來的，那隻狗想要搜尋一隻鼴鼠，把洞挖得很深。

瑪麗看着這個洞，實在不明白為甚麼會有這麼一個洞，看着看着，她發現一件東西幾乎被埋在新挖出來的泥土裏。這東西像是一個生鏽的鐵戒指或銅戒指，這時知更鳥飛到了附近的一棵樹上，瑪麗伸出手去把戒指撿起來。然而，這不是一個戒指；這是一把舊鑰匙，看起來被埋了很久。

瑪麗小姐站起來，看着掛在手指上的鑰匙，一張小臉簡直像受到了驚嚇一樣。

"也許它被埋了十年了，"她喃喃地說。"也許這就是那個花園的鑰匙。"

第八章

知更鳥指路

她看着鑰匙，看了很久，把它翻來翻去，思考着它的來龍去脈。我前面已經說過，她這個女孩要做甚麼事情從來不懂得徵求別人同意，也不會與大人們商量。關於這把鑰匙，她一心想的只是，如果它是那個被關閉的花園的鑰匙，她就能找到花園的門，也許她能打開它，看看圍牆裏面到底有些甚麼，那些老玫瑰樹怎麼樣了。就因為它被關閉得這麼久，她才一心想着要進去看看。看起來它跟別的地方一定大不一樣，十年來裏面肯定發生了奇怪的變化。另外，如果她喜歡它的話，她每天都可以進去，把門關起來，一個人在裏面盡情玩耍，因為沒人會知道她在哪裏，他們會以為那扇門仍然鎖着，鑰匙還是被埋在地底下呢。想到這裏她高興極了。

　　她一個人住在一幢有一百個神秘地鎖起來的房間的大屋裏，整天沒有甚麼有趣的事情可做，迫使她開動起原本懶惰的腦，激發起她的想像力。毫無疑問，曠野上清純濃烈的空氣起了很大作用。就像這種空氣使她胃口大開，與風搏鬥使她血液暢通一樣，同樣的事情使她的腦也活了起來。在印度時，她總是太熱、太倦怠、太虛弱，對任何事情都不太關心，但是在這裏，她開始關心起來，並想要做一些新奇的事情。她已經感覺到不那麼"倔強"了，雖然並不知道是為甚麼。

她把鑰匙放進口袋，繼續在小路上走來走去。除了她之外，似乎沒人到這裏來，所以她盡可以慢慢地走，打量圍牆，或者不妨說，打量牆上的常春藤。常春藤是礙事的東西，不管她怎樣仔細打量，都只能看見厚厚的、有光澤的、暗綠色的葉。她非常失望。她在小路上走着，看着前面牆裏邊的樹梢，倔強脾氣又有點發作起來了。真是太傻了，她對自己說，就在它旁邊，卻進不去。她帶着放在口袋裏的鑰匙回到屋裏，她打定主意，每當到屋外去的時候都要把鑰匙帶在身上，這樣不管甚麼時候發現了那扇隱蔽的門她都可以進去。

梅洛太太允許瑪莎在她家的小屋裏住一晚，但是她第二天一早就回來工作了，她的臉頰比以往更紅，興致高得不能再高。

"我四時就起牀了，"她說。"哦！曠野上真美，小鳥飛、兔子跑、太陽升。我並不是一路走來的，有一個人用車載了我一段路，我好快活呢。"

關於她的這個休息天，她有一肚子有趣故事要說。她媽媽看見她回家很高興，她們烤好了食物，洗刷了所有東西。她甚至給每個孩子做了一個麵餅，裏面加了一點紅糖。

"當他們從曠野上玩耍回來時，我把餅烘得燙燙的。小屋裏瀰漫着一股吸引人的、香噴噴、滾燙的烘餅香味,屋裏的火生得很旺,孩子們高興得大叫。我們的狄肯說,我家的小屋給一個國王住都夠好的了。"

晚上大家都圍坐在壁爐旁,瑪莎和她媽媽縫補衣服和襪,瑪莎給弟弟妹妹們說從印度來的小女孩的事情,她一向都由瑪莎稱之為"黑人"的人伺候,弄得連襪都不會穿。

"嗨!他們真喜歡聽我說你的事情,"瑪莎說。"他們都想知道關於黑人和你坐的大輪船的故事。我說的那些他們都聽不夠。"

瑪麗思考了一下。

"等下次你再回去的時候,我會說很多很多給你聽,"她說,"這樣你就能告訴他們更多了。我肯定他們喜歡聽騎大象和駱駝的事情,還有軍官們打老虎的事情。"

"哇!"瑪莎興奮地叫了起來。"這樣他們會高興得發瘋的。你真的會這麼做嗎,小姐?這將跟我們曾經聽說過的約克的一次野獸展覽一樣令人高興。"

"印度跟約克郡大不一樣,"瑪麗一邊慢吞吞地說,一邊仔細思考這件事。"我從沒這麼想過。狄肯和你媽媽真的喜歡聽你說我的事情嗎?"

"當然了,我們狄肯的眼睛瞪得圓極了,簡直都要掉出來了,"瑪莎答道。"但是媽媽嘛,當她聽說你好像只有一個人,沒人跟你作伴時,她有點想不通。她說,'克拉文先生沒有給她找個家庭教師或者保姆嗎?'我說,'沒有,他沒有找,雖然梅洛太太說,等他想到的話他會找的,但是她說,他恐怕再過兩三年也想不到呢。'"

"我不要甚麼家庭教師，"瑪麗尖刻地説。

"但是媽媽説，像你這樣的歲數應該學習讀書識字了，也應該有個女人來照料你，她説：'其實，瑪莎，你只要想一想，如果是你的話，一個人住在那麼大的地方，逛來逛去，沒有媽媽照料，你會有甚麼感覺呢。你要盡力使她開心，'她説，我説我會的。"

瑪麗眼睛一眨不眨地盯着她看了很久。

"你的確使我開心，"她説。"我喜歡聽你説話。"

不一會瑪莎走出房間，回來時雙手用圍兜盛着一件東西。

"你看，"她歡樂愉快地咧嘴一笑。"我帶了一份禮物給你！"

"一份禮物！"瑪麗小姐驚喜地叫道。一個擁擠着十四個飢餓的人的小屋裏，怎麼拿得出甚麼禮物來呢！

"一個小販駕着車經過曠野，"瑪莎解釋説，"他把車停在我家門口。他的車上有罈罈罐罐和別的雜貨，但是媽媽沒有錢，甚麼也買不起。正當他要離開時，伊麗莎白·艾倫叫道，'媽媽，他有紅藍木柄的跳繩呀。'媽媽突然叫道，'停一下，先生！跳繩要多少錢？'小販説，'兩個便士。'媽媽就開始在口袋裏翻起來，她對我説，'瑪莎，你是個好女孩，每次都把工錢拿回來給我，我把每一個便士都要分成四瓣花，但是我要拿出兩個便士來，給那個女孩買一根跳繩，'於是她就買了下來，喏，給你。"

她從圍兜裏拿出跳繩，非常自豪地展開來。這是一根結實、細長的繩，兩頭各有一個紅藍條紋的木柄，但是瑪麗·倫諾斯以前從沒見到過跳繩。她注視着繩，臉上露出困惑不解的神色。

"這是怎麼用的？"她好奇地問。

"怎麼用！"瑪莎叫了起來。"你該不是説印度人沒有跳繩吧，儘管他們有大象、老虎和駱駝！怪不得他們大多是黑人，這是這麼用的，看着我。"

她奔到房間中央，兩手各握着一隻木柄，跳了起來，一下，兩下，三下，瑪麗在椅裏轉過身來，目不轉睛地看着她，畫像上那些奇怪面孔好像也在盯着她看，並且疑惑：這個來自小屋裏的普通女孩怎麼這麼大膽，竟敢在她們的眼皮底下這麼放肆。但是瑪莎根本就沒看她們。瑪麗小姐臉上顯示出來的興趣和好奇令她高興，她不停地跳着，邊跳邊數數，一直跳到一百下。

"我還能跳下去，"她停下來後說。"我十二歲的時候能跳五百下呢，但那時候我沒有現在這麼胖，而且那時候我經常鍛煉。"

瑪麗從椅上站起身體，感到興奮起來。

"看起來真有趣，"她說。"你媽媽是個好人。你覺得我也能像你那樣跳嗎？"

"你來試試吧，"瑪莎催促道，把跳繩遞給她。"一開始你跳不了一百下，但是如果你練下去，就會越跳越多的。媽媽就是這麼說的。她說，'沒有甚麼比跳繩對人更有好處的了。這是一個孩子所能擁有的最實用的玩具。讓她在屋外的新鮮空氣裏跳繩，這會使她手腳長得很長，讓它們有力。'"

瑪麗小姐剛剛開始跳的時候，她的手腳顯然沒有多大的力氣。她跳得不太好，但是她非常喜歡跳，不願意停下來。

"穿好衣服，到外面去跳，"瑪莎說。"媽媽說我必須告訴你，要盡可能堅持在屋外活動，哪怕下點雨也沒關係，只要把衣服穿暖和了就行。"

瑪麗穿上外衣，戴上帽，把跳繩搭在手臂上。她打開房門走出去，突然想起了甚麼事情，又慢慢地退回來。

"瑪莎，"她説，"這根繩是你的工資買的。這兩個便士其實是你的。謝謝你。"她説得很尷尬，因為她從來不習慣謝謝別人，或注意到別人在為她做事情。"謝謝你，"她説，並且伸出手去，因為她不知道此外她還該做些甚麼。

瑪莎笨拙地輕輕握了一下她的手，似乎她也不習慣做這樣的事情。然後她笑了起來。

"哈哈！你真是個怪東西，像個老婆婆似的，"她説。"如果這是我家伊麗莎白・艾倫的話，她會親我一下的。"

瑪麗看來更尷尬了。

"你要我親你嗎？"

瑪莎又笑了起來。

"不，不是我要你親，"她回答説。"如果你變了另一個人的話，你自己就會親我了。可是你沒變。跑到外面去，玩你的跳繩去吧。"

瑪麗小姐走出房間時，感到有點困惑。約克郡人好像怪兮兮的，瑪莎對她總是個謎。一開始的時候，瑪麗很不喜歡她，但是現在不一樣了。

這根跳繩真是件寶貝。她邊數邊跳，邊跳邊數，直到臉頰發紅；從出生到現在，她從來沒有像這樣對一件事情感興趣。陽光燦爛，微風輕吹——風不猛，而是令人愜意地一陣陣輕輕拂來，吹來了新翻起來的泥土的清香。她圍着噴泉花園跳，跳到了一條又一條小路上。她最後跳進了菜園裏，看見本・威瑟斯塔夫在挖土並跟知更鳥說話，知更鳥在他腳邊跳躍。她順着小路朝他跳去，他抬起頭來，看着她，臉上露出奇怪表情。她很想知道他是不是會注意到她。她要使他看到她在跳繩。

"哦！"他叫道。"說實在話，也許你畢竟還是個小女孩，也許你的血管裏流淌的是孩子的血，而不是酸奶。你跳繩跳得臉都紅了，千真萬確，就像我的名字叫本・威瑟斯塔夫一樣。我真不相信你會跳繩。"

"我以前從來沒跳過，"瑪麗說。"我剛剛開始學。我只能跳二十下。"

"你接着跳，"本說。"你一個跟野蠻人一起生活的女孩，學得夠好的了。只要看看牠盯着你看的樣子就知道了，"他把頭往知更鳥那裏一歪。"昨天牠一直跟着你。今天還會跟着你。牠會打定主意要弄清這根跳繩是甚麼東西。牠從來沒見過跳繩。哦！"他朝小鳥搖搖頭，"要是不留神的話，你的好奇心早晚會要了你的命。"

瑪麗跳着繩繞遍了花園和果園，沒過兩三分鐘就休息一下。最後她踏上了她自己的那條特別的小路，打定主意試試能不能從小路的一頭跳到另一頭。這段距離很長，開始她跳得很慢，一半距離沒跳到，她就氣喘吁吁，熱得不行，只好停了下來。她並不太在意，因為她已經數到了三十下。她停下來時還高興地笑了一下，還有，看，那隻知更鳥在一根常春藤的長枝條上搖晃着。牠一直跟蹤着她，啾鳴了一聲算是跟她打招呼。她跳着繩朝牠走去，這時她感到口袋裏有樣沉甸甸的東西，她每跳一下，那東西就朝她身上撞一下，當她看見知更鳥時她又笑了。

"昨天你引路到放鑰匙的地方，"她説。"今天你應該引路到門的地方；但是我看你也不知道！"

知更鳥從牠在那裏搖晃的常春藤枝條上飛到了牆頭上，牠張開嘴巴，發出一聲響亮、可愛的囀鳴，純粹是為了炫耀。世界上沒有一樣東西比一隻在炫耀的知更鳥更可愛——而知更鳥幾乎總是在炫耀自己。

瑪麗在聽她的保姆説故事時，常常聽到魔法，她經常説那時候發生的事情幾乎都是魔法。

一小股令人舒適的風吹過小路，這股風比其他的風要強勁一點。風力足以吹動樹枝，而且還能把懸垂在牆上、未經修剪的常春藤枝條吹得搖擺起來。瑪麗走近了知更鳥，突然這陣風把一些鬆散的常春藤枝條吹開，更為突然的是，瑪麗朝枝條跳去，一把抓住了它。因為她看見了枝條下面有樣東西——一個圓球，被掛在它上面的枝葉遮擋着。這是一個門球。

她把手伸到枝葉下面，把它們往旁邊拉。雖然垂懸着的常春藤顯得很厚，其實就是個鬆散搖晃的門簾，儘管有些已經爬過了木頭和鐵的框架。瑪麗既欣喜又激動，她的心開始跳了起來，手也發抖了。知更鳥依然在啾鳴，牠的頭歪在一邊，似乎像她一樣激動。她的手下有一個方方的、用鐵做成的東西，她的手指在那上面發現了一個洞，這是甚麼？

這是一扇鎖了十年的門上的門鎖，瑪麗將手伸進了口袋，掏出那把鑰匙，發現正好跟鎖眼吻合。她把鑰匙插進去，轉了一下。她用兩隻手來轉，鎖轉動了。

然後她深深地吸了口氣，回頭朝小路的那頭看看是不是有人過來。看起來沒有人過來，她情不自禁地又深深吸了口氣，把搖晃的常春藤簾撩起來，把門往後推，門慢慢地打開了——慢慢地。

她悄悄地進了門裏，把門關上，背對着門站在那裏，打量四周；由於興奮、好奇和欣喜，她的呼吸加快了。

她站在了秘密花園裏面。

第九章

最奇怪的屋

誰都無法想像世界上會有看來這麼可愛、這麼神秘的地方。四周高高的牆上爬着沒有葉的玫瑰梗，密密的像是編織的地席把牆壁覆蓋住。瑪麗·倫諾斯知道這些是玫瑰，因為她在印度時見到過許多玫瑰。地上全都覆蓋着枯黃的草，枯草裏長出一叢叢灌木，如果這些灌木能活的話，一定是玫瑰叢。那裏有許多標準的玫瑰，它們的枝葉很舒展，好像小樹。花園裏還有別的樹，所有的樹上都爬滿了玫瑰藤，它們長長的捲鬚拖下來，看來像是輕輕搖晃的簾，隨處可見它們互相交接，或與伸展出來的枝葉連接，從一棵樹爬到另一棵樹上，有時它們本身就搭起一座座可愛的橋，正是這種爬藤玫瑰使這個地方看來那麼奇怪，那麼可愛。現在這些藤蔓上既沒有葉也沒有玫瑰，瑪麗不知道它們是死的還是活的，但是它們大大小小灰色、褐色的枝椏像一片迷霧籠罩着一切，牆壁，樹木甚至枯草，它們從它們攀附的東西上掉落下來，在地上往前延伸。正是這種纏繞着一棵又一棵樹的迷霧般的枝椏使這裏顯得如此神秘。瑪麗原先以為這裏肯定跟其他的花園不一樣，畢竟它們不像它這麼久沒人料理；的確，它與她有生以來見到過的任何地方都不一樣。

"這裏多麼安靜啊！"她喃喃自語。"多安靜啊！"

然後她等待了片刻，在一片寂靜中諦聽着動靜。那隻飛到了樹梢上去的知更鳥像其他一切一樣安靜。甚至沒拍動翅膀；牠蹲在那裏，一動不動，看着瑪麗。

"怪不得牠這麼安靜，"她又喃喃自語道。"十年來，我是第一個在這裏説話的人。"

她從門前走開，躡手躡腳地走着，好像怕吵醒甚麼人似的。她很高興腳下有草，這樣她走路時就不會發出聲響。她像在童話裏似的，走在一條灰色樹木之間的拱廊下面，抬頭看着搭成拱廊的枝椏和捲鬚。

"不知道它們是不是都死掉了，"她説。"這是一座死花園嗎？希望它不是。"

如果她是本‧威瑟斯塔夫，她只要看一眼就能知道這裏的樹木是死的還是活的，但是她只能看見這裏只有灰色和褐色的大小枝椏，連一點花蕾的影子都沒有。

但是她畢竟到了這座神奇的花園的裏面，她隨時都可以從常春藤下的門裏進來，她感到自己像是發現了一個完全屬於她自己的世界。

園內陽光普照，高懸在米塞爾斯威特莊園的這塊特殊地方的藍色天空，似乎比懸在曠野上的天空更加明媚，更加柔和。知更鳥從樹梢上飛了下來，跟在她後面跳躍，或者從一叢灌木飛到另一叢灌木。牠啾鳴個不停，一副忙碌的樣子，好像正在向她指點這裏的種種。一切都顯得奇怪和寂靜，她似乎與任何人都相隔千里，但她卻一點都不覺得孤獨。唯一讓她為難的是，她想知道這些玫瑰是不是都死了，是不是有些可能還活着，隨着天氣轉暖，還會長出花蕾來。她不願意這是個死花園。如果這是個活花園，那將是件多麼奇妙的事啊，四面八方將會開出多麼數不盡的玫瑰啊！

她進來時，把跳繩搭在了手臂上，走了一段路後，心想不妨跳着繩繞遍整個花園，如果想看甚麼東西時就停下來。這裏似乎隨處可見長着草的小徑，在一兩個角落裏，有常春藤搭成的涼亭，裏面有石凳和蒙着苔蘚的高高的花甕。

她走進第二個涼亭，停止跳繩。那裏曾經有一個花壇，她覺得自己看見有樣東西從黑土地上竄了出來——原來是一些淡綠色的尖尖小苗。她還記得本·威瑟斯塔夫説的話，就跪下來看那些東西。

"對，這些是細小的植物，也許是番紅花，也可能是雪花蓮或黃水仙，"她喃喃自語道。

她把腰彎得很低，看着它們，嗅着潮濕的土地清新的氣味。她非常喜歡這種氣味。

"也許在別的地方還有別的東西竄出來，"她説。"我要繞遍花園看一看。"

她沒有跳繩，而是徒步。她走得很慢，眼睛盯着地上，看着舊的路邊花壇和草叢裏面；她繞了一圈，試圖一樣東西都不要漏掉，結果看見了更多淡綠色的尖尖小苗，她又變得非常激動起來。

"這不是一個甚麼都死掉的花園，"她輕輕地叫了起來。"就算玫瑰都死了，還有別的東西活着呢。"

她對種花方面的事情一無所知，但是在那些綠苗往外竄的地方，草似乎很密，她覺得苗沒有足夠的地方生長。她四處尋找，找到了一根尖木棍，就跪下來，把一些野草挖出來清除掉，在苗的周圍清理出一小塊空地。

"現在它們看來可以呼吸了，"清理好第一塊後。她說，"我還要做很多這樣的工作。只要看見有苗的地方我都要這樣做。要是今天來不及，我就明天再來。"

她在花園裏走來走去，挖掘，清除野草，做得滿有樂趣的，走過了一個又一個花壇，走到了樹木下面的草叢裏。這番活動使她渾身發熱，她先是脫掉了外衣，然後摘掉了帽，而且她不知不覺地一直朝着腳下的草和淡綠色苗微笑。

知更鳥忙得不可開交。看見在牠自己的土地上開始了養花種草，牠很高興。牠常常對本·威瑟斯塔夫感到好奇。在養花種草的地方，所有好吃的東西都隨着泥土翻了出來。現在這裏來了一個陌生人，她的身材只有本的一半，但是她很聰明，進入了牠的花園，而且立刻就做了起來。

瑪麗在她的花園裏一直做到吃午飯的時候。事實上，她很晚才想起該吃飯了，當她穿上外衣，戴上帽，拿起跳繩的時候，她簡直不敢相信自己已經做了兩三個小時了。她始終從心底裏感到愉快；在被清理乾淨的地方，可以看見許多淡綠色的小苗，比起原來野草阻礙它們生長時的樣子，它們現在看來精神了一倍。

"今天下午我還要來，"她說，四處打量着她這個新的王國，跟那些樹木和玫瑰叢說話，好像它們能聽懂似的。

然後她輕盈地奔過草地，慢慢地推開那扇舊門，從常春藤下面出去。她的臉頰紅通通，兩眼亮晶晶，午飯吃得又多又快，令瑪莎欣喜不已。

"兩塊肉，兩份大米布丁！"她說。"哦！要是我告訴媽媽，說跳繩對你起了這麼好的作用，她會很高興的。"

瑪麗小姐在用尖木棍挖野草的過程中，挖出了一個白色的根，樣子很像洋蔥頭。她把它放回原地，仔細地把土培好，現在，她很想知道瑪莎能不能告訴她那是甚麼東西。

"瑪莎，"她說，"那些看來像洋蔥頭的東西是甚麼？"

"是球莖，"瑪莎回答說。"許多春季的花都是從球莖裏長出來的。很小的那種是雪花蓮和番紅花，大的那種是水仙、長壽花和黃水仙。最大的是百合以及紫菖蒲。哦！這些花都很好看。我們家那個小花園裏這些花都有，都是狄肯種的。"

"這些花狄肯都認識嗎？"瑪麗問，一個新的想法佔據了她的腦海。

"我家狄肯能使花從磚頭小道上長出來。媽媽說，他用喃喃自語的辦法就能使東西從地裏長出來。"

"球莖生活的時間長嗎？如果沒人幫助它們，它們能一年一年活下去嗎？"瑪麗擔心地問。

"它們能夠靠自己活起來，"瑪莎說。"所以窮人也種得起。如果你不去騷擾它們，它們中的大多數會一輩子在地底下往外掙扎，伸展開來，沒有甚麼樂趣。這裏的林苑裏有成千上萬的雪花蓮。春天來臨時，它們是約克郡最美麗的景色。沒人知道它們最早是甚麼時候種下去的。”

“希望春天現在就來到這裏，”瑪麗說。“我希望看到在英格蘭生長的所有東西。”

她吃完飯，到壁爐地毯前她習慣坐的位置坐下。

“我希望——我希望有一把小鏟，”她說。

“你要鏟做甚麼？”瑪莎笑呵呵地問。“你要挖地嗎？我一定把這件事也告訴媽媽。”

瑪麗看着爐火，沉思了一會。如果她要為她的秘密王國保密的話，就必須處處小心。她沒有做傷害甚麼的事情，但是如果克拉文先生發現她打開了秘密花園的門，一定會大大光火，並且會配一把新鑰匙，再一次將門永遠鎖上。這一點她可實在忍受不了。

“這真是個又大又偏僻的地方，”她慢慢地說，好像在腦裏權衡着一件件事情。“這幢屋是偏僻的，這個林苑是偏僻的，這些花園是偏僻的。許多地方好像都被關了起來。我在印度從來沒做過多少事情，但是可以看見的人比這兒多，傭人以及行軍走過的軍隊——有時候還有樂隊演奏，我保姆說故事給我聽。在這裏，除了你和本·威瑟斯塔夫之外，我連一個可以和我說話的人都沒有。而你要做你的工作，本·威瑟斯塔夫又不常跟我說話。我想，如果我有一把鏟的話，我就可以像他一樣找個地方挖挖土，如果他願意給我一點種子的話，我還可以做個小花園呢。”

瑪莎的神情豁然開朗。

“嘿！”她叫道。“這正是媽媽說的呢。她說，‘那裏地方那麼大，為甚麼不給她一塊呢，就算她甚麼都不種，只種些西芹和小蘿蔔也好呀。她可以挖土、鬆土，她會做得很高興的。'這是我媽媽的原本說的話。"

"是嗎？"瑪麗說。"她懂得的事情真多，不是嗎？"

"哦！"瑪莎說。"正像她說的那樣：'一個養大了十二個孩子的女人，除了知道一些最基本的知識外，還要學一些別的東西。小孩子在幫助你解答難題方面，像四則運算一樣管用。'"

"一把鏟要多少錢——一把小鏟？"瑪麗問。

"嗯，"瑪莎想了一下，"斯威特村裏有一間店，我看見那裏放着一套花匠用的小工具，有鏟、耙和叉，紮在一起，賣兩個先令。這些工具很結實，用它們工作肯定沒有問題。"

"我錢包裏的錢不止兩先令，"瑪麗說。"莫里森太太給了我五先令，梅洛太太也替克拉文先生給了我一些錢。"

"他竟然還記得給你錢？"瑪莎叫道。

"梅洛太太說我每週有一先令的零用錢。她每個星期六給我一先令。我不知道該怎麼花。"

"哇！真闊啊，"瑪莎說。"你可以買到這個世界上你想要的任何東西。我們家小屋的租金只有一先令三便士，我們要得到這筆錢真費力呢。嘿，我想起了一件事情，"她把手擱在臀部。

"甚麼事？"瑪麗急切地問。

"斯威特的店舖裏有袋裝的花種子出售，每一便士一袋，我家狄肯知道甚麼花最好，怎樣種。他經常徒步到那裏去，就是為了好玩。你會用印刷體寫信嗎？"她問得很突然。

"我會用手寫體寫，"瑪麗回答說。

瑪莎搖搖頭。

"我家狄肯只認得印刷體的字。如果你能寫印刷體,我們就可以寫封信給他,請他去買你要的種花用的工具和種子。"

"哦!你是個好女孩!"瑪麗叫道。"你真好!我以前不知道你這麼好。我知道如果我試一試的話,是能寫印刷體的。我們去跟梅洛太太要筆、墨水和紙。"

"我自己就有一點,"瑪莎說。"我買了一點,是為了星期天能給媽媽寫寫信。我現在就去拿。"

她奔出房間,瑪麗站在壁爐旁,興奮地扭着細小的雙手。

"如果我有一把鏟,"她喃喃地說,"我就能把泥土弄得又鬆又軟,並能把野草鏟掉。如果我有種子並能使花長出來,這個花園就再也不會這樣死氣沉沉了——它會活過來。"

那天下午她沒有再出去,因為瑪莎拿着筆、墨水和紙回來後,不得不把桌整理乾淨,把盤、碟甚麼的拿到樓下去,當她走進廚房時,梅洛太太正在那裏,她讓瑪莎做件事情,瑪麗只好等待,似乎等了很久,瑪莎才回來。接着就是給狄肯寫信,這可是一件嚴肅認真的工作。由於瑪麗的家庭教師很不喜歡她,不願意跟她在一起,所以瑪麗學到的東西實在有限。她的拼寫不太好,但是她試了試,發現自己能夠寫印刷體。下面就是瑪莎口述,她用印刷體寫下的信:

親愛的狄肯:

見信好。瑪麗小姐有很多錢,她想請你到斯威特去跑一趟,給她買一些花種子和一套種花工具,她要做一個花壇。選一些最好看、最容易生長的,因為她以前從沒做過這種事,她原來住在印度,那裏跟這裏大不一樣。代我向媽媽和所有的弟弟妹妹問好。瑪麗小姐要給我說更多的事情，這樣我下次回家時你們就能聽到關於大象、駱駝以及先生們獵獅子老虎的事情了。

愛你們的姐姐

瑪莎・菲比・索爾比

"我們把錢裝在信封裏，我讓肉店員工的車載去。他是狄肯的好朋友，"瑪莎說。

"狄肯買好之後我怎樣才能拿到呢？"

"他自己會送來給你。讓他走這麼一趟他才高興呢。"

"哦！"瑪麗驚喜地叫道。"那樣我就能見到他了！我從沒想過我能見到狄肯。"

"你想見他嗎？"瑪莎突然問，因為瑪麗看來非常高興。

"是的，我想。我從沒見到過一個讓狐狸和烏鴉都喜歡的男孩子。我非常想見到他。"

瑪莎顯得有點驚訝，似乎是想起了甚麼事情。

"看我，"她脫口說道，"看我竟然忘了這件事；我本來打算今天早上把它當做第一件事告訴你的呢。我問過媽媽——她說她會親自對梅洛太太說的。"

"你是說——"瑪麗說。

"就是我星期二說的事嘛。問問她能不能讓你坐車到我們的小屋去，嚐一嚐我媽媽做的麥餅、牛油，喝上一杯牛奶。"

好像所有令人開心的事情都在一天裏發生了。想想吧，她竟然能在大白天裏，天空蔚藍的時候穿過曠野！想想吧，她竟然能到擠住着十二個孩子的小屋裏去！

"她覺得梅洛太太會讓我去嗎？"她非常擔心地問道。

"哎，她認為梅洛太太會答應的。梅洛太太知道我媽媽多麼愛清潔，她把小屋收拾得多麼整潔。"

"如果我去的話，我不但能見到狄肯，還能見到你的媽媽，"瑪麗說，仔細回味着這件事，別提有多高興了。"她似乎跟印度的那些媽媽不一樣。"

那天下午她在花園裏的工作結束了，那股興奮的心情過去了，這時她感到很平靜，很沉穩。瑪莎陪她留到喝午茶的時候，但是她們只是舒服地坐着，很少說話。就在瑪莎準備下樓去拿茶托時，瑪麗提了一個問題。

"瑪莎，"她說，"今天那個廚房裏做粗重工作的傭人又牙痛了嗎？"

瑪莎當然微微吃了一驚。

"你為甚麼這麼問？"她問道。

"因為我剛才等你等了那麼長時間你都沒有回來，我就開門出去，沿走廊往前走，想看看你是不是回來了。我又聽見了遠處的哭聲，跟那天晚上聽見的一樣。今天又沒有風，絕對不會是風聲的。"

"哦！"瑪莎不安地說。"你千萬不能在走廊裏走來走去地聽動靜。克拉文先生會生氣的，到時候誰也不知道他會做出甚麼。"

"我不是有意聽的，"瑪麗說。"我只是在等你——結果就聽見了。已經有三次了。"

"糟糕！梅洛太太搖鈴叫我了，"瑪莎說，幾乎是跑着出了房間。

　　“誰也沒住過這麼奇怪的屋，”瑪麗懶洋洋地説，把頭枕在了身邊扶手椅的軟墊上。新鮮的空氣、挖土以及跳繩使她感到了一種渾身舒服的疲倦，她睡着了。

第十章

狄肯

將近一個星期以來，秘密花園裏始終是陽光普照。"秘密花園"是瑪麗的叫法，她想到這個花園時就這麼叫它。她喜歡這個叫法，當美麗的舊圍牆將她包圍在花園裏面，誰也不知道她在哪裏的時候，這種感覺更讓她喜歡。這種時候簡直就像是在與世隔絕的仙境裏。她讀過的為數不多而又喜歡的書都是童話故事，在這些故事裏就有關於秘密花園的。有時候，有人在那裏面睡覺，一睡就是一百年，她覺得這樣做肯定很傻。她可不想睡覺，事實上，她在米塞爾斯威特的日子裏一天比一天清醒。她開始變得願意到屋外去了；她不再討厭風，而是喜歡它了。她奔得比以前快，跑的距離比以前遠，跳繩能跳一百下。秘密花園裏的那些植物的球莖一定非常驚訝，它們的周圍被整理得這麼乾淨，它們可以自由自在地呼吸，說實在的（但願瑪麗小姐能夠知道），它們開始在黑暗的地底下甦醒過來，努力掙扎着往外生長了。太陽可以照耀到它們，讓它們溫暖，雨一下來馬上就能下到它們身上，所以它們感到渾身充滿了活力。

瑪麗是個奇怪的、堅定的女孩，現在她有了一件有趣的、讓她下決心去做的事情，她的確十分投入。她不停地工作，把雜草挖掉，每做一個小時，勞累就增加一分，而她也就更感到高興。對她來說，這就像是一種令人着迷的遊戲。她發現了許多正在發芽的淡綠色的苗，她根本沒想到會有這麼多。它們好像到處都在往外長，她每天都很有把握會發現新的細小的苗，有些實在太細小，就像剛長出地面。苗太多了，她想起了瑪莎說過的"漫天雪花"，以及球莖蔓延，長出新的球莖。這些東西自生自滅已有十年，也許它們蔓延開來，像雪花一樣，成千上萬。她不知道要過多久這些東西才能顯出花的樣子來。她不時地停下手中的工作，環顧花園，想像一下，如果這裏被成千上萬朵美麗的花覆蓋的話，會是怎樣的情景。

在那個陽光燦爛的星期裏，她跟本·威瑟斯塔夫更熟絡了。她有好幾次突然躥到他的身邊，好像是從地底下蹦出來似的，把他嚇一大跳。其實呢，是因為她害怕他看見她後會收拾起工具離開，所以她總是盡可能輕手輕腳地走到他跟前。但是，事實上，他並不像剛開始那樣討厭她。而她明顯地想要他這個大人陪伴，他說不定還暗自得意呢。再說呢，她也比原來要文雅多了。他不知道，當她第一次看見他時，跟他說話的口氣就像跟一個當地人說話一樣，她也不知道一個壞脾氣的、結實的約克郡老人只會聽命令工作，而不習慣於討好他的主人。

"你就像知更鳥一樣，"有一天早晨，當他抬起頭來看見她正在他身旁時，他說。"我從來不知道甚麼時候會看見你，或者你從哪個方向來。"

"牠現在是我的朋友了，"瑪麗說。

"牠就是這樣的，"本‧威瑟斯塔夫突然打斷了她的話。"傻乎乎的，愛虛榮，所以老是巴結女人。為了炫耀和擺動牠尾巴上的羽毛，牠甚麼都願意做。牠的自負甚麼都比不了。"

他難得說很多的話，有時候甚至不回答瑪麗的問題，最多只是哼哼鼻子，但是這個早晨他的話比平時來得多。他把一隻穿着釘有平頭釘的靴子的腳擱在鏟上，打量着瑪麗。

"你來這裏有多久了？"他突然說。

"大概有一個月了吧，"她答道。

"這已經可以看出米塞爾斯威特的好處來了，"他說。"你比原來胖了，臉色也不像原來那麼黃了。你第一次進這個花園時，看樣子像個醜八怪。我對自己說，我從沒見過比你更難看、更令人討厭的小女孩。"

瑪麗沒有沾沾自喜，由於她從來不多考慮自己長得怎麼樣，所以本的話也沒有使她感到煩惱不安。

"我知道我胖了，"她說。"我的襪越來越緊。以前可老是要起皺的。知更鳥來了，本‧威瑟斯塔夫。"

果然是知更鳥來了，她覺得牠比原來更好看了。紅背心像緞子一樣光滑，牠拍打着翅膀，搖晃着尾巴，把頭歪到一邊，跳來跳去，做出種種活潑俏皮的樣子，可愛極了。牠似乎打定了主意要讓本‧威瑟斯塔夫羨慕牠，可是本卻嘲笑牠。

"啊，是你啊！"他說。"你總要在找不到更好的同伴時才想到我。這兩個星期來，你老是把你的背心越弄越紅，把羽毛越擦越亮。我知道你想做甚麼。你在追求某個大膽的小姐，對她撒謊，說你是米塞爾曠野上最好的雄知更鳥，隨時準備與所有其他的雄知更鳥搏鬥。"

"哦，看！"瑪麗叫了起來。

此時的知更鳥顯然又迷人又活躍，牠越跳越近，越來越可愛地看着本·威瑟斯塔夫。牠飛到最近的醋栗叢裏，歪着頭，對着他唱起一支小調。

"你以為你這麼做就能使我原諒你，"本説，拼命把臉皺起來，瑪麗相信他是故意做出不高興的樣子。"你認為沒有誰能超越你——你肯定是這麼想的。"

知更鳥張開翅膀——瑪麗簡直不敢相信自己的眼睛。知更鳥徑直飛到了本·威瑟斯塔夫的鏟柄上，停了在鏟柄頂端。這時老人的臉慢慢地皺成了另外一種表情。他一動不動地站在那裏，好像連呼吸都不敢了——好像他害怕自己哪怕稍微動彈一下就會把知更鳥嚇跑。他説話的聲音放得很輕。

"喲，我太驚訝了！"他説，聲音輕得根本聽不出表示驚訝的意思。"你真會討人喜歡——真的！你這麼懂事，真叫人不可思議。"

他一動不動地站在那裏，幾乎呼吸也不敢，直到知更鳥又拍了拍翅膀，飛走了。他就站在那裏看着鏟柄，好像那裏有魔法似的，然後又挖起土來，好幾分鐘沒説話。

因為他時不時地露出齜牙咧嘴的傻笑，瑪麗跟他説話不覺得害怕。

"你有自己的花園嗎？"她問。

"沒有。我是個單身漢，跟看門的馬丁一起住。"

"如果你有花園的話，"瑪麗問道，"你會種甚麼？"

"捲心菜、馬鈴薯和洋蔥。"

"但是如果你有一個花園的話，"瑪麗接着問道，"你會種甚麼呢？"

"球莖植物和味道好聞的東西——但主要是玫瑰。"

瑪麗臉色一亮。

"你喜歡玫瑰？"她説。

本·威瑟斯塔夫回答前先拔起一根野草，扔到一邊。

"嗯，是的，我喜歡玫瑰。我是從一個小姐那裏聽説玫瑰的，我是她的花匠。在她喜歡的一個地方有許多玫瑰，她像喜歡孩子或知更鳥一樣喜歡它們。我看見過她彎腰親它們。"他又拔出一根野草，對它皺着眉頭。"那是十年前的事了。"

"她如今在哪裏？"瑪麗饒有興趣地問。

"天堂，"他答道，把鐵鏟深深地插進泥土裏，"照人們的説法。"

"那些玫瑰怎麼樣了呢？"瑪麗又問，興趣更大了。

"沒人照顧了。"

瑪麗變得非常焦急。

"它們都快死了嗎？玫瑰如果沒人照顧會不會死呢？"她大膽地問。

"嗯，我也喜歡上它們了——我喜歡她——她喜歡它們，"本·威瑟斯塔夫勉強承認説。"我一年到那裏去一兩次，照料它們一下——給它們剪剪枝、鬆鬆土。它們枯萎了，但是它們的土壤很肥沃，所以有些還活着。"

"當它們沒有枝葉，看來是灰色、褐色和乾枯的，你怎麼知道它們是死的還是活的呢？"瑪麗問。

"等到春天來臨——等到陽光照着它們，雨水淋到它們，雨水淋到它們，陽光照着它們，你就會看出來了。"

"怎麼看——怎麼看？"瑪麗顧不得謹慎，叫了起來。

"沿着枝椏看過去，如果看見這裏那裏有一個個褐色的疙瘩，那就等下過一場暖烘烘的雨後再去看，就會看到發生了甚麼。"他突然打住，奇怪地看着她那張焦急的臉。"你怎麼突然間對玫瑰這麼關心起來了呢？"他問道。

瑪麗小姐感到自己臉紅了。她幾乎不敢回答。

"我——我想種那個——如果我有個屬於我自己的花園的話，"她結結巴巴地說。"我——我沒事情做。我甚麼也沒有——也沒有花園。"

"哦，"本·威瑟斯塔夫看着她，慢慢地說，"這倒是真的。你是沒有。"

他說話的樣子怪極了，瑪麗心想，不知道他是不是有點為她感到難受。她從來沒為自己感到難受。她只是感到累和煩，因為她實在不喜歡跟人交往和做事。但是現在，這個世界好像變了，變得可愛起來了。如果沒有人發現這個秘密花園，她就永遠都能自得其樂了。

她在他身邊又留了十多分鐘，大膽地問了許多問題。他用那種奇怪的、嘟嘟噥噥的聲音一一作了回答，看起來他並沒真的生氣，沒有拔出鐵鏟離她而去。就在她快要離開時，他說了一些關於玫瑰的話，使她想起他說過他一直非常喜歡的那些玫瑰。

"你現在還去看那些玫瑰嗎？"她問。

"今年沒去過。我的風濕病使我的關節非常僵硬。"

他嘟嘟噥噥地說了這句話，然後，突然之間，他好像對她生起氣來，她弄不懂是甚麼原因。

"你聽着！"他厲聲說。"別問這麼多的問題。你是我見到過的最壞的女孩，問這麼多的問題。離開這裏，一個人去玩吧。我今天不想再說話了。"

他說這話時很生氣，瑪麗知道哪怕再逗留一分鐘都是自討沒趣。她慢慢地朝外面的小路走去，心裏仍然在想着他，並對自己說，雖然很奇怪，但本・威瑟斯塔夫確實像換了一個人，他發這麼大的脾氣，她還是喜歡他。她喜歡本・威瑟斯塔夫。不錯，她真的喜歡他。她還開始相信，關於花的事情，他甚麼都懂。

秘密花園周圍有一條栽着月桂樹籬的小路，小路的盡頭是一扇門，門的那邊是林苑的一片林子。她想，她不妨在這條小路上繞一圈，到林子裏去看看會不會有兔子跳來跳去。她很喜歡這麼慢慢地繞，當她終於走到那扇小門前時，就把門推開，走了進去，因為她聽見了一個奇怪的、輕輕的嘯聲，想要弄明白到底是甚麼聲音。

這真是件奇怪的事情。她屏住了呼吸，停下腳步來看。只見一個男孩子坐在一棵樹下，背靠着樹，吹着一根粗木笛。他大約十二歲，長得怪模怪樣。人倒是挺乾淨的，鼻往上翹，臉頰紅得像罌粟，瑪麗小姐從沒見過一個男孩子有這麼圓、這麼藍的眼睛。在他背靠着的樹幹上，棲息着一隻褐色麻雀，注視着他，旁邊灌木叢後面，有一隻雄的山雞正伸長着頸項往外偷看，就在那個男孩的身邊，有兩隻兔子蹲在那裏，用大得出奇的鼻子嗅着——説真的，牠們看起來好像都被吸引到他身邊來，注視他，聽他的木笛發出的那種奇怪的、輕輕的哨子似的聲音。

他看見了瑪麗，舉起手來，跟她説話，那聲音簡直跟他的笛聲一樣又輕又怪。

"別動，"他説。"會把牠們嚇跑的。"

瑪麗一動不動。他的笛聲停了下來，他開始從地上站起來。他的動作很慢，簡直看不出他在動，但他最終站了起來，於是那隻麻雀飛回了樹上，山雞縮回了頭，兔子四腳着地，蹦跳着跑開，雖然牠們看起來一點都不害怕。

"我是狄肯，"那男孩説。"我知道你是瑪麗小姐。"

這時瑪麗才意識到，不知怎麼一回事，她一開始就斷定他是狄肯。除了他，還有誰能吸引兔子和山雞，就像印度人能吸引蛇一樣呢？他有弧線優美的、紅通通的大嘴，他的臉上蕩漾着笑意。

"我站起來時動作很慢，"他解釋説，"因為如果你動作快的話，會嚇着牠們的。當身邊有野生動物的時候，人應該動作輕柔，説話輕聲。"

他跟她説話的口氣根本不像是剛剛認識的樣子，倒像是非常熟悉似的。瑪麗從來沒跟男孩子打過交道，她很害羞，説話就有點僵硬。

"你收到瑪莎的信了嗎？"她問。

他點了一下長着鬈髮、鐵銹色的頭。"我就是為這個來的。"

他彎腰撿起剛才吹笛子時放在旁邊的東西。

"我把栽花種草的工具帶來了。有鏟、耙、叉和鋤頭。喏！都是好東西。還有一把小鏟。我買種子的時候，女店員還給了我一包白罌粟和一包藍翠雀。"

"你能讓我看看種子嗎？"瑪麗說。

她恨不得自己能像他一樣說話。他說起話來又快又從容。聽起來他好像很喜歡她，而且一點都不怕她會不喜歡他，雖然他只是一個很普通的曠野上的孩子，穿着打補丁的衣服，有一張怪模怪樣的臉，一個毛糙的、鐵銹紅頭髮的頭。她走近他，注意到他身上散發出一種清新的歐石楠和草葉的香味，好像他就是這些東西做成的。這令她十分喜歡，她仔細打量他那張紅臉頰、藍眼睛的滑稽的臉，竟然忘了自己是個害羞的人。

"我們坐在這根圓木上看，"她說。

他們坐了下來，狄肯從外衣口袋裏掏出一個皺巴巴的褐色紙包。他解開紮包的繩，裏面有許多更乾淨更小的包，每個包上有一幅畫，畫的是花。

"這裏有許多木犀草和罌粟，"他說。"木犀草是味道最好聞的東西，不管你把它們撒在哪裏，它們都能生長，就跟罌粟一樣。只要你對它們吹笛子，它們就會發芽、開花，它們是最好的東西。"

他停下來，一下子轉過頭去，那張像罌粟一樣紅的臉紅光滿面。

"那隻在叫喊我們的知更鳥是哪裏來的？"他說。

啾鳴聲來自一個茂密的冬青叢，冬青叢上結滿鮮亮、猩紅的草莓，瑪麗心想，我知道這是誰的啾鳴。

"牠真的是在叫我們嗎？"她問道。

"是啊，"狄肯說，好像這是世界上最自然的事情，"牠是在叫牠的朋友。就像是在說，'我來了。看我啊。我要跟你們聊聊。'牠在那兒的灌木叢裏。牠是誰的知更鳥？"

"牠是本·威瑟斯塔夫的，但是我想牠也有點認識我，"瑪麗回答說。

"噢，牠認識你，"狄肯說，聲音又輕了下來。"而且牠喜歡你，跟你交了朋友。牠馬上就會把你的事都告訴我。"

他用瑪麗先前注意到的慢動作走到緊挨着灌木叢的地方，然後發出一個聲音，簡直跟知更鳥自己的啾鳴一樣。知更鳥凝神聽了片刻，然後像回答問題似的回叫了一聲。

"噢，原來牠是你的朋友，"狄肯咯咯地笑着說。

"你覺得牠是嗎？"瑪麗急切地叫道。她迫不急待地想要知道。"你真的覺得牠喜歡我嗎？"

"如果不喜歡你，牠就不會靠近你，"狄肯回答說。"鳥可愛挑剔了，一隻知更鳥有時比人更能看不起一個人。看，牠在巴結你呢。牠在說，'你就不能來見見老朋友嗎？'"

看起來真像是這麼一回事。牠在灌木上跳躍着、啾鳴着，側着身體，歪着頭走來走去。

"鳥說的話你都能聽懂嗎？"瑪麗說。

狄肯擦着毛糙的頭，呵呵地傻笑，那張紅通通的、曲線優美的大嘴幾乎都合不攏了。

"我想我能聽懂，別人也覺得我能聽懂，"他說。"我在曠野上跟牠們一起生活了這麼久。我曾看着牠們從蛋殼裏鑽出來，長出豐滿的羽毛，學會飛翔，開始唱歌，到後來我覺得我成為了牠們中的一份子。有時候我覺得自己也許就是隻鳥，或者是隻狐狸、兔子、麻雀，甚至是個甲蟲，而我自己卻不知道。"

他哈哈大笑，回到圓木那裏，又説起那些花的種子來。他向她描述它們開花後會是甚麼樣子，告訴她怎麼種花，看護它們，給它們澆水。

"聽着，"他突然説，轉身看着她。"我要親自給你把花種上。你的花園在哪裏？"

瑪麗握緊兩隻手，擱在大腿上。她不知道該説甚麼，整整一分鐘甚麼都沒説。她從沒想到過這件事。她覺得很傷心，覺得臉上紅一陣白一陣的。

"你有一個小花園，是嗎？"狄肯説。

她的臉上的確紅一陣白一陣。狄肯看出來了，見她仍然甚麼都不説，狄肯開始覺得糊塗了。

"他們一個小花園都不給你？"他問道。"你根本就沒有花園？"

她把手握得更緊，眼睛朝他看去。

"我對男孩子一點都不了解，"她慢慢地説。"如果我告訴你一個秘密，你能保守秘密嗎？這可是個大秘密。如果給人發現了這個秘密，我不知道該怎麼辦。我相信我會死的！"説最後一句話時她簡直是咬牙切齒。

狄肯更加莫名其妙，又擦起毛糙的頭來，但是他的回答很友善。

"我一向都很能保守秘密的，"他說。"如果我不能向別的男孩子保密，保守狐狸窩、鳥巢、野獸甚麼的秘密，在曠野上就沒有安全了。相信我，我是能夠保守秘密的。"

瑪麗小姐沒有打算伸出手去拉他的袖，但是她卻這麼做了。

"我偷了一個花園，"她很快地說。"那個花園不是我的。它不是任何人的。誰也不要它，誰也沒有曾經進去。也許裏面所有東西都已經死了，我不知道。"

她開始感到熱起來，像以往一樣感到彆扭。

"我不管，我不管！既然只有我來關心它，別人都不關心它，任何人都沒有權利把它從我手裏奪走。他們聽任它死去，讓它自我關閉，"她說到最後動起了感情，雙手捧住了臉，哇一聲哭了起來——可憐的瑪麗小姐。

狄肯好奇的藍眼睛越瞪越圓。

"嗨——嗨！"他慢慢地吐露着驚嘆，既表示驚訝，又表示同情。

"我沒事做，"瑪麗說。"我甚麼也沒有。我發現了那個花園，就走了進去。我只是像知更鳥一樣，而他們不會把它從知更鳥手裏奪走。"

"花園在哪裏？"狄肯壓低嗓子問。

瑪麗一下子從圓木上站了起來。她知道自己又感到彆扭起來，又發了倔強脾氣，她才不管三七二十一呢。她是傲慢的人，是個印度人，同時她感到又熱又難受。

"跟我來，我帶你去看，"她說。

她領着狄肯繞過兩邊栽着月桂的小路，朝常春藤長得很密的小路走去。狄肯跟在她後面，臉上帶着奇怪的，幾乎是可憐的神情。他覺得自己像是被領着去看一個陌生的鳥巢，必須放輕腳步。當她走到牆跟前，掀起垂下來的常春藤時，他吃了一驚。牆上出現了一扇門，瑪麗慢慢地把它推開，他們一起走了進去，然後瑪麗站在那裏，挑釁似的朝四面揮着手。

"就是這裏，"她說。"這是個秘密花園，我是世界上唯一希望它活過來的人。"

狄肯一遍又一遍地打量着它。

"嗨！"他幾乎耳語道，"這是個奇怪的、漂亮的地方！好像在做夢一樣。"

第十一章

米塞爾畫眉鳥的巢

他站在那裏朝四處打量了兩三分鐘，而瑪麗則看着他，然後他開始輕輕地走動，甚至比瑪麗第一次發現自己進入這裏時的走動還要輕。他的眼睛好像要把一切都看進去——灰色的樹和爬在樹上覓食、吊在樹枝上灰色的鳥，牆上和草裏的枝椏，常春藤遮掩下的涼亭，裏面放着石凳和花壇。

"我從沒想到會看見這樣的地方，"他最後說，像耳語一樣。

"你知道這個地方嗎？"瑪麗問。

她的聲音很響，他向她做了個手勢。

"我們一定要低聲說話，"他說，"要不然別人會聽見，並會奇怪我們在這裏做甚麼。"

"噢！忘了！"瑪麗說，嚇得連忙用手捂住嘴巴。"你知道這個花園嗎？"她鎮定下來後又問道。

狄肯點點頭。

“瑪莎跟我説，有這麼一個從來沒人進去的花園，”他答道。“我們常常好奇，不知道那是甚麼樣子的。”

他停下來，看看四處那些可愛的灰枝椏，那雙圓眼睛裏透露着奇怪的欣喜。

“哎！來年春天這些鳥巢肯定還在，”他説。“這裏將是全英格蘭最安全的築巢地方。絕對不會有人走近這裏，樹木的枝椏和玫瑰可以用來築巢。我奇怪的是曠野所有的鳥都沒來這裏築巢。”

瑪麗小姐又不知不覺地把手擱在他的手臂上。

“會有玫瑰嗎？”她喃喃地説。“你説得準嗎？我看它們也許都已死了。”

“哦！不！不是——不是都死了！”他答道。“看這裏！”

他朝最近的那棵樹走去——那是一棵很老很老的樹，樹皮上全都是灰色苔蘚，但是卻頂着一片纏結在一起的樹枝和枝叉。他從衣袋裏拿出一把多刃折刀，打開其中一片刀刃。

“有很多死樹枝應該被割掉，”他説。“還有很多老樹枝，但是去年又長出了一些新的。這兒就有一些新的，”他碰了碰一根嫩枝，它是一種褐綠色，而不是那種乾枯的灰色。

瑪麗也急切、虔敬地碰碰它。

“這根？”她説。“就這根還活着——活得挺好？”

狄肯咧開大嘴笑了。

“就像你和我一樣有活力，”他説。瑪麗記得瑪莎跟她説過，“活力”就是“活的”或“活潑”的。

“我高興它有活力！”她低聲叫道。“我希望它們都有活力。我們在花園裏繞一圈，看看有多少有活力的東西。”

她急得直喘氣，狄肯像她一樣急不可待。他們走過一棵又一棵樹，一叢又一叢灌木。狄肯手裏握着刀，向她指點着各種各樣的東西，在她看來這些東西都是奇妙的。

"它們變得荒蕪了，"他說，"但是那些最強壯的長得很旺盛。嬌嫩的已經死了，但是其他的還在不斷生長，到處蔓延，直到成為一種令人驚嘆的景象。看這裏！"他摘下一根看來已經枯死的灰色粗樹枝。"有人會認為這是一棵死樹，但我不相信它一直到樹根都是死的。我要割斷下面的看看。"

他跪下去，用刀割斷靠近地面的那根看來毫無生氣的樹枝。

"看！"他激動地說。"我跟你說過的吧。那棵樹裏面還有綠色。你看。"

瑪麗在他說話前就已經跪下，全神貫注地看着。

"像這樣有點綠色並且有點汁，就說明它是活的，"他解釋說。"如果裏面是乾的，而且一折就斷，就像我剛才割斷的那根，那就完了。這裏有一個粗大的根，一切有生命的樹枝就從那裏竄出來，如果把老的樹枝割掉，四面的土挖鬆，仔細地照顧，今年夏天就會有——"說到這兒他停了一下，抬頭看看那些往上攀爬的和往下垂掛的小樹枝——"好大一片玫瑰。"

他們走過一叢叢灌木，一棵棵樹。他又有力氣又聰明，知道怎樣用手中的刀割掉枯死的樹枝，能看出哪些似乎已經沒有希望的枝條裏面還有綠色的生命。半個小時之後，瑪麗覺得自己也能看出來了，當狄肯割去一根看來毫無生氣的樹枝，她看見一絲濕潤的綠色時，也會屏着氣息興奮地叫起來。那鏟、鋤頭和叉非常有用。他教她使用叉，他自己則用鏟挖樹根，鬆土，讓空氣往裏面灌。

他們圍着一叢最大的玫瑰興致勃勃地做着，這時他看見了一樣東西，不由得驚喜地叫了起來。

"喲！"他叫道，指着兩三步外的草叢。"那是誰做的？"

原來是瑪麗自己的一塊塊小空地，空地裏面是一簇簇淡水綠色的苗。

"是我做的，"瑪麗説。

"哦，我還以為你一點都不懂種花呢，"他驚叫道。

"我是不懂呀，"她答道，"但是它們那麼小，而那些雜草又密又強壯，它們看來好像連氣都透不過來。所以我給它們弄這麼一塊地方。我甚至都不知道它們是甚麼東西。"

狄肯走過去，在它們旁邊跪下，咧開大嘴笑了起來。

"你做得對，"他説。"一個花匠也不會做得比你更好。現在它們長得就像傑克的豆莖。它們是番紅花和雪花蓮，還有水仙，"他轉身朝另一塊地走去，"這個叫黃水仙。哦，它們會變得非常好看。"

他從一塊空地奔向另一塊空地。

"你一個小女孩，做得夠多的了，"他看着她説。

"我正在長胖，"瑪麗説，"我的力氣也越來越大。我以前動不動就感到累。可我在挖土的時候一點都不累。我喜歡泥土被翻起來時的那種氣味。"

"你能這樣想真好，"他説，很內行地點點頭。"沒有甚麼氣味能比乾淨的泥土味更好聞的了，除了雨下在剛長出來的東西上。天一下雨我就到曠野上去，躺在一叢灌木下面，聽着雨點輕輕地打在石楠上，我只是不停地嗅着鼻子。媽媽常説，我的鼻尖像知更鳥似的抖個不停。"

"你從來不感冒嗎？"瑪麗盯着他，問道。她從沒見過這麼有趣的男孩，或這麼友善的男孩。

"是的，"他咧嘴一笑説。"我從生下來就沒有試過感冒。我從來不怕冷。我像知更鳥一樣，不管甚麼樣的天氣都在曠野上四處奔跑。媽媽説我十二年來吸進了太多的新鮮空氣，所以再也吸不進感冒了。我結實得像山楂樹做的圓頭棒一樣。"

他邊説邊做，瑪麗一邊跟着他，一邊用叉和小鏟給他幫忙。

"這裏有很多事要做！"他興奮地抬起頭來説了一句。

"你能再到這裏來幫我做嗎？"瑪麗請求説。"我肯定也能幫忙。我可以挖土、拔草，你要我做甚麼就做甚麼。哦，來吧，狄肯！"

"如果你要我來，不管下雨還是出太陽，我每天都能來，"他乾脆地説。"這是我一輩子最有趣的事情——關閉在這裏，讓這個花園甦醒過來。"

"如果你能來，"瑪麗説，"如果你能來幫我讓它活過來，我要——我都不知道我要做甚麼了，"她無可奈何地説。面對這樣一個男孩，你能怎麼辦呢？

"我會告訴你該做些甚麼，"狄肯説，高興地咧嘴而笑。"你會長胖，你會像隻小狐狸一樣感到餓，你會像我一樣跟知更鳥説話。哎，我們會有很多很多的樂趣。"

他開始四處走動，抬頭看樹，看牆和灌木叢，一臉沉思的樣子。

"我不想讓它看來像個花匠的花園一樣,把一切都修建得整整齊齊、乾乾淨淨,你呢?"他説。"像這樣多好啊:各種各樣的東西自由生長,互相糾纏在一起。"

"我們不要把它弄得整整齊齊,"瑪麗急切地説。"整整齊齊就不像秘密花園了。"

狄肯擦着他那鐵銹紅的頭髮,一臉的困惑。

"這當然是個秘密花園,"他説,"但是既然它是十年前關閉的,那麼除了知更鳥外,肯定還有別的甚麼人到過裏面。"

"可是門被鎖上了,鑰匙也被埋掉了,"瑪麗説。"沒人能夠進來。"

"這倒是的,"他答道。"這是個奇怪的地方。在我看來,這裏很多地方都被修剪過,不像是十年前做的。"

"這怎麼可能呢?"瑪麗説。

他正在檢查一根莖幹挺直的玫瑰的樹枝,搖了搖頭。

"是啊!這怎麼可能呢!"他喃喃地説。"門鎖着,鑰匙埋掉了。"

瑪麗小姐始終感到,不管她活多久,她永遠都不會忘記她的花園開始甦醒的第一個早晨。當然,在她看來,這天早晨花園似乎就開始甦醒了。當狄肯開始清理場地準備播種時,她想起了巴茲爾想要取笑她時對她唱的歌。

"有一種像鈴鐺一樣的花嗎?"她問道。

"鈴蘭就像,"他答道,用小鏟挖着土,"還有風鈴草、圓葉風鈴草。"

"我們就種一點吧,"瑪麗説。

"鈴蘭這裏已經有了；我看見了。它們會長得太密，我們要把它們分開一點，但是數量很多。其他的花從種子長到開花要兩年時間，不過我可以從我們家的花圃裏帶一點來給你。你為甚麼要這些呢？"

於是瑪麗給他説了印度的巴茲爾和他的弟弟妹妹，她多恨他們，以及他們叫她"倔強瑪麗"的事情。

"他們常常圍着我又跳又唱。他們是這樣唱的——

> 瑪麗，瑪麗，真倔強，
>   你的花園甚麼樣？
> 銀鐘花和海扇殼，
>   還有萬壽菊排成一行。

我始終記着這件事，並且常常在想，是不是真的有像銀鐘那樣的花。"

她微微皺了皺眉頭，把小鏟狠狠地插進泥土裏。

"我才不像他們那樣倔強呢。"

狄肯卻哈哈大笑起來。

"哎！"他説，瑪麗看見他一邊把肥沃的黑土捏碎，一邊嗅着泥土的芬芳。"只要有花，有這麼多這樣友好的野生東西四處蔓延，為牠們自己築巢壘窩，歌唱，啾鳴，那麼誰都沒必要變得倔強，你説是嗎？"

瑪麗捧着種子跪在他的旁邊，看着他，眉頭舒展了。

"狄肯，"她説，"你像瑪莎説的一樣好。我喜歡你，你成為第五個人。我從沒想過我會喜歡五個人。"

狄肯像瑪莎擦壁爐格柵時那樣蹲坐在腳跟上。瑪麗看着他那藍色的圓眼睛、紅臉頰和看着就令人高興的翹鼻子，心想，他看來真是又滑稽又可愛。

"你只喜歡五個人嗎？"他説。"那另外四個是誰呢？"

"你的媽媽和瑪莎，"瑪麗掰着手指説，"還有知更鳥和本・威瑟斯塔夫。"

狄肯樂不可支，只好捂着嘴巴把笑聲壓住。

"我知道你認為我是個怪男孩，"他説，"但是我覺得你是我見過的最怪的小女孩。"

接着，瑪麗做了一件奇怪的事情。她把身體湊向前去，向他問了一個她以前做夢都想不到會向任何人問的問題。她試着用約克話來問這個問題，因為這是他的語言，在印度，如果你懂一個當地人説的話，他會十分高興。

"你喜歡我嗎？"她説。

"哎！"他由衷地回答説，"我喜歡。我很喜歡你，我相信，知更鳥也喜歡你！"

"那就有兩個了，"瑪麗説。"有兩個喜歡我了。"

然後他們比原來更加興致勃勃、更愉快地做了起來。當瑪麗聽到庭院的大鐘敲響，告訴她該吃午飯了時，她嚇了一跳，同時感到遺憾。

"我要走了，"她傷心地説。"你也要走了，是嗎？"

狄肯咧嘴一笑。

"我的午飯很簡單，隨身帶着呢，"他説。"媽媽老是讓我在口袋裏放點東西。"

他從草地上拿起外衣，從口袋裏掏出一個用一條非常乾淨粗糙的、藍白相間的手帕包着的包裹，裏面有兩塊厚厚的麵包，當中夾着一樣東西。

"這是我最常吃的麵包，"他說，"但我今天在裏面夾了一塊很肥的熏肉。"

瑪麗覺得這是一種奇怪的午飯，但他好像已經準備好好享用了。

"快跑回去吃你的飯吧，"他說。"我先吃了。我要在回家前再多做點。"

他背靠一棵樹坐了下來。

"我要把知更鳥叫來，把熏肉的皮給牠啄。牠們可喜歡吃肥肉了。"

瑪麗實在不想離開他。好像他會突然變成一個樹精靈，等她再回到花園時他就離開了。他實在太好了，好得令人難以相信。她慢慢向牆上的那扇門走去，剛走到一半就停了下來並且往回走。

"不管發生了甚麼，你——你絕對不會說出去嗎？"她說。

他剛咬了一大口麵包和熏肉，那罌粟似的臉頰鼓鼓的，但是他努力擠出一個讓她感到鼓舞的笑容。

"如果你是一隻米塞爾畫眉鳥，告訴了我你的巢在哪兒，你想我會告訴任何人嗎？不會的，"他說。"你就像一隻米塞爾畫眉鳥一樣安全。"

她非常相信自己是安全的。

"可以給我一小塊土地嗎？"

瑪麗跑得很快，跑到房間時已經上氣不接下氣了。她的頭髮亂糟糟地貼在額頭上，雙頰發亮，泛着紅暈。飯菜已經放在桌上，瑪莎在餐桌旁等她。

"稍微晚了點，"她說，"你去哪兒了？"

"我見到狄肯了！"瑪麗說。"我見到狄肯了！"

"我知道他會來的，"瑪莎興奮地說。"你覺得他怎麼樣，喜歡他嗎？"

"我覺得——我覺得他很英俊！"瑪麗用不容置疑的口氣說。

瑪莎好像嚇了一跳，但她看來也很高興。

"哦，"她說，"他的確是最好的男孩，不過我們從來不覺得他英俊。他的鼻翹得太厲害了。"

"我就喜歡它往上翹，"瑪麗說。

"他的眼睛太圓，"瑪莎有點困惑地說。"不過顏色挺不錯的。”

“我喜歡圓眼睛，”瑪麗説。“它們的顏色跟曠野上的天空一樣。”

這話説到了瑪莎的心上，高興得她滿臉放光。

“媽媽説那是因為他總是抬頭看鳥和天空的緣故。但是他的嘴很大，是嗎？”

“我喜歡他的大嘴巴，”瑪麗固執地説。“我巴不得我的嘴巴跟他一樣大呢。”

瑪莎高興得咯咯笑了起來。

“你的小臉上要是有一張大嘴巴，那看起來一定非常滑稽，”她説。“但是我知道，你看見他一定也有這樣的感覺。你喜歡那些種子和種花的工具嗎？”

“你怎麼知道他把那些東西帶來了呢？”瑪麗問。

“我從沒想過他會不帶。只要那些東西在約克郡，他就一定會帶來。他可是個靠得住的男孩。”

瑪麗擔心她會問一些難以回答的問題，但是她沒有問。她感興趣的是那些種子和種花的工具。只有一刻讓瑪麗覺得非常緊張，那就是當瑪莎問她該把花種在哪裏的時候。

“這件事你問過誰沒有？”瑪莎問。

“我誰也沒問過，”瑪麗遲疑地答道。

“哦，我不能去問花匠頭，他太一本正經了，羅奇先生真的很一本正經。”

“我從沒見過他，”瑪麗説。“我只見過他手下的花匠和本·威瑟斯塔夫先生。”

"如果我是你的話，我就會問本‧威瑟斯塔夫先生。"瑪莎建議說，"雖然他老愛生氣，又是一臉的惡相，可其實一點也不像看樣子那麼壞。克拉文先生甚麼都由他，是因為克拉文太太還活着的時候他就來這裏了，他最能逗太太開心了。太太很喜歡他。或許他能給你找一個不引人注目的角落呢。"

"如果是不引人注目的角落，那麼就沒人會要它，如果我有了它，也沒人會在意，是嗎？"瑪麗急切地說。

"你說得有道理，"瑪莎答道，"你又不會弄壞甚麼東西。"

瑪麗連忙吃完飯，然後離開餐桌跑回臥室，再把帽戴上，但是瑪莎攔住了她。

"我有件事情要告訴你，"她說。"我是想讓你先把飯吃完再說的。今天早上克拉文先生回來了，我想他要見見你。"

瑪麗一下子臉色發白。

"哦！"她說。"為甚麼！為甚麼！我剛來的時候他不想見我。我聽匹契爾先生說他不想見我。"

"是這樣的，"瑪莎解釋說，"梅洛太太說那是因為我媽媽的緣故。她到斯威特村來，見到了他。他以前從沒跟她說過話，但是克拉文太太到我們家去過兩三次。他忘記了，可我媽媽沒忘記，她大着膽攔住他。我不知道她怎樣跟他提起了你，不過她說的話讓他想到在他明天再次離家前見見你。"

"哦！"瑪麗叫道，"他明天要走了嗎？我太高興了！"

"他要離家很長一段時間呢。或許要到秋天甚至冬天才回來。他要到外地去旅行。他經常旅行。"

"哦！我真高興——真高興！"瑪麗千謝萬謝地說。

如果他要冬天才回來，或者就算秋天回來，她就有時間看着秘密花園活過來。到那時就算讓他發現，甚至再把它收回，她也心滿意足了。

"你看他打算甚麼時候見——"

她沒把話說完，因為這時門開了，梅洛太太走了進來。她穿着最好的黑色連衣裙，戴着帽，領上別着一根大胸針，胸針上有一個人的頭像。這是數年前去世的梅洛先生的彩色畫像，每當她盛裝打扮的時候，總會將它戴上。她看來激動不安。

"你的頭髮亂糟糟的，"她急匆匆地說。"去梳一下。瑪莎，幫她把最好的衣服穿上。克拉文先生讓我來帶她去他的書房。"

瑪麗臉上的紅暈完全消失了。她的心怦怦地跳了起來，她覺得自己又變成了那個僵硬、平庸、沉默寡言的小女孩。她沒理睬梅洛太太，而是轉身進了自己的臥室，瑪莎跟了進去。換衣服、梳頭髮的時候她沒說話，整理乾淨之後她跟着梅洛太太一聲不吭地走進走廊。她有甚麼可說的呢？她是被迫去見克拉文先生的，他肯定不喜歡她，她也不會喜歡他。她知道他會怎麼看她。

她被帶進屋裏的一個地方，以前她從沒來過這裏。最後梅洛太太敲敲一扇門，有人說，"進來，"她們一起走了進去。一個男人坐在壁爐前的大椅上，梅洛太太對他說：

"先生，這就是瑪麗小姐。"

"讓她留在這裏，你可以走了，"克拉文先生說。

梅洛太太出去，把門關上，這時候瑪麗只好站在那兒等着，一個相貌平平的小女孩，絞着兩隻細小的手。她能看出，坐在椅上的那個人背駝得並不十分厲害，儘管高聳的雙肩相當彎曲；一頭黑髮裏夾雜着絲絲白髮。他把頭從高聳的雙肩上轉過來，跟她說話。

"過來，"他說。

瑪麗朝他跟前走去。

他並不醜。要不是臉容那麼悲傷，他的臉本來是很英俊的。他的樣子好像在說，看見她讓他又擔心又發愁，不知道該拿她怎麼辦。

"你好嗎？"他問。

"好的，"瑪麗答道。

"他們對你照顧得好嗎？"

"好的。"

他仔細打量她，同時發愁地擦着額頭。

"你很瘦，"他說。

"我開始胖起來了，"瑪麗用她所知道的自己最僵硬的態度答道。

他的臉色多不高興啊！他的黑眼睛好像並沒看見她，而是看着別的甚麼，他的心思也很難集中在她身上。

"我忘記你了，"他說。"我怎樣才能記住你呢？我本來打算給你請一個家庭教師或保姆甚麼的，但我忘了。"

"請別，"瑪麗説。"請別——"說到這兒，她的嗓子像是被堵住了，再也説不下去。

"你想説甚麼？"他問道。

"我——我夠大了，不要用保姆，"瑪麗説。"也別——也別請家庭教師給我。"

他又擦起額頭，並盯着她看。

"正像那個叫索爾比的女人説的那樣，"他心不在焉地喃喃道。

突然，瑪麗鼓起了勇氣。

"她是——她是瑪莎的媽媽嗎？"她結結巴巴地説。

"對，我想是的，"他答道。

"她理解孩子，"瑪麗説。"她有十二個孩子。她理解他們。"

他好像振作起來。

"你想做甚麼呢？"

"我想到屋外去玩，"瑪麗答道，希望自己的聲音別發抖。"我在印度的時候從來不喜歡在屋外玩，可在這裏，我在屋外一玩肚子就餓，所以人就胖了。"

他打量着她。

"索爾比太太説這對你是有好處的。也許真的有好處，"他説。"她説在給你請家庭教師前最好先讓你健壯一點。"

"當我在外面玩，風從曠野那裏吹來的時候，我就覺得自己很健壯，"瑪麗爭辯説。

"你在哪裏玩呢？"他接着問。

"到處，"瑪麗緊張地説。"瑪莎的媽媽送給我一根跳繩。我又跳又跑——我到處張望，看看有沒有東西從泥土中竄出來。我沒做甚麼壞事。"

"別這麼害怕，"他聲音焦慮地説。"像你這樣的孩子，不會做任何壞事！你可以高興做甚麼就做甚麼。"

瑪麗激動得心都快跳到喉嚨口了，她怕他看出來，就用手摀住喉嚨。她朝他走近了一步。

"我可以嗎？"她聲音發顫地問道。

她那張激動不安的笑臉好像更讓他焦慮了。

"別這麼害怕，"他大聲說。"你當然可以。我是你的監護人，雖然對任何孩子來說，我都是個不好的監護人。我不能把時間花在你的身上或為你操心。我的身體太差了，心裏苦惱、煩躁不安；但是我希望你過得高興舒服。我一點都不明白孩子，不過你有甚麼事儘管跟梅洛太太說，她會打點你的一切。我今天叫你來，是因為索爾比太太說我應該見見你。她的女兒跟她提起過你。她認為你需要新鮮的空氣和四處跑動。"

"孩子的事她甚麼都懂，"瑪麗又忍不住說。

"那是應該的，"克拉文先生說。"我覺得她在曠野上攔住我的行為很大膽，但是她說──克拉文太太生前向對她很好。"提到他去世的太太的名字他好像很難受。"她是個令人尊敬的女人。現在我已經見到了你，我覺得索爾比太太的話很有道理。只要你高興，你就盡量到屋外去玩吧。這裏地方很大，你願意去哪裏就去哪裏，願意怎麼玩就怎麼玩，只要高興就好。你需要些甚麼嗎？"他好像突然想到了甚麼。"你想要玩具、書和洋娃娃嗎？"

"可以──"瑪麗聲音發抖地說，"可以給我一小塊土地嗎？"

情急之下，她也不知道自己的話聽起來有多怪，而且這也不是她本來要說的話。克拉文先生看來很驚訝。

"土地！"他重複道。"你是甚麼意思？"

"種一點東西──讓一些東西生長──看着它們活過來，"瑪麗結結巴巴地說。

他盯着她看了一會，然後迅速用手去抹眼睛。

"你真的——這麼喜歡花園嗎？"他慢慢地説。

"我在印度的時候根本就不懂，"瑪麗説。"我老是生病、疲倦，那裏也很熱，我有時候在沙地裏壘一些小花壇，把花插在裏面。但是這兒跟那裏可不一樣。"

克拉文先生站起來，在書房裏慢慢地踱步。

"一小塊土地，"他自言自語道，瑪麗覺得自己應該提醒他點甚麼。當他停下來，跟她説話時，那雙黑色的眼睛看來幾乎是溫柔慈祥的。

"你要多少地都可以，"他説。"你讓我想到了一個人，她跟你一樣喜歡地，喜歡看着東西生長起來。要是你看見了你想要的那塊地，"他幾乎帶着笑意説，"你要吧，讓它活過來。"

"隨便哪裏的土地，只要沒用的，我都可以要嗎？"

"隨便哪裏都可以，"他答道。"行了，現在你要走了，我累了。"他按鈴叫梅洛太太進來。"再見。我整個夏天都不在家。"

梅洛太太很快就進來了，瑪麗猜想她肯定一直等在走廊裏。

"梅洛太太，"克拉文先生説，"現在我見過了這個孩子，總算明白索爾比太太的意思了。在她開始讀書識字前不要太寵她。給她吃簡單的、有益健康的食物。讓她到花園裏瘋跑。不要把她照顧得太周到。她需要自由和新鮮的空氣、需要四處奔跑。索爾比太太可以時常來這裏看看，也可以讓瑪麗到她的小屋去。"

梅洛太太看來挺高興。聽説她不必太多地"照顧"瑪麗，她不由得鬆了口氣。她一直覺得瑪麗是個討厭的累贅，並且已經盡可能偷懶不去管她。此外，還因為她喜歡瑪莎的媽媽。

"謝謝你，先生，"她説。"蘇珊·索爾比和我是同學，正像你白天跟她散一會步就能發現的那樣，她是個理智的、好心腸的女人。我自己沒有孩子，而她有十二個，沒有比她的孩子更健康更好的了。瑪麗不會受到他們的傷害。關於孩子方面的事情，我本人就常常請教蘇珊‧索爾比。你不妨把她稱為健康專家——如果你懂我的意思。"

"我懂，"克拉文先生答道。"現在把瑪麗小姐帶走，叫匹契爾來。"

梅洛太太把瑪麗帶到她的臥室所在那條走廊的盡頭後就離開了，瑪麗連忙跑回臥室。她發現瑪莎正等在那裏。其實瑪莎剛把碗碟收拾好之後就趕來了。

"我有自己的花園了！"瑪麗叫道。"我願意要哪裏的花園就要哪裏的花園！我要過很久很久才會有家庭教師！你媽媽可以來看我，我也可以去你家！他說像我這樣的小女孩不會做甚麼壞事，我可以願做甚麼做甚麼——願去哪裏去哪裏！"

"哦！"瑪莎興奮地說，"他真好，是嗎？"

"瑪莎，"瑪麗一本正經地說，"他真是個好人，就是他的臉太難看，眉頭皺得太緊。"

她以最快的速度跑到花園。她離開的時間比她預計的要長得多，她知道狄肯回家要走五英里路，所以一定要早點動身。當她從常春藤下面的門鑽進去時，看見狄肯並沒在她離開他時的那個地方工作。種花的工具全都放在一棵樹下。她朝它們奔去，朝那四處打量，但是看不見狄肯的影子。他已經走了，秘密花園裏空無一人——只有那隻剛飛過牆頭的知更鳥停在玫瑰叢上看着她。

"他走了，"她傷心地說。"哦！難道他——難道他——難道他只是個樹精靈嗎?"

　　一個繫在玫瑰叢上的白東西吸引了她的目光。那是一張白紙,原來就是她寫好後讓瑪莎帶給狄肯的那封信。它被一根長枝條繫在玫瑰叢上,她馬上明白過來,是狄肯把它留在那裏的。上面有數個很粗糙的字,還有一幅畫。起初她弄不懂是怎麼一回事。隨後她就明白過來,原來畫的是一個鳥巢,上面蹲着一隻鳥。下面有一句話:

　　"我會回來的。"

第十三章

"我是柯林。"

回去吃晚飯時，瑪麗把狄肯的畫帶了回去，並給瑪莎看。"嗨！"瑪莎非常自豪地說。"我從沒想到我們家狄肯原來這麼聰明。這畫上有一個米塞爾畫眉鳥在巢裏，像活的一樣，有兩隻真米塞爾畫眉鳥那麼大。"

接着瑪麗知道狄肯把這幅畫當成一個信息。他的意思是讓她放心，他一定會保守她的秘密。她的花園就是她的巢，她就像一隻米塞爾畫眉鳥。哦，她多喜歡那個又怪又平凡的男孩啊！

她希望他第二天能夠再來，她盼望着早晨的來臨，進入了夢鄉。

但是約克郡的天氣說變就變，特別是在春天。夜裏，她被粗大的雨點打在窗玻璃上的聲音吵醒。大雨如注，狂風在又老又大的屋的四角和煙囱裏呼嘯。瑪麗從牀上坐起來，感到傷心和氣憤。

"我從沒見過這麼搗亂的雨，"她說。"它偏偏在我不需要它的時候下。”

她躺回去，把臉埋在枕頭裏。但是她沒有哭，而是躺在那裏，詛咒着那沉重的雨點聲，她詛咒狂風和它的呼嘯。她無法重新入睡。那哭喪似的聲音讓她久久地醒着，因為她自己感到悲傷。如果她感到高興，那雨聲就會催她入眠。那風呼嘯得多狂，粗大的雨點多麼兇猛地打在窗玻璃上啊！

“聽起來就像一個人在曠野裏迷了路，一遍遍地繞着圈，大喊大叫，”她說。

她躺在牀上輾轉反側將近一個小時，始終無法入睡，突然有一件事情讓她從牀上坐了起來，把頭轉向門那邊，側耳傾聽。她聽啊，聽啊。

“這次不是風聲了，”她嘀咕道。“這不是風聲。這聲音跟風聲不一樣。這就是我上次聽到的哭聲。”

她臥室的門半掩着，聲音從走廊那頭傳來，是一種很微弱的傷心的哭泣聲。她聽了數分鐘，一分鐘比一分鐘更確定。她覺得自己應該去弄清到底是怎麼一回事。這似乎比秘密花園和埋在地裏的鑰匙更奇怪。也許這會她正是在發倔強脾氣的時候，所以膽也就特別大。於是她下了牀，站在地板上。

“我要去看看是怎麼一回事，”她說。“所有的人都上牀了，我不怕碰到梅洛太太——我不怕！”

她的牀邊有一支蠟燭，她拿上蠟燭，輕輕地走出臥室。走廊黑漆漆的，看來很長，不過她太興奮了，根本顧不了這個。她覺得自己還記得要拐過哪些轉角才能找到那個短走廊，沿走廊開着一扇門，門上掛着掛毯——那天她迷路的時候正好看見梅洛太太從那扇門裏出來。聲音是從那裏傳來的，於是她憑着昏暗的燭光，幾乎是摸索着朝前走，心怦怦地跳着，她感覺自己都能聽到。遠處微弱的哭聲還在傳來，給她引路。有時候，哭聲會稍停片刻，然後又響起來。是不是要在這裏轉彎呢？她停下來思忖。是的，是這裏。順着這個走廊往前走，然後左轉，走上兩極寬闊的梯級，再往右。對，掛着掛毯的門就在前面。

她輕輕把門推開，進去後又關上；她站在走廊裏面，可以非常清楚地聽見哭聲，雖然不是很響。聲音來自她左邊牆的另一頭，再往前一點又有一扇門。她看見一縷燈光從門底下滲出來。有人在那間屋裏哭，是個很小的人。

於是她走過去，把門推開。她站到了房間裏。

這是個大房間，擺放着古色古香的漂亮傢具。有一個矮壁爐，爐牀裏泛着微弱的火光，一張雕花的四柱牀上掛着織錦帳幔，牀邊放着一盞夜燈，牀上躺着一個男孩，正在傷心地哭泣。

瑪麗弄不清自己是在一個真的地方呢，還是她又睡着了，不知不覺地做起夢來。

那男孩有一張瘦削、柔和的臉，臉色蒼白，兩隻眼睛大得好像整張臉都容不下。他還有一頭濃密的頭髮，一大團一大團亂糟糟地堆在額頭上，使他的瘦臉顯得更小。他看來像是個一直在生病的孩子，但是聽他的哭聲，倒不太像是因為病痛，而更像是因為疲倦和生氣。

瑪麗拿着蠟燭站在門邊，屏住呼吸。然後她輕輕地走上前去，隨着她越走越近，燭光吸引了孩子的注意，他在枕頭上轉過頭來，凝視着她，灰色的眼睛瞪得滾圓，好像其大無比。

"你是誰？"他帶點驚嚇地低聲問道。"你是鬼嗎？"

"不，我不是鬼，"瑪麗答道，她的耳語聲聽上去也像受到了一點驚嚇。"你是鬼嗎？"

他拼命盯着她看。瑪麗不由得注意到他的眼睛有多奇怪。那眼睛灰得像瑪瑙，大得整個臉幾乎容不下，因為眼睛四周都是黑色的睫毛。

"不，"他等了一會之後回答說。"我是柯林。"

"柯林是甚麼人？"她結結巴巴地說。

"我是柯林·克拉文。你是誰？"

"我是瑪麗·倫諾斯。克拉文先生是我的姑丈。"

"他是我爸爸，"男孩說。

"你爸爸！"瑪麗大吃一驚。"從沒人跟我說過他有個兒子！他們為甚麼不說呢？"

"過來，"他說，那雙奇怪的眼睛仍然緊盯着她，流露出焦慮的神情。

她走近牀前，他伸出手去摸她。

"你是真的，是嗎？"他說。"我經常做一些很逼真的夢。你或許就是其中的一個。"

瑪麗在離開自己的臥室時披上了一件羊毛晨衣，這會她把晨衣的一角塞到他的手指間。

"摸摸看，它多厚、多暖和啊，"她說。"如果你願意的話，我可以捏你一下，讓你知道我有多真。我有那麼一會還以為你是我夢裏的人呢。"

"你從哪裏來？"他問。

“從我自己的房間呀。風颳得呼呼的，我睡不着，聽見有人在哭，就來看看到底是誰。你為甚麼哭？”

“因為我也睡不着，我頭痛。再說一遍你的名字。”

“瑪麗‧倫諾斯。從來沒人跟你說過我來這裏住的事嗎？”

他還在撫摩着她晨衣的皺褶，但看來似乎有點相信她是真的人了。

“不，”他答道。“他們不敢說。”

“為甚麼？”瑪麗問。

“因為我會害怕讓你看見我。我不想別人看見我，跟我說話。”

“為甚麼？”瑪麗又問，越來越覺得神秘。

“因為我向來都是這個樣子，病懨懨的，只能躺着。我爸爸也不准別人跟我說話。傭人不准提起我。如果我能活下去，那將是個駝子，不過我活不長的。我爸爸想都不願想我會跟他一樣。”

“哦，這是個多麼奇怪的家啊！”瑪麗說。“多麼奇怪的家啊！每件事情都是一個秘密。房間被鎖着，花園被鎖着——還有你！你也被鎖着嗎？”

“不。我是因為不喜歡被帶到外面去，才留在這間房裏的。出去太累了。”

“你爸爸常來看你嗎？”瑪麗大膽地問。

“有時候會來。一般都是在我睡着之後。他不想看見我。”

“為甚麼？”瑪麗禁不住又問。

他的臉上掠過一絲惱怒的陰霾。

“我媽媽在生下我後就死了，所以他看見我就生氣。他以為我不知道，但我常聽別人説起。他幾乎恨我。"

　　"他恨那花園，因為她死了，"瑪麗有點像是自言自語。

　　"甚麼花園？"那男孩問。

　　"哦！就是——就是她生前喜歡的那個花園，"瑪麗結結巴巴地説。"你一直住在這裏的嗎？"

　　"差不多吧。有時候我被帶到海邊去，但是我留不下去，因為那裏的人老是盯着我看，我常常戴着一個鐵支架，讓我的腰挺直，但是有一個大醫生從倫敦來看我，説這樣做很傻。他要我把那東西拿走，要我經常呼吸新鮮空氣。我討厭新鮮空氣，我不願意到外面去。"

　　"我剛來這裏的時候，也不願意到外面去，"瑪麗説，"你為甚麼老是那樣盯着我看？"

　　"因為那些夢太逼真了，"他很傷心地答道。"有時候我睜開眼睛時，不敢相信自己醒着。"

　　"我們兩個都醒着呢，"瑪麗説。她四周打量了一下房間，高高的天花板，陰暗的角落和微弱的火光。"看起來倒真像是在夢裏，而且現在是半夜，家裏所有的人都睡着了——只有我們兩個除外。我們可清醒着呢。"

　　"我不想這是個夢，"男孩不安地説。

　　瑪麗一下子想起了一件事情。

　　"要是你不願意讓別人看見你，"她説，"那要不要我離開呢？"

　　他仍然抓着她晨衣的一角，輕輕地拉了一下。

　　"不，"他説。"要是你走了，那我肯定會認為你是一個夢了。

如果你是真實的，就坐在那個大的踏腳凳上，跟我說話。我想聽聽你的事情。"

瑪麗把蠟燭放在牀邊的桌上，在有墊的凳上坐下。她一點都不想走開。她想留在這個神秘、隱蔽的房間裏，跟這個神秘的男孩說說話。

"你要我告訴你甚麼呢？"她說。

他想知道她來米塞爾斯威特有多久了；他想知道她的房間在哪一條走廊裏；他想知道她一直都做甚麼；她是不是像他一樣不喜歡曠野；她來約克郡之前住在哪裏。她一一回答了所有這些問題，還有很多別的問題，他躺在枕頭上聽着。他讓她說了很多關於印度的事情，說了她在海上航行的事情。她發現，由於他是個經常生病的孩子，所以不像別的孩子那樣懂事。他很小的時候，一個保姆就教他認字，他就經常唸書，看一些很漂亮的書上的圖畫。

雖然在他醒着的時候他爸爸不常來看他，但是爸爸給了他各種各樣有趣的玩具讓他一個人玩。不過，他從來不覺得好玩。他可以要甚麼有甚麼，不喜歡做甚麼就不用做甚麼。

"每個人都要做能夠讓我開心的事，"他滿不在意地說。"這讓我想生氣都不行。沒人相信我能活下去並長大。"

他說話的口氣好像是對這樣的想法早已習慣，一點都沒甚麼可以大驚小怪的。他好像喜歡瑪麗的聲音。在她說話的時候，他就像被催眠似的入神地聽着。有那麼一兩次他懷疑自己是不是打盹了。但是最後他問了一個問題，於是他們開始聊起了一個新的話題。

"你多大了？"他問。

"十歲，"瑪麗答道，一時有點忘乎所以，"你也十歲。"

"你怎麼知道？"他驚訝地問。

"因為當你出生的時候，那花園門是鎖着的，鑰匙被埋掉了。那門鎖了有十年了。"

柯林半坐了起來，靠在手臂肘上，把臉轉向她。

"哪個花園門是鎖着的？是誰鎖的？鑰匙埋在哪裏？"他好像突然來了興趣，大聲地説。

"是——是克拉文先生討厭的那個花園，"瑪麗緊張地説。"他鎖上了門。沒人——沒人知道他把鑰匙埋在了哪裏。"

"那是個甚麼樣的花園呢？"柯林追問道。

"十年來誰都不准進去，"瑪麗小心地回答説。

但是她的小心為時已晚。他太像她了。他也同樣沒別的事情需要操心，所以一個秘密花園像吸引她一樣地吸引着他。他問了一個又一個問題。花園在哪裏？她從沒找過那扇門嗎？她從沒問過花匠嗎？

"他們不願説這件事，"瑪麗説。"我猜他們得到過吩咐，不能回答任何問題。"

"我會讓他們回答的，"柯林説。

"是嗎？"瑪麗遲疑地説，開始感到害怕。如果他能讓人們回答問題，誰知道會出甚麼事呢！

"所有的人都巴不得討我喜歡。我跟你説過，"他説。"如果我能活下去，這個地方早晚就是我的。這個他們都知道。我會讓他們告訴我的。"

瑪麗不知道她自己被寵壞了，但是她清楚地看出這個神秘的男孩一直受到溺愛。他以為整個地球都是他的。他多特別啊，説起活不下去的時候多冷靜啊。

　　"你覺得自己活不下去嗎？"她問道，一方面是因為好奇，另一方面是想讓他忘記那個花園。

　　"我是這樣想的，"他像剛才一樣滿不在乎地説。"自從我懂事起，我就總聽別人説我活不了多久。起初他們認為我太小，聽不懂他們的話，現在，他們以為我聽不見。但是我都聽見了。我的醫生是我爸爸的堂兄。他很窮，如果我死了，那麼等我爸爸也死了之後，整個米塞爾斯威特就是他的。我有理由認為他不想讓我活下去。"

　　"你想活下去嗎？"瑪麗問道。

　　"不想，"他答道，生氣、疲倦的樣子。"但我也不想死。當我感到自己身體不舒服的時候，我就躺在這裏，想這件事情，想啊想啊，想到後來就哭個不停。"

　　"我有三次聽見你哭，"瑪麗説，"但我不知道是誰。你是為這件事情哭嗎？"她多麼想讓他忘記那個花園啊。

　　"我想是的，"他答道。"我們來説點別的事情吧。説説那個花園。你不想去看看嗎？"

　　"想的，"瑪麗小聲回答説。

　　"我也想，"他不依不饒地説。"以前我從沒想過我會真的想要看看甚麼東西，但是我要看看那個花園。我要把那把鑰匙挖出來。我要把那扇門打開。我要他們用我的輪椅把我推到那裏去。這樣就會吸到新鮮空氣。我要讓他們把門打開。"

他變得非常激動，那雙奇怪的眼睛像星星似的閃光，看來比原來更大了。

"他們非得討好我不可，"他說。"我會讓他們把我推到那裏去，我要讓你也去。"

瑪麗雙手緊握着。一切都完了——一切！狄肯再也不會回來。她再不是一隻米塞爾畫眉鳥，躲在安全隱蔽的鳥巢裏了。

"哦，別——別——別這樣！"她叫道。

他直愣愣地看着，好像認為她瘋了！

"為甚麼？"他驚奇地說。"你說過你要看的。"

"我是要看的，"她回答說，嗓子幾乎哽咽了一下，"但是如果你讓人把你推去的話，那就再也不是甚麼秘密了。"

他把身體再往前靠。

"秘密，"他說。"你是甚麼意思？告訴我。"

瑪麗結結巴巴的好像連話都說不完整了。

"你知道——你知道，"她氣喘吁吁地說，"如果除了我們外，別人誰都不知道——如果那裏有一扇門，藏在一些常春藤裏面——如果有——我們就能找到；如果我們能一起偷偷進去，把門關上，誰也不知道裏面有人，我們把它叫做我們自己的花園，我們就當——就當自己是米塞爾畫眉鳥，而那裏是我們的巢，如果我們幾乎每天都在那裏玩，挖土種花，讓那裏再活過來——"

"那是死的嗎？"柯林打斷了她。

"如果沒人去關心它，它很快就要死了，"她接着說。"那些球莖植物會活過來，但是那些玫瑰——"

柯林又打斷了她，像她一樣激動。

“甚麼叫球莖植物？”他很快地插進來說。

“比如像黃水仙，百合，還有雪花蓮。現在它們在地底下生長——把嫩綠的芽伸出地面，因為春天來了。”

“春天來了嗎？”他說。“春天是甚麼樣子的呢？如果你病了，留在房間裏，那就不知道春天是甚麼樣子了。”

“就是陽光照在雨上，雨下在陽光上，植物在地底下活動，往外生長，”瑪麗說。“如果那個花園是個秘密，我們就可以進去，看着那些植物一天天長大，看到有多少玫瑰活了過來。你還不明白嗎？哦，你還不明白，如果我們保守那個花園的秘密，那該有多好嗎？”

他躺回枕頭上，臉上有一種奇怪的表情。

“我從來不曾有過秘密，”他說，“除非關於我不能長大這件事。他們不知道我知道這件事，所以這也算是個秘密。但我更喜歡這個秘密。”

“如果你不讓他們把你推進花園，”瑪麗保證說，“也許——我幾乎可以肯定，總有一天我能找到進去的方法。然後——如果醫生希望你坐在輪椅上到外面去活動，如果你可以想做甚麼就做甚麼，也許——也許我們可以找一個男孩來給你推輪椅，我們就可以獨自到那裏去，那就將永遠是個秘密花園。”

“我應該——喜歡——這樣，”他慢慢地說，眼睛裏流露出夢幻似的感覺。“我應該喜歡這樣。我不應該介意秘密花園裏的新鮮空氣。”

瑪麗開始恢復了正常的呼吸，感覺安全了，因為柯林對於保守秘密的想法似乎也挺高興。她幾乎肯定，如果繼續說下去，就會讓他在心裏對那個花園的看法跟她的看法一樣，就會非常喜歡它，想到任何人都可以隨心所欲地進去，他肯定受不了。

"如果我們能進去的話，我會告訴你它是甚麼樣子的，"她說。"那裏關閉得太久，裏面的東西可能都變得荒蕪了。"

他靜靜地躺在那裏，聽她不停地說着：玫瑰本來應該從一棵樹爬到另一棵樹，然後懸掛下來——很多鳥應該在那裏築巢，因為那裏很安全。然後她跟他說起了那隻知更鳥和本·威瑟斯塔夫，關於知更鳥，要說的話可就多了，而且說起來又容易又安全，所以她也不再害怕。知更鳥讓柯林十分高興，他不停地微笑，到後來幾乎讓人感到他是個漂亮的孩子，起初瑪麗看他那一雙大眼睛，一頭濃密的頭髮，覺得他長得比自己還要平凡。

"我沒想到鳥會是那個樣子，"他說。"不過，要是你總是留在房裏，那麼有許多事情你是看不見的。你懂得真多啊。我覺得你好像一直留在那個花園裏似的。"

她不知該說甚麼，所以甚麼也沒說。他顯然沒指望她會回答，緊接着他就讓她吃了一驚。

"我要讓你看一樣東西，"他說。"你看見壁爐那邊牆上掛着的玫瑰色的絲簾嗎？"

瑪麗原先並沒注意，但她這時抬起頭來一看，看見了。那是一塊柔軟的絲簾，掛在一個好像是畫像的東西上面。

"看見了，"她回答說。

"那上面有一根繩，過去拉一下。"

瑪麗一頭霧水地站起來，找到了繩。當她拉動繩時，簾往旁退去，露出了裏面的一幅畫。那是一個女孩的畫像，女孩有一張笑吟吟的臉，亮麗的頭髮用一根藍絲帶紮着，充滿喜悅的、可愛的灰瑪瑙色眼睛跟柯林那雙悲傷的眼睛一模一樣，由於四周圍着黑色睫毛，看來有實際的兩倍那麼大。

"她是我媽媽，"柯林哀怨地說。"我不知道她為甚麼要死。有時候我因為她這麼做而恨她。"

"多奇怪啊！"瑪麗說。

"要是她還活着，我相信我就不會老這麼生病，"他嘀咕道。"我敢說，我也會活下去。我爸爸也不會恨得連看都不願看我。我敢說，我就會有一個健壯的背部。把簾拉上。"

瑪麗照辦後又坐回腳凳上。

"她比你漂亮多了，"她說，"但是她的眼睛跟你的一樣——至少形狀和顏色是一樣的。為甚麼要把簾拉起來罩住她呢？"

他難受地動着身體。

"是我讓他們這麼做的，"他說。"有時候我不喜歡她看着我。當我生病難受的時候，她老那麼笑着，太過份了。再說，她是我的，我不想讓每個人都看見她。"

兩三分鐘的沉默之後，瑪麗說話了。

"要是梅洛太太發現我來過這裏，那怎麼辦呢？"她問道。

"她會照我說的去做，"他答道。"我要對她說，我想讓你每天都來跟我說話。我很高興你能來。"

"我也是，"瑪麗說。"我會盡量常來，可是，"——她遲疑了一下——"我每天都要去找那個花園的門。"

"是的，你必須這樣做，"柯林說，"你找到後要告訴我。"他躺在那裏想了一會，像剛才一樣，然後又說起話來。

"我想把你也當成一個秘密，"他説。"在他們發現之前，我不會告訴他們。我可以一直把保姆關在門外，説我喜歡一個人。你認識瑪莎嗎？"

"認識，我跟她很熟絡，"瑪麗説。"她服侍我。"

他朝外面的走廊點點頭。

"她就住在那個房間裏。保姆昨天跟她姐姐一起過夜去了，她每次外出就讓瑪莎來照顧我。當我要你來的時候會讓瑪莎告訴你。"

這時瑪麗才明白，當她提到那個哭聲的時候，瑪莎為甚麼會那麼緊張。

"瑪莎早就認識你嗎？"她問道。

"是啊；她常常照顧我。保姆老是離開我，所以就由瑪莎來頂替。"

"我來這裏很久了，"瑪麗説。"我現在該走了吧？看你的眼睛好像要睡覺了。"

"我希望我能在你離開之前睡着，"他非常羞怯地説。

"那就把眼睛閉上，"瑪麗説，把腳凳往他跟前拖，"我要像在印度時我的保姆做的那樣。我要拍你的手，摩擦它，輕輕地唱一首歌。"

"也許我會喜歡這樣，"他帶着睡意説。

她有點為他感到難受，不想讓他躺在那裏卻睡不着覺，於是她就俯在牀上，開始撫摩、拍他的手，用印度語輕輕地唱起一首歌。

"真好，"他説，睡意更濃了，她不停地唱着，拍着，當她抬起頭來看他時，他的黑色睫毛已經貼在臉頰上，他睡着了。於是她輕輕地站起來，拿起蠟燭，悄悄地走了出去。

第十四章

小酋長

早晨來臨時，曠野被籠罩在迷霧裏，雨一刻不停地傾盆而下。今天是無法出門了。瑪莎很忙，瑪麗沒有機會跟她說話，但是到了下午，她讓瑪莎過來跟她一起坐在兒童室裏。瑪莎來的時候帶着她正在編織的襪，每當沒事做的時候，她總是織個不停。

"你怎麼了？"她們一坐下她就問道。"你看來好像有話要說。"

"我是有話要說。我發現是誰在哭了，"瑪麗說。

瑪莎正在編織的襪掉在了腳跟，她目瞪口呆地看着瑪麗。

"你沒有！"她驚叫道。"絕對沒有！"

"我在夜裏聽見了哭聲，"瑪麗接着說。"我就起牀去看哭聲是從哪裏來的。原來是柯林。我找到了他。"

瑪莎嚇得滿臉通紅。

"哎！瑪麗小姐！"她簡直帶着哭音説。"你不該那樣做——你不該！你會給我找麻煩的。我從來沒跟你説過他的事情——但你會給我找麻煩的。我會失去這份工作，我媽媽該怎麼辦呢！"

"你不會失去工作，"瑪麗説。"他見到我去很高興。我們説了很長時間的話，他見到我去可高興了。"

"是嗎？"瑪莎叫道。"你能肯定嗎？你不知道，一旦有甚麼事情惹惱了他，他會是甚麼樣子。他是個大男孩，可哭起來像個嬰兒，但是當他發脾氣的時候，那尖叫聲會把我們嚇壞。他知道我們都做不了主。"

"他沒有生氣，"瑪麗説。"我問他，要不要我走開，可他讓我留下來。他問我問題，我坐在一個大的踏腳凳上跟他説印度、知更鳥和花園。他不讓我走。他讓我看他媽媽的畫像。我離開他之前給他唱了歌，哄他睡着了。"

瑪莎驚呆了。

"我實在不敢相信你的話！"她反駁説。"聽起來你就像是直接走進了一個獅子籠裏。如果他像他大部份時間那樣，肯定會大發脾氣，把整幢屋都吵醒。他不願意讓陌生人看見他。"

"可他讓我看着他。我一直都看着他，他也看着我。我們互相對望！"瑪麗説。

"我不知道該怎麼辦！"瑪莎不安地叫道。"如果梅洛太太發現了，她會認為我破壞了規矩，把柯林的事告訴了你，然後我就要收拾行李回我媽媽家去了。"

"這件事他一點都不會告訴梅洛太太的。這事剛剛開始，應該是一種秘密，"瑪麗堅定地説。"他説每個人都要巴結他，讓他高興。"

"嗯，這倒是千真萬確的——那是個壞孩子！"瑪莎嘆了一口氣說，用圍兜擦擦額頭。

"他說梅洛太太必須讓他高興。他要我每天都去跟他說話，並說他想見我的時候會讓你來告訴我。"

"我！"瑪莎說。"我會失去工作的——我可以肯定！"

"如果你照他說的去做，就不會失去工作，每個人都被命令要服從他，"瑪麗說。

"你難道是說，"瑪莎瞪大眼睛叫道，"他對你很好！"

"幾乎可以說是喜歡我，"瑪麗答道。

"那你肯定是迷住了他！"瑪莎斷定說，長長地吸了口氣。

"你是說用魔法？"瑪麗問道。"我在印度聽說過魔法，但是我不會。我只是進了他的房間，看見他我嚇了一跳，我站在那裏盯着他看。然後他轉過身來，盯着我看。他以為我是一隻鬼或是一個夢，而我以為他是隻鬼或是一個夢。深更半夜的留在那裏，兩個人互不相識，真是怪怪的。我們開始互相問問題。當我問他我要不要離開時，他說我不能走。"

"世界末日到了！"瑪莎喘着氣說。

"他是怎麼一回事？"瑪麗問。

"誰也說不準，"瑪莎說。"他剛生下來，克拉文先生好像就神志失常了，醫生們說應該送他去精神病院，這是因為克拉文太太死了，像我跟你說過的那樣。他一眼都不看那個孩子。他只是胡言亂語，說孩子將來肯定跟他一樣是個駝子，還不如死掉的好。"

"柯林是駝子嗎？"瑪麗問。"看來不像嘛。"

"現在還不是，"瑪莎說。"但是他開始感到處處都不對勁。我媽媽說，這屋裏的麻煩和怒氣足以讓任何一個孩子感到不對勁。大家害怕他的背脊虛弱，於是就對他小心照顧——老是讓他躺着，不讓他走路。有一次他們讓他戴上一個鐵支架，可是他非常惱火，於是就徹底大病了一場。然後一個醫生來看他，讓他們把鐵支架拿走。他非常直率地跟另一個醫生交談——倒是很有禮貌。他說，給這個孩子用的藥太多，對他也太溺愛了。"

"我覺得他是個被寵壞的孩子，"瑪麗說。

"從沒見過像他那樣沒用的孩子！"瑪莎說。"我倒不是說他從沒得過大病。有兩三次他因為傷風感冒而差點要了命。有一次他患了風濕熱，又有一次患了傷寒。嗨！那一次梅洛太太可給嚇壞了。當時他神志不清，她以為他甚麼都不知道，就跟保姆說，'這次他是死定了，這對他和對每個人都是再好不過的。'她看着他，卻見他睜着大眼睛，凝視着她，像她自己一樣清醒。她不知道發生了甚麼事情，但見他凝視着她說，'給我拿點水來，別說話。'"

"你認為他會死嗎？"瑪麗問道。

"我媽媽說，任何孩子要是不呼吸新鮮空氣，或者甚麼也不做，只是躺在牀上看圖畫書、吃藥，都不可能活下去。他非常虛弱，不願意別人把他帶到屋外，他很容易感冒，他說這讓他非常惱火。"

瑪麗坐在那裏看着爐火。

"我在想，"她慢慢地說，"要是讓他出門到一個花園裏去，看看各種各樣的東西生長，會不會對他有好處。這對我是很有好處的。"

"他生過的一場最嚴重的疾病，"瑪莎説，"是有一次他們帶他到噴泉旁的玫瑰叢去。他曾在一張報紙上看到，人們會患一種叫'玫瑰熱'的疾病，他就開始嗅鼻子，並説他感染上了這種疾病，這時一個不懂規矩的新花匠從他身邊走過，好奇地看着他。他一下子發作起來，説那人之所以看他是因為他將成為一個駝子。他哭得發起了高燒，整晚都病。"

"要是他對我發脾氣，我以後再也不去看他，"瑪麗説。

"他想見你的話總能見到你，"瑪莎説。"你一開始就應該知道這一點。"

緊接着鈴聲響了起來，瑪莎把正在編織的東西捲起來。

"肯定是保姆要我陪一陪柯林，"她説。"但願他沒發脾氣。"

她去了大約十分鐘，然後帶着一臉的困惑回來。

"哦，你讓他入迷了，"她説。"他起了牀，在沙發上看圖畫書呢。他叫保姆離開，六時再回去。我要等在隔壁房間裏。保姆剛走他就叫我進去並説，'我要瑪麗來跟我説話，記住，不要告訴其他任何人。'你最好盡快過去。"

瑪麗很想快點過去。她去見柯林的心情不像去見狄肯那樣迫切；但她同樣很想見他。

她走近柯林的房間，那裏壁爐裏的爐火很旺，在日光中她看見那是個非常漂亮的房間。儘管外面大雨傾盆，天色灰濛濛的，但房間牆上的掛毯、掛件、畫像和書本五顏六色，簡直讓房間裏熠熠生輝、舒適宜人。柯林本人看來就像一幅畫。他裹着一件絲絨晨衣，坐在沙發上，背靠一個錦緞大靠墊。兩邊臉頰上各有一個紅點。

"進來，"他説。"我整個早上都在想你。"

"我也一直在想你，"瑪麗答道。"你不知道瑪莎嚇成甚麼樣子。她説梅洛太太會以為是她把你的事情告訴了我，然後她就會被解僱。"

他皺起了眉頭。

"去叫她過來，"他説。"她就在隔壁房間裏。"

瑪麗過去把她帶了過來。可憐的瑪莎直發抖。柯林仍然皺着眉頭。

"你願不願意做讓我高興的事情？"他問道。

"我不得不做讓你高興的事情，少爺，"瑪莎吞吞吐吐地説，臉變得通紅。

"梅洛太太是不是也要做讓我高興的事情呢？"

"每個人都要做，少爺，"瑪莎説。

"嗯，那就好，要是我命令你把瑪麗帶來見我，就算梅洛太太發現了，她又怎麼能解僱你呢？"

"請別讓她知道，少爺，"瑪莎懇求道。

"要是對這件事情她敢説一個字，我就請她離開，"克拉文少爺傲慢地説，"我可以告訴你，她不會喜歡這樣。"

"謝謝你，少爺，"瑪莎説着行了個屈膝禮，"我會盡忠職守的，少爺。"

"我需要的就是你盡忠職守，"柯林更傲慢地説。"我會照顧你的。現在你出去吧。"

當房門在瑪莎身後關上後，柯林發現瑪麗小姐正凝視着他，好像他讓她驚訝不已。

"你為何那樣看着我？"他問。"你在想甚麼？"

"我在想兩件事。"

"哪兩件事？坐下來告訴我。"

"第一件是這樣的，"瑪麗說，在踏腳凳上坐下。"從前在印度的時候，有一次我看見一個男孩，他是個酋長，渾身上下戴滿紅寶石、翡翠和鑽石。他跟他的人民說話的樣子就像你跟瑪莎說話的樣子一樣。所有的人都要照他吩咐的去做——馬上就要做。要是不做，我想他們就會被殺死。"

"我待會要你跟我說說酋長，"他說，"但現在先說說第二件事。"

"我在想，"瑪麗說，"你跟狄肯多麼不同。"

"狄肯是誰？"他說。"多怪的名字啊！"

她想，她不妨告訴他。她可以在說到狄肯的時候不提那個秘密花園。她一直都喜歡聽瑪莎提起他。再說，她渴望提起他。這樣好像能讓他離自己近一點。

"他是瑪莎的弟弟。他十二歲，"她解釋說。"他跟世界上任何一個人都不一樣。他可以像印度人馴蛇一樣馴狐狸、麻雀和鳥。他在笛子上吹出很輕的音調，牠們就會跑來聽。"

他身邊的桌上有一些大書，他突然把其中一本拖到跟前。

"這裏就有一張馴蛇師的照片，"他解釋說。"過來看看。"

這是一本很漂亮的書，裏面有色彩艷麗的插圖，他翻到其中一張。

"他能這麼做嗎？"他急切地問。

"他用笛子吹出輕柔的音調，牠們就過來聽，"瑪麗解釋説。"但是他説這不是魔法。他説這是因為他經常在曠野上，他知道牠們的習性。他説有時候他覺得自己就是一隻鳥或兔子，他非常喜歡牠們。我覺得他還會向知更鳥問問題呢。看起來他們就像在用輕柔的啾鳴交談。"

柯林躺回到靠墊上，眼睛越瞪越大，臉上的斑點灼燒得滾燙。

"再跟我説説他，"他説。

"他對蛋啊巢的甚麼都知道，"瑪麗接着説。"他知道狐狸、獾和水獺都住在哪裏。他保守着牠們的秘密，所以別的男孩找不到牠們的洞穴，也就不能讓牠們受到驚嚇。他對生長或生活在曠野上的一切都知道得清清楚楚。"

"他喜歡曠野嗎？"柯林説。"那是個光禿禿的、可怕的地方，他怎麼會喜歡它呢？"

"那是個最美麗的地方，"瑪麗反駁説。"那裏生長着成千上萬種可愛的東西，那裏有成千上萬隻小動物忙着築巢疊窩，或互相啾鳴歌唱。牠們在地底下或樹上、石楠間忙碌，開心過生活。那是牠們的世界。"

"這一切你都是怎麼知道的呢？"柯林説，用手臂肘支起身體看着她。

"其實我一次也沒去過那裏，"瑪麗突然想了起來。"我只是夜裏坐馬車從那裏經過。我原來覺得那裏很可怕。最先是瑪莎跟我提起那裏，然後是狄肯。當狄肯説起它的時候，你會覺得就像自己看見了那些東西，聽見了牠們的聲音，好像你就站在石楠間，陽光照耀着你，荊豆像蜂蜜一樣好聞——到處都有蜜蜂和蝴蝶。"

"要是你在生病，那就甚麼也看不見，"柯林不安地說。他那個樣子就像在聽從遠處傳來的一把陌生的聲音，弄不懂那是甚麼聲音。

"要是你留在房間裏，同樣看不見，"瑪麗說。

"我不能到曠野上去，"他怨恨地說。

瑪麗沉默了一會，然後她大膽地說了一句。"你可以——在某些時候。"

他像受驚似的動彈了一下。

"去曠野！怎麼去呢？我快要死了。"

"你怎麼知道？"瑪麗毫不留情地說。她不喜歡他說到死亡時的那種樣子。她不太同情他，甚至覺得他是在吹噓這件事。

"哦，從我懂事起就聽說這件事，"他粗聲粗氣地答道。"別人老是嘀咕這件事，還以為我不知道呢。他們也希望我死。"

瑪麗小姐的倔強脾氣又來了，她撅起了小嘴。

"要是別人希望我死，"她說，"那我就偏不死。誰希望你死？"

"那些傭人——當然還有克拉文醫生，因為他能繼承米塞爾斯威特，成為富人，不再窮困。他不敢這麼說，但是每當我病情嚴重的時候，他就高興。當我患了傷寒的時候，他的臉上就長肉。我覺得我爸爸也希望我死。"

"我不信，"瑪麗固執地說。

柯林又轉過頭去看她。

"是嗎？"他說。

然後他躺在靠墊上，一動不動，好像在想心事。沉默了很久。也許兩人都在想着孩子們不太會想的一些新鮮的事情。

"我喜歡倫敦來的那個大醫生，因為是他讓他們把你後背的鐵支架拿走了，"瑪麗最後說。"他說過你要死了嗎？"

"沒有。"

"他怎麼說？"

"他沒有輕聲細語地說，"柯林回答說。"也許他知道我討厭輕聲細語地說話。我聽見他大聲地說一件事情。他說，'這個孩子要是下定決心活下去，就能活下去。讓他振作起來。'聽起來他像是在發脾氣。"

"也許我可以告訴你，誰會讓你振作起來，"瑪麗沉思着說。她感到自己好像願意用某種方法把這件事情弄妥。"我相信狄肯可以做到。他總是談論活的東西。他從來不談死的或有病的東西。他老是抬頭看鳥在天空中飛行——或低頭看地上的東西生長起來。他有一雙圓滾滾的藍眼睛，朝四處看的時候睜得好大好大。他喜歡張開大嘴發出爽朗的大笑——他的臉頰紅得就像——就像草莓。"

她把凳朝沙發跟前拖拖，一想到那張大嘴和那雙大眼睛，她的表情完全變了。

"行了，"她說。"我們別再說死啊死的了；我不喜歡。我們還是來說說話吧。我們來說說狄肯。然後我們再來看你的畫。"

這是她能想到的最好的話題。談論狄肯就意味着談論曠野，談論小屋以及靠每週十六個先令的收入住在小屋裏的十四個人

——那些孩子像野馬一樣吃着曠野上的草就長胖了。還有狄肯的媽媽——以及那根跳繩——太陽照耀下的曠野——以及竄出黑土地的嫩綠色的小苗。這裏充滿了活力，瑪麗從來沒有說過像現在這麼多的話——柯林也從沒像現在這樣又是說又是聽。他們兩個開始莫名其妙地哈哈大笑，就像在一起玩得開心的孩子們常做的那樣。他們笑得忘乎所以，就像兩個普通、健康的十歲的孩子一樣——而不是一個尖刻的、不討人喜歡的女孩和一個病懨懨的、總認為自己快要死的男孩。

他們玩得開心極了，忘記了畫和時間。他們為本·威瑟斯塔夫和知更鳥放聲大笑。柯林坐了起來，好像忘記了自己的背脊很虛弱。這時他突然想起了一件事情。

"你知道嗎，有一件事情我們從沒想到過，"他說。"我們是表姊弟。"

說起來真怪，他們說了這麼多的話，竟然沒有想到過這麼簡單的一件事情，他們笑得更厲害了，因為他們現在情緒好極了，對甚麼事情都覺得好笑。就在他們笑得開心的時候，門打開了，克拉文醫生和梅洛太太進了房間。

克拉文醫生實實在在地吃了一驚，而梅洛太太幾乎後退了一步，因為醫生不小心撞了她一下。

"天哪！"可憐的梅洛太太驚叫道，眼珠都快掉出來了。"天哪！"

"怎麼了？"克拉文醫生走上前去說。"這是怎麼一回事？"

於是，瑪麗又想起了那個小酋長。柯林的答話似乎根本沒把醫生的驚慌和梅洛太太的恐懼放在眼裏。他絲毫沒受干擾和驚嚇，好像走進房間的只是一隻老貓和一隻老狗。

"她是我的表姐，瑪麗·倫諾斯，"他說。"我請她來跟我說話。我喜歡她。只要我派人去請她，她就要來跟我說話。"

克拉文醫生轉向梅洛太太，面露責備的神色。

"哦，先生，"她緊張地說。"我不知道這是怎麼一回事。這裏的僕人誰都不敢說——他們都接過命令。"

"沒人告訴過她甚麼，"柯林說。"她自己聽見了我的哭聲，找到了我。我很高興她來陪我。別傻，梅洛。"

瑪麗看見克拉文醫生一臉的不痛快，但很明顯，他不敢跟他的病人作對。他在柯林身邊坐下，給他聽診。

"恐怕你剛才激動過度了。激動對你沒好處，孩子，"他說。

"要是她一直不來，我就要激動了，"柯林答道，他的眼睛裏開始閃爍出逼人的目光。"我好多了。她讓我好多了。一定要讓保姆把她的點心跟我的一起拿來。我們要一起吃點心。"

梅洛太太和克拉文醫生互相看着，不知道怎麼辦才好，但是顯然甚麼也做不了。

"他看來並不怎麼好，先生，"梅洛太太大膽地說。"但是，"她仔細想了一想——"今天早上在她進房間前，他的氣色是好了一點。"

"她昨天晚上就來了。她跟我在一起很久。她給我唱了一支印度歌，讓我睡着了，"柯林說。"我醒來後感覺就好多了。我要吃早餐。我現在要吃點心。去告訴保姆，梅洛。"

克拉文醫生沒有逗留很久。保姆來了之後，他跟保姆說了數分鐘話，又告誡了柯林兩三句，要他千萬別多說話；千萬不能忘記自己還是個病人；千萬不能忘記他很容易疲勞。瑪麗心想，他好像有很多令人難受的事情不能忘記。

柯林看來挺不耐煩的，那雙黑睫毛的怪眼睛死死地盯着克拉文醫生的臉。

"我就是要忘記，"最後他説。"她讓我忘記了這些。所以我要她來。"

克拉文醫生離開房間時很不高興。他困惑地看了一眼坐在踏腳凳上的那個小女孩。他一進房間她就又變成了那個僵硬的、一聲不吭的孩子，他看不出她有甚麼吸引力。不過，那男孩的確開朗多了——醫生走進走廊，沉重地嘆着氣。

"我不想吃東西的時候，他們總是要我吃，"保姆把點心端進來，放在沙發旁邊的桌上時，柯林説。"現在，只要你們吃東西，我就吃。那些鬆餅看來香噴噴的，還是熱的呢。跟我説説關於酋長的故事。"

第十五章

築巢

又下了一個星期的雨之後，高高在上的藍色的拱形天空終於又出現了，陽光直射下來，熱辣辣的。雖然沒有機會看到秘密花園和狄肯，瑪麗小姐還是很能自得其樂。一個星期好像很快就過去了。她每天跟柯林在一起數小時，談論酋長、花園或狄肯，以及曠野上的小屋。他們一起看漂亮的書和畫，有時候瑪麗唸一點東西給柯林聽，有時候柯林唸給瑪麗聽。當他興致勃勃的時候，瑪麗覺得他一點都不像病人，只不過臉上一點血色都沒有，而且總是躺在沙發上。

"你這個小孩真狡猾，所以能聽到哭聲，那天晚上還從牀上爬起來去查個明白，"有一次梅洛太太這樣說她。"但這對我們很多人來說倒是一件好事。自從你跟他交上朋友後，他就再沒發過一次脾氣，也沒哭哭啼啼。保姆剛剛打算辭職，因為她實在受不了他。但是現在她覺得留下來也沒甚麼，因為你已經替她當值了，"説到這兒她還笑了笑。

　　瑪麗在跟柯林説話時，一直非常小心避免提到那個秘密花園。她有很多事情要向他打聽，但是她覺得千萬不能直接向他提問。首先，由於她開始喜歡跟他在一起，她想弄清他是不是那種你可以向他透露秘密的男孩。他一點都不像狄肯，但是他顯然對一個沒人知道的花園很感興趣，就憑這點，她覺得他也許是信得過的。但是她認識他的時間不長，所以還沒把握。她要弄清楚的第二件事情是：如果他是信得過的——如果他真的是信得過的——那有沒有可能把他帶到那個花園去而不讓其他任何人知道？那位大醫生説過，必須讓他呼吸新鮮空氣，柯林説如果到秘密花園裏去呼吸新鮮空氣，那他不介意。也許，要是他吸進了大量的新鮮空氣，認識了狄肯和知更鳥，看見了東西的生長，他就不會再那麼老想着死不死的。近來瑪麗照鏡的時候，發現自己跟剛從印度來的時候大不一樣了。現在鏡裏的孩子看來比較可愛。就連瑪莎也從她身上看出了變化。

　　"來自曠野的空氣已經讓你受益，"她説。"你不再那麼面黃肌瘦。就連頭髮也不再那麼有氣無力地平攤在頭上。你的頭髮有了點生氣，所以就蓬鬆了一點。"

　　"就像我的身體一樣，真的，"瑪麗説。"我強壯了，也胖了。我肯定，我的頭髮也多了一點。"

　　"看起來是這樣的，可以肯定，"瑪莎説，把圍着她臉蛋的頭髮稍稍弄亂。"你不再像原來那麼難看，臉上也有了一點血色。"

　　如果種花和新鮮空氣對瑪麗有益，那麼對柯林或許也是有益的。但話又説回來，要是他不喜歡讓別人看見他，那麼他也可能不願意看見狄肯。

"為甚麼當別人看着你的時候你會生氣呢？"有一天她這樣問道。

"我從來都是這樣的，"他答道，"我很小的時候就是這樣。那時候，我被帶到海邊去，每天躺在搖籃裏，瞪着眼睛發呆，一些太太小姐們就會停下腳步，跟我的保姆説話，然後她們就説悄悄話，我知道她們是説，我長不大。有時候，她們會拍拍我的臉説，'可憐的孩子！'有一次，當一位太太這麼做的時候，我大叫一聲，咬了她的手。她嚇壞了，拔腿就跑。"

"她覺得你像一隻瘋狗，"瑪麗説，口氣裏卻透着欽佩。

"我才不管她怎麼想，"柯林皺着眉頭説。

"那麼我當時進你房間，你為甚麼沒叫也沒咬我呢？"瑪麗説。然後她慢慢地笑了起來。

"我以為你是隻鬼或是個夢，"他説。"人怎麼可以咬鬼或夢呢，就算你大聲尖叫它們也不怕。"

"要是——要是一個男孩看着你，你會討厭嗎？"瑪麗猶疑地問。

他躺回靠墊上，沉思起來。

"有這麼一個男孩，"他慢慢地説，好像每個字都要經過深思熟慮，"有這麼一個男孩，我相信我是不介意的。就是那個知道狐狸住在哪裏的男孩，他叫——狄肯。"

"我相信你是不會介意他的，"瑪麗説。

"小鳥和其他動物都不介意，"他説，仍然字斟句酌，"也許這就是我也不介意的原因。他是個令動物着迷的人，而我就是隻小動物。"

說到這兒他哈哈大笑起來,瑪麗也笑了起來;結果兩個人笑成一團,覺得他把自己比喻為一個小動物、藏在自己的巢裏,實在非常有趣。

事後讓瑪麗感到的是,她不必再為狄肯擔心了。

當天空再次變藍的第一個早晨,瑪麗很早就醒來。陽光斜斜地射下來,穿進了窗簾。看見陽光,瑪麗喜上眉梢,她跳下牀,奔到窗跟前,拉起窗簾,打開窗,一股清新芬芳的空氣撲面而來。曠野上一片湛藍,整個世界好像被施了魔法。這裏那裏,到處都有輕柔的長笛般的聲音,好像是成群成群的鳥準備去參加一場音樂會。瑪麗把手伸出窗外,伸在陽光裏。

"天氣真暖和——真暖和!"她說。"這樣的天氣會讓綠色的苗不停生長,球莖和根也會在地底下用盡全力地活動。"

她跪下來,身體盡可能探出窗外,大口地吸着、嗅着空氣,這時她想起狄肯的媽媽說他的鼻尖像知更鳥似的顫抖,不由得笑了起來。

"現在肯定還很早,"她說。"那一小朵一小朵的雲都是粉紅色的,我從沒見過這樣的天空。誰也沒有起牀。甚至連小馬夫都還沒有動靜。"

一個突如其來的想法讓她站了起來。

"我等不及了!我要去看我的花園!"

這時候她已經學會了自己穿衣服,她在五分鐘內就穿好了衣服。她知道有一扇小邊門,她可以自己撥開門閂。她穿着襪悄悄下樓去,在門廳裏把鞋穿上。她解開鎖鏈,撥開門閂,打開門,然後一躍跳過了門階，來到了草地上。草好像已經開始返青，陽光直射在她身上，暖烘烘的香味包圍着她。每一叢灌木、每一棵樹上都傳來鳥的啾鳴和歌唱。她打從心底裏感到高興，十指緊緊交叉，抬頭看天，天空藍裏帶紅，紅裏帶着珠色和白色，彌漫着滿目春光，她覺得自己真想放聲歌唱，而且知道畫眉鳥、知更鳥和雲雀也會情不自禁地亮開歌喉。她繞過一個個灌木叢，沿着小路朝秘密花園跑去。

"一切都已大不一樣，"她說，"草比原來綠了，處處都有東西往外竄，舒枝展葉。我相信今天下午狄肯會來的。"

矮牆旁的小路邊有一片綠草帶，那場下得很久的溫暖的雨讓這片綠草帶發生了奇妙的變化。不斷有小苗從一叢叢植物的根部竄出來，藏紅花的莖上隨時可以瞥見深紫色和黃色的花在綻放。六個月前，瑪麗小姐是絕對不會看見世界是如何甦醒過來的，而現在，她把一切都看在了眼裏。

當她來到那片藏着門的常春藤跟前時，一把奇怪、響亮的聲音把她嚇了一跳。那是烏鴉的叫聲，來自牆頂上。她抬頭去看，只見一隻羽毛光潔、藍黑相間的大烏鴉，朝下俯視着她，一副非常傲慢的樣子。她以前從沒這麼近地見過一隻烏鴉，牠讓她有點緊張，但是緊接着牠就張開翅膀，撲棱着飛過了花園。她希望牠不要留在花園裏，帶着這樣的疑慮，她把門推開。當她進到裏面的時候，發現那烏鴉原來是打算留在裏面的，因為牠已經飛到了一棵矮小的蘋果樹上，蘋果樹下躺着一個帶點紅色的小動物，拖着根毛茸茸的尾巴，牠們兩隻都看着狄肯彎曲的身體和鐵銹紅的頭，他正跪在草地上賣力地工作。

瑪麗飛跑過草地，朝他跑去。

"哦，狄肯，狄肯！"她叫道。"你怎麼來得這麼早呢！你怎麼來的呢！太陽才剛剛升起！"

他站起來，笑呵呵的，滿臉發光，一頭亂髮。他的眼睛有點像天空。

"嗨！"他說。"我比太陽起得早多了。我怎麼能夠留在牀上呢！今天早晨世界又開始完全甦醒過來了，是的。它在活動，在哼唱，在發出刮擦聲和呼嘯聲，在築巢，在吐出香味，我再也躺不住了，於是就下了牀。當太陽跳躍着升起的時候，曠野興奮得發瘋，我到了石楠叢中，像發瘋似地奔跑，大聲叫喊、歌唱。我直接就來到了這裏，我不能到別的地方去。哦，這花園正等着我呢！"

瑪麗的手攔在胸前，喘着氣，好像她也一直在奔跑似的。

"哦，狄肯！狄肯！"她說，"我高興得氣都喘不過來了！"

那只有一隻尾巴毛茸茸的小動物看見他跟一個陌生人說話，就從樹底下牠趴着的地方站起來，跑到他跟前；那烏鴉叫了一聲，從樹枝上飛下來，悄悄地停在他的肩上。

"這是一隻小狐狸，"他說，撫摩着紅兮兮的小動物的頭。"牠的名字叫隊長。這隻烏鴉叫煤煙。煤煙跟我飛過曠野，而隊長跑起來就像後面有獵狗在追似的。牠們都跟我有一樣的感覺。"

這兩隻小東西看來一點都不怕瑪麗。當狄肯說話時，煤煙仍然棲息在他的肩上，而隊長則緊挨着他悄悄地走來走去。

"看這裏！"狄肯說。"看這些都已經發芽，還有這些，這些！還有，哦！看這裏這些！"

他啪的一聲跪了下去，瑪麗也跟着在他身旁跪下。他們面前是一大簇藏紅花，開出了紫色、橙色和金色的花。瑪麗把臉湊到那些花上，一遍又一遍地親吻着。

"你從來不會這樣親吻一個人，"她抬起頭來說。"花跟人就是不一樣。"

他一臉的困惑，但依然帶着笑容。

"哎！"他說，"我像那樣親吻過媽媽好多次呢，當我在曠野上玩耍了一天後回家，媽媽站在陽光下的屋門口，看來又高興又舒服，這時候我就會親吻媽媽。"

他們從花園的一處奔到另一處，看見了許多奇妙的景象，弄得他們不得不提醒自己一定要把說話的聲音壓低。他指給她看那些好像已經死掉的玫瑰樹枝上開出的花蕾。他指給她看成千上萬株鑽出地面的嫩綠的小苗。他們把急迫稚嫩的鼻湊近地面，吮吸着它那溫暖的春天的氣息；他們一邊挖土、拔草，一邊充滿欣喜地低聲嬉笑，到後來瑪麗小姐的頭髮像狄肯的一樣亂成一團，臉頰也像狄肯的那樣紅得像罌粟殼似的。

那天早晨的秘密花園裏，一切都充滿喜悅，而其中有一件事更是令人高興，因為它更奇妙。只見一個東西嗖地飛過牆頭，唰……穿過樹木，停在一個花草茂密的角落，原來那是一隻鮮亮的紅胸脯的小鳥，嘴上掛着一個東西。狄肯一動不動地站在那裏，手搭在瑪麗身上，好像突然發現他們兩個剛才在教堂裏哈哈大笑似的。

"我們千萬不能動，"他用約克話悄悄地對瑪麗說。"我們甚至連呼吸都要屏住。我上次給牠餵食的時候就發現牠在求偶。牠是本·威瑟斯塔夫的知更鳥。牠在築巢。要是我們不嚇着牠，牠就會在留在這裏。"

他們輕輕地坐到了草地上，一動不動。

"我們千萬不能盯着牠看，"狄肯說。"要是牠發現我們在打擾牠，牠就會離開。直到這件事完全過去之前，牠會很不開心。牠正在打理家務。牠會比原來更害羞，也更容易生氣。牠沒時間去聽些閒言碎語。我們一定要保持絕對的安靜，要裝得像是草啊樹啊灌木叢啊似的。這樣等牠看慣了我們，我就可以學牠叫上兩三聲，牠就會知道我們並不想打擾牠。"

瑪麗小姐一點都不知道怎樣才能讓自己裝得像草、樹或灌木叢。不過狄肯好像知道，而且他說起奇怪的事情來就像是天底下最簡單最自然的事一樣，所以她覺得這件事對他來說肯定很容易。的確，她仔細看了他數分鐘，心想不知他是否真的能悄悄地變成綠色，長出枝葉。但是他只是一動不動地坐着，說話時聲音也壓得很低，她能聽見才是怪事，可她偏偏就能聽見。

"築巢是春天的一部份，"他說。"我敢肯定，自從有了世界，每年就都是這樣的。牠們有牠們想事情和做事情的方法，人最好不要打擾。如果你太好奇，那麼在春天比在別的季節更容易失去朋友。"

"要是我們在牠身邊走動，我就會忍不住去看牠，"瑪麗盡可能輕輕地說。"我們必須說點其他事。我有件事要告訴你。"

"要是我們說件別的事情，牠肯定更高興，"狄肯說。"你有甚麼事要告訴我？"

"哦——你認識柯林嗎？"她輕輕地說。

他轉過頭去看她。

"你也認識他？"他問。

"我見過他。這個星期我每天都去跟他說話。他希望我去。他說我讓他忘記了他是個病得快要死的人，"瑪麗答道。

驚訝之情從狄肯的圓臉上褪去，他立刻鬆了口氣。

"我聽了很高興，"他叫道。"我太高興了。這樣一來我就輕鬆了。本來我知道，關於他的事我甚麼都不能說，可我又不喜歡隱藏。"

"你不喜歡把花園藏起來嗎？"瑪麗說。

"我絕對不會說出去，"他答道。"但是我對媽媽說，'媽媽，'我說，'我有一個秘密需要保守。這不是一個壞的秘密，這你知道。這不比把鳥巢藏起來更糟。你不要在意，你會在意嗎？'"

瑪麗一直想聽他媽媽的事情。

"她怎麼說？"她問，一點都不怕會聽到些甚麼。

狄肯溫和地咧嘴一笑。

"她說的話一點都不出我的意料，"他答道。"她輕輕地擦擦我的頭，呵呵笑笑，然後說，'哎，孩子，你願意保守甚麼樣的秘密都可以。我認識你可有十二年了。'"

"你怎麼認識柯林的呢？"瑪麗問。

"每個認識克拉文先生的人都知道他有個孩子將會成為殘疾人，大家知道克拉文先生不喜歡別人談論他。大家都為克拉文先生難過，因為克拉文太太那麼年輕漂亮，他們那麼恩愛。梅洛太太每次去斯威特村總要來我家坐坐，她不介意當着我們的面跟我媽媽說話，因為她知道我們都是誠實的孩子。你是怎麼發現他的呢？瑪莎上次回家的時候可緊張了。她説你聽見了他的哭聲然後問她，她不知道怎樣回答。”

瑪麗跟他説起那個半夜，她被狂風驚醒，聽見遠處傳來微弱的哀哭聲，她就拿着蠟燭，順着黑漆漆的走廊找去，最後推開一扇房門，裏面點着昏暗的燈，角落裏有一張四條柱的牀。當她形容起那張跟象牙一樣白的小臉，帶着黑眼圈的奇怪眼睛時，狄肯搖搖頭。

“他的眼睛跟他媽媽的眼睛一模一樣，只不過大家都説他媽媽的眼睛永遠都在笑，”他説。“別人説克拉文先生不願在他醒着的時候看見他，因為他的眼睛跟他媽媽的眼睛那麼像，但是嵌在他那張傷心的臉上又顯得那麼怪異。”

“你覺得他想死嗎？”瑪麗輕輕地問。

“不，但是他希望自己根本就沒生出來。媽媽説這對一個孩子來説是天底下最糟糕的事情。沒人想要的孩子很難長得壯實。克拉文先生給那個可憐的孩子買了用錢所能買到的一切東西。而他寧願忘記這個孩子生活在世界上。因為他害怕自己總有一天會看着孩子，發現他變成了駝子。”

“柯林對自己一點信心都沒有，所以他不願坐起來，”瑪麗説。“他説他總是在想，要是發現他的背上長出一個瘤，他肯定會發瘋，並會大哭大鬧，直到死去。”

“嗨！他不該老躺在那裏想這樣的事情，”狄肯説。“任何一個孩子老想這樣的事情都不會健康。”

狐狸緊挨着他躺在草地上，不時地抬起頭來讓他拍一下，狄肯彎腰擦着牠的頸項，默默地思考了數分鐘。然後他抬頭打量花園。

"我們第一次進來的時候，這裏的一切都好像是灰色的。現在你四處看看，然後告訴我，是不是看見了變化。"

瑪麗看了一下，不由得稍稍屏了一下氣。

"哎！"她叫道，"那灰色的牆正在變。好像有一層綠色的霧從它上面拂過。幾乎像是一塊綠色的薄紗面罩。"

"是啊，"狄肯說。"它會越來越綠，越來越綠，直到灰色全部褪去。你能猜到我在想甚麼嗎？"

"我知道肯定是好的事情，"瑪麗急切地說。"我相信是關於柯林的事。"

"我在想，要是柯林到這裏來，他就不會看着自己的背上長出瘤；他會看着玫瑰叢裏花蕾的綻放，他也會變得很健康，"狄肯解釋說。"我在想，我們能不能想辦法讓他有興致到這裏來，躺在樹底下，他的輪椅裏。"

"我也一直在想這件事。幾乎每次跟他說話的時候我就在想這件事，"瑪麗說。"我一直在想，不知道他能不能保守秘密，我們能不能把他帶到這裏來而又不讓別人看見我們。我想也許你可以幫他推輪椅。醫生說他一定要呼吸新鮮空氣，要是他想讓我們推他出來，沒人敢反對。他不會因為別人而出來，要是他肯跟我們出去，別人也許會高興的。他可以命令花匠走開，這樣就沒人會發現我們了。"

狄肯一邊撓着隊長的背，一邊用心想着。

"我能肯定，這樣對他會有好處的，"他說。"我們決不會覺得他還是沒生下來的好。只有我們兩個孩子看着一個花園生長，再加上他一個。兩個男孩和一個女孩看着春天。我肯定這比醫生的藥方還要好。"

"他在房間裏躺了那麼長時間,一直害怕自己的背會出問題,所以弄得神經兮兮的,"瑪麗説。"他從書本上知道很多東西,但是別的甚麼都不懂。他説他病得太厲害,顧不上注意別的東西,他討厭出門,討厭花園和花匠。但是他喜歡聽這個花園的事情,因為這是個秘密花園。我不敢告訴他太多,但是他説他要來看看。"

"我們總有一天肯定會把他帶到這裏來,"狄肯説。"我可以幫他推輪椅。我們坐在這裏的時候,你注意到知更鳥和牠的伴侶怎樣工作嗎?看牠停在樹枝上,好像在考慮該把牠銜在嘴裏的小枝條放在哪裏。"

狄肯輕輕地吹了聲口哨,知更鳥轉過頭去,用好奇的目光看着他,嘴裏仍然銜着枝條。狄肯像本·威瑟斯塔夫那樣跟牠説話,但是狄肯用的是那種友好建議的語氣。

"不管你把它放在哪裏都挺好的,"他説,"你在鑽出蛋殼前就知道怎樣築巢了。接着做吧,小東西。你沒時間可浪費了。"

"哦,我很喜歡聽你跟牠説話!"瑪麗説,高興地笑着。"本·威瑟斯塔夫老是責罵牠,拿牠開玩笑,牠跳來跳去,像是聽得懂每一句話似的,我知道牠喜歡這樣。本·威瑟斯塔夫説牠非常自負,寧願別人拿石頭砸牠也別不把牠當一回事。"

狄肯也笑了起來,接着説話。

"你知道我們不會打擾你,"他對知更鳥説。"我們自己也跟野生的東西差不多。我們也在築巢,上帝保佑你。小心別把我們的事洩露出去。"

知更鳥的嘴裏銜着東西，所以沒有答話，但是當牠銜着枝條飛到花園裏牠自己的角落的時候，瑪麗從牠晶瑩透亮的眼睛裏看出，牠是絕對不會把他們的秘密透露給任何人的。

"我就不來！"瑪麗説。

瑪麗説那天早晨他們發現有很多事情要做，瑪麗很晚回到家裏，又匆忙趕回去工作，忙到最後才突然想起了柯林。

"去告訴柯林，就説我現在沒時間去看他，"她對瑪莎説。"我在花園裏忙不過來。"

瑪莎看來一臉的惶恐。

"哎！瑪麗小姐，"她説，"要是我跟他説了，他也許會生氣的。"

但是瑪麗可不像別人那麼怕他，她也不是個願意放棄自己主意的人。

"我沒時間留下來，"她答道。"狄肯等着我呢，"説完她就跑走了。

那天下午甚至比早晨還要可愛。花園裏幾乎所有的雜草都被拔掉，大部份玫瑰和樹木都被修剪過或鬆過土。狄肯把自己的鏟帶來，他教會了瑪麗使用她的所有的工具，所以現在已經很明顯，雖然這個可愛的荒蕪之地不會變成一個"花匠的花園"，但它會在春天過去之前變成一個雜亂但又有花生長的地方。

"頭頂上會有蘋果花和草莓花，"狄肯說，拼命工作着。"牆邊的桃樹和李樹也會開花，草地會變成一張花的地毯。"

小狐狸和禿鼻烏鴉像他們一樣忙碌和歡快，知更鳥和牠的伴侶像兩道細小的閃電飛來飛去。有時候烏鴉會振動黑色的翅膀，從林苑中的樹梢上一衝而過。每次飛回來時，總是停在狄肯的身旁，呱呱地叫着，像是在講述牠的歷險，狄肯跟牠說話，就像跟知更鳥說話一樣。有一次，狄肯實在太忙，一開始沒顧上搭理牠，牠就飛到了狄肯的肩上，用牠的大嘴輕輕地啄狄肯的耳朵。當瑪麗提出休息一下的時候，狄肯就跟她一起坐在一棵樹下，他還從口袋裏掏出笛子，輕輕吹出一段奇妙的音符，兩隻麻雀出現在牆頭，看着他們並且靜靜地聽着。

"你現在比過去強壯多了，"他看着正在挖土的瑪麗說。"你看來跟原來不一樣了，真的。"

瑪麗因為工作再加上興致勃勃，臉上紅彤彤的。

"我一天比一天胖，"她很興奮地說。"梅洛太太都要給我準備大一點的衣服了。瑪莎說我的頭髮比原先濃密了。不像原來那樣捲鬈似的平攤在頭上。"

當他們分別的時候，太陽開始落山，金色的陽光斜斜的射到樹底。

"明天會是好天氣，"狄肯說，"我會在太陽升起的時候回來工作。"

"我也會來。"瑪麗説。

她盡快地跑回家裏。她要把小狐狸和禿鼻烏鴉的事告訴柯林，要把春天做的事情告訴他。她相信柯林會喜歡聽的。可是當她推開房門時，卻看見瑪莎苦着一張臉站在那裏等着她，這可不太有趣了。

"怎麼了？"她問道。"你跟柯林説我不能去看他的時候，他説了甚麼？"

"嗨！"瑪莎説。"我真希望你能去。他差點就要大發脾氣。為了讓他安靜，我可沒少費力。他老是不停地看鐘。"

瑪麗的嘴唇緊緊地抿着。她像柯林一樣不會為別人着想，她不明白為甚麼一個壞脾氣的男孩子要干涉她最喜歡的事情。這個男孩一向有病而且神經質，他不知道自己應該控制脾氣，不要弄得別人也有病而且神經質，這樣的人其實是很可憐的，但是瑪麗一點也不知道。住在印度的時候，每當她頭痛時，她就會想方設法讓其他所有的人也頭痛或讓他們感到同樣難受。她覺得自己做得很對；但是現在她當然覺得柯林是錯的。

她走進他的房間時，他沒躺在沙發上，而是平躺在牀上；她進去時他並沒把頭轉向她。這是個糟糕的開頭，瑪麗以她那種僵硬的態度大步走到他跟前。

"你為甚麼不起來？"

"今天早晨當我以為你會來的時候，我是有起來的，"他看都沒看她。"下午我才讓他們把我送回牀上。我的背脊很痛，我累了。你為甚麼不來？"

"我跟狄肯在花園裏工作，"瑪麗説。

柯林皺着眉頭，全神貫注地看着她。

"要是你不來跟我説話，而是去跟他在一起，我就不讓他到這裏來，"他説。

瑪麗的怒火一下子爆發了。她生氣可以一點聲響都沒有。她只是變得乖戾、固執，對發生的事情不管不顧。

"要是你把狄肯趕走，我就再也不進這個房間！"她回嘴説。

"我要你來你就非來不可，"柯林説。

"我就不來！"瑪麗説。

"我會要你來，"柯林説。"我會讓人把你拖進來。"

"他們可以這麼做，酋長先生！"瑪麗尖鋭地説。"他們可以把我拖進來，但是就算我進來了，他們也不能讓我跟你説話。我會坐下來，咬緊牙關，一件事也不告訴你。我甚至看都不會看你。我會盯着地板！"

他們互相怒視，真是匹配的一對。要是他們是兩個街頭男孩，那準會大打出手。事實上，他們的爭吵跟打架也差不了多少。

"你是個自私鬼！"柯林叫道。

"你是甚麼？"瑪麗説。"自私的人總是説別人自私。任何不做別人想做的事情的人就是自私鬼。你比我更自私。你是我見過的最自私的男孩。"

"我不是！"柯林厲聲説。"我才沒有你的好狄肯那麼自私！他明明知道我只有一個人在房間，卻讓你跟他一起玩泥巴。他才是自私鬼，要是你喜歡這麼説的話！"

瑪麗的眼睛都冒出火來。

"他比世界上任何一個男孩都好！"她説。"他像——他像天使！"這樣的話聽起來肯定很傻，但她才不管呢。

"一個好天使！"柯林嘲諷説。"他只是曠野旁邊一座小屋裏的一個普通的孩子！"

"他比一個平凡的酋長好！"瑪麗反駁説。"他比酋長要好一千倍！"

因為她比柯林強壯一點，所以開始佔了上風。事實上，他一輩子都沒跟他一樣的人爭吵過，總的來説，這對他是有好處的，雖然他和瑪麗都不知道這一點。他把頭轉向枕頭，閉上眼睛，一顆豆大的淚珠擠了出來，順着臉頰往下淌。他開始為自己感到可悲、可憐——決不是為了其他人。

"我沒你那麼自私，因為我一直都在生病，我相信我的背上會長出一個瘤，"他説。"再説我馬上就要死了。"

"你不會死！"瑪麗毫不同情地跟他唱反調。

他氣得把眼睛瞪得滾圓。他以前從沒聽見過這樣的話。他又氣又有點高興，要是一個人可以同時擁有這樣兩種感覺的話。

"我不會？"他叫道。"我快要死了！你知道我快要死了！每個人都這麼説。"

"我不信！"瑪麗尖鋭地説。"你這樣只是要讓別人同情你。我知道你為此而自滿。我不信！如果你是個好孩子，這就有可能是真的——但你太令人討厭了！"

柯林不顧自己的背脊軟弱無力，帶着一肚子怒氣從牀上坐了起來。

"滾出房間去！"他叫道，抓起枕頭朝她扔去。他的力氣不夠大，枕頭沒扔遠，落在了她的腳跟前，但是瑪麗的臉皺縮得像個瘋嘴似的。

"我走了，"她説。"我再也不會回來了！"

她朝門口走去，到了那裏又轉過身來，説道：

"我本來想要告訴你很多有趣的事情。狄肯把他的狐狸和烏鴉帶來了，我本來要把牠們的事情都告訴你的。現在我甚麼也不會告訴你了！"

她大步走出門去，把門帶上，這時她驚訝地發現那個專職保姆正站在門口，好像一直都在偷聽，更讓她吃驚的是——保姆還在笑呢。保姆是個身材高大的漂亮少婦，照理根本不該做一個專職保姆，因為她對病人沒有耐心，老是找藉口把柯林扔給瑪莎或其他任何能夠頂替她的人照料。瑪麗一點都不喜歡她，她直愣愣地站在那裏看着保姆，而保姆則對着一塊手帕咯咯地笑。

"你笑甚麼？"瑪麗問道。

"笑你們兩個孩子，"保姆説。"對一個被寵得不成樣子的人來説，有一個像他一樣被寵的人來對付他，那是再好不過的了；"她又對着手帕哈哈大笑起來。"要是他有個刁蠻的小姐姐來跟他打架，那倒能救他一命。"

"他要死了嗎？"

"我不知道，這不關我的事，"保姆説。"他的病痛有一半是來自歇斯底里發作和脾氣。"

"甚麼是歇斯底里？"瑪麗問。

"要是你在這件事之後惹他生氣了，你就會明白甚麼叫歇斯底里了——但是不管怎麼説，你已經使他歇斯底里了，我很高興。"

瑪麗回到自己的房間，從花園回來時的高興心情早已蕩然無存。她感到惱火、失望，但一點都不為柯林難過。她本來一直盼着能給他說許多事情，她還真心想要問問自己，把那個了不起的秘密告訴他是不是安全。她已經開始認為這樣做是安全的，但是現在她完全改變了主意。她永遠不會告訴他，既然他喜歡，就讓他留在他的房間裏，永遠不要呼吸新鮮空氣，然後就死掉吧！他應該如此！她憋着一肚子的火，恨得牙癢癢，有那麼數分鐘裏幾乎忘記了狄肯，忘記了那拂過萬物的綠色面罩和從曠野吹來的微風。

瑪莎正在等她，臉上的焦慮一時間被關切和好奇替代。

桌上有一個木箱，蓋已被拿走，能看出裏面是一個個放得整整齊齊的包裹。

"這是克拉文先生送給你的，"瑪莎説。"裏面好像是圖畫書。"

瑪麗想起來那天去他房間時，他曾問過她的話。"你要甚麼東西嗎——洋娃娃——玩具——書？"她邊打開包裹，邊想，他會不會送她一個洋娃娃，又在想，要真是一個洋娃娃，她該怎麼辦。但他沒送洋娃娃。裏面有數本漂亮的書，像柯林的那些書一樣，其中兩本是關於園藝的，有很多插圖。有兩三個字謎遊戲，一個漂亮的文具盒，上面有金的交織字母，還有一支金筆和一個墨水台。

每樣東西都很精美，她的高興開始把氣憤從心裏擠出去。她一點都沒指望他會記着她，那顆幼小冰冷的心變得溫暖起來。

"我用手寫體寫字可以比用印刷體寫得更好，"她説，"我最先要用這支筆給他寫一封信，告訴他我很感激他。"

如果她是柯林的朋友，她就會馬上跑到柯林那裏給他看她收到的禮物，他們會一起看那些插圖，唸一點關於園藝的書，或許還會玩字謎遊戲，他會非常高興，一點都不會想到他就要死了，或把手放在脊椎上看看那裏是不是長出了瘤。他那樣做實在叫她受不了。這會給她一種很不舒服的受驚嚇的感覺，因為他自己老是那麼受驚嚇的樣子。他說有一天哪怕他只是感覺到一個小小的瘤，他都會知道他的背開始駝了。他曾聽到梅洛太太跟保姆嘀咕的那些話，讓他有了這樣的念頭，他暗地裏再三思考過這件事，最終讓這個念頭在心裏牢牢地扎了根。梅洛太太說過他父親的駝背就是在他還是個孩子時以那樣的方式顯示出來的。他只對瑪麗一個人說過，別人所說的他的那些"脾氣"，大部份就是這種歇斯底里般的暗藏恐懼造成的。當他告訴瑪麗的時候，她真為他難過。

"每當他發脾氣或者疲倦的時候，就會想到這件事，"她對自己說。"今天他就在發脾氣。也許——也許他一個下午都在想這件事。"

她靜靜地站在那裏，俯視着地毯，想着心事。

"我說過我再也不去了——"她眉頭打結地猶豫道——"但也許，僅僅是也許，早上我還是應該去看看——如果他要我去的話。也許他又會用枕頭擲向我，但——我想——我還是要去。"

第十七章
發脾氣

她一早就起了牀，在花園裏賣力地工作，現在又累又倦；瑪莎把晚飯拿來，她端起就吃，然後高興地上牀睡覺。頭挨着枕頭的時候，她嘀咕道：

"我要在早餐前出去跟狄肯一起工作，然後——我相信——我會去看他。"

她被一陣非常可怕的聲音吵醒，一骨碌下了牀，她以為這時候是在半夜。是甚麼聲音——甚麼聲音？緊接着她就確信自己知道了。一扇扇門被打開又關上，走廊裏響起匆匆的腳步聲，與此同時有人在又哭又鬧，又鬧又哭，簡直嚇死人。

"是柯林，"她說。"他在發脾氣，就是保姆說的歇斯底里發作。聽起來真嚇人。"

她聽着那種帶着抽泣的尖叫，心想，怪不得別人會嚇得寧願一切都由着他，而不願聽到這種聲音。她用手摀住耳朵，感到不適並禁不住抖了起來。

"我不知道該怎麼辦。我不知道該怎麼辦，"她不停地説。"我受不了。"

她一度想道，要是她大膽走到他跟前，不知道他會不會停下來，接着她就想起他怎樣把她趕出房間，心想，也許看見她會讓他的怒火更盛。當她把耳朵捂得更緊時，仍然無法把那可怕的聲音擋開。她對那些聲音又恨又怕，突然間讓她生起氣來，她覺得自己也要像他一樣發脾氣，像他嚇唬她一樣地嚇唬他。她從來只習慣自己發脾氣，不能忍受別人發脾氣。她把手從耳朵上拿開，跳起來，用力跺腳。

"應該讓他停下，要有人讓他停下！要有人揍他一頓！"她大聲叫道。

就在這時，她聽見急促的腳步聲從走廊過來，緊接着她的門被推開，保姆衝了進來，這回她可一點沒有笑的意思。她甚至顯得很蒼白。

"他歇斯底里發作了，"她心急慌忙地説。"他會傷害自己。誰都拿他沒辦法。好孩子，你去試試。他喜歡你。"

"他今天早上把我趕出了他的房門，"瑪麗説，激動地跺着腳。

她這一跺腳可把保姆逗樂了。保姆本來就怕會看見瑪麗把頭藏在被裏哭呢。

"這就對了，"她説。"你的情緒正合適。你去罵他。給他點新的玩意去想想。去吧，孩子，快點去吧。"

直到後來瑪麗才意識到，這件事不但可怕，而且滑稽——滑稽的是所有的大人都被嚇壞，他們來找一個小女孩幫忙，只因為他們猜想這個小女孩幾乎像柯林一樣壞。

她沿着走廊飛奔，越接近哭鬧聲，她的怒火就越盛。到了門口時，她都快忍不住了。她一手推開門，朝四柱牀衝過去。

"你閉嘴！"她幾乎是吼道。"你閉嘴！我討厭你！所有的人都討厭你！但願所有的人都跑出這間屋，讓你一個人叫到死！你不到一分鐘就會叫到死，但願你叫到死！"

一個有同情心的好孩子既不會想到也不會說出這樣的話來，但巧的是，聽到這番話後的震驚或許是對這個歇斯底里的孩子的最好的藥方，沒有人曾經膽敢阻止他或違背他。

他一直趴在牀上，用手捶打着枕頭，他還差點一躍而起，一聽到那個奇怪、稚嫩的聲音他就迅速轉過頭來。他的臉看來挺嚇人，又白又紅又腫，他喘得透不過氣來；但是冷酷的小瑪麗絲毫不為所動。

"你要是再叫一聲，"她說，"我也叫——我叫得比你還響，我會嚇倒你，我會嚇倒你！"

這一下他吃驚不小，果然就停止了哭叫。那堵在喉嚨口的叫聲差點讓他噎住。他渾身發抖，眼淚從臉上淌下來。

"我不能停下來！"他又喘氣又抽泣。"我不能——我不能！"

"你能！"瑪麗大喝一聲。"折磨你的病痛一半來自歇斯底里發作和你的脾氣——就是歇斯底里——歇斯底里——歇斯底里！"每說一遍就跺一下腳。

"我摸到了瘤——我摸到了，"柯林哽咽着說。"我知道我會摸到的。我會變成駝子，然後就會死掉，"他又開始痛苦地扭動起身體，轉過臉去，抽泣、慟哭，但沒有尖叫。

"你沒有摸到瘤！"瑪麗尖銳地反駁說。"就算你摸到了，那也是個歇斯底里的瘤。只有歇斯底里才會生出瘤。你那討厭的背脊根本沒事——根本沒事，就是歇斯底里！轉過來讓我看看！"

她喜歡"歇斯底里"這個詞，覺得這個詞好歹對他起了點作用。他或許像她一樣，以前從沒聽說過這個詞。

保姆、梅洛太太和瑪莎一直在門口擠做一團注視着她，三個人的嘴巴都半張着，不止一次地嚇得大喘氣。保姆走上前來，好像她害怕的程度只有她們的一半。柯林泣不成聲，胸口起伏得厲害。

"也許——他不會讓我看，"她遲疑地低聲說道。

不過，柯林聽見了她的話，在兩次抽泣之間拼出一句話來：

"那就給——給她看！"

脫去衣服後，柯林的背脊瘦得慘不忍睹。每一根肋骨，每一個脊椎的關節處都清晰可數，雖然瑪麗並沒有數，而是彎着腰，繃着一張蠻橫的小臉，仔細打量着。她看得那麼專心那麼做作，逗得保姆轉過臉去，生怕給人看出她嘴角抽動的樣子。沉默了一分鐘，就連柯林也盡量屏住了呼吸讓瑪麗上上下下，下下上上地檢查，那副專心的態度活像那個從倫敦來的了不起的醫生。

"根本就沒甚麼瘤！"最後她說。"連個針頭那麼大的瘤也沒有——只有脊骨上突起的骨頭，因為你太瘦了，所以才會摸到這些骨頭。本來我自己的脊骨上也有疙瘩，像你的一樣突出來，後來我開始發胖，不過還沒胖到遮住它們的程度。這些疙瘩沒一個像針頭那麼大！要是你再說有甚麼瘤，我可要笑你了！"

只有柯林自己知道，這些帶着孩子氣的怒沖沖地說出來的話對他產生了甚麼樣的作用。只要曾經有人能夠聽他說說他內心的恐懼——只要他曾經有膽量讓自己問一些問題——只要他能有一些同齡的夥伴，不是老躺在這個封閉的大屋裏，呼吸混雜着大人們的恐懼的沉重空氣（他們中的大多數對他漠不關心，視他為一個麻煩），他就會發現，他的大多數恐懼心理和疾病都是自找的。但是他時時刻刻、年年月月地躺在那裏，想着自己和自己的病痛，越想越覺得無聊。現在這個怒氣沖沖、毫無同情心的小女孩固執地堅持認為他的病不像他自以為的那麼嚴重，他倒覺得她也許說的是真話。

"我不知道，"保姆大膽地說，"他認為他的脊椎上有個瘤。他的背脊一向很弱，因為他從來不試着坐起來。我本來可以告訴他，他的背上根本沒有瘤。"柯林哽住了，把頭稍微轉過來看着她。

"真——真的嗎？"他可憐兮兮地說。

"是的，少爺。"

"真是的！"瑪麗說，她也哽住了。

柯林又把臉轉過來，靜靜地躺了一會，間中大喘一口氣，表明這場暴風雨般的發作已近尾聲，不過豆大的淚珠從臉上淌下，弄濕了枕頭。其實，這淚珠奇怪的意味着他感到如釋重負。不一會他又轉過來看着保姆，實在奇怪的是，當他跟她說話的時候一點都不像是個酋長。

"你認為——我可以——長大？"他說。

保姆既不聰明，也沒有慈悲心腸，但是她可以重複倫敦醫生的一些話。

"只要你照吩咐去做，不要老發脾氣，盡量多呼吸新鮮空氣，那就有可能長大。"

柯林發完脾氣了，因為又哭又叫，弄得他虛弱不堪，筋疲力盡，不過也許正因為這麼一來，他變得溫和了。他稍稍向瑪麗伸出手去，我可以很高興地說，她也發完脾氣了，她也變得溫和起來，同樣伸出手去，兩人就算和好了。

"我要——我要跟你一起出去，瑪麗，"他說。"我不討厭新鮮空氣，只要能夠找到——"他突然記起要保密，於是及時停住，沒有說出"只要我們能找到那個秘密花園"，而是說，"只要狄肯願意來給我推輪椅，我就跟你們一起出去。我太想見到狄肯和他的狐狸、烏鴉了。"

保姆把弄皺的牀重新鋪好，把枕頭拍鬆弄挺。然後她給柯林端來一杯牛肉茶，也給了瑪麗一杯。經過剛才那麼激動，這杯茶對瑪麗來說來得正是時候。梅洛太太和瑪莎高興地靜靜走了，當一切都歸於平靜，恢復正常之後，保姆看來也要高興地走了。她是個健康的小婦人，最討厭被人打擾睡眠。她肆無忌憚地打着哈欠，看着瑪麗。瑪麗已經把踏腳凳移到四柱牀跟前，正抓着柯林的手。

"你必須回去，補一補眠，"她說。"他要過一會才能睡着——如果他不是太煩惱的話。到時候我就去隔壁房間躺一會。"

"要我給你唱我從印度保姆那裏學來的那首歌嗎？"瑪麗悄悄地對柯林說。

他輕輕地拉着她的手，充滿倦意的眼睛渴求地看着她。

"哦，要的！"他答道。"這首歌很輕柔，我一會就能睡着。"

"我會令他入睡的，"瑪麗對哈欠連連的保姆說。"你想走就走吧。"

"好的，"保姆說，裝出很勉強的樣子，"要是他半小時之內還沒睡着，你可要來叫我。"

"行，"瑪麗說。

保姆轉眼就出了房間，她剛一走，柯林就又抓住了瑪麗的手。

"我差點說出來，"他說；"幸虧及時止住了。我不說話了，我要睡覺。但是你說你有很多好玩的事情要告訴我。你有沒有——你是不是認為你找到了任何進入那個秘密花園的方法？"

瑪麗看着他那張可憐的、疲倦的小臉，紅腫的眼睛，心裏充滿憐憫。

"是——的，"她答道，"我想我是找到了。要是你乖乖地睡覺，明天我就告訴你。"

他的手很厲害地顫抖起來。

"哦，瑪麗！"他說。"哦！瑪麗！要是我能進去，我想我就能長大了！你能不能不要唱歌，而是像第一天那樣輕輕地告訴我，你想像中那裏是甚麼樣子？我肯定那會讓我睡着的。"

"好吧，"瑪麗說，"閉上眼睛。"

他閉上了眼睛，靜靜地躺在那裏，瑪麗抓住他的手，慢慢地，輕輕地開始說。

"我想它被廢棄了那麼長的時間——裏面的枝椏肯定纏結在一起了。我想玫瑰已經爬啊，爬啊，爬到了樹枝上和牆頭上，從那裏掛下來，而且爬得滿地都是——幾乎像是一片灰色的、奇怪的迷霧。有些已經死了，但是有許多——活着，等到夏天，就會有像簾和噴泉似的玫瑰。我想，黃水仙、雪蓮花、百合和蝴蝶花會從黑暗中鑽出來，開滿一地。現在春天已經來了，——也許——也許——"

她溫柔的聲音讓他越來越安靜，她看了出來，接着往下説。

"也許它們正從草裏鑽出來——也許那裏有一串串紫色和金色的番紅花——可能現在就有。也許葉芽已經開始露出來，並開始舒展——也許——灰色正在變化，一切都在被染綠。鳥飛來觀看——因為那裏——非常安全，安靜。也許——也許——也許——"瑪麗的聲音的確又輕又溫柔，"知更鳥找到了伴侶——正在築巢。"

柯林睡着了。

第十八章

"你決不能浪費時間。"

第二天早晨瑪麗當然沒有很早醒來。她睡了個大懶覺，因為她太累了，瑪莎把早餐端來時，告訴瑪麗説，柯林雖然挺安靜的，但是他病了，發起高燒；每次因為大叫一陣而累垮了之後，就免不了要發燒。瑪麗邊聽邊慢慢地吃早餐。

"他説他希望你能盡快去看他，"瑪莎説。"他對你這麼癡迷，真是怪事。昨天晚上你着實訓了他一頓，是嗎？別人誰都不敢這麼做。嗨，可憐的孩子！他被寵得沒藥可救了。媽媽説，有兩件事對孩子最有害，一是不讓他們做自己想做的事，二是事事都由着他們。她不知道哪一樣更有害。你自己就有很大的脾氣，可當我進他房間時他對我説，'請問瑪麗小姐她願不願意來看我，跟我説話？'想一想吧，他居然説了'請'字！你想去嗎，小姐？"

"我先要跑去看狄肯，"瑪麗説。"不，我還是先去看柯林，告訴他説——我知道我該告訴他甚麼，"突然靈機一動。

她戴着帽來到柯林的房間，他一時間顯得很失望。他躺在牀上，臉色白得可憐，眼睛四周是黑眼圈。

"我很高興你來了，"他說。"我頭痛，我渾身都痛，因為我太累了。你還要去別的地方嗎？"

瑪麗走上前去，倚在他的牀上。

"我不會去太久的，"她說。"我要去狄肯那裏，但我會回來的。柯林，這是——這是關於那個花園的事。"

他的整個臉色為之一亮，並且稍微有了點血色。

"哦，是嗎？"他叫道。"我整個晚上都夢見這件事。我聽見你說甚麼灰色變成了綠色，我夢見自己站在一個充滿搖搖擺擺的綠色小枝葉的地方——那裏到處都有鳥在巢裏，牠們看來那麼溫柔、安靜。我會躺在這裏想着這件事，直到你回來。"

不過五分鐘，瑪麗就在花園裏找到了狄肯。狐狸和烏鴉又來到他的身邊，這次他還帶來兩隻溫順的麻雀。

"今天早上我騎着小馬上了曠野，"他說。"嗨！我的小馬叫'跳躍'，他是個好的小東西！我把這兩個小東西放在口袋裏帶來。這隻叫'堅果'，另一隻叫'果殼'。"

當他說到'堅果'時，那隻麻雀跳到了他的右肩上，而當他說'果殼'時，另一隻麻雀跳到了他的左肩上。

他們在草地上坐下來，隊長蜷縮在他們腳跟前，煤煙停在一棵樹上，一本正經地聽着，堅果和果殼緊挨着他們，東張西望。這副其樂融融的景象令瑪麗簡直不忍離去。但是當她向狄肯講述了自己前一天的經歷後，狄肯那張怪臉上的表情，慢慢地改變了她的想法。她能看出，狄肯比她更為柯林感到難過。他抬頭看看天空和四周。

"聽那些鳥在叫——好像滿世界都是鳥——一個個都在啾鳴，"他說。"看牠們飛來飛去，聽牠們互相叫喚。每當春天來臨，這世界好像就充滿了牠們的叫喚聲。枝葉都在舒展，所以你能看見牠們——而且，相信我，沒錯的，到處都是好聞的氣味！"他那高興的翹鼻子嗅了嗅，"而那個可憐的孩子躺在封閉的房間裏，甚麼都看不見，於是就胡思亂想，結果就大哭大叫。嗨，我說，我們一定要把他帶到這裏來——我們一定要讓他到這裏來看，來聽，來聞聞這裏的空氣，讓他整個人沐浴在陽光裏。我們再也不能浪費時間了。"

每當他高興的時候，就會說一口約克話，儘管平時他總是盡力掩飾自己的方言，好讓瑪麗盡量聽懂他的話。但是瑪麗喜歡聽他的約克話，甚至盡力學他的話，所以現在她也能說一點了。

"對，我們必須這麼做。我要告訴你，我們首先要做甚麼，"她接着說，狄肯咧一咧嘴，因為每當那小女孩捲着舌頭說約克話的時候，他都會覺得十分好笑。"他對你非常着迷。他想見你，想見煤煙和隊長。等會我回去之後，我要去問他，能不能讓你明天早上去看他——帶着你的那些動物——然後——過段時間，等葉長得更多，碰巧還有一兩簇花蕾，我們就帶他到這裏來，你幫他推輪椅，我們帶他到這裏來，把一切都指給他看。"

說完後，她很為自己感到驕傲。她以前從沒用約克方言說過這麼一大段話，她記得非常清楚。

"你一定要像這樣跟柯林說點約克話。"狄肯咯咯地笑着說。"你會逗得他哈哈大笑，對病人來說，哈哈大笑是有好處的。媽媽説，她相信，每天早上大笑半個小時，就能治好一個可能患斑疹傷寒的人。"

"我今天就跟他説約克話，"瑪麗也咯咯地笑着説。

如今的秘密花園已經到了這樣的境地：每天每夜都像有魔術師用魔杖點過，把它的可愛從地底下和樹枝間顯示出來。從它那裏走開或徹底離開是難以忍受的，尤其是堅果爬到了她的衣服上，果殼順着蘋果樹的樹幹往下爬（他們就坐在蘋果樹下），在那裏用好奇的目光盯着她看。但是她回到了屋裏，當她緊挨着柯林的牀坐下時，他聞了聞，就像狄肯一樣，只是不如狄肯那麼熟練。

"你像花——和新鮮的東西一樣好聞，"他欣喜地叫道。"你身上到底是甚麼氣味？清涼、溫暖，又香甜。"

"是曠野裏吹來的風，"瑪麗説。"它過來跟狄肯和隊長還有煤煙、堅果、果殼一起坐在一棵樹下的草地上。春天來了，屋外的陽光聞上去可香了。"

她盡可能説出約克話的土味，除非你親耳聽人説，否則你根本無法想像約克話有多土。柯林哈哈大笑起來。

"你這是做甚麼？"他説。"我以前從沒聽過你像這樣説話。這聲音聽起來真怪。"

"我在跟你説約克話，"瑪麗得意地説，"可惜我不像狄肯和瑪莎説得那麼好，但你能看出來，我也能説一點。你能聽懂一點約克話嗎？你是個土生土長的約克人！嗨！我真奇怪你怎麼不覺得臉紅。"

接着她也哈哈大笑起來。兩人都笑了起來，笑得停都停不住。整個房間裏都蕩漾着笑聲。梅洛太太打開房門，站在走廊裏聽着，一臉的疑惑。

"哦，天哪！"她也用很土的約克話説，因為沒人能聽見，再説她也太驚訝了。"誰聽見過這樣的笑聲！這到底是甚麼人啊！"

要説的話很多。柯林好像總也聽不夠關於狄肯、隊長、煤煙、堅果、果殼和那匹名叫跳躍的小馬的事情。瑪麗曾經和狄肯一起奔進樹林裏去看跳躍。牠是匹一身粗毛的曠野小馬，粗毛從眼睛上垂下來，牠有一張英俊的臉和愛摩擦的光滑鼻子。牠靠曠野上的草為生，長得很瘦，但是非常結實，那小腿肚子上的肌肉好像都是鋼彈簧做的。當牠看見狄肯時，抬起頭來，輕輕地嘶鳴了一聲，篤篤地跑到他跟前，把頭擱在他的肩上，然後狄肯湊着牠的耳朵跟牠輕輕地説起話來。跳躍也用奇怪的低聲嘶鳴和噴鼻息來回答他。狄肯讓牠向瑪麗抬起小前蹄，並用牠光滑的口鼻吻她的臉頰。

"牠真的能聽懂狄肯的話？"柯林問道。

"好像能聽懂，"瑪麗回答説。"狄肯説，只要交上朋友，任何東西都是可以互相理解的，但你必須與牠們交上朋友。"

柯林安靜地躺了一會，那雙怪異的灰眼睛好像在盯着牆看，但是瑪麗能看出他在思考。

"我希望我能跟牠們交上朋友，"最後他説，"但我現在沒有做到。我從來沒有一個朋友，我容不了人。"

"你容得了我嗎？"瑪麗問。

"是的，我能，"他答道。"説來真怪，我甚至喜歡上了你。"

"本·威瑟斯塔夫説我像他，"瑪麗説，"他説他敢保證，我和他有一樣的臭脾氣。我看你也像他。我們三個很相像——你、我和本·威瑟斯塔夫。他說我們中沒一個長得好看。我們一看就是尖酸刻薄的人。但我覺得我已經不像認識知更鳥和狄肯之前那麼尖酸刻薄了。"

"你是不是覺得你好像恨別人？"

"是的，"瑪麗平淡地說。"要是我在看見知更鳥和狄肯之前看見你，我肯定會討厭你。"

柯林伸出細小的手摸了摸她。

"瑪麗，"他說，"我真希望我沒說過要把狄肯趕走。當你說他像天使的時候，我真恨你，並且笑你——但是——但是他也許真的是天使。"

"是啊，説起來真好笑，"她坦率地承認說，"因為他有一個翹鼻子，一張大嘴巴，衣服上全是補釘，説一口約克土話，但是——但是如果真有一個天使來到約克，住在曠野上——如果真有一個約克郡天使——我相信他會懂得那些綠色的東西，知道怎樣讓它們生長，他會像狄肯一樣懂得怎樣跟那些野生動物説話，牠們肯定會知道他是牠們的朋友。"

"我不會介意狄肯看着我，"柯林說，"我想見他。"

"我很高興你這麼說，"瑪麗答道，"因為——因為——"

突然間，她想到，現在是告訴他的時候了。

柯林知道新的事情就要發生了。

"因為甚麼？"他急切地叫道。

瑪麗心急難耐，她從凳上站起來，走到他跟前，緊緊抓住他的雙手。

"我能相信你嗎？我相信狄肯，因為鳥都相信他。但我能相信你嗎——肯定——肯定能相信嗎？"她懇切地追問道。

他的臉色非常嚴肅，幾乎是用耳語說出了自己的回答。

"是的——是的！"

"那好，明天早上狄肯會來看你，他會把他的動物帶來。"

"哦！哦！"柯林欣喜地叫了起來。

"還不止這個呢，"瑪麗接着說，激動得幾乎臉都發白了。"更好的消息還在後面：有一扇進花園的門，我找到了，它在牆上的一片常春藤下面。"

如果柯林是一個健壯的男孩，他也許就會大叫三聲"好啊！"，可他是個虛弱並且歇斯底里的孩子，他的眼睛越瞪越大，喘得氣都透不過來。

"哦，瑪麗！"他帶着哽咽叫道。"我能看看它嗎？我能進去嗎？我能活着進去嗎？"他抓着她的手，把她拉到自己跟前。

"你當然能看見它！"瑪麗帶着怒氣厲聲說。"你當然能活着進去！別傻了！"

她這麼正常、自然、充滿孩子氣，讓他也冷靜下來。他開始笑自己，數分鐘之後，她又坐在凳上，告訴他花園是甚麼樣的，這次不是她的想像，而是真實情況。柯林全然忘記了病痛和疲倦，聚精會神地聽着。

"這正是你想像中的樣子，"最後他說。"聽起來真的像你以前曾經進去一樣。你知道，當你第一次跟我說的時候，我就這麼說過。"

瑪麗猶豫了兩分鐘，然後大膽地說出了真相。

"我是見過它——我是曾經進去，"她說。"數個星期前我就

找到了鑰匙並且進去了。但我不敢告訴你——因為我怕不能完全
相信你，所以不敢告訴你。"

第十九章

"它來了！"

那天早上柯林發過脾氣後，克拉文醫生當然就被叫來了。每當發生這樣的事情他就會被叫來。而每當他趕到，總會看見一個臉色發白、渾身發抖的孩子躺在牀上，一臉怒色，依然那麼歇斯底里，只要一句話，就會讓他爆發出一次新的哭叫。事實上，克拉文醫生對這樣棘手的差事又怕又恨。這一次，他是下午才到米塞爾斯威特莊園的。

"他怎麼樣了？"他來到後不耐煩地問梅洛太太。"他這樣發作，早晚有一天會弄得血管爆裂的。這個孩子因為歇斯底里和自我放縱，已經有一點神經錯亂了。"

"是啊，先生，"梅洛太太答道，"你看見他的時候，肯定會很難相信自己的眼睛。那個幾乎像他一樣壞、又難看又尖酸刻薄的小女孩剛剛給他施了魔力。誰也不知道她是怎麼做的。誰都知道她長得一點都不好看，你也難得聽見她說話，可她做了我們誰都不敢做的事情。她昨天晚上像隻貓似的竄到他的跟前，踮着腳命令他停止哭叫，不知怎麼一回事，她居然就把他給唬住了，他真的就停了下來，今天下午——行了，還是去看看吧，先生。光說沒人會相信。"

克拉文走進病人房間時見到的情景的確讓他目瞪口呆。梅洛太太打開房門，他聽見了笑聲和閒聊聲。只見柯林穿着晨衣坐在沙發上，坐得筆直，正在看一本園藝書上的一張畫，同時在和那個相貌平平的女孩説話，當時那個女孩真不能説是相貌平平，因為她那充滿喜悦的臉上紅光滿面。

"那些藍色的細長幼葉——我們會有很多，"柯林説。"它們叫飛燕草。"

"狄肯説它們是翠雀，會開很大的花，"瑪麗小姐叫道。"花園裏已經有好幾簇了。"

這時他們看見了克拉文醫生，就停了下來。瑪麗變得非常安靜，而柯林一臉的苦相。

"聽説你昨晚病了，孩子，我很難過，"克拉文醫生帶點緊張地説。他是個相當神經質的人。

"我現在好了——好多了，"柯林答道，神情很像一個酋長。"如果可以的話，過一二天我要坐輪椅出去。我需要呼吸一點新鮮空氣。"

克拉文先生在他身邊坐下，一邊給他聽診，一邊好奇地看着他。

"那一定是個大晴天，"他説，"而且你一定要非常注意，別把自己弄得太累。"

"新鮮空氣不會令我感到累的，"小酋長說。

以前曾經有過這樣的事情：同樣是這位小紳士，尖聲哭叫，大發脾氣，說甚麼新鮮空氣會讓他着涼，會害死他；所以，他現在的這番話讓醫生大吃一驚也就不足為奇了。

"我以為你向來都不喜歡新鮮空氣的，"他說。

"我一個人的時候是不喜歡，"酋長答道，"但我表姊要跟我一起去。"

"當然還有保姆了？"克拉文醫生建議說。

"不，我不要保姆去，"他說得那麼莊重，瑪麗不由得想起那個印度小王子珠玉滿身，小黑手上戴着巨大的紅寶石，招手向奴僕發令，讓他們邊行額手禮邊跑來接受他的命令時的神情。

"我表姊知道怎樣照顧我。只要她跟我在一起，我就會好得多。昨天晚上就是她讓我好起來的。我認識的一個很壯實的男孩會為我推輪椅。"

克拉文醫生相當驚慌。要是這個疲憊而又歇斯底里的孩子的身體健康起來，他本人就失去了繼承米塞爾斯威特莊園的機會；但他儘管心術不正，倒也不是個肆無忌憚的人，所以他並不打算讓他陷入真正的危險。

"他一定是個壯實穩重的男孩，"他說。"我要對他有所了解。他是誰？叫甚麼名字？"

"是狄肯，"瑪麗突然大聲說。她有種感覺：凡是知道曠野的人肯定都認識狄肯。她的感覺很對。她看見，克拉文醫生那張嚴肅的臉一下子鬆弛下來，露出了微笑。

"哦，是狄肯，"他說。"如果是狄肯，那你們就安全了。他壯實得像一頭曠野小馬。"

"而且他很可靠,"瑪麗説,"他是全約克最可靠的男孩。"她一直在用約克方言跟柯林説話,都有點忘乎所以了。

"是狄肯教你的嗎?"克拉文醫生一邊開懷大笑一邊問。

"我學約克話就像學法語一樣,"瑪麗相當冷淡地説。"它像印度人的方言,非常聰明的人都想學它們。我喜歡它,柯林也喜歡。"

"是啊,是啊,"他説。"既然能讓你覺得高興,那也許就不會有甚麼害處。你昨晚吃了安眠藥了嗎,柯林?"

"沒有,"柯林答道,"起初是我不想吃,後來瑪麗讓我安靜下來。她用很輕的聲音跟我説話,説春天滲透進花園,説着説着我就睡着了。"

"聽起來很舒服,"克拉文説,比先前更困惑,不時地瞥一眼瑪麗,她正坐在凳上,默默無聲地朝下看着地毯。"你顯然好多了,但必須記住——"

"我不要記住,"柯林打斷他説,酋長氣派又出來了。"當我一個人躺着並試圖記住的時候,我就開始全身疼痛,當我要想一些事情的時候,我就開始尖叫,因為我太討厭那些事情。要是有這麼一個醫生,他不是老要讓你記住你在生病,而是要你忘記它,我就要找人去把他叫來。"他揮舞着一隻瘦小的手,這隻手上照理應該戴着紅寶石做的王室圖章戒指。"就是因為我表姊讓我忘了我是病人,我才感覺好多了。"

克拉文醫生從來沒有在這麼一場"火氣發作"之後只留這麼短的時間就離開;通常他要留在這裏很長時間,做很多事情。這個下午他既沒有做任何治療，也沒留下任何新的醫囑，他也沒遭遇任何不愉快的場面。他下樓時一臉沉思的樣子，在書房裏跟梅洛太太談話時，梅洛太太覺得他像是被甚麼難倒了。

"哦，先生，"她斗膽問道，"你能相信嗎？"

"這當然是一種新的狀態，"醫生說。"不可否認的是，這種狀態比原來的好。"

"我相信蘇珊·索爾比是對的——我真的相信，"梅洛太太說。"昨天我去斯威特村時順便去了她家，跟她說了一會話。她對我說，'哦，薩拉·安，她也許不是個好孩子，她也許不是個漂亮的孩子，但她是個孩子，孩子需要孩子。'蘇珊·索爾比和我，我們是同學。"

"她是我認識的最好的護士，"克拉文醫生說。"當我在她家的小屋第一次遇見她的時候，我就知道我的病人有救了。"

梅洛太太笑了。她很喜歡蘇珊·索爾比。

"蘇珊有她自己的一套辦法，"她滔滔不絕地說。"我一上午都在想她昨晚說的一件事。她說，'每當孩子們打完架，我教訓他們的時候，我就說，'我在上學的時候，從地理課上學到，地球像個橙，我在十歲之前就懂得，這個橙不屬於任何一個人。每個人都只能擁有屬於他的一個角落，有時候，你會覺得這個角落太小，你無法自由走動。但是你們——你們所有的人——不要以為你們擁有整個橙，否則你們會發現你們是錯的，當然，不經過嚴重挫折你們不會懂得這個道理。'孩子們從孩子們那裏學到的道理是，'她說，'要想擁有整個橙——連皮帶肉——是荒唐的。要是你想這麼做，很可能連種子都得不到，而種子是很苦的，根本不能吃。'"

"她是個精明的女人，"克拉文醫生邊說邊穿大衣。

"是啊，她說話很有一套，"梅洛太太最後說，顯得很高興。"有時候我跟她說，'嗨！蘇珊，如果你是別的女人，不說這麼一口約克土話，我有朝一日真的該說你是個聰明的人。'"

那天晚上柯林一覺睡到天亮，早晨醒來後，他靜靜地躺着，不知不覺地笑着——因為他覺得格外舒服。醒着真好，他翻過身來，愜意地伸展四肢。他覺得把他緊緊捆住的繩索自動解除了，放開了他。他的神經已經鬆弛，安靜下來，他不知道克拉文醫生對此會怎麼說。他不再像以往那樣躺在那裏死盯着牆壁，希望自己不要醒來，他的腦裏盡想着昨天跟瑪麗訂好的計劃，盡是那個花園和狄肯以及他的野生動物的畫面。心裏有東西掛念真好。醒來後不到十分鐘，他就聽見腳步聲從走廊傳來，瑪麗來到了門口。緊接着她進了房間，奔到他的牀前，帶進來一股充滿清晨氣息的新鮮空氣。

"你剛才出去了！你剛才出去了！你身上有好聞的草葉氣味！"他叫道。

她一直在奔跑，頭髮散開來，飄曳着，清新的空氣讓她滿臉發光，一張小臉紅撲撲的，雖然他看不出來。

"太漂亮了！"她說，因為跑得太快，有點氣喘。"你從沒見過這麼漂亮的東西。它已經來了！前一天早晨我就以為它已經來了，其實剛剛才來。現在它已到了這裏！它來了，春天！是狄肯說的！"

"是嗎！"柯林叫道，儘管他其實甚麼都不懂，但也覺得自己的心在怦怦地跳。他從牀上坐了起來。

「打開窗！」他說，哈哈大笑，一方面是出於充滿喜悅的激動之情，另一方面是出於自己的幻想。「也許我們可以聽見金喇叭聲！」

雖然他哈哈大笑，瑪麗在窗前站了一會，又過了一會之後，窗才完全打開，清新的空氣、香味和百鳥的啾鳴撲面而來。

「這是新鮮空氣，」她說。「仰面躺在牀上，做深呼吸。狄肯躺在曠野上的時候就是這樣做的。他說他感覺到新鮮空氣進入他的血管，讓他變得健壯，好像他能永遠活下去。呼吸，再呼吸。」

她只是在重複狄肯告訴她的話，但她引起了柯林的幻想。

「『永遠』！新鮮空氣真的讓他有這樣的感覺嗎？」他說，並且照她說的那樣，一次又一次地深呼吸，果然有了一種新的令人喜悅的感覺。

瑪麗又來到他身邊。

「好多東西都鑽出了地面，」她急匆匆地往下說。「花在綻放，嫩芽處處可見，原來的一片灰色幾乎都被染綠，鳥在鳥巢四周忙碌，因為害怕遲到後在秘密花園佔不到一席之地，有些鳥甚至打了起來。玫瑰叢看來精神得不能再精神。小道上和樹林裏都充滿了希望，我們播下的種子也已經發芽，狄肯帶來了狐狸、烏鴉、麻雀和一隻新生的羔羊。」

這時她停下來喘口氣。那隻新生的羔羊是狄肯在三天前發現的，當時牠正躺在曠野上荊豆叢間牠死去的羊媽媽旁邊。這已不是他發現的第一頭失去媽媽的羔羊了，他知道怎麼照顧牠。他用自己的外套把牠裹好，帶到自己家裏，讓牠躺在爐火旁，用熱牛奶餵牠。這是個軟綿綿的小東西，有一張可愛的、傻乎乎的娃娃臉，跟身體比較之下，腳顯得很長。狄肯懷抱着牠，口袋裏放着奶瓶，來到了曠野上，還帶來了一隻麻雀，這時瑪麗坐在一棵樹下，那頭軟綿綿的羔羊帶着體溫蜷縮在她的大腿上，她心裏充滿一種奇異的喜悅感，簡直連話都說不出來了。一頭羔羊——一頭羔羊！一頭活生生的羔羊像個孩子似的躺在你的大腿上！

她興奮不已地向柯林描述着那種情景，柯林一邊聽一邊大口呼吸新鮮空氣，這時保姆進來了。見到開了窗，她微微吃了一驚。在很多個溫暖的日子裏，她都曾坐在這個房間裏，感覺氣都透不過來，因為她的病人相信開窗會令人着涼。

"你肯定不覺得冷嗎，柯林少爺？"她問道。

"不冷，"柯林答道。"我在大口呼吸新鮮空氣。這樣會令人健壯。我要坐到沙發上去吃早餐。我表姊要跟我一起吃。"

保姆離開房間，去吩咐準備兩個人的早餐。她發現傭人房間是個比病人房間有趣得多的地方，這時候大家都想聽樓上的消息。關於那個不合群的小隱士，有很多的笑話，廚師說他"找到了他的師傅，對他是有好處的"。傭人們都受夠了他的脾氣，男管家（他是個有家庭的人）不止一次地表示，那個病人最好"徹底藏起來"。

當柯林坐在沙發上，供兩個人吃的早餐擺上桌之後，柯林用他十足的酋長氣派宣佈說：

"今天早上將有一個男孩、一隻狐狸、一隻烏鴉、兩隻麻雀和一頭新生的羔羊要來看我。他們一到就帶他們上樓，"他說。"你們不能把那些動物扣在傭人房裏玩耍。我要牠們上來。"

保姆微微倒抽一口冷氣，隨即咳嗽了一聲加以掩飾。

"是，少爺，"她答道。

"我會告訴你，你該怎麼做，"柯林接着説，揮了揮手。"你要告訴瑪莎把他們帶到這裏來。那男孩是瑪莎的弟弟。他叫狄肯，他是馴獸師。"

"但願那些動物不會咬人，柯林少爺，"保姆説。

"我跟你説過他是個馴獸師，"柯林一本正經地説。"馴獸師的動物從來不咬人。"

"印度有馴蛇師，"瑪麗説，"他們敢把蛇頭放進嘴裏。"

"天哪！"保姆打了個冷顫。

他們在晨風吹拂中吃着早餐。柯林的早餐很豐盛，瑪麗饒有興趣地看着他。

"你會像我一樣開始變胖的，"她説。"我在印度的時候從來不想吃早餐，現在我每個早上都想吃。"

"今天早上我也想吃，"柯林説。"也許這是新鮮空氣的緣故。你説狄肯甚麼時候能到？"

他不久就來了。大概十分鐘之後，瑪麗舉起手來。

"聽！"她説。"你聽見烏鴉的叫聲了嗎？"

柯林豎起耳朵聽，果然聽見了，這是在屋裏所能聽到的世界上最怪的聲音，一種粗的"呱呱"聲。

"聽到了，"他説。

"那是煤煙，"瑪麗説。"再聽。你聽到一個'咩咩'的聲音了嗎？——很輕很輕。"

"哦，聽到了！"柯林叫道，臉漲得通紅。

"那就是新生的羔羊，"瑪麗説，"他來了。"

狄肯的曠野靴又厚又笨拙，雖然他盡力想把腳步放輕，但那雙靴還是在長走廊裏發出啪嗒啪嗒的聲響。瑪麗和柯林聽着他一步步過來，經過了那扇掛着壁毯的門，來到了柯林的房間所在的鋪着軟地毯的走廊。

"請聽我説，少爺，"瑪莎推開門通報説，"請聽我説，少爺，狄肯和他的動物到了。"

狄肯帶着他最好看的咧開大嘴的笑容進來了。那頭羔羊抱在他的懷裏，紅色的小狐狸走在他的身邊。堅果坐在他的左肩上，煤煙坐在他的右肩上，果殼的頭和爪從他的外衣袋裏探出來。

柯林慢慢坐起來，不停地注視着——就像第一次看見瑪麗時那樣；但這次是一種帶着驚奇和喜悦的注視。事實上，儘管他聽説了那麼多關於狄肯的事情，他仍然一點都不知道這個男孩會是甚麼樣子，他的狐狸、烏鴉、麻雀、羔羊靠他這麼近，像他一樣友善，幾乎成了他的一部份。柯林這輩子從沒跟一個男孩子説過話，他的喜悦和好奇讓他不知所措，甚至想不到要説些甚麼。

但是狄肯絲毫不覺得害羞或窘迫。當初他和烏鴉第一次相遇，烏鴉因為聽不懂他的話，只會死盯着他看而沒有跟他説話，他也沒有感到尷尬。動物們在真正了解你之前都是這樣的。他走到柯林的沙發跟前，輕輕地把羔羊放在他的大腿上，那小東西立刻轉向溫暖的天鵝絨晨衣，開始一遍遍地將鼻往衣服的皺褶裏摩擦，略帶急切地將牠那捲毛頭朝他的腰部撞。這時候，當然任何一個男孩都會忍不住要開口説話。

"牠在做甚麼？"柯林叫道。"牠要甚麼？"

"牠要找媽媽,"狄肯説,越笑越開懷。"我故意讓牠餓着肚子,因為我知道你想看我餵牠食物。"

他在沙發旁跪下,從衣袋裏掏出奶瓶。

"過來,小乖乖,"他説,用一隻溫柔、褐色的手把那隻毛茸茸的白色小頭撥過來。"你要的是這個。你從這裏得到的比從絲綢外衣上得到的要多。吃吧,"他把橡皮奶嘴塞進正在摩擦的嘴裏,羔羊狂喜地吸吮起來。

此後就沒甚麼新奇事可説了。等羔羊入睡後,便連珠爆發地問問題,狄肯一一作了回答。他説了三天前太陽升起時他發現羔羊的經過。當時他正站在曠野上聽雲雀歌唱,看着牠越飛越高,飛進了天空中,成為藍色蒼穹中的一個斑點。

"要不是牠的歌聲,我差點就找不到牠了,我正在奇怪,牠轉眼間就好像飛出了地球,一個人怎麼可能聽到牠的歌聲——就在這時,我聽見從遠處荊豆叢中傳來的另外一種聲音。那是一種微弱的咩咩聲。我知道那是一頭餓壞了的羔羊,我還知道,要不是失去了媽媽,牠是不會餓着的。所以我就開始尋找。嗨,我找得好苦啊。我在荊豆叢裏進進出出,繞了一圈又一圈,好像總是轉錯方向。但最後我在曠野頂端一塊岩石旁邊看見了一塊白色的東西,我爬上去,看見了這頭又冷又餓、半死不活的羔羊。"

在他説話的時候,煤煙一本正經地從開着的窗飛進飛出,發出呱呱的叫聲,算是對窗外景色的評論,而堅果和果殼則飛到窗外的大樹上,順着樹幹爬上爬下,探查着一根根樹枝。隊長蜷縮在狄肯身邊,狄肯出於偏好,坐在爐前地毯上。

他們看着園藝書裏的插圖,狄肯説得出所有那些花的名稱,並且知道哪些已經在秘密花園裏生長。

"我説不出它這個名字，"他指着一種花説，那朵花下面印着"Aquilegia"，"不過我們叫它耬斗菜，這一種叫金魚草，它們都是野生的綠籬植物，但也有長在花園裏的，比野生的要大。秘密花園裏有大簇大簇的耬斗草。它們生長出來之後就像大片飛舞的藍白蝴蝶。"

"我要去看看它們，"柯林叫道，"我要去看看！"

"好啊，你一定要去，"瑪麗認真地説。"你絕對不能再浪費時間。"

"我要永永遠遠活下去！"

但是他們不得不等待一個多星期，因為首先，接連數天颳起大風，其次，柯林出現了感冒的症狀，這兩件事情先後發生，照理無疑會讓柯林大發其火，幸好他們有很多仔細的、神秘的計劃要做，而且狄肯幾乎每天都來，哪怕只逗留數分鐘，說一說曠野上、小路上以及樹籬、小河兩邊發生的事情。他要講述水獺、獾和水老鼠的窩，當然還要說說鳥巢、田鼠和牠們的洞穴。當你聽一個馴獸師給你詳細講述這些事情的時候，你準會激動得幾乎發抖，並意識到整個忙碌的地下世界以何等扎心的熱切和緊張在工作。

"牠們跟我們一樣，"狄肯說，"只不過牠們每年都要築巢。這讓牠們非常忙碌，所以就難免匆匆忙忙，草草了事。"

不過，最讓他們費心的事情是準備非常機密地把柯林帶到花園裏去。在狄肯和瑪麗把柯林的輪椅推過一個轉角，走上常春藤牆外面那條小路之後，絕對不能給人看見他們。隨着日子一天天過去，柯林越來越相信，環繞着花園的那種神秘才是它最大的魅力之一。絕對不能讓任何事情來破壞它。不能讓任何人猜到他們有一個秘密。一定要讓別人以為他只是因為喜歡瑪麗和狄肯他們，不反對讓他們看着他，所以才跟他們一起出去。他們高高興興地討論了很久要走的路線。他們要走上這條小路，走下那條小路，穿過另一條小路，在噴泉花圃之間繞行，好像他們是在照着花匠頭羅奇先生的安排，查看適合花壇種植的花草。這件事看起來是非常順理成章的，誰也不會想到這裏有甚麼秘密。他們會轉向灌木小道，然後會迷路，最後走到長牆前。他們這些嚴肅詳盡的計劃簡直就像戰爭時期的大將軍們的作戰計劃一樣。

發生在這個病人房間裏的這些新奇的事情，當然從傭人房裏流傳到馬廄裏，又傳到了花匠們的耳裏。儘管如此，當羅奇先生有一天接到從柯林少爺的房間裏傳來的命令時，還是大吃一驚，少爺說有話要跟他說，叫他去少爺的房間，但絕對不能讓外人看見。

"哦，哦，"他邊換外衣邊自言自語道，"現在該怎麼辦？少爺殿下從來不召見一個他從沒見過的人。"

羅奇先生不無好奇。他從沒見過少爺一眼，但關於他的奇怪的相貌和行為以及臭脾氣的故事倒是聽說了十來個。他最常聽說的是，他隨時可能死掉，那些從沒見過他的人常常活靈活現地描述他的駝背和無力的四肢。

"這間屋裏的事情發生了變化，羅奇先生，"梅洛太太一邊領他走上後樓梯，一邊說，後樓梯上那條走廊就通向目前充滿神秘感的那個房間。

"但願它們越變越好，梅洛太太，"他答道。

"總不會變得更壞，"她接着說，"奇怪的是，有一些人發現，他們的職責比原來輕鬆多了。羅奇先生，要是你發現自己置身在一群動物之間，瑪莎·索爾比家的狄肯留在這屋裏的時間比你我都多，你難道不覺得驚訝嗎？"

正如瑪麗私下相信的那樣，狄肯真的有一種魔力。當羅奇先生聽到他的名字的時候，他非常溫和地笑了。

"他在白金漢宮和在煤礦底下都是一樣自在，"他說。"不過這也不算冒失無禮。他是個好孩子。"

或許因為他做好了充份的準備，否則準會大吃一驚。當臥室門一打開，就見一隻大烏鴉棲息在一隻雕花椅高高的椅背上，像在自己的巢裏一樣自在，非常響亮地"呱呱"叫了兩聲，通報有客人到。儘管有梅洛太太的警告在先，羅奇先生還是差點嚇得狼狽地往後一跳。

那小酋長既不在牀上，也不在沙發上。他正坐在一張扶手椅裏，一頭小羔羊站在他的旁邊搖着尾巴，狄肯跪在地上用奶瓶給牠餵奶。一隻麻雀站在狄肯彎着的背上，專心致志地啃着一個堅果。那個印度來的小女孩坐在一隻踏腳凳上看着。

"羅奇先生來了，柯林少爺，"梅洛太太說。

小酋長轉過身來仔細打量他的男僕——至少這位花匠頭認為柯林是在打量他。

"哦，你就是羅奇，是嗎？"他說。"我叫你來，是要給你下一些非常重要的命令。"

"很好，少爺，"羅奇答道，心想，不知會不會接到把林苑裏的橡樹全部砍掉或把果園改建成水上園林的命令。

"今天下午我要坐輪椅到外面去，"柯林說，"要是新鮮空氣讓我感到舒服的話，我每天都要出去。在我去的時候，任何花匠都不能留在花園牆那裏的長路附近。誰都不能到那裏。我大概二時去，所有的人都必須迴避，直到我下令，他們才可以回去工作。"

"很好，少爺，"羅奇先生答道，聽說橡樹可以得到保留，果園也平安無事，大大鬆了口氣。

"瑪麗，"柯林轉向她說，"你在印度的時候，當你話說完了要把人打發走的時候，你是怎麼說的？"

"你就說，'你得到了我的允許，可以走了，'"瑪麗答道。

小酋長揮揮手。

"你得到了我的允許，可以走了，羅奇，"他說。"但是，記住，這件事非常重要。"

"呱—呱！"烏鴉發出嘶啞但有禮貌的叫聲。

"很好，少爺。謝謝你，少爺，"羅奇說，梅洛太太帶他離開了房間。

來到外面的走廊裏，這個好脾氣的人一直在微笑，最後幾乎哈哈大笑起來。

"哎呀！"他說，"他真有一股王者的氣派，是嗎？你會以為他是整個王室的化身——王夫加上其他人。"

"哎！"梅洛太太反駁說，"自從他長出腳來，我們就只能讓他把我們每一個人都踩在腳底下，他以為別人生下來就是讓他踩的。"

"如果他能活下去的話，也許會有所改變的，"羅奇先生説。

"哦，有一件事情是很肯定的，"梅洛太太説。"如果他真能活下去，而那個印度來的小女孩也能留在這裏，我可以保證，她就會教他懂得，整個橙並不屬於他一個人，就像蘇珊・索爾比説的那樣。他早晚會發現屬於他自己的那份到底有多大。"

房間裏，柯林正斜靠在靠墊上。

"現在一切都安全了，"他説。"這個下午我就將看見它——這個下午我就可以進去了！"

狄肯帶着他的動物回到了花園裏，瑪麗留在柯林身邊。她沒有覺得他很累，不過午飯端來前他很安靜，他們吃飯時他也很安靜。她很奇怪，就問他是怎麼一回事。

"你的眼睛多大啊，柯林，"她説。"當你在思考的時候，它們大得就像茶碟一樣。你現在在想甚麼呢？"

"我禁不住在想，它會是甚麼樣子的，"他答道。

"你是説花園？"瑪麗問。

"我是説春天，"他説。"我在想，我以前真的從沒見過春天。我甚至難得到屋外去，就算出去，我也從來不看它。我甚至從沒想起過它。"

"我在印度的時候也從沒見過，因為那裏根本沒有春天，"瑪麗説。

儘管柯林過着與世隔絕的生活，他卻比瑪麗更有想像力，至少他有很多時間來看那些奇妙的圖書和圖畫。

"那天早上你跑進來説，'它已經來了！它已經來了！'我當時感到很奇怪。聽起來就像是有大隊的人馬在音樂伴奏下過來了。我的書裏有一張這樣的畫——一群群的大人和小孩，戴着花環和開花的樹枝，每個人都笑呵呵地跳着舞，推推搡搡，吹奏着笛子。所以我説，'也許我們會聽見金喇叭'，並要你推開窗。"

"多有趣啊！"瑪麗説。"的確就是那樣的感覺。要是所有的花、葉、綠色的東西，以及鳥和野生動物一起跳着舞經過這裏，那將有多大一群啊！我相信他們會跳舞唱歌吹笛子，那會合成一陣陣的音樂。"

兩人都大笑起來，但並不是因為他們的想法有多好笑，而是他們喜歡笑。

過了一會，保姆來給柯林穿衣服。她發現，柯林不像以往那樣跟木頭似的躺在那裏讓保姆給他穿衣服，而是坐了起來，並努力自己穿，同時他不停地跟瑪麗説笑。

"今天他的精神很好，先生，"她對來給柯林診視的克拉文醫生説，"他的精神實在太好，所以力氣也大點了。"

"下午等他回來後我再來看看，"克拉文醫生説。"我要看看到外面去對他有多大的好處。我希望，"他放低聲音，"他會讓你跟他一起去。"

"我寧願當場離開，也不願留在這裏聽你提出這個建議。"保姆突然堅定地説。

"其實我並沒真的決定要提出這個建議，"醫生有點緊張地説，"我們要做個實驗。狄肯這孩子，就是把一個嬰兒交給他我都信得過。"

家裏力氣最大的男僕把柯林背下樓，放進了輪椅裏，狄肯就在外面等着。男僕人把毯子、靠墊甚麼的都整理好之後，小酋長朝他和保姆揮了揮手。

"你們得到了我的允許，可以走了，"他說，他們兩人都迅速退下，必須承認的是，兩人安全退回屋後都咯咯地笑了起來。

狄肯開始慢慢地穩穩地推起輪椅。瑪麗小姐走在輪椅旁邊，柯林靠在輪椅上，抬頭看着天空。拱形的天空看來很高，在那晶瑩透明的藍色映襯下，雪白的小雲塊像鳥張開翅膀在飛翔。輕柔的微風從曠野吹來，帶來一種格外清新的香味，令人感覺到陌生。柯林始終挺着瘦弱的胸膛，吮吸着這股香甜的空氣，他的大眼睛看來像是代替了耳朵的功能，在傾聽——傾聽。

"好多的聲音啊，有歌聲、嗡嗡聲和叫喚聲，"他說，"風吹來的是甚麼香味？"

"是曠野上正在開花的荊豆的香味，"狄肯回答說。"嗨，今天那裏的蜜蜂可高興極了。"

他們經過的小路上看不見一個人影。事實上，所有的花匠或花匠的孩子都被趕走了。但是他們按照事先周密安排好的線路在灌木叢和噴泉花圃之間繞來繞去，要的就是那份神秘感帶給他們的快樂。最後他們折進常春藤牆旁邊的長路，出於一種無法解釋的奇怪原因，一種眼看就要發生的驚險遭遇引起的興奮感讓他們放低了說話的聲音。

"到了，"瑪麗幽幽地說。"這裏就是我經常來來去去，一次又一次感到驚訝的地方。"

"就是這裏嗎？"柯林叫道，他的目光帶着急迫的好奇搜索起常春藤。"但我甚麼也看不見，"他悄悄地說。"這裏沒有門。"

"我原先也是這麼想的，"瑪麗說。

接着是一陣可愛得連呼吸都聽不見的沉默，輪椅繼續向前。

"這裏是本·威瑟斯塔夫工作的地方，"瑪麗說。

"是嗎？"柯林問。

再往前走了數碼，瑪麗又悄悄地說起話來。

"知更鳥就是從這裏飛過牆頭的，"她說。

"是嗎？"柯林叫道。"哦！我希望牠回來！"

"那裏，"瑪麗帶着正經的愉快神情指着丁香花叢下面說，"就是牠站在小土堆上把鑰匙指給我看的地方。"

這時柯林坐了起來。

"哪裏？哪裏？是那裏？"他叫道，他的眼睛大得就像童話《小紅帽》裏面的狼的眼睛一樣，在童話裏，狼的大眼睛曾引起小紅帽的警覺。狄肯一動不動地站在那裏，輪椅也停了下來。

"還有這裏，"瑪麗走到常春藤旁邊的花壇上，"就是知更鳥在牆頭上朝我唱歌時我跟牠說話的地方。這裏就是被風吹開的常春藤，"她抓住了那個懸掛下來的綠色簾。

"哦！是這裏——是這裏！"柯林喘着氣說。

"這裏是門把手，這裏是門。狄肯推他進去——快推他進去！"

狄肯有力、平穩、優雅地一推，把柯林推了進去。

但是柯林卻往後一仰倒在了靠墊上，不過他高興地喘着氣，用雙手捂住眼睛，不讓自己看見任何東西，直到進了花園，輪椅像變魔術似的停了下來，門被關上。直到這時他才把手拿開，像狄肯和瑪麗第一次進來時一樣，一遍又一遍朝四處打量。幼嫩的小枝葉像綠色的面紗罩住了牆頭、地面、樹木、晃悠悠的小樹枝和椴权；樹木下面的草地上、涼亭的灰色花缽裏以及這裏那裏，到處都有一抹抹的金色、紫色和白色，他頭頂上的樹木閃爍着粉色和雪白色，那裏有翅膀的撲騰聲，隱隱約約的鳥鳴聲以及一股又一股的香味。太陽溫暖地照在他的臉上，好像一隻手在親切地撫摩他。瑪麗和狄肯驚訝地站在那裏注視着他。他看來那麼不同往常，因為一種亮麗的粉色爬滿了他的全身——象牙白的臉上和頸項上，手上以及全身。

　　"我會康復的！我會康復的！"他叫道。"瑪麗！狄肯！我會康復的！我會永永遠遠活下去！"

第二十一章

本・威瑟斯塔夫

　　個人生活在世界上，有一件事情是不可思議的：你只是偶爾才覺得確信自己可以永遠永遠活下去。有時候，當你在溫柔蕭穆的黎明時份起牀後，走出家門，孤獨地站着，把頭盡力往後仰，往天上看，看着蒼白的天空慢慢變化，變得通紅，一些奇妙的、不可知的事情開始發生，直到旭日東昇——這是千萬年來每天早晨都發生的事情——當時那種永恆的莊嚴讓你情不自禁地大聲叫喊，讓你的心臟停止跳動，這時你就會有這樣的感覺。這時候你的這種感覺是短暫的。有時候，當你在日落時獨自站在樹林裏，夕陽的金色光輝斜射過樹枝或灑落在樹枝下面，給樹林平添一分神秘的寧靜，好像在慢慢地反覆敘述着一件事情，無論你怎樣努力都無法聽清，這時候，你也就會有這樣的感覺。有時候，深藍色的夜空中一片寂靜，成千上萬的星星在等待、注視，這同樣會讓你確信你將永遠永遠活下去；有時候遠處的音樂聲會讓這種感覺成真；有時候某人的一個目光就行。

當柯林第一次在一個隱閉的花園的高牆裏看見、聽見並感覺到春天的時候，就是這樣。那天下午，整個世界好像都在為了一個男孩而努力讓自己完美，光彩耀人、和善可親。也許春天正是出於純粹的無比的善意，盡其所能把一切美好的東西都聚集在這一個地方。狄肯不止一次地停下來，靜靜地站着，輕輕地搖頭，眼睛裏流露出越來越驚訝的神色。

"哦，太奇妙了，"他說。"我是十二歲多快十三歲的人了，十三年裏有許多個下午，但我好像從沒見過一個像今天這樣奇妙的下午。"

"是啊，真是個奇妙的下午，"瑪麗說，快樂地舒了口氣。"我敢說，這是世界上最奇妙的一個下午。"

"你不覺得，"柯林帶着夢幻般的小心說，"這一切全都是為了我嗎？"

"天哪！"瑪麗羨慕地叫道，"你也說得一口地道的約克話了。你說得真好——十分好。"

這些孩子沉浸在快樂中。

他們把輪椅推到李子樹底下，樹上開着雪白的花，蜜蜂在嗡嗡地鳴叫。那就像是國王的華蓋，一個童話中國王的華蓋。附近有開花的草莓樹、蘋果樹，花蕾是粉紅的和白色的，隨處可見有些花蕾已經綻開。在華蓋上開花的樹枝之間，可以看見星星點點藍色的天空像神奇的眼睛往下俯瞰。

瑪麗和狄肯這裏那裏地做點工作，柯林看着他們。他們拿東西給他看——綻放的花蕾，緊緊包裹着的花蕾，葉剛剛泛綠的枝條，一隻啄木鳥掉在草地上的一根羽毛，一隻鳥早先孵過的空蛋殼。狄肯推着輪椅慢慢地在花園裏繞圈，不時地停下來，讓他看看奇蹟從地底下蹦出來，或從樹上垂下來。這就像是巡遊一個會魔法的國王和王后所擁有的王國，參觀他們的神秘財寶。

"我們會看見知更鳥嗎？"柯林問。

"過一會就能讓你看個夠，"狄肯回答說。

"等鳥蛋孵出小鳥來，牠就會忙得頭昏腦脹。你會看見牠叼着像牠一樣大的蟲飛來飛去，當牠飛到鳥巢裏的時候，那裏一片喧鬧，牠自己同樣緊張不安，都不知道該把蟲最先餵給哪一張大嘴。牠的四周都是流着饞涎的嘴巴和呱呱的叫聲。媽媽說，當她看見一隻知更鳥為了餵飽牠那些飢餓的孩子而辛苦工作時，她就覺得自己簡直是個不用做的闊太太。她說她看見那些小東西的時候，好像有汗水從牠們身上滴下來，儘管人們看不見。"

這些話說得大家開心地咯咯笑起來，這時他們想起不能被人聽見，就不得不用手把嘴巴捂住。柯林數天前就學過要低聲說話，他喜歡這樣的神秘氣氛，並盡力這樣去做，但是在興奮之中，要想不大聲笑出來實在是很困難的。

這個下午的每時每刻都充滿新奇的事物，陽光每個小時都變得更加燦爛。輪椅被推回到樹陰下面，狄肯坐在草地上，剛掏出木笛，柯林就看見了他剛才沒時間去注意的東西。

"那棵樹已經很老了，是嗎？"他說。

狄肯的目光越過草地朝那棵樹看去，瑪麗也朝那裏看去。一時間大家都沉默了。

"是的，"隨後狄肯壓低嗓門說，聲音非常柔和。

瑪麗凝視着那棵樹，想着心事。

"那些樹枝很灰，一片葉都沒有，"柯林接着説。"它已經死得差不多了，是嗎？"

"是啊，"狄肯説。"但是等到爬滿樹身的玫瑰長滿葉，開出花來的時候，就可以把死樹全部遮住。到那時它就看不出是死的了。它會是最漂亮的。"

瑪麗還在凝視並想着心事。

"看來好像有一根大樹枝被折斷了，"柯林説。"不知道是怎麼一回事。"

"那是好多年前的事了，"狄肯回答説。"哎！"他突然覺得放輕鬆，把手搭在柯林的身上。"看那隻知更鳥！牠在那兒呢！牠一直在找伴侶。"

柯林差點沒看見，他只瞥見一隻紅胸脯的鳥嘴裏叼着東西一閃而過。牠箭一般穿過一片綠色，飛進了一個草木生長過密的角落，轉眼間就沒有了蹤影。柯林又倚在靠墊上，笑了一笑。

"牠在送點心給她。現在大概五時，我也想吃點心了。"

這麼一來，狄肯和瑪麗可就安全了。

"是魔法把知更鳥送來的，"事後瑪麗悄悄地對狄肯説。"我知道是魔法。"因為她和狄肯都害怕柯林會問十年前斷了樹枝的那棵老樹的事情。他們一起談論過這件事，當時狄肯站在那裏尷尬地直抓頭皮。

"我們必須裝得好像那棵樹跟別的樹沒甚麼兩樣，"他説。"我們千萬不能告訴他樹是怎麼斷的，可憐的孩子。要是他提起了這件事情，我們必須——我們必須裝得很開心的樣子。"

"對，我們必須這樣做，"瑪麗答道。

但是當她凝視着那棵樹的時候，並沒有感到自己顯得很開心的樣子。在那些為數不多的時刻，她一次又一次地疑惑，狄肯説的另外一件事是不是真的。他一直搔着那頭鐵銹紅的頭髮，一臉困惑的樣子。但他的藍眼睛開始出現令人欣慰的神色。

"克拉文太太是個非常可愛的年輕夫人，"他相當遲疑地説。"媽媽説，也許她到米塞爾斯威特來過好多次，來照顧柯林少爺，就像所有去世的媽媽們都會做的那樣。你知道，她們一定要回來。正是她一直在這個花園裏。正是她讓我們工作，要我們把他帶到這裏來。"

瑪麗覺得他説的是魔法。她非常相信魔法。私下她非常相信狄肯對任何靠近他的東西都施了魔法，當然是好的魔法，所以大家才這麼喜歡他，野生動物也知道他是牠們的朋友。她非常想知道的是，當柯林問到那個危險的問題時，會不會正是他的天賦把知更鳥招來，為他們解了圍。她覺得他的魔法一下午都在起着作用，讓柯林看來完全換了個人，一點都不像是那個大喊大叫、捶打枕頭的發瘋的人。就連他象牙似的蒼白好像也在變。他剛進花園時隱約出現在他臉上、頸項上和手上的一絲血色始終沒有完全褪去。他看來像是用血肉做成的，而不再是用象牙或蠟做的了。

他們有兩三次看見知更鳥給牠的伴侶送去食物，這大大地刺激了他們的食慾。柯林覺得一定要吃一些點心。

"去叫一個男傭人把點心放在籃裏，送到杜鵑路上來，"他説。"然後由你和狄肯把它拿到這裏來。"

這是個好主意，很容易辦到。當一塊白布鋪在草地上，熱茶、牛油麵包和烤麵餅擺在上面之後，孩子們就高高興興、狼吞虎嚥地吃了起來。數隻正在辦家事的鳥停下來，看看這裏正在做甚麼，並且興致勃勃、唧唧喳喳，像是在作調查。堅果和果殼叼着數塊餅輕盈地飛到樹上，煤煙叼着整整半塊牛油烤餅飛進了一個角落，先是啄啄它，檢查一下，把它翻過來，嘶啞地叫兩三聲，好像是表示自己的看法，然後才決定高高興興地一口把它吞下。

下午悄悄地過去。陽光的金色越來越深，蜜蜂開始回家，來往的鳥越來越少。狄肯和瑪麗坐在草地上，把點心籃重新包好，準備帶回屋裏去。柯林躺在靠墊上，濃密的頭髮從額頭往後垂下，臉上出現了很自然的血色。

"我不想讓這個下午過去，"他說，"但我明天還要來，後天、大後天、大大後天我都要來。"

"你會吸入很多新鮮空氣，是嗎？"瑪麗說。

"我別的甚麼都不吸了，"他答道。"現在我看見了春天，我還要看夏天。我要看所有生長在這裏的東西。我自己也要在這裏成長。"

"你會的，"狄肯說。"用不了多久，我們就會讓你在這裏走來走去，像別人一樣挖土甚麼的。"

柯林的臉刷地變得通紅。

"走路！"他說。"挖土！我能嗎？"

狄肯小心地瞥了他一眼。他和瑪麗都沒問過他，他的腳到底有沒有病。

"當然能，"他堅定地說。"你——你自己長着腳，像別人一樣！"

瑪麗嚇了一跳，聽到柯林的回答才放下心來。

"我的腳其實沒病，只是又瘦又乏力，而且抖個不停，所以我不敢站立。"

瑪麗和狄肯都鬆了口氣。

"只要你不再害怕，你就能站立了，"狄肯說，"而你馬上就會不再害怕了。"

"我能嗎？"柯林說，他靜靜地躺着，好像在想着甚麼心事。

他們着實安靜了一會。太陽越來越低了。現在正是一切都寂然無聲的時候，他們已經度過了一個忙碌的下午。柯林看來像是在愜意地休息，就連那些動物也不再走動，而是聚在一起，在他們身邊休息。煤煙棲在一根低樹枝上，一條腿抬起來，灰色的眼簾垂在眼睛上，昏昏欲睡。瑪麗暗暗地想，牠看來馬上就要打鼾了。

就在這片沉寂中，柯林半抬起頭，突然發出一聲低低的驚叫，把大家都嚇了一跳。

"那人是誰？"

狄肯和瑪麗騰地跳起來。

"人！"兩人同時急促地輕輕叫出聲來。

柯林朝高牆那裏指去。

"看！"他激動地低聲說道。"看！"

瑪麗和狄肯車轉身來，朝那裏看去。原來是本·威瑟斯塔夫，只見他站在梯上，隔着牆，一臉怒氣地注視着他們！他還朝瑪麗揮着拳頭。

"我要不是個鰥夫，而你又是我的閨女的話，"他叫道，"我就要狠狠揍你一頓！"

他咄咄逼人地朝上蹬了一步，好像要從梯上跳下來對付她；但是當她朝他走去時，他顯然又考慮了一下，站在梯的最高一級上，往下朝她揮着拳頭。

"我一直就看不慣你！"他氣憤地說。"我第一次看見你的時候就受不了你。一個瘦骨嶙峋的，面色蒼白的小女孩，老是問東問西。我怎麼也沒想到你會這麼麻煩。要不是因為那隻知更鳥——討厭的東西——"

"本·威瑟斯塔夫，"瑪麗終於喘過氣來叫道。她站在他下面，喘着氣抬頭叫他。"本·威瑟斯塔夫，是知更鳥指路的！"

這時，本好像真的要從梯上往下跳到她的身邊；他氣壞了。

"你這個壞小鬼！"他朝她叫道。"把你做的壞事賴在知更鳥身上——雖然牠也是個無禮的東西。牠給你指的路！牠，嘿！你這個小東西，"——她可以看見他的下一句話蹦出來，因為他心裏充滿了好奇——"你到底是怎麼進來的？"

"是知更鳥給我指路，"她固執地反駁說。"牠不知道牠在做這件事，但牠確實做了。你這樣對我揮拳頭，我就不告訴你。"

瑪麗話音剛落，他的拳頭就突然停止了揮動，下巴也垂下來。原來他的目光越過瑪麗的頭頂，看着一樣東西越過草地朝他飛來。

剛一聽到本的怒吼聲時，柯林嚇愣了，他只是坐起來，像是着了迷似地聽着。但是聽到一半，他恢復了過來，氣沖沖地朝狄肯示意。

"推我過去！"他命令道。"推我過去，靠近那裏，就在他面前停下！”

而這正是本‧威瑟斯塔夫所看見並讓他下巴垂下來的事情。一輛輪椅朝他推來，看來就像是王室的馬車，因為一個小酋長斜躺在裏面，那雙黑眼圈的大眼睛發出王家的命令，一隻細小的白手高傲地指向他，直到他的鼻底下才停住。怪不得他的嘴巴張得那麼大。

“你知道我是誰嗎？”酋長問。

本‧威瑟斯塔夫好一副張嘴結舌的樣子！他的紅眼睛愣愣地盯着前面這個人，像是見到了鬼一樣。他久久地注視着，好像吞下一塊東西堵住了喉嚨口，一句話也説不出來。

“你知道我是誰嗎？”柯林更加盛氣凌人地問道。“回答！”

本‧威瑟斯塔夫舉起那隻粗糙的手，舉過眼睛，又舉過額頭，然後用奇怪、發抖的聲音作了回答。

“你是誰？”他説。“啊，我想起來了——你媽媽的眼睛長在你的臉上，你用它們盯着我。天知道你是怎麼到這裏來的。但你就是那個可憐的癱子。”

柯林忘記了他一直有一個後背。他的臉漲得通紅，刷地坐起來，坐得筆直。

“我不是癱子！”他憤怒地叫道。“我不是！”

“他不是！”瑪麗氣得幾乎朝着牆頭怒吼。“他連個針頭般大的瘤都沒有！我看過，根本就沒有——一個也沒有！”

本‧威瑟斯塔夫又把手舉過額頭，注視着他，好像看不夠似的。他的手在抖，嘴在抖，聲音也在抖。他是個自負的老人，一個缺心眼的老人，他只記得他聽説過的事情。

"你——你沒有曲背？"他嘶啞地問。

"沒有！"柯林吼道。

"你——你沒有瘸腿？"本顫抖着說，聲音更粗了。

太過份了。柯林那股通常轉化為怒氣的力量現在以一種新的方式在他身上快速產生。從來沒人罵他是瘸子，哪怕是背地裏也沒有人這麼説——而聽本・威瑟斯塔夫那言之鑿鑿的口氣，好像他真的是個瘸子，這下子酋長不論是精神上還是肉體上都承受不住了。他的怒氣和被侮辱的自尊促使他忘掉了一切，只記得現在這個時刻，令他產生了一種前所未有的力量，一種近乎超自然的力量。

"過來！"他朝狄肯吼道，並拉掉下肢上的遮蓋物，把自己掙脫出來。"過來！過來！馬上過來！"

狄肯馬上來到他的身邊。瑪麗短短地倒抽一口氣，隨後將氣息屏住，她感到自己臉色發白了。

"他做到了！他做得到！他做得到！他做得到！"她用快得不能再快的速度像連珠砲似的自言自語道。

隨着一陣短促的手忙腳亂的行動，毯子被扔到了地上，狄肯扶住柯林的手臂，一雙細腿伸了出來，踩在草地上。柯林站得筆直——筆直——直得像一支箭，看來格外地高——他的頭往後仰，眼睛閃爍着奇怪的火花。

"看着我！"他對着本・威瑟斯塔夫叫道。"好好看着我——你！好好看着我！"

"他站得像我一樣直！"狄肯叫道。"他像約克郡的任何一個男孩站得一樣直！"

本・威瑟斯塔夫接下來的行為在瑪麗看來怪得不能再怪。他先是哽咽了一下，隨後吞嚥了一下，最後眼淚突然順着他那飽經風霜的老臉流了下來，他狠狠地拍打着那雙老手。

"嘿！"他脫口而出。"別人都在說謊！你的確瘦得像根板條，白得像隻鬼魂，但你身上根本沒有瘤，你能長成一個男人。上帝保佑你！"

狄肯牢牢地扶着柯林的手臂，但柯林已不再搖搖晃晃了。他站得越來越直，直視着本・威瑟斯塔夫的臉。

"我爸不在的時候，"他說，"我就是你的主人。你要服從我。這是我的花園。不要膽敢提到它，一個字也不行！你從梯上下來，到長路上去，瑪麗小姐會去接你，帶你過來。我有話跟你說。我們並不需要你，但現在你不得不捲入這個秘密。快！"

本・威瑟斯塔夫那張怒氣沖沖的老臉上仍然掛着在那陣古怪的衝動中淌下的淚水。他好像無法把目光從柯林身上移開，只見瘦削的柯林站得筆直，頭往後仰着。

"嘿！孩子，"他幾乎是耳語道。"嘿！我的孩子！"接着他想起了該做的事情，就突然用花匠的方式碰了一下帽，說，"是，少爺！是，少爺！"順從地走下梯，人也就不見了。

第二十二章

太陽下山時

等他的頭落下去，看不見之後，柯林轉向瑪麗。

"去接他，"他説；瑪麗奔過草地朝常春藤下面的那扇門跑去。

狄肯目光敏鋭地看着他。他的臉上有猩紅的斑點，看來很驚訝，但一點都沒有要摔倒的樣子。

"我能堅持，"他説，他的頭依然抬得高高的，説話時一臉的嚴肅。

"我跟你説過，你馬上就會不再害怕了，"狄肯回答説。"你現在就不怕了。"

"是的，我不怕了，"柯林説。

然後，突然間，他想起了瑪麗説過的話。

"你在施展魔力嗎？"他尖鋭地問。

狄肯張開了一張笑臉。

"是你自己在施展魔力，"他説。"就像把這些東西從地底下變出來的魔力一樣，"他用厚靴碰了碰草叢裏的番紅花。

柯林朝下看着它們。

"是啊，"他慢慢地説，"沒有甚麼魔力比那更厲害了——肯定沒有。"

他把腰挺得比從前任何時候都直。

"我要走到那棵樹跟前去，"他説，指着離他數英尺遠的地方。"我要站在那裏等威瑟斯塔夫過來。願意的話，我可以倚在樹上休息。想坐下的時候我就坐下，但一定要在走到那棵樹跟前之後。把輪椅裏的毯子拿給我。"

他走到樹前，雖然狄肯扶着他的手臂，但他走得出奇地穩當。當他背靠樹幹站立的時候，很難看出他是倚在樹幹上的，他仍然挺得筆直，看來很高。

當本・威瑟斯塔夫從門口進來時，看見柯林站在那裏，又聽見瑪麗在低聲跟他説着甚麼。

"你在説甚麼？"他很暴躁地問，因為他不想把注意力從這個又高又瘦、站得筆直的男孩子和他那張驕傲的臉上移開。

但瑪麗沒理他。她説的是這個：

"你能做到！你能做到！我説過你能做到！你能做到！你能做到！你能！"

她這麼對柯林説，是因為她想施展魔力，讓柯林這樣繼續站立。要是他在本・威瑟斯塔夫面前放棄，她可受不了。她突然覺得，儘管他很瘦，卻很俊美。他用那種滑稽的威嚴神態注視着本・威瑟斯塔夫。

“看着我！”他命令道。“看看我的全身！我是駝背嗎？我有瘸腿嗎？”

本‧威瑟斯塔夫的激動還沒有完全平息，但已經稍微冷靜了一點，他幾乎是用平常的態度回答。

“不是，”他說。“一點都不。你在做甚麼！——老是躲着人，讓別人以為你是個瘸子和蠢人？”

“蠢人！”狄肯氣憤地說。“誰這麼想？”

“很多人，”本說。“這世界上多的是笨蛋，他們只會造謠。你為甚麼要把自己藏起來呢？”

“所有的人都說我要死了，”柯林簡潔地說。“我不會死！”

他說得這麼堅決，本‧威瑟斯塔夫不由得從上到下、從下到上地仔細打量起他來。

“你會死？”他帶着乾巴巴的笑意說。“一點都看不出呢！你的精神好着呢。我看見你那麼利落地把腳踩到地上的時候，我就知道你沒事。少爺，你在毯子上坐一會，給我下命令吧。”

他的態度裏有一種難以捉摸的溫柔和深刻的理解，兩者奇怪地混合在一起。他們一起順着長路往前走的時候，瑪麗連珠砲似的說着話，語速快得不能再快。她告訴他，首先要記住的是，柯林正在好起來——越來越好。是花園讓他好起來的。任何人都不能讓他覺得自己身上長着瘤，快要死了。

酋長屈尊地坐在樹下的一塊毯子上。

“你在花園裏做甚麼，威瑟斯塔夫？”他問道。

“要我做甚麼就做甚麼，”老本答道。“我一直受到寵愛——因為她喜歡我。”

"她？"柯林説。

"就是你的媽媽，"本·威瑟斯塔夫説。

"我媽媽？"柯林説，他悄悄地打量着四周。"這是她的花園，是嗎？"

"是啊，是她的，"本·威瑟斯塔夫也打量着四周，"她很喜歡它。"

"現在這是我的花園。我喜歡它。我每天都要來這裏，"柯林宣佈説。"但是這件事要保密。我的命令就是：不能讓任何人知道我們來這裏。狄肯和我表姐在這裏工作，讓它活了過來。有時候我會叫你來幫忙——但是你一定要在沒人看見的時候來。"

本·威瑟斯塔夫的老臉扭曲，擠出一個乾巴巴的笑容。

"以前我就在沒人看見的時候來過這裏，"他説。

"甚麼！"柯林驚叫道。"甚麼時候？"

"我最後一次來這裏，"他擦着下巴，打量四周，"大概在兩年前。"

"但是這裏已經十年沒人來過了！"柯林叫道。"這裏又沒門！"

"我不是一般的人，"老本乾巴巴地説。"我也不是從門裏進來的。我是爬牆過來的。自以後我患了風濕病，就沒再來過。"

"你進來做過一點修剪！"狄肯叫道。"我實在弄不明白是怎麼一回事。"

"她非常喜歡它——真的！"本·威瑟斯塔夫慢慢地説。"她是個那麼漂亮的小夫人。有一次她對我説，'本，'她笑着説，'要是我病了或我走了，你要照顧好我的玫瑰。'在她真的走了之後，主人卻吩咐說，誰也不准接近這裏。但我還是來了，"他的固執裏帶着怒氣。"爬過牆進來了——直到患了風濕病才罷休——我一年來修剪一次。是她原先吩咐的。"

"要不是你先來打理過，這兒不會這麼有活力，"狄肯說，"我本來就很奇怪。"

"我很高興你這麼做，威瑟斯塔夫，"柯林說。"你會知道怎樣保守秘密的。"

"是啊，我知道，少爺，"本答道。"一個有風濕病的人從門口進來要容易得多了。"

瑪麗把小鏟扔到樹旁的草地上。柯林伸手把它拿起來。他的臉上出現一種奇怪的表情，他開始在地上挖起來。他細小的手實在太沒有力氣，但是在大家的注視下——瑪麗饒有興趣地看着——他把鏟插進了泥土裏，把一些泥土挖了起來。

"你能做的！你能做的！"瑪麗對自己說。"我告訴過你，你能的！"

狄肯的圓眼睛裏充滿迫切的好奇心，但是他甚麼也沒說。本·威瑟斯塔夫饒有興趣地看着。

柯林堅持着。挖出了數鏟泥土之後，他用最標準的約克話興奮地對狄肯說，"你說過你會讓我像別的人一樣在這裏走來走去——你說過你會讓我挖土。我當時還以為你只是逗我開心呢。我今天第一次走路——我還在這裏挖土。"

聽到他的話，本·威瑟斯塔夫的嘴巴張得老大，但最後卻咯咯地笑了起來。

"嗨！"他說，"聽起來你好像聰明多了。你肯定是個約克郡孩子。你還會挖土。種一點東西怎麼樣？我可以給你拿一盆玫瑰來。"

"快去拿！"柯林一邊興奮地挖着一邊說。"快！快！"

本的速度的確夠快的。他完全忘了自己有風濕病。狄肯拿起鏟，把洞挖得很深很大，一個雙手細小蒼白的新手是做不了的。瑪麗奔過去拿來一個水罐。當狄肯把洞挖深時，柯林繼續一次次地把柔軟的泥土翻過來。他抬頭看着天空，這種從沒有過的運動讓他臉色微微紅潤、發亮。

"我想在太陽落得——落得很低之前做這件事，"他說。

瑪麗覺得太陽好像有意拖延了數分鐘下山的時間。本·威瑟斯塔夫從溫室裏把玫瑰連同花盆一起拿來。他也開始興奮起來，盡快一瘸一拐地從草地上跑過來，跪倒在洞旁，把花盆砸碎。

"過來，孩子，"他說，把玫瑰遞給柯林。"你親手把它種下去，就像一個國王每到一個新的地方都要做的一樣。"

柯林那雙細白的小手微微顫抖，臉也更紅了，他把玫瑰放進土裏，扶着它，讓老本給它培土。土先被填進洞裏，然後壓實，讓玫瑰不再搖晃。瑪麗手腳着地，身體靠前。煤煙飛了下來，走上前來看看這裏在做甚麼。堅果和果殼在一棵草莓樹上唧唧喳喳地聊着這件事。

"種好了！"柯林最後說。"太陽剛剛開始下山。扶我起來，狄肯。我要站着看它下山。這是魔力的一部份。"

狄肯把他扶了起來，而魔力——或者不管它是甚麼——給了他這麼大的力量，當太陽下山，這個可愛奇妙的下午結束時，他確確實實地靠兩條腿站立着，並且哈哈大笑。

第二十三章

魔力

當他們回到家裏時，克拉文醫生已經等了好一會。他確實已經在想，是不是應該派人到通往花園的各條小路上去看看。當柯林被送回房間時，可憐的醫生仔細地上下打量他。

"你不應該在外面逗留那麼長的時間，"他說。"你不該太勞累。"

"我一點都不累，"柯林說。"我感覺很好。明天我早上下午都要去。"

"我不敢答應，"克拉文醫生回答說。"我怕這樣做不太妥當。"

"想要阻止我才不妥當呢，"柯林很認真地說。"我就要去。"

就連瑪麗也發現，柯林的一個怪異之處就是，他一點都不知道當他在向別人發號施令時多像一個粗魯的小霸王。他一輩子都生活在一個荒島上，因為他是這個荒島的國王，於是就養成了自己的行事方法，而且沒有別人可作比較。瑪麗以前的確很像他，但自從來到米塞爾斯威特之後，她慢慢地發現，自己的那套方式多麼不合常規。發現了這一點之後，她當然覺得跟柯林交流一下是很有趣的。於是等克拉文醫生走了之後，她坐在那裏看了他數分鐘。她很想讓他來問她，為甚麼要這樣做，她當然如願了。

"你為甚麼看着我？"他說。

"我在想，我非常為克拉文醫生感到難過。"

"我也是，"柯林平靜地說，但透露着一點滿意的神氣。"現在我不會死，他也就得不到米塞爾斯威特了。"

"我當然也是為這個而替他感到難過，"瑪麗說，"但是我剛才在想，要十年如一日地對一個總是粗暴魯莽的孩子客客氣氣，那一定是非常可怕的。我決不會這麼做。"

"我粗魯嗎？"柯林問，絲毫沒感到不安。

"如果你是他自己的孩子，而他是個愛打人的爸爸，"瑪麗說，"他肯定會打你。"

"可他不敢，"柯林說。

"是啊，他是不敢，"瑪麗小姐回答說，絲毫不帶偏見地思考着這件事情。"任何人都不敢做你不喜歡的事情——因為你要死了甚麼的。你是個這麼可憐的東西。"

"但是，"柯林固執地說，"我不再是個可憐的東西了。我不會讓別人認為我可憐。今天下午我用自己的腳站了起來。"

"就是因為你老是自行其是，才讓你變得這麼怪，"瑪麗把心裏想的說了出來。

柯林轉過頭去，皺起了眉頭。

“我怪嗎？”他責問道。

“是的，”瑪麗回答說，“非常怪。但你不必發怒，”她不偏不倚地補充說，“因為我跟你一樣怪——還有本·威瑟斯塔夫。現在我開始喜歡起別人來，並且找到了秘密花園，所以我不像以前那樣怪了。”

“我不想做個怪人，”柯林說。“我不想，”他又皺起眉頭，顯得很有決心。

他是個非常驕傲的孩子。他躺在那裏想了一會，然後瑪麗看見他美麗的笑容出現了，並且慢慢地改變了整張臉。

“要是我每天都到花園裏去，”他說，“我就不會再是怪人了。那裏有魔力——好的魔力，你知道，瑪麗。我肯定那裏有的。”

“我也肯定，”瑪麗說。

“就算不是真的魔力，”柯林說，“我們也可以假裝它是。那裏有一種東西——一種東西！”

“那就是魔力，”瑪麗說，“但不是壞的黑魔力，而是好的白魔力，像雪一樣白。”

他們總是稱它為魔力，的確，在接下來的數個月裏，它好像就是魔力。那可是奇妙的數個月、充滿歡樂的數個月、驚人的數個月。哦！那個花園裏發生的事情啊！要是你沒有一個花園，你就不能明白，要是你有一個花園，你就會知道，要把那裏面發生的一切描繪出來，要寫整整一本書。一開始，那些綠色的東西好像再也不會停止從土裏往外竄的勢頭，青草裏、花牀裏，甚至牆縫裏，到處看得見它們。接着，那些綠色的東西開始長出花蕾，接着花蕾開始綻放，呈現出顏色，深淺不同的藍色、紫色、濃淡各異的猩紅色。在那些快樂的日子裏，花在每一個角落裏開放。本·威瑟斯塔夫見過這樣的情景，也曾把磚牆縫裏的灰泥刮掉，補上很多泥土，讓那些可愛的攀附植物生長。彩虹色和白色的百合花一簇一簇地挺立在草叢裏，綠色的涼亭裏長着多得驚人的高高的飛燕草，耬斗菜和風鈴草，它們開着藍色和白色的花。

"她特別喜歡它們——真的，"本·威瑟斯塔夫說。"她常說，她喜歡那些東西總是不停地指向藍天。她倒不是那種厭惡塵世的人——不是的。她說她喜歡藍天就是因為藍天看起來總是那麼開開心心的。"

狄肯和瑪麗播下的種子像得到仙女的照料似的長了出來。五顏六色的柔滑的罌粟迎着微風起舞，與那些已經在花園裏生長了數年的愉快、高傲的花爭奇鬥艷，那些花也許會覺得好奇，不知這些陌生人是怎麼進來的。還有那些玫瑰——玫瑰！從草叢裏長出來，與羽扇豆纏結在一起，爬滿了樹幹，從樹葉上懸掛下來，爬上牆頭，長長的花環佈滿牆面，像瀑布似的垂掛下來——它們一天比一天、一小時比一小時更有生氣。鮮嫩的葉，花蕾——還有花蕾——開始時很細小，但是不斷生長，像施了魔力一樣，最後終於怒放出杯狀的花，清香溢出杯口，瀰漫在花園的空氣裏。

柯林看見了這一切，注視着每一個變化。他每個早晨都被帶到外面，白天只要不下雨，他每時每刻都在花園裏度過。即使是灰濛濛的天氣也讓他高興。他會躺在草地上，"看着東西生長，"他說。他還鑿鑿有據地說，要是你看得時間夠長，就會看見花蕾綻放開來。你還可以結交那些忙得不可開交的昆蟲，牠們東奔西跑，不知在忙些甚麼，但對牠們來說顯然是很重要的工作，有時候拖數根稻草或羽毛，拉一點吃的東西，有時候爬到葉瓣上，就像你爬到大樹頂上俯瞰整個鄉野一樣。一隻鼴鼠把洞口的土頂開，終於鑽了出來，牠爪上指甲很長，活像小精靈的手，柯林聚精會神地看了整整一個早上。螞蟻的生活、甲蟲的生活、蜜蜂的生活、青蛙的生活、鳥的生活、植物的生活，這些都在他面前打開一個嶄新的世界，當狄肯向他揭示了這一切，又加上狐狸的生活、水獺的生活、雪貂的生活、麻雀的生活、鱒魚和水老鼠以及獾的生活時，他就有沒完沒了的事情可以談論和思考了。

這還沒有顯示出魔力的一半。他曾經真正地站起來過一回，這個事實讓柯林思緒萬千，當瑪麗告訴他，她曾經使用過的咒語時，他非常激動，並表示極大的贊同。他不停地說着這件事。

"當然了，世界上有好多魔力，"有一天他聰明地說，"但人們不知道它是甚麼樣子的，怎樣使用它。也許一開始就是不停地說你希望會發生的美好的事情，直到它真的發生為止。我要做個試驗。"

第二天早晨，當他們進入秘密花園之後，他立刻派人去叫本·威瑟斯塔夫來。本馬上就趕來了，只見小酋長站在一棵樹下，看來挺威嚴，不過同樣帶着甜美的微笑。

"早上好，本·威瑟斯塔夫，"他說。"我要你和狄肯、瑪麗小姐站成一排，聽我說話，因為我有件非常重要的事情要告訴你們。"

"是，是，少爺！"本·威瑟斯塔夫碰了碰額頭答道。（本·威瑟斯塔夫有一個保存了很久的秘密：他小時候曾經偷偷到海邊並跟船出海。所以他能像個水手那樣回答柯林的話。）

"我要做一個科學實驗，"酋長解釋説。"等我長大後我要做出偉大的科學發現，我就從現在這個實驗開始。"

"是，是，少爺！"本·威瑟斯塔夫立即説，儘管他還是第一次聽説科學發現這個詞。

瑪麗也是第一次聽説，但即使這樣，她仍然開始意識到，柯林儘管很怪，但他讀過很多講述奇妙事物的書，是個很能令人相信的男孩。當他用那雙奇怪的眼睛直愣愣地盯着你的時候，你就會情不自禁地相信他，儘管他只有十歲——將近十一歲。此刻他特別令人信服，因為他突然產生一種強烈的慾望，像一個真正的大人那樣説話。

"我將要做的科學發現，"他接着説。"是關於魔力。魔力是個偉大的東西，除了古書上少數數個人之外，幾乎沒人了解它——瑪麗也了解一點，因為她出生在印度，那裏有假冒懂得魔力的人。我相信狄肯懂一點魔力，但也許他自己都不知道自己懂得魔力。他能讓動物和人着迷。如果他不是個馴獸師，我就不會讓他來看我——他還是個馴男孩師，因為男孩也是動物。我相信任何東西都有魔力，只不過我們沒有足夠的悟性去把握它，讓它為我們做事——像電、馬和蒸氣一樣。"

這段話太有説服力了，連本·威瑟斯塔夫都變得非常激動起來，實在難以保持鎮靜。

"是，是，少爺，"他説道，並開始站得筆直。

"當瑪麗發現這個花園的時候，它看來像死的一樣，"那個雄辯家接着説。"接着有樣東西開始讓一些東西從土裏長出來，而且憑空造出一些東西來。今天這裏還沒有東西，隔天就有了。

我以前從沒盯着甚麼東西看過，這使我非常好奇。科學家總是好奇的，而我將要成為科學家。我總是對自己說，'這是甚麼？'這總是某種東西。不會甚麼也不是！我不知道它的名字，所以我就叫它魔力。我從沒看見過日出，但是瑪麗和狄肯看見過，根據他們告訴我的，我相信，這也是魔力。有個東西把它往上推又往下拉。有時候，當我在花園裏的時候，我抬頭透過樹枝往天上看，會有一種奇怪的愉快感覺，好像有一種東西在我心裏往上推又往下拉，讓我呼吸加快。魔力總是把東西往上推、往下拉，並且憑空造出東西。一切東西都是由魔力造出來的，不管是樹葉還是樹，花還是鳥，獾還是狐狸，麻雀還是人。所以它肯定就在我們周圍。在這個花園裏，——在所有的地方。這個花園裏的魔力使我站了起來，並且知道我將活下去，成為一個大人。我將做一個科學實驗，提取出一些魔力，將它輸入我的身體，讓它在我身體裏往上推往下拉，讓我強壯起來。我不知道我該怎麼做，但我想，只要你不停地想這件事，叫喚它，它也許就會來。也許我是第一個用孩子的方式獲取魔力的人。我第一次試圖站起來的時候，瑪麗不停地盡可能快地對自己說，'你能做到！你能做到！'而我真的做到了。當然，當時我自己也在努力，但是她的魔力幫助了我——還有狄肯的魔力。每天早晨和晚上以及我能記得住的白天，我總要說，'魔力在我身體裏面！讓我康復起來！我要變得跟狄肯一樣強壯，跟狄肯一樣強壯！'你們也一定要這樣做。這是我的實驗。你會幫助我嗎，本·威瑟斯塔夫？"

"是，是，少爺！"本·威瑟斯塔夫說。"是，是！"

"要是你每天像士兵出操那樣正規地堅持這麼做，我們就會看到將有甚麼樣的結果，看看實驗是不是成功。你學習的時候，總是反覆唸你要學的東西，不斷地思考它，直到它長留在你的心裏，我覺得魔力也是這樣。要是你不停地叫喚它，讓它來到你的身邊，幫助你，它就會成為你的一部份，它會留下來，為你做事。”

“我在印度的時候，有一次聽見一個軍官對我媽媽說，印度有些苦行者，把一些話重複上千遍，”瑪麗說。

“我聽見過傑姆·費特華斯的妻子把同樣一句話重複上千遍——罵傑姆是醉鬼，”本·威瑟斯塔夫乾巴巴地說。“傑姆常常喝醉，這倒是真的。他會狠狠揍她一頓，然後到‘藍獅子’酒館去，把自己灌得酩酊大醉。”

柯林皺着眉頭思考了數分鐘，然後又露出了笑容。

“哦，”他說，“你看出一點名堂來了。她使用了錯誤的魔力，弄得傑姆揍了她。要是她使用了正確的，跟他說一些好話，或許他就不會把自己灌得酩酊大醉——或許他還會給她買一頂新帽呢。”

本·威瑟斯塔夫咯咯地笑了起來，那雙又小又老的眼睛裏流露出對柯林由衷的敬佩。

“你不但是個雙腳筆直的孩子，還是個聰明的孩子，柯林少爺，”他說。“下次我見到貝絲·費特華斯的時候，我會暗示她，魔力會為她做些甚麼。要是你的科學實驗成功的話，她肯定會非常高興的——傑姆也會非常高興。”

狄肯一直站着聽柯林演講，那雙圓眼睛裏閃爍着好奇、喜悅的光芒。堅果和果殼停棲在他的肩上，他的懷裏抱着一個長耳大白兔，輕輕地，輕輕地撫摩着牠，牠的耳朵垂在背上，自得其樂。

"你覺得實驗會成功嗎？"柯林問他，不知他在想些甚麼。每當看見狄肯帶着他那歡快的笑容看着他或他的某隻"動物"時，他就想知道狄肯在想些甚麼。

這時候他就在笑，笑得比平時更歡樂。

"是啊，"他答道，"我覺得會成功。就像太陽照在種子上一樣。它肯定會成功。我們現在就開始嗎？"

柯林很高興，瑪麗也很高興。憑着對插圖中那些苦行者和宗教信徒的記憶，柯林建議大家盤腿坐在一棵華蓋似的樹下。

"這就像坐在廟裏一樣，"柯林説。"我太累了，想坐一會。"

"哎！"狄肯説，"你不能用'我累了'這樣的話來開頭。你這樣會損壞魔力的。"

柯林轉身看着他——看着那雙天真的圓眼睛。

"説得對，"他慢慢地説。"我一定要只想着魔力。"

他們團團圍坐在樹下，顯得又莊嚴又神秘。本·威瑟斯塔夫覺得自己像是被領去參加了一個禱告會。通常他對他所謂的"老掉牙的禱告會"是不屑一顧的，但這次是酋長的事情，他不但不覺得討厭，反而因為能夠應邀參與而受寵若驚。瑪麗小姐有一種完全入迷的感覺。狄肯懷抱着兔子，也許他悄悄説了一些馴獸師的咒語，當他像其他人一樣盤腿坐下時，烏鴉、狐狸、麻雀和羔羊都慢慢地走上前來，好像自覺自願似的各自佔了一個地方，加入到他們圍成的圈子裏。

"動物們來了，"柯林莊重地説。"牠們想幫助我們。"

柯林看來真的很俊美，瑪麗心想。他高高地昂着頭，似乎覺得自己是個牧師，那雙奇怪的眼睛裏有一種奇妙的神色。陽光透過樹枝照在他的身上。"現在我們要開始了，"他說。"假如我們是苦行僧，我們要不要前後搖擺呢，瑪麗？"

"我可不會前後搖擺，"本·威瑟斯塔夫說。"我有風濕病。"

"魔力會把風濕病趕走，"柯林像個祭司長那樣說，"但是我們在魔力把你的風濕病趕走之前是不用搖擺的。我們只要唱歌就行。"

"我也不會唱歌，"本·威瑟斯塔夫有點不耐煩地說。"我只試着在教堂唱詩班唱過一次，結果就被趕了出來。"

沒有人笑。大家都太認真了。柯林的臉上甚至沒有一絲陰影。他只想着魔力。

"那我來唱吧，"他說。接着就唱了起來，看來像個陌生的男精靈。"太陽在發光——太陽在發光。那就是魔力。花在開放——根在搖晃。那就是魔力。魔力有活力——魔力多強壯。魔力在我身上——魔力在我身上。它在我身上——它在我身上。它在我們每個人身上。它在本·威瑟斯塔夫的背上。魔力！魔力！快來幫忙！"

他把這段話重複了很多很多遍——不說它有上千遍吧，反正也夠多的。瑪麗入迷地聽着。她覺得這些話似乎既奇怪又好聽，她要他不斷地說下去。本·威瑟斯塔夫開始有了一種夢幻似的舒適感覺。花叢裏蜜蜂的嗡嗡聲與歌聲混雜在一起，產生了一種催眠的效果。狄肯盤腿坐着，兔子睡在他的懷裏，他的一隻手搭在羔羊的背上。煤煙擠走了一隻麻雀，蜷縮在他的肩上，灰色的薄眼簾垂在眼睛上。最後柯林停了下來。

"現在我要繞着花園走一圈，"他宣佈説。

本·威瑟斯塔夫的頭剛剛往前垂，聽見這句話，猛地一下子又抬了起來。

"你剛才睡着了，"柯林説。

"根本不是，"本喃喃地説。"你的講道很精彩——可我要在募捐之前出去。"

他還沒完全清醒。

"你不是在教堂裏，"柯林説。

"當然不是，"本直起腰來説。"誰説我是在教堂裏呢？我聽清了你説的每一句話。你説魔力在我背上。醫生説這就是風濕病。"

酋長搖搖頭。

"那是錯誤的魔力，"他説。"你會好起來的。現在我同意你去工作。但是明天你還要來。"

"我倒是想看看你繞着花園走一圈，"本嘀咕道。

這聲嘀咕沒有甚麼不友好的意思，但總還是嘀咕。事實上，作為一個固執的老人，對魔力又不完全信服，他已打定主意，一旦他被支走，就要爬上梯，從牆頭上張望，這樣假如柯林被絆倒的話，他就可以一瘸一拐地趕回去幫忙。

酋長沒有反對他留下來，於是一個行列就組成了。這的確是一個行列。柯林領頭，狄肯和瑪麗在他兩邊。本·威瑟斯塔夫走在後面，"動物們"跟在他們後面，羔羊和小狐狸緊挨着狄肯，白兔在一邊時而蹦蹦跳跳，時而停下啃東西，煤煙跟在後面，臉上那種一本正經的樣子就像個自以為重任在肩的人那樣。

這個行列移動得很慢，但非常莊嚴。每走兩三碼就停下歇一會。柯林倚在狄肯的手臂上，本・威瑟斯塔夫暗地裏格外留神，但是柯林時不時地把手從狄肯的手臂上拿開，獨自走上兩三步。他的頭始終高高昂起，看來非常有氣勢。

"魔力在我身上！"他不停地說。"魔力讓我健壯！我能夠感覺到！我能夠感覺到！"

似乎可以非常肯定的是他身上有樣東西在支撐着他。他坐在涼亭裏的椅上，有一兩次坐在草地上，好幾次停在小路上，倚在狄肯身上，但他堅持着繞花園走了一圈。當他回到那棵華蓋似的大樹下時，臉蛋紅撲撲的，看來很得意。

"我成功了！魔力奏效了！"他叫道。"這是我的第一個科學發現。"

"克拉文醫生會怎麼説呢？"瑪麗脫口問道。

"他甚麼也不會説，"柯林答道，"因為沒人會告訴他。這將是個最大的秘密。在我健壯得可以像任何男孩子一樣走路、奔跑之前，誰也不准把這件事説出去。我每天照樣坐輪椅來這裏，坐輪椅回去。在這個實驗完全成功之前，我不想讓別人竊竊私語，東問西問，也不想讓我爸爸聽說這件事。到那時，等他回到米塞爾斯威特，我就要走進他的書房，對他説，'我來了；我跟任何一個男孩一樣。我很健康，我會長成一個大人。這全是科學實驗的功勞。'"

"他會以為他是在做夢，"瑪麗叫道。"他不會相信他的眼睛。"

柯林得意得臉都紅了。他讓自己相信他會好的，要是他能明白的話，可以説，這實在不亞於一場戰鬥。給他刺激最大的一個念頭是，想像一下他的爸爸看見他有一個跟別人的孩子一樣腰桿筆直、一樣健壯的兒子，他會有甚麼樣的表情。在以往病魔纏身的日子裏，最令他傷心的就是，自己是一個有病的，腰都挺不直的孩子，連自己的爸爸都不敢看他，為此他對自己充滿了怨恨。

"他非相信不可，"他説。

"在魔力奏效之後，在我從事科學發現之前，我要做的一件事情就是，成為一個田徑運動員。"

"過一個星期左右，我們就可以讓你參加拳擊比賽，"本·威瑟斯塔夫説。"你會贏得金腰帶，成為全英格蘭的拳擊冠軍。"

柯林的目光緊緊地盯着他。

"威瑟斯塔夫，"他説，"你這樣做是不尊重我們。你不能亂説話，因為你要保守秘密。不管魔力的威力有多大，我都不會成為冠軍。我要做個從事科學發現的科學家。"

"對不起——對不起，少爺，"本回答説，碰碰前額，做出敬禮的姿勢。"我應該知道，這不是開玩笑的事情，"但他的眼睛眨動着，心底裏不知有多高興呢。既然柯林這樣斥責他意味着這孩子有了力氣和精神，那麼他才不把這斥責放在心上呢。

第二十四章

"讓他們笑吧。"

秘密花園並不是狄肯在裏面工作的唯一地方。曠野上的小屋四周有一塊空地，被一面亂石牆包圍着。每天一大早和暮色降臨的黃昏，以及柯林和瑪麗看不見他的整天，狄肯都要在那裏幫他媽媽種植或照料馬鈴薯、捲心菜、甘藍、胡蘿蔔以及芳草。在他的"動物"的陪伴下，他在那裏播種奇蹟，而且好像樂此不疲。在挖土和播種的時候，他常常會吹口哨，或唱一點約克郡曠野上的歌曲，再不就跟煤煙、隊長或他叫來幫忙的弟弟妹妹們聊天。

"多虧了狄肯的園子，"索爾比太太說，"要不我們決不會像現在這樣舒服。他種甚麼都能活。他種的馬鈴薯和捲心菜比任何人種的都要大一倍，還有一種別人都沒有的香味。"

有空的時候，她就會出去跟他說話。晚飯後他還可以借着暮色做很長時間，這也是她清靜的時候。她可以坐在矮牆上，看着孩子工作，聽聽白天裏發生的事情。她喜愛這個時刻。這個園子裏不僅有蔬菜。狄肯還不時地買來一些一便士一包的花的種子，在荊豆叢，甚至捲心菜中間種下一些鮮豔芳香的花，他還圍上木犀草、石竹、圓三色堇和其他東西，他一年又一年地把這些東西的種子留下來，它們的根每年春天都會開花，到了一定的時候就會繁衍成花團錦簇。矮牆也是約克郡最美麗的景色之一，因為他給每一條牆縫裏都塞進了毛地黃的種子，等到它長到最茂盛的時候，連牆上的石頭都難以看見了。

"一個人要想讓它們長得紅紅火火，媽媽，"他會這麼説，"就要真心地跟它們交朋友。它們就像動物一樣。它們渴了，就給它們喝水，餓了，就給它們吃東西。它們要像我們一樣生活。要是它們死了，我就會覺得自己是個壞孩子，沒心沒肺地對待它們。"

就是在這些黃昏時刻，索爾比太太聽説了米塞爾斯威特莊園裏發生的一切。起初她只是聽説"柯林少爺"幻想着要跟瑪麗小姐一起到外面去，這樣對他會有好處。但不久兩個孩子就一致同意要讓狄肯的媽媽"參與這個秘密"。不知怎麼一回事，他們絲毫不懷疑她是"信得過"的人。

因此，在一個美麗靜謐的黃昏，狄肯把整個故事告訴了她：埋在地裏的鑰匙、那隻知更鳥、那片好像枯死的灰色霧以及瑪麗小姐打算永遠不説出去的秘密，狄肯的到來，怎樣聽説了這個秘密，柯林的懷疑，狄肯最後被引進那個隱秘王國的戲劇性故事，加上本·威瑟斯塔夫那張憤怒的臉在牆頭偷看，以及柯林少爺因為發脾氣而突然產生的力氣，直説得索爾比太太的臉色變了好幾回。

"哎呀！"她説。"這個小女孩來到莊園倒是件好事情。既改變了她自己，又挽救了柯林。柯林站了起來！而我們都以為他是個可憐的半癡半呆的孩子，身上沒有一根骨頭是直的。"

她問了很多問題，那雙藍眼睛裏佈滿了沉思。

"他們在莊園裏都做了些甚麼——把他變得這麼好，整天開開心心的，再也不發牢騷了？"她問道。

"他們也不知道是怎麼一回事，"狄肯答道。"他的臉每天都在變化。它變得飽滿了，不再那麼瘦削，蠟一樣的臉色也在消褪。但他還要發點牢騷，"狄肯調皮地咧嘴一笑。

"這到底是怎麼一回事呢？"索爾比太太問。

狄肯咯咯地笑起來。

"他這樣做是不讓別人產生懷疑。要是醫生發現他可以站起來了，就會寫信告訴克拉文先生。柯林少爺是要親口告訴他這個秘密。他要每天站着練習他的魔力，直到他爸爸回來，然後他就要大步走進爸爸的房間，讓他看到，他像別的孩子一樣腰桿筆直。但是他和瑪麗小姐認為現在最好還是不時地哼上數聲，不要讓別人產生懷疑。"

索爾比太太沒等他説完，就忍不住高興地輕聲笑了起來。

"嗨！"她説，"我敢肯定，那兩個孩子挺會自得其樂的。他們肯定會演一齣好戲，孩子們最喜歡演戲了。説説看，狄肯乖孩子，他們都做了些甚麼。"

狄肯停止了除草，蹲坐在腳跟上，跟她説了起來。他的眼睛快樂地眨動着。

"柯林少爺每次外出時都要被從樓上抱到樓下他的輪椅上，"

他解釋説。"他總是責罵男僕約翰,怪他抱他時不夠小心。在我們走到沒人看見的地方之前,他總是盡力裝出一副無能為力的樣子,從來不把頭抬起來。在被抱到輪椅上時,他總是大聲地哼哼。他和瑪麗小姐都為此樂個不停,當他哼哼並且責罵時,她就説,'可憐的柯林!'——但麻煩的是,有時候他們實在忍不住要笑出來。當我們安全地進入秘密花園之後,他們就拼命地笑,直到笑得喘不過氣來。要是附近有花匠的話,為了不讓他們聽見,他們不得不把臉埋在輪椅的墊裹。"

"他們笑得越厲害,對他們越有好處!"索爾比太太説,她自己也在笑個不停。"對健康的孩子來説,任何一天,笑聲總比藥丸好。那兩個孩子肯定會長胖的。"

"他們已經長胖了,"狄肯説。"他們總是餓得不知怎樣才能吃飽,吃飯的時候連話都不説。柯林少爺説要是他老是叫人拿吃的來,別人就不相信他是病人了。瑪麗小姐説他可以吃她的那份,但是他説,要是她餓着的話,就會瘦下去,他要他們一起胖起來。"

索爾比太太聽他講述這個難題,不由得發出由衷的歡笑,她穿着藍披風,笑得前仰後翻,狄肯跟着笑起來。

笑過之後,索爾比太太終於能夠説話了。她説,"孩子,我告訴你,我想到了一個幫助他們的辦法。明天早上你去那裏的時候,帶上一桶新鮮牛奶,我給他們烘點葡萄乾麵包甚麼的,就是你們兄弟姐妹喜歡吃的那些東西。沒有甚麼比新鮮牛奶加麵包更好吃的了。這樣他們在花園裏時就不會太餓,而回家後吃的好東西能塞塞牙縫就行了。"

"哦！媽媽！"狄肯欽佩地說，"你真了不起！甚麼都難不倒你。昨天他們才煩惱呢。他們不知道怎麼辦才能既吃飽肚子，又不叫人拿更多的食物來——他們覺得肚子裏空空的。"

"他們是兩個長得很快的孩子，健康很快就會回到他們兩個身上。這樣的孩子就像狼一樣，對他們來說，食物就像是肉和血，"索爾比太太說。然後她像狄肯那樣咧開大嘴笑起來。"哎！不過他們肯定玩得很開心，"她說。

她說得很對，這個令人寬慰的、了不起的媽媽——她說他們的"表演"會讓他們開心時，這話真是對得不能再對了。柯林和瑪麗都覺得這是最令他們激動的娛樂來源。保護自己，不讓自己受到懷疑的想法，最先是由那個困惑的保姆和克拉文醫生在不自覺中提議的。

"你的胃口大多了，柯林少爺，"保姆有一天這麼說。"你以前甚麼都不吃，很多東西都不合你的胃口。"

"現在也沒甚麼合我的胃口，"柯林答道，然後，看見保姆在注視他，他突然想起，也許他現在還不能顯得太好。"至少很多吃的東西不是經常對我的胃口。還是新鮮空氣對我有好處。"

"也許是這麼一回事，"保姆說，依然神秘兮兮地看着他。"但我必須和克拉文醫生談談這件事。"

"她肯定嚇倒你了！"她走後瑪麗說。"好像她覺得肯定有甚麼秘密要揭穿似的。"

"我不會讓她發現任何東西，"柯林說。"誰也別想發現任何東西。"

那天早上克拉文醫生來的時候，好像也很困惑。他問了很多問題，弄得柯林很不耐煩。

"你常在花園裏，"他説。"你去了哪裏？"

柯林擺出他最喜歡的對別人的意見不屑一顧的那種神態。

"我不會讓任何人知道我去了哪裏，"他答道。"我去了一個我喜歡去的地方。所有的人都接到避開的命令。我不想被人盯着我看。這你是知道的！"

"你好像整天都在外面，可我看不出這對你有甚麼壞處——我不這麼認為。保姆説你現在吃得比以前多得多了。"

"也許是的，"柯林説，突然產生了一個想法，"也許我的胃口不太正常。"

"我不這麼認為，因為你的食物好像很對你的胃口，"克拉文醫生説。"你的肉長得很快，面色也越來越好。"

"也許——也許我是浮腫、發燒呢，"柯林説，裝出一副悶悶不樂的樣子。"一個眼看就要活不下去的人看來總是兩樣的。"

克拉文醫生搖搖頭。他正握着柯林的手腕，拉起他的袖，感受他的脈搏。

"你沒發燒，"他沉思地説，"你長的肉是健康的。要是你能保持這樣，孩子，我們就不用再説會死了。你爸爸要是聽見你的這種令人驚喜的進步，準會高興的。"

"我不想別人告訴他！"柯林突然尖利地説。"要是我又變糟了，那只會讓他失望——我今天晚上就會變糟。我會發高燒。我覺得我現在就要發燒了。我不想別人給爸爸寫信——我不想——我不想！你讓我生氣，你知道這對我是不好的。我已經感到熱了。我討厭別人在信裏談論我，就像討厭別人盯着我看一樣！"

"噓！孩子，"克拉文醫生安慰他。"沒有你的同意，任何人都不會寫信談論你。你對事情太敏感了。你已經有了好的開頭，千萬不能再毀了它。"

他沒有再提給克拉文先生寫信的事情，當他見到保姆時，悄悄地警告她說，千萬不能向病人提起寫信的事。

"這個孩子康復得令人驚訝，"他說。"他康復的速度簡直不太正常。當然了，他現在是自覺自願地在做鍛煉，這一點我們以前是沒法讓他做的。不過，他很容易激動，千萬別說任何會讓他發怒的話。"

瑪麗和柯林非常驚慌，他們一起焦慮地交談着。他們的"表演"從現在就算開始了。

"我不得不發一次脾氣，"柯林後悔地說。"我不想發脾氣，我現在也沒甚麼傷心的事情非要發一場大脾氣不可。也許我根本就發不出脾氣。現在我已經沒有了那種像骨頭哽在喉嚨裏的感覺，我總是想好的事情，而不是可怕的事情。但是如果他們說要給我爸爸寫信的話，我就要給他們點顏色看看。"

他打定主意要少吃一點，但不幸的是，這個絕妙的想法根本不可能執行，每天早晨醒來，肚子都餓得咕咕叫，而沙發旁邊的桌上放着早餐，有自製的麵包和新鮮牛奶、雪白的蛋、草莓醬和濃縮忌廉。瑪麗總是跟他一起吃早餐，當他們發現自己坐在餐桌邊——特別是當滾燙的銀罩下飄出嗞嗞作響的火腿肉片的誘人香味時——他們就會垂涎欲滴、大眼瞪小眼地看着對方。

"我覺得今天早上我們要把它全吃掉，瑪麗，"柯林最後總是這樣說。"我們可以送回一點午餐和大部份晚餐。"

但是他們怎麼也無法送回任何東西，被吃得乾乾淨淨的盤拿回到餐具室之後，引起很多的議論。

　　"我真希望，"柯林會這麼說，"我真希望火腿肉片能再厚一點，而每人一張鬆餅對任何人來說都是不夠的。"

　　"對一個快要死的人來說足夠了，"瑪麗第一次聽見他這麼說的時候回答說，"但對一個要活下去的人來說是不夠的。有時候，當曠野上那些石楠和荊豆的香味從打開的窗撲進來的時候，我覺得自己能吃下三塊。"

　　那天早上，當柯林和瑪麗在花園裏玩了大約兩個小時之後，狄肯提着兩個桶從玫瑰叢後面走了過來。一個桶裏裝滿新鮮牛奶，上面漂着一層油脂；另一個桶裏裝着狄肯家做的葡萄乾麵包，裹在一塊乾淨的藍白相間的圍裙裏，麵包被裹得很小心，現在還是熱的，孩子們發出一片驚喜的歡呼聲。索爾比太太想得多周到啊！她是個多麼慈祥、多麼聰明的女人啊！這些麵包多好吃啊！牛奶多香啊！

　　"她身上就像狄肯身上一樣有魔力，"柯林說。"魔力讓她想到做事情——好事情——的辦法，她是個有魔力的人。對她說，狄肯，我們很感謝她——非常感謝。"

　　有時候，他愛用大人的口氣說話。他喜歡這樣。他非常喜歡大人的口吻，並且不斷改進。

　　"對她說，她非常慷慨，我們感激不盡。"

　　隨後他就忘記了他的架子，狼吞虎嚥地吃起麵包，並就着奶桶大口大口地喝起牛奶，就像一個做了大量的運動、呼吸着曠野上的空氣、要過兩三個小時才能吃早餐的小男孩一樣。

這是許多有趣的小插曲的開始。他們想到了這樣一個事實，即索爾比太太要養活十四個人，她沒有那麼多的食物每天都來滿足他們兩個人大得出奇的胃口。於是他們問她，能不能出錢買她的東西。

狄肯有了一個令人振奮的發現，在林苑裏面，花園外面，也就是瑪麗第一次看見狄肯給動物們吹笛的地方，有個很深的小坑，他們可以用石頭砌一個小爐灶，在上面烤馬鈴薯和蛋。烤蛋是一種無人知道的美味食物，而熱乎乎的烤馬鈴薯加上鹽和新鮮牛油，別說一般人吃起來會津津有味，就算給一個森林之王吃也很適合。你可以用錢去買馬鈴薯和蛋，想吃多少就吃多少，而不會覺得像是從十四個人的嘴裏搶東西吃。

每一個美麗的早晨，李樹下就有一個神秘的圈子在施魔力，那李樹在短暫的花期過後，濃密的綠樹葉好似一個華蓋。儀式過後，柯林就鍛煉走路，整天他都斷斷續續地練習使用他新發現的魔力。他的力氣每天都在增長，走路越來越穩，距離越來越長。他對魔力的信念也是一天比一天更堅定。他做了一個又一個實驗，感到自己越來越有力氣，而最好的辦法是狄肯教他的。

"昨天，"一天早上狄肯在缺席了一次晨練之後說，"我去斯威特看媽媽，在'藍牛旅館'附近我看見了鮑伯·霍沃斯。他是曠野上最健壯的人。他是摔跤冠軍，他比任何人跳得都高，擲鏈球擲得最遠。很多年來他都特地到蘇格蘭去參加運動會。我很小的時候他就認識了我，他很友好，我問了他一些問題。別人稱他是運動員，我想到了你，柯林少爺，我說，'你怎麼才讓你的肌肉這樣結實的，鮑伯？你有沒有做過甚麼特別的事情讓你變得這麼健壯？'他説，'哦，是的，孩子，我做過。以前有個劇團來斯威特表演，其中有個很健壯的人，他教我怎樣鍛煉我的手臂、腿以及身上的每一處肌肉。'我説，'一個嬌嫩的孩子也可以練得健壯嗎，鮑伯？'他哈哈大笑説，'你就是那個嬌嫩的孩子嗎？'我説，'不，但我認識一個小紳士，生了很久的病，剛剛開始康復，我希望我能知道一些鍛煉的技巧好告訴他。'我沒告訴他你的名字，他也沒問。他就像我説的一樣友好，站起來耐心地指點我，我模仿他的動作，直到把它們全都記在了心裏。"

柯林一直激動地聽着。

"你能教我嗎？"他叫道。"能嗎？"

"噢，當然能，"狄肯站起來答道。"但他説你一開始先要悠着點，小心別讓自己累着。兩次鍛煉之間要休息一下，做做深呼吸，別過量。"

"我會注意的，"柯林説。"教我吧！教我吧！狄肯，你是世界上最有魔力的男孩！"

狄肯站在草地上，慢慢地做起一套實用而簡單的肌肉練習。柯林睜大眼睛看着。他坐在地上時已經會做數個動作了。一會之後，他站了起來，兩條腿已經相當穩定。他悠悠地做了數個動作。瑪麗也做了起來。一直在看着他們表演的煤煙不安份了，牠從樹枝上飛下來，在周圍跳來跳去，直恨自己不能學他們一樣。

從那時起，這些練習就像魔力一樣成為每天的必修課。柯林和瑪麗每次的訓練量都在增加，結果胃口也就大開，要不是狄肯每天早上來的時候都把食物籃放在灌木叢後面，只怕他們會餓死。但是那個坑裏的小灶以及索爾比太太提供的食物盡夠他們吃的了，所以梅洛太太、保姆和克拉文醫生又一次摸不着頭腦了。要是你吃飽了烤蛋和馬鈴薯、泡沫豐富的牛奶、燕麥餅和麵包以及蜂蜜和濃縮忌廉，你當然就可以少吃點早餐，並對晚餐表示厭惡了。

"他們幾乎甚麼都沒吃，"保姆說。"要是不說服他們吸收點營養，他們會餓死的。可是你看他們的臉色多好啊。"

"看！"梅洛太太氣憤地叫道。"哎！我都被他們弄得困惑死了。他們真是一對小壞蛋。今天還吃得差點把外衣撐破，明天又對廚師做得最好的飯菜翹起鼻不理不睬。昨天那些可口的小雞肉和牛奶調味汁他們一口都沒吃——那個可憐的廚娘特意給他們做了布丁——又被送了回去。她簡直要哭了。她是擔心他們餓死的話，她要捱罵。"

克拉文醫生過來看柯林，看了很久，也很仔細。當保姆跟他說話，並指給他看那盤幾乎沒有碰過的早餐時（這是她特意留着給他看的），他的表情很憂慮，但是當他坐在柯林的沙發旁邊給他檢查時，更加憂慮了。他被叫到倫敦去公幹，將近兩個星期沒見到柯林了。小孩子一旦開始長力氣，那速度是很快的。蠟黃的膚色已經不見，取而代之的是暖玫瑰色；美麗的眼睛晶瑩透亮，眼睛下面以及臉頰和太陽穴上的凹陷也已長滿了肉。原先又黑又密的髮鬢開始變得柔軟溫暖，充滿活力，像是從額頭上健康地蹦出來似的。嘴唇也顯得豐滿，色澤自然。事實上，作為一個被證實有病的孩子，他裝得實在不像。克拉文醫生托着下巴，心事重重地打量着他。

"我很遺憾地聽說你不吃東西，"他說。"這可不行。你會失去你已經獲得的一切——你獲得的一切是驚人的。不久以前你的胃口還很好嘛。"

"我跟你說過,那種胃口是不正常的,"柯林答道。

瑪麗坐在旁邊的凳上,突然發出一種很怪的聲音,她的力氣用得實在太大,差點噎住。

"甚麼事?"克拉文醫生轉身看着她說。

瑪麗一臉的嚴肅。

"一種令人像是打噴嚏又像是咳嗽的東西,"她繃着臉惱怒地答道,"進入了我的喉嚨。"

"但是,"她事後對柯林說,"我克制不住自己。它一下子就衝了出來,因為我不由自主地想起了你吃的最後一個大馬鈴薯,還有你在咬那塊塗着果醬和濃縮忌廉的可口的厚麵包片時嘴唇動起來的樣子。"

"那些孩子有沒有可能偷吃東西呢?"克拉文醫生問梅洛太太。

"不可能,除了從地裏挖東西或從樹上摘東西吃,"梅洛太太答道。"他們整天都在外面,怎麼看都只有他們兩個。要是他們對端給他們的飯菜不滿意,想吃點別的,那只要開口就行。"

"哦,"克拉文醫生說,"假如真的只是因為沒有食物對他們的胃口,我們就沒有必要自尋煩惱。那男孩完全變了。"

"那女孩也是,"梅洛太太說。"自從開始長肉,那張苦瓜似的小臉不見了之後,她就變得漂亮了。她的頭髮長密了,看來健康了,膚色也亮了。原先她是個最悶悶不樂的、脾氣惡劣的小女孩,現在她常和柯林少爺在一起哈哈大笑,像一對小瘋子。也許他們就是因為笑才變胖的呢。"

　　"也許是的，"克拉文醫生說。"那就讓他們笑吧。"

第二十五章

簾

秘密花園的花越開越盛，每天早晨都有新的奇蹟出現。知更鳥的巢裏有了蛋，知更鳥的伴侶蹲在牠們上面孵蛋，用她羽毛豐滿的小胸脯和小心翼翼的翅膀給牠們保暖。開始時她很緊張，知更鳥則非常警惕。那些天裏，就連狄肯也不能接近那個花草繁茂的角落，而是等待着，直到他用某種神秘的符咒似乎讓那對小小的心靈明白，花園裏沒有甚麼不像牠們一樣——沒有甚麼不能理解牠們正在發生的奇妙事情——那些鳥蛋無與倫比的、溫柔的、非同尋常的、儡人魂魄的美麗和莊嚴。要是花園裏有個人不完全理解知更鳥或牠的伴侶的心思——要是有一個蛋被拿走或打碎，整個世界就會天崩地裂，世界末日就將來臨——要是有人連這點都感覺不到並相應行事，那麼就算是在金色的春天裏，也沒甚麼快樂可言了。但是他們都明白這一點，感覺到這一點，知更鳥和牠的伴侶也知道他們知道這一點。

開始的時候，知更鳥非常焦慮地看着瑪麗和柯林。出於某種神秘的原因，牠知道牠不用防着狄肯。牠那雙晶瑩透亮的黑眼睛第一次看見狄肯的時候，就知道他不是異類，而是個沒有喙和羽毛的知更鳥。他可以說知更鳥的話（這是一種非常清晰的語言，決不會跟別的任何語言混淆）。跟一隻知更鳥說知更鳥的話，就像跟一個法國人說法語一樣。狄肯總是跟知更鳥說知更鳥的話，所以他跟人說話時的那種怪腔調就一點也不礙事了。知更鳥覺得，他之所以用那種怪腔調跟人說話，是因為他們的智力不足以理解羽毛類動物的語言。他的動作也跟知更鳥一樣。牠們從來不用突然做出似乎有危險或威脅的動作令人受驚。每隻知更鳥都理解狄肯，所以他的出現絲毫不影響牠們。

　　但剛開始的時候，似乎有必要提防一下另外兩個人。首先，那個男孩沒有用自己的雙腳走進花園。他是坐在一個有輪子的東西上被推進來的，他的身上蓋着野生動物的皮。這本身就值得懷疑。其次，當他開始站起來並四處走動的時候，那動作看來怪怪的，其他人好像不得不幫助他。知更鳥總把自己藏在一個灌木叢裏，不安地看着這個場景，牠的頭來回晃動。牠以為那個人的慢動作表明他接下來就要跳躍了，就像貓一樣。當貓準備跳躍時，先會在地上慢慢地爬行。知更鳥跟牠的伴侶就這件事談論了好幾天，但此後牠決定不再談論這個話題，因為牠太害怕了，牠擔心這會讓牠們的蛋受到傷害。

　　當那男孩開始自己走路，甚至走得比較快的時候，知更鳥大大地放下心來。但在很長一段時間裏——或者對知更鳥來說是很長一段時間——他仍然讓知更鳥感到不安。他的行為跟其他人不一樣。他好像很喜歡走路，但走兩三步就要坐下來或躺下來，然後用很不協調的動作站起來再往前走。

有一天，知更鳥想起來，當初牠的爸爸媽媽教牠飛行的時候，牠也常做這樣的事情。牠只能飛短短數碼，就不得不休息一下。所以，牠想，這個男孩大概是在學飛行——或者不如說是在學走路。牠向牠的伴侶提起這件事，當牠告訴牠的伴侶，等牠們的蛋孵成小鳥，小鳥羽毛豐滿之後，或許會有良好的表現，她感到很寬慰，甚至在鳥巢邊看着那個男孩時顯示出濃厚的興趣並感受到極大的快樂——雖然牠的伴侶總覺得牠的蛋要比他聰明得多，學起東西來也要快得多。但後來牠很寬容地説，人總是比蛋要笨拙和遲鈍，而且大多數似乎永遠也學不會飛行。你從來不會在空中或樹梢上遇見他們。

過了一段日子，那個男孩開始像其他孩子一樣四處走動，但是這三個孩子不時會做一些奇怪的事情。他們會坐在樹下，揮揮手、踢踢腿，再不就搖搖頭，那樣子既不是走路，奔跑，也不是坐下。他們每天都要重複兩三次這樣的動作，知更鳥實在無法向牠的伴侶解釋他們在做甚麼或想做甚麼。牠只能説，牠們的蛋將來決不會這樣拍動雙翼；但是既然那個經常説知更鳥話的男孩也這麼做，那些鳥就可以肯定，這些行為是無害的。當然了，知更鳥和牠的伴侶都從沒聽説過摔跤冠軍鮑伯・霍沃斯，以及他為了讓肌肉突起而進行的鍛煉。知更鳥跟人不一樣；牠們一生出來就要鍛煉肌肉，所以牠們用一種自然的方式發展。要是不得不為每天的食物四處飛行，你的肌肉自然就不會萎縮。

當那男孩像其他孩子一樣四處走動、奔跑、挖土、鋤草的時候，角落裏的鳥巢呈現出一片安寧祥和的氣氛。擔心鳥蛋受到傷害已經成了過去的事情。知道自己的蛋像鎖在銀行保險櫃裏一樣安全，並且能夠看見那麼多新奇有趣的事情發生，這倒讓孵蛋成為一項最有趣味的職業。雨天裏，那些孩子不到花園裏來，鳥媽媽甚至會覺得有點乏味。

但就算是下雨天，瑪麗和柯林也不感到乏味。一天早晨，大雨不停地往下倒，柯林開始感到有點煩躁，這種天氣到外面去可不太安全，所以他只好被困在沙發上，這時瑪麗突然靈機一動。

"現在我是個真正的男孩了，"柯林說，"我的腳、手臂和全身都是魔力，一刻也不能停。它們每時每刻都要做事。你知道嗎，瑪麗，我一早就醒來的時候，鳥剛剛開始歡叫——所有的東西好像都剛剛開始歡叫——甚至那些我們其實聽不見聲音的東西，比方說樹啊甚麼的——我感到我一定要從牀上跳起來，也要歡叫。要是我這麼做了，你覺得會發生甚麼事呢！"

瑪麗咯咯咯地癡笑起來。

"保姆會跑過來，梅洛太太會跑過來，她們肯定會認為你發瘋了，會去叫醫生來，"她說。

柯林也咯咯地笑起來。他可以預見她們會是怎樣一副神態——他的發作會令她們感到多麼害怕，看見他站得筆直時，她們又會多麼驚訝。

"我希望我爸爸能回來，"他說。"我想親口告訴他。我老在想這件事——但是再也不能這樣下去了。我不想再這樣一動不動地躺着裝病，而且我現在的樣子跟以前也大不一樣了。希望今天不要下雨。"

就在這時瑪麗有了靈感。

"柯林，"她神秘兮兮地說，"你知道這棟屋裏有多少個房間嗎？"

"我猜有一千間吧，"他答道。

"大概有一百間，從來沒人進去，"瑪麗說。"有一個下雨天，我闖進了其中很多間。誰也不知道，雖然差點被梅洛太太撞見。我回來時迷了路，就在你的走廊盡頭停了下來。那是我第二次聽見你哭。"

柯林在他的沙發上跳了起來。

"一百個從沒人進去的房間，"他說。"聽起來簡直就像是個秘密花園嘛。也許我們可以去看看。你用輪椅推着我，誰也不會知道我們去哪裏。"

"我正是這樣想的，"瑪麗說。"沒人敢跟着我們。那裏有好多長廊，你可以在那裏奔跑。我們可以鍛煉。那裏有一個印度小房間，裏面放滿牙雕的大象。那裏有各種各樣的房間。"

"按鈴，"柯林說。

保姆應聲而來，柯林下了命令。

"把我的輪椅推來，"他說。"瑪麗小姐和我要去看看屋裏沒有使用過的地方。約翰可以一直把我推到畫廊那裏，因為路上要爬數段梯。然後他要離開，不要管我們，直到我再派人去叫他。"

那天早上，雨天不再顯得那麼可怕。當男傭人將輪椅推進畫廊，照着吩咐讓他們兩個留在那裏之後，柯林和瑪麗欣喜地互相注視着。一等瑪麗確信約翰回到了樓下他自己的地方，柯林就跳出了輪椅。

"我要從畫廊的一頭奔到另一頭，"他說，"然後我就要跳躍，然後我們一起像鮑伯·霍沃斯那樣練習。"

他們做了這一切事情，還做了別的事情。他們看肖像，發現那個相貌平庸的女孩穿着綠色的纖錦裙子，手上捧着鸚鵡。

柯林說，"這些全都是我的親戚。他們生活在很久以前。那個手上拿着鸚鵡的人，我相信，是我的一個曾、曾、曾、曾姨婆。她長得挺像你的，瑪麗——不是現在的你，而是你剛來這裏時的你。現在你胖多了，也漂亮多了。"

"你也是，"瑪麗說，兩人哈哈大笑起來。

他們走進印度房間，玩弄起象牙雕的大象。他們發現了用玫瑰色纖錦裝飾的閨房，椅墊上的老鼠洞，但是老鼠已經長大，悄悄走了，所以洞是空的。他們看見了更多的房間，有了比瑪麗第一次朝聖時更多的發現。他們發現了新的走廊和轉角，一段段的樓梯，他們喜歡的老畫像以及他們不知道有甚麼用處的怪東西。這是一個充滿奇妙趣味的早晨，他們在這間屋裏遊覽，雖然屋裏還住着其他人，但覺得像是與他們相隔千里，這種感覺真令人陶醉。

"我很開心我們來了，"柯林說。"我從來不知道我住在這麼一個又大又怪的舊屋裏。我喜歡它。我們每個下雨天都要四處逛逛。我們每次都要發現新的角落和新的東西。"

那天早晨他們發現的東西中還包括非常好的胃口，回到柯林的房間後，不可能再把送來的午飯動也不動地就打發走了。

保姆把盤拿下樓去，啪地放在廚房的備餐桌上，廚娘盧米斯太太看見了被舔得乾乾淨淨的碟和盤。

"你看！"她説。"這真是一間謎一樣的大屋，而那兩個孩子就是最大的謎。"

"要是他們每天都保持這樣，"年輕健壯的男傭人約翰説，"就難怪他今天要比一個月前重一倍了。我早晚要辭職，免得一不小心傷了筋骨。"

那天下午瑪麗注意到柯林的房間裏發生了一件新的事情。她前天就注意到了，但是甚麼也沒説，因為她想或許會有變化。今天她也甚麼都沒説，而是坐在那裏，死死地盯着壁爐上方的那張肖像。因為簾拉到了一邊，所以她能看見。這就是她注意到的變化。

"我知道你要我告訴你甚麼，"在她盯着那張肖像看了數分鐘後柯林説。"每次你想讓我告訴你甚麼的時候，我都能看出來。你在想，這簾為甚麼被拉開。我想讓它一直保持那個樣子。"

"為甚麼呢？"瑪麗問。

"因為一看到她笑呵呵的模樣，我就不會生氣了。兩天前的那個晚上，我醒來時，只見月光很明亮，我感到魔力好像充滿了整個房間，讓一切都顯得那麼輝煌，我再也不能靜靜地躺着了。我爬起來，朝窗外看去。房間裏很亮，簾上有一縷月光，我不知不覺地走上前去，拉動繩。她俯視着我，好像在朝我笑，因為很高興我站在那裏。我好喜歡看着她。我想看着她永遠都那樣笑呵呵的。我想她可能也是個有魔力的人。"

"你現在很像她，"瑪麗説，"有時候我想你也許是她鬼魂的化身。"

這個想法似乎深深打動了柯林。他仔細想了想，然後慢慢地回答她。

"假如我是她的鬼魂——我爸爸就應該喜歡我。"

"你想他喜歡你嗎？"瑪麗問道。

"我以前總是因為他不喜歡我而不開心。要是他變得喜歡我了，我想我會告訴他關於魔力的事情。這會讓他高興起來。"

第二十六章

"是媽媽！"

他們對魔力的信念是持久不變的。有時候，做過晨練之後，柯林會給他們作魔力講座。

"我喜歡這樣做，"他解釋説，"因為等我長大並開始做偉大的科學發現之後，我總是要作演講的，所以，現在只當是練習。現在我只能作些短的演講，因為我還很小，再説，本·威瑟斯塔夫會以為他是在教堂裏，所以會睡着的。"

"關於演講，最大的好處就是，"本説，"一個人可以站起來，説他想説的任何話，而不需要任何人回答。有時候，我自己也不反對做點演講。"

但是當柯林在樹下滔滔不絕地演講時，本把那雙眼睛死死地盯着柯林的臉。他用挑剔的目光仔細打量他。令他感興趣的並不全是演講本身，而是那雙看起來一天比一天更直更有力的腳，那個高高昂起的孩子的頭，那個原先尖細的下巴和凹陷的雙頰，而今已經變得圓滾滾的、肉嘟嘟的，還有那雙眼睛裏的光，他記得從另一雙眼睛裏看到過這樣的光。有時候，當柯林感覺到本那認真的目光表明他已被深深地打動時，他真想知道他此刻在想些甚麼。有一次，在他看起來已經入迷的時候，柯林問起他來。

"你在想甚麼呢，本·威瑟斯塔夫？"他問道。

"我在想，"本答道，"我曾向你保證過，這個星期你會再重三四磅。我在看你的腿肚子和你的肩膀。我真想把你放到秤上去稱稱。"

"這是魔力——是索爾比太太的麵包和牛奶甚麼的功勞，"柯林説。"你知道，科學實驗成功了。"

那天早上狄肯來晚了，沒聽到演講。他來的時候，跑得那張有趣的臉上紅通通的，看來比平時更有光彩。因為雨後有很多草要鋤掉，所以他們馬上就做了起來。每當下過一場暖和的大雨後，他們總有很多工作要做。潮濕的空氣對花是有益的，對雜草同樣如此，它們的細枝嫩葉不斷地往外長，必須在它們的根扎牢之前把它們拔掉。這些天來，柯林拔草的技術變得像其他人一樣熟練，而且他還能邊做邊演講。

"你，你親自做事的時候，魔力是最有效的，"今天早上他説。"你可以從你的骨頭和肌肉裏感覺到它。我將要閱讀關於骨頭和肌肉的書，但是我要寫一本關於魔力的書。我現在就在作準備。我要不斷地發現東西。"

就在説過這段話後不久，他把小鏟放下，用雙腳站立，沉默了數分鐘。他們知道他在想他的演講詞，他常常都這樣做。每當他放下小鏟並筆直地站立時，瑪麗和狄肯就會覺得是一種突如其來的強烈的念頭讓他這樣做的。他把身體挺直。直得不能再直，興奮地伸出雙臂。臉上容光煥發，奇怪的眼睛瞪得滾圓，透着欣喜。突然之間，他徹底明白了一件事情。

"瑪麗！狄肯！"他叫道。"看着我！"

他們停止除草，看着他。

"你們還記得第一次帶我來這裏的那個早晨嗎？"他問道。

狄肯緊緊看着他。作為一個馴獸師，他比大多數人能看出更多東西，而有很多東西他從來沒説過。現在從這個孩子身上，他就看到了一些這樣的東西。

"是啊，我們記得，"他答道。

瑪麗也緊緊看着，但是甚麼也沒説。

"就在這一刻，"柯林説，"我突然想了起來——當我看着自己的手握着鏟在挖土時——當我用雙腳站立，看看這是不是真的時。這是真的！我的病好了——我好了！"

"是啊，你是好了！"狄肯説。

"我好了！我好了！"柯林又説，他滿臉通紅。

他以前就在某種程度上知道這一點，他曾經希望過這一點，感覺到這一點，思考過這一點，但就在那個時刻，某種東西衝擊了他的全身——某種如癡如醉的信念和認識，——這種東西如此強烈，使他不由自主地叫了起來。

"我會永遠永遠活下去！"他莊嚴地叫道。"我會發現成千上萬的東西。我會發現人、動物和一切生長的東西——跟狄肯一樣——我永遠不會停止施展魔力。我好了！我好了！我想要——我想要大聲呼喊——用呼喊表示我的謝意，表示我的快樂！"

本·威瑟斯塔夫一直在一個玫瑰叢旁邊做事，這時他轉過身來朝柯林瞥了一眼。

"你不妨唱一唱《榮耀頌》，"他用乾巴巴的咕嚕聲建議說。他沒有對《榮耀頌》發表評論，在提這個建議時也沒顯示出特別的崇敬。

但是柯林喜歡刨根究底，何況他對《榮耀頌》一無所知。

"那是甚麼歌？"他問道。

"我敢肯定，狄肯可以唱給你聽，"本·威瑟斯塔夫答道。

狄肯帶着他那馴獸師的微笑作了回答。

"就是人們在教堂裏唱的歌，"他說。"媽媽說她相信雲雀們早上醒來時唱的就是這首歌。"

"如果她是這麼說的，那一定是一首好歌，"柯林答道。"我從沒進過教堂。我總是病得太重。唱吧，狄肯。我想聽。"

狄肯在這件事上很單純、很真摯。他比柯林更了解柯林。他以一種非常自然的本能了解他，而他並不知道這就是了解。他摘下帽，依然微笑着打量四周。

"你必須摘下帽，"他對柯林說，"還有你，本——你知道，你必須站起來。"

柯林摘下帽，太陽照着他的頭髮，暖烘烘的，他專注地看着狄肯。本·威瑟斯塔夫從地上站起來，也摘下帽，那張老臉上流露出帶點怨憤的神色，好像他弄不懂他為甚麼要做這件奇怪的事情。

狄肯站在樹木和玫瑰叢之間，用一種簡單而平淡的方式和男孩子的有力嗓音唱了起來：

"讚美真神慈愛最深，

　　讚美真神恩及萬人，

　　讚美真神聲達天庭，

　　讚美聖父、聖子、聖靈。

　　阿門。"

　　他唱完後，本・威瑟斯塔夫固執地緊閉嘴巴站在那裏，但是眼睛裏有一種不安的神色，凝視着柯林。柯林一臉的沉思和讚賞。

　　"這是一首很好聽的歌，"他說。"我喜歡。也許它表示的正是我想要高呼感謝魔力時所表示的一樣。"他停下來，困惑地思考着。"也許這本來就是兩件同樣的事情。我們怎麼可能知道每樣東西的確切名稱呢？再唱一遍，狄肯。我們也來試試，瑪麗。我也想唱，這是我的歌。開頭怎麼唱？'讚美真神慈愛最深'？"

　　他們又唱了一遍，瑪麗和柯林盡可能悦耳地提高了嗓門，狄肯的聲音也越來越響，並且非常動聽——唱到第二句時，本・威瑟斯塔夫刺耳地清了清嗓子，到了第三句時，他也唱了起來，那聲音非常高亢，簡直像是在發怒一樣，當唱到"阿門"的拖音結束時，瑪麗注意到當初他發現柯林不是瘸子時的那一幕又出現了——他的下巴扭動着；他凝視着，眨巴着眼睛，飽經風霜的臉頰濕潤了。

　　"我以前從沒想到《榮耀頌》有甚麼意義，"他嘶啞地說，"但是這次我要改變看法了。我可以說這個星期你的體重會增加五磅，柯林少爺——增加五磅就因為這首歌！"

　　花園對面有個東西吸引了柯林的目光，他露出吃驚的表情。

　　"誰往這邊來了？"他急促地說。"他是誰？"

常春藤牆上的門被輕輕地推開，一個女人走了進來。她在他們唱到最後一句時就已經進來，靜靜地站在那裏看着他們。常春藤在她身後，陽光透過樹葉，使她那件藍色的披風花花搭搭，她穿過青草地時，那張美麗清醒的臉上始終帶着笑容，就像柯林的書中的一幅色彩淡雅的插圖。她有一雙很有感染力的眼睛，似乎能把一切都看進去——所有的一切，甚至包括本·威瑟斯塔夫和那些"動物"以及每一朵正在盛開的花。儘管她那麼出人意料地出現，但誰也不覺得她是個不速之客。狄肯的眼睛像燈泡一樣發亮。

"是我媽媽——是她！"他叫着朝對面跑去。

柯林也開始朝她走去，瑪麗跟他一起過去。他們兩個都覺得自己的心跳加速了。

"是媽媽！"當他們在半路上相遇時，狄肯又説。"我知道你們想見她，就告訴了她門在哪裏。"

柯林非常害羞地伸出手去，但是他的眼睛死死地盯着她的臉。

"我在生病的時候都想見你，"他説，"你和狄肯和這個秘密花園。我以前從沒想過要見任何人或任何東西。"

看見他高高抬起的頭，她也暗暗吃驚。她的臉紅了，嘴角抽搐，眼睛好像蒙上了一層霧氣。

"嗨！親愛的孩子！"她聲音顫抖地脫口叫道。"嗨！親愛的孩子！"好像她不知道自己要説這句話。她沒有説"柯林少爺"，而是突如其來的"親愛的孩子"。要是她在狄肯的臉上看到令她感動的神色，她也會用同樣的方式對他説同樣的話。柯林喜歡她這麼説。

"你吃驚是因為我身體很健康,對嗎?"他問道。

她把手攔在他的肩上,微微一笑,擠走了眼睛裏的霧氣。

"哎,是啊!"她説;"但是你太像你媽媽了,讓我的心怦怦地直跳。"

"你是不是覺得,"柯林有點窘迫地説,"這樣會讓我爸爸喜歡我呢?"

"是啊,這是肯定的,親愛的孩子,"她答道,輕輕地拍了一下他的肩膀。"他一定會回來——他一定會回來。"

"蘇珊·索爾比,"本·威瑟斯塔夫走近她身邊説。"你能看看這個孩子的腳嗎?兩個月前,它們穿在襪裏就像鼓槌一樣——我聽別人説,那兩條腿又是膝內翻又是膝外翻。現在你看!"

蘇珊·索爾比欣慰地笑了。

"要不了多久它們就會變成男孩子的有力的雙腳,"她説。"讓他在花園裏玩耍,工作,敞開肚子吃東西,喝很多很多香甜的牛奶,它們就會成為約克郡裏的一雙難得一見的好腳,感謝上帝。"

她把雙手攔在瑪麗小姐的肩上,像媽媽似的仔細打量她。

"還有你!"她説。"你長得像我們家伊麗莎白·艾倫一樣健壯了。我敢説你也像你的媽媽。我們家瑪莎告訴我説,梅洛太太聽人説她是個漂亮的女人。等你長大後會像一朵紅玫瑰,我的小女孩,祝福你。"

她沒有提到那天瑪莎"休假"回家向她説起那個相貌平庸、臉色蠟黃的女孩時,她説,不管梅洛太太聽到些甚麼,她都不信。"一個漂亮的女人不可能是這樣一個令人討厭的小女孩的媽媽,"她固執地補充説。

瑪麗沒有時間去注意她臉色的變化。她只知道她看來"不一樣了"，好像有了很多的頭髮，頭髮長得很快。但是想起過去看見夫人時的愉悦，她很高興聽説自己將來會長得像她。

　　蘇珊・索爾比跟他們一起在花園裏繞了一圈，聽他們講述了關於這個花園的整個故事，在他們的指點下看了每一個活過來的灌木叢和每一棵樹。柯林和瑪麗走在她的兩邊。兩人都不時地抬頭看她那張令人舒服的玫瑰似的臉，為她帶給他們的那種愉快的感覺而暗暗稱奇——這是一種溫暖而令人振奮的感覺。她好像理解他們，就像狄肯理解他的"動物"一樣。她向花俯下身去，像談論自己的孩子一樣談論它們。煙煤跟着她，朝她叫了一兩聲，飛到她的肩上，就像那是狄肯的肩膀一樣。當孩子們告訴她關於知更鳥以及牠的小寶寶們的第一次飛行時，她的喉嚨裏發出充滿母愛的那種輕輕的愉快的笑聲。

　　"我看牠們學飛行就像孩子們學走路一樣，但是假如我的孩子長的是翅膀而不是腳的話，那我可要擔心了，"她説。

　　這個住在曠野小屋裏的女人，舉動如此優雅，真是個神奇的女人，孩子們最後跟她提起了魔力。

　　"你相信魔力嗎？"柯林向她解釋了印度苦行僧的情況後問道。"我希望你相信。"

　　"我的確相信，孩子，"她答道。"我從來不知道它叫甚麼名字，但是叫甚麼名字又有甚麼關係呢？我肯定在法國和在德國它們的叫法都不一樣。讓種子發芽的東西和讓你變成一個健康孩子的陽光都是同樣的東西，是個好東西。它不像我們這些可憐的傻子，以為令人叫得出名字來有多麼大不了似的。大的好東西不會停下來憂慮，上帝保佑你。它不停地創造出上百萬個世界——像我們這樣的世界。你千萬不要放棄對大的好東西的信念，要知道這個世界上到處都是好東西——你想怎麼稱呼它就怎麼稱呼它。剛才我進花園的時候你們正在為它歌唱。"

"我好高興啊，"柯林說，瞪大漂亮怪異的眼睛看着她。"我突然感覺完全變了一個人——你知道我的手臂和腳多有力啊——我多麼能夠挖土、站立啊——我跳躍，我要向任何願意聽我叫喊的東西叫喊。"

"在你們唱《榮耀頌》的時候，魔力在聽着呢。重要的是讓自己開心。哎！孩子，孩子——對開心製造者來說，名字又算得了甚麼，"她輕輕地又拍了一下他的肩膀。

這天早晨她又帶來了一個籃，裏面照樣裝着那些好吃的東西，當大家都感到餓了的時候，狄肯把籃從藏着的地方拿了出來，索爾比太太跟大家一起坐在樹下，看他們狼吞虎嚥地吃着，他們的好胃口讓她笑口大開，滿心歡喜。她有一肚子的奇聞逸事，讓他們哈哈大笑。她用一口約克話給他們說故事，並教他們新的約克話。當他們告訴她說，他們越來越難讓柯林繼續裝病的時候，她笑得前仰後翻，好像剎不了車似的。

"你看，我們在一起的時候就總是忍不住要哈哈大笑，"柯林解釋說。"這種聲音根本不像在生病。我們想要克制，但它總是蹦出來，而且聽起來更不像生病。"

"有一件事老是闖進我的心裏，"瑪麗說，"每次突然想到它，我就控制不住自己。我老是在想，柯林的臉或許會變得像滿月一樣。現在還不像，但是他每天都會胖一點——或許到了某個早晨它看來就像了——到那時我們該怎麼辦呢！"

"保佑我們大家，我知道你們還要好好裝下去，"蘇珊・索爾比說。"但是你們裝不了多久了。克拉文老爺就要回來了。"

"你覺得他會回來嗎？"柯林問道。"為甚麼？"

蘇珊・索爾比輕輕地笑了笑。

"要是在你們親口告訴他之前，他自己先看出來的話，我看你們準會傷心死的，"她說。"為了這個計劃，你們肯定數個晚上沒睡好覺。"

"其他任何人告訴他我都受不了，"柯林說。"我每天都在想不同的方法，現在我想我要跑進他的房間裏去。"

"這會讓他大吃一驚的，"蘇珊・索爾比說。"我倒想看看他的臉，孩子。我真想看！他一定會回來——一定。"

他們談論的事情之一就是到小屋去探望她。他們作了周全的計劃。他們要駕車上曠野，在屋外的石楠叢裏吃午餐。他們要看看所有十二個孩子和狄肯的花園，直到累了才回家。

蘇珊・索爾比終於站了起來，回屋去見梅洛太太。柯林也該坐輪椅回去了。但是在坐進輪椅前，他站在蘇珊・索爾比跟前，眼睛緊盯着她，流露出敬畏的神情；他突然抓住她的藍色披風的皺褶，抓得緊緊的。

"你正是——正是我想要的，"他說。"我希望你不僅是狄肯的媽媽，也是我的媽媽！"

蘇珊・索爾比突然俯下身去，用溫暖的雙臂摟住他，讓他緊貼自己藍色披風裏面的胸脯——好像他是狄肯的弟弟似的。她的眼睛很快就濕潤了。

"哎！親愛的孩子！"她說。"我相信，你的親媽媽就在這個花園裏。她不會離開這裏。你的爸爸一定會回來——一定！"

第二十七章

在花園裏

自從有了世界以來，每個世紀都有奇妙的東西被發現。上個世紀被發現的令人驚訝的東西比以前任何一個世紀都多。在這個新世紀裏，許多更加令人驚嘆的東西將曝光。起初人們不願相信一件奇怪的事情可以做到，然後他們希望能夠做到，接着他們知道這可以做到——再接着它就被做到，而全世界都在疑惑，為甚麼數個世紀之前未能做到。上個世紀人們的一個新發現就是，思想——只不過是些思想——像電池一樣有力量——好的力量好似陽光，壞的力量壞如毒藥。讓一個壞的思想進入你的腦，就像讓一個猩紅熱病毒進入你的身體一樣危險。要是它進入後你還讓它留在那裏，那麼，只要你活着，它就不會讓你安寧。

只要瑪麗小姐的腦裏裝滿與她不喜歡的東西和別人尖酸刻薄的意見格格不入的彆扭念頭，對任何事情都不高興、不感興趣，她就是個病懨懨、尖酸刻薄的黃臉傭人。不過，命運對她很仁慈，儘管她一點都沒意識到。它們開始把她往對她有益的方向推。當她的腦裏慢慢地裝滿知更鳥、曠野小屋和裏面的孩子，裝滿性格乖戾的老花匠和普通的約克郡小傭人，裝滿春天和一天一天恢復生機的秘密花園，並且裝滿一個曠野的男孩和他的"動物"時，就容不下與他人格格不入的彆扭念頭，她的肝臟和消化器官就不會受到影響，她也就不會臉色蠟黃、渾身乏力了。

只要柯林把自己關在房間裏，只想着他的恐懼、虛弱和對那些看着他的人的憎恨，老是想着駝背和早死，他就是個歇斯底里的半瘋的小疑心病患者，對陽光、春天甚麼的一無所知，也不知道他可以康復，只要試着去做，就可以用雙腳站立。當新的思想開始把舊的醜陋的思想擠出去之後，他就開始恢復了生氣，他的血液健康地在血管裏流淌，力氣像潮水一樣湧入他的身體。他的科學實驗非常實用，簡單，沒有任何怪異的地方。任何人，當那種令人討厭或令人萎靡不振的思想鑽進腦裏的時候，一定要有意識地用積極進取的思想來把它擠走，這樣一來，更令人驚喜的事情就會發生在他身上。兩種東西不能同時在一個地方並存。

"在你種了玫瑰的地方，我的孩子，薊就不能生長。"

隨着秘密花園再生，兩個孩子也一天天健康起來，有一個人在千里之外的挪威峽灣風景名勝和瑞士的幽谷高山間漫遊，這個人十多年來心裏一直藏着黯淡的和令人心碎的念頭。他沒有勇氣；他從來沒有試過用別的念頭來替代這些黯淡的念頭。他徘徊在藍色的湖泊邊，滿腦都是這樣的念頭；他躺在高山上，四周盛開着深藍色的歐龍膽，空氣中瀰漫着花香，而他滿腦還是那些念頭。當年正當他享受着幸福的時候，一種可怕的悲哀落到了他的身上，他的心裏從此裝滿了黑暗，他固執地拒絕任何光亮穿透它。他忘記並摒棄了自己的家和責任。當他四處漫遊的時候，黑暗深深地籠罩着他，他的出現對別人來說就像是個罪孽，因為他好像用憂鬱毒化了周圍的空氣。大多數陌生人認為他要麼是個半瘋子，要麼就是靈魂裏有見不得人的罪孽。他身型很高大，有一張長臉、塌肩膀，他登記住旅店常用的名字是：“阿奇博爾德·克拉文，英格蘭約克郡，米塞爾斯威特莊園。”

自從在書房裏見過瑪麗小姐，告訴她可以“有一小塊地”之後，他就出遠門去了。他到過歐洲最美麗的地方，雖然在任何一個地方逗留的時間都沒三四天。他選擇的是最僻靜的地方。他曾在日出時爬上雲霧繚繞的山頂，俯瞰其他的山峰；陽光撫摩着群山，令人覺得世界像是一個新生兒。

但是這陽光似乎從沒照射到他，直到有一天，他意識到，這十年來，發生了一件奇怪的事情。當時他在奧地利蒂羅爾的一個奇妙的山谷裏，他在這美麗的景致中獨自而行，這樣的美景足以讓任何人走出心靈的陰影。他走了很長的路，卻沒有走出心靈的陰影。但最後他感到累了，就倒在一條小溪旁的青苔上休息。這是一條清澈的小溪，溪水愉快靜謐地流淌在狹窄的河牀裏，在芬芳潮濕的滿目青綠中穿行。有時候溪水汩汩地流過卵石，會發出一種聲響，很像輕輕的笑聲。他看見鳥飛來，喝數口溪水，然後拍拍翅膀又飛走。這條小溪好像是個活生生的東西，但是它那細小的噪音讓靜謐更加深邃。這個山谷非常非常靜謐。

阿奇博爾德·克拉文坐在那裏凝視着晶瑩清澈的涓涓細流，慢慢地覺得自己的心靈和身體都變得安寧了，像山谷本身一樣安寧。他懷疑自己是否會睡着，但是沒有。他坐在那裏，凝視着陽光照耀下的溪水，他的眼睛開始看見生長在小溪旁邊的東西。只有一片可愛的藍色勿忘我草緊挨着小溪，草葉被溪水打濕，看着這些，他想起多年前他曾看到過同樣的東西。他眷戀地想着，它是多麼可愛，它那成百上千朵花藍得多麼令人心醉。他不知道，正是這個簡單的想法慢慢地充斥着他的腦——不斷地充斥，直到別的想法被輕輕地推開。好像有一股清澈香甜的泉水從一個死水池裏升起，它不斷地往上升，最後將原先烏黑的池水排開。但是當然了，他自己並沒這麼想。他只知道山谷似乎越來越靜謐，他坐在那裏凝視着那片明亮柔和的藍色。他不知道在那裏坐了多久，也不知道自己出了甚麼事，但是最後他像甦醒過來一樣，慢慢地站起來，站在青苔地上，長長地、深深地、輕輕地吸了一口氣，好像對自己都感到陌生了。某種東西悄然地在他的心裏得到釋放。

"怎麼一回事？"他幾乎是用耳語說道，用手摸摸額頭。"我簡直感到——我原來活着！"

我對未被發現的事物的神奇性所知不多，無法解釋發生在他身上的事情。其他任何人一時也無法解釋。他本人一點都沒理解——但時隔數個月之後，當他回到米塞爾斯威特時，他還記着這個奇怪的時刻，當時他偶然地發現，就在這一天，柯林走進秘密花園時叫道：

"我會永遠活下去，永遠永遠活下去！"

那天晚上的其餘時間裏，他保持着這份獨特的寧靜，踏踏實實地睡了一覺，這對他來說實在是件新鮮事；但是這份寧靜沒有保持多久。他不知道這是可以保持的。到了第二天晚上，他又向那些暗淡的念頭打開了大門，它們就大舉進攻，殺了個回馬槍。他離開了山谷，繼續漫遊。但是令他感到奇怪的是，有那麼數分鐘——有時候是半個小時——莫名其妙的，他的背又會突然挺直起來，他知道自己是個活人而不是死人。慢慢地——慢慢地——他不知道出於甚麼原因——他和花園一起"活了過來"。

隨着金色的夏天變成了深金色的秋天，他去了科莫湖。他在那裏發現了做夢的可愛。那數天他不是在晶瑩湛藍的湖上度過，就是走進樹木蔥蘢、層林盡染的山丘，不停地跋涉，直到身疲力乏，這樣就能睡一個好覺。但是到這時他的睡眠已經不錯，他知道，他的夢對他來説已不再恐怖。

"也許，"他想道，"我的身體正在強壯起來。"

他的身體的確是在強壯起來，但是——因為在他的思想轉變過程中的難得的寧靜時刻——他的心靈也在慢慢地變得強壯起來。他開始想念起米塞爾斯威特，並在考慮要不要回家去。他不時地隱約想到他的兒子，並且問自己，假如他回去之後，站在雕花的四柱牀前，看着兒子睡着時那刀刻斧鑿般瘦削、慘白的臉，以及緊閉的雙眼四周那些黑得驚人的睫毛，自己會有甚麼樣的感覺。這個念頭讓他不寒而慄。

有一天，他走得很遠，回來時一輪圓月高懸在空中，萬物猶如紫色的陰影，或閃着銀光。湖面、岸上以及樹林裏一片寂靜，令人稱奇，他沒有回到住的別墅裏面，而是走到湖邊一個涼台上，坐在一張椅裏，吸吮着夜晚沁人心脾的芬芳。他感覺到那種奇妙的寧靜侵入他的心底，越來越深沉，最後他睡着了。

他不知道自己是甚麼時候睡着，甚麼時候開始做夢的；他的夢非常逼真，他沒有感到自己是在做夢。事後他回想起，當時他認為自己是多麼清醒和警覺。他認為當時他坐在那裏，吸吮着夜玫瑰的芬芳，傾聽湖水在腳邊的拍打聲，他聽到了一把聲音在叫喚。那聲音甜美、清晰、愉快、遙遠。聽起來好像很遠，但是他覺得非常清晰，就像是在自己的身邊。

"阿奇！阿奇！阿奇！"那聲音叫道，接着又叫了起來，比剛才還要甜美和清晰，"阿奇！阿奇！"

他感到自己跳了起來，甚至都沒覺得驚訝。這是一個如此真實的聲音，他能聽見似乎也非常自然。

"莉莉婭絲！莉莉婭絲！"他答道。"莉莉婭絲！你在哪裏？"

"在花園裏，"那聲音好像出自一支金笛。"在花園裏！"

接着夢結束，但是他沒有醒來。那個可愛的晚上他一直呼呼地睡得很甜。當他最後醒來時，已經是陽光明媚的早晨，一個傭人正站在旁邊呆呆地看着他。他是個意大利傭人，像別墅裏所有的傭人一樣，對於他的這位外國主人可能做出的任何怪事都毫無疑問地全盤接受。沒人知道他甚麼時候出去或回來，他想在哪裏睡覺，會不會在花園裏漫遊或整晚躺在湖裏的小船上。傭人端着個托盤，裏面放着一些信件，他默默地等候着，直到克拉文先生伸手去拿。等他走後，克拉文先生拿着信坐了一會，看着湖面。他還保持着那份奇怪的寧靜，而且還有新的發展——成為一種輕鬆，好像那件殘酷的事情並沒像他認為的那樣發生——好像某件事發生了變化。他還記得那個夢——那個逼真的——逼真的夢。

"在花園裏！"他說，暗自疑惑。"在花園裏！但是那門是鎖着的，鑰匙被深深地埋掉了。"

數分鐘後他瞥了一眼手裏的信，看見最上面那封是用英文寫的，寄自約克郡。一看就知道出自一個普通女人的手筆，但是並非出自認識的人。他把信打開，根本沒去想寫信的人到底是誰，但是開頭數句話就一下子吸引了他的注意力。

親愛的先生：

我是蘇珊·索爾比，曾經在曠野上冒昧地跟您說過話。我說的是關於瑪麗小姐的事情。我要再一次冒昧地跟您說話。對不起，先生，假如我是您的話，我就會回家。我想您會高興回家的——請恕我直言，先生——假如您的太太還在的話，她會請您回家的。

您溫順的僕人
蘇珊·索爾比

克拉文先生把這封信唸了兩遍，然後才塞回信封。他還在想着那個夢。

"我要回米塞爾斯威特，"他說。"我馬上就要回去。"

他穿過花園回到別墅，命令匹契爾為他回英格蘭做好準備。

沒過數天，他回到了約克郡，在坐火車的長途旅行中，他發現自己在想兒子，這是過去整整十年來從沒有過的事情。在那些年裏，他總是巴不得自己能忘記他。現在，雖然他並不刻意要想他，對他的記憶卻總是浮現在腦海裏。他想起在那些陰暗的日子裏，他老是像個瘋子似的咆哮，因為兒子活着，媽媽卻死了。他拒絕看他，當他最後不得不去看他時，他已經成了一個殘疾的小孩，所有的人都肯定他活不了數天。但是讓那些照料他的人驚訝的是，日子一天天過去，他卻依然活着，然後所有的人又相信他會成為一個畸形的瘸子。

他不是有意要做一個壞爸爸，但是他一點都沒有做爸爸的感覺。他給兒子請來醫生、保姆，讓他應有盡有，但是他連想都不敢想這個兒子，把自己深深地埋在自己的悲哀裏。在他外出一年後的第一次回家時，這個一臉苦相的小子沒精打采、漫不經心地抬起頭來，那雙四周有黑睫毛的灰色大眼睛像極了那雙令他崇敬的愉快眼睛，但是長在他的臉上卻是那麼令人可怕，他不忍看見它們，就轉過身去，臉色像死人一樣慘白。從那以後，他很少再見他，除非在他睡覺的時候，他只知道他是個畸形的病人，脾氣惡劣、歇斯底里，像個瘋子。只有一切都依着他，才能避免他發瘋到傷害自己的程度。

所有這些都是令人消沉的回憶，但是隨着火車載着他穿過高山和金色的平原，這個"活過來"的人開始用一種新的方式思考，他思考了很久，很平穩、很深沉。

"也許這十年來我全錯了，"他對自己說。"十年是段很長的時間。現在也許做甚麼都太遲了——實在太遲了。我一年到頭都在想些甚麼！"

當然了，這是一種錯誤的魔力——一開頭就說"太遲了"。連柯林都可以這樣對他說。但是他對魔力一無所知——不管是壞的還是好的。關於魔力他還要學起來。他在想，蘇珊·索爾比之所以敢給他寫信，或許是因為這個母愛強烈的女人意識到那男孩的情況越來越糟糕——已經病入膏肓。要不是那種佔據了他的心靈的奇怪的寧靜鎮住了他，他或許會比任何時候都更痛苦。但是這種寧靜帶來了勇氣和希望。他沒有再去想那些糟糕的事情，而是發現自己正在努力想那些令人振奮的事情。

"難道她看出我能夠幫助他，控制他的情緒？"他想道。"我要在去米塞爾斯威特的路上去看看她。"

但是在穿越曠野的路上，他在小屋門口停下馬車時，七八個正在附近玩耍的孩子聚過來，友好而禮貌地向他行了七八個屈膝禮，並告訴他，他們的媽媽一早去曠野的另一頭，幫一個剛剛生孩子的女人。""我們家狄肯，"他們主動說，"去了莊園，在那裏的花園之一工作，他每週去數天。"

克拉文先生看着這些結實的小身體和紅撲撲的圓臉蛋，每張臉都咧嘴而笑，但又各不相同，他意識到他們是一群健康的、逗人喜愛的孩子。他向他們報以微笑，從衣袋裏掏出一塊金幣，給了年齡最大的"我們家的"伊麗莎白·艾倫。

"你們把它分成八份，每人可以得到半個克朗，"他說。

孩子們有的咧嘴而笑，有的咯咯地笑，並紛紛向他行屈膝禮，他駕着車離開了那裏，孩子們在他身後歡呼雀躍，蹦跳着。

馬車順利穿過神奇的曠野。他好像有了一種回家的感覺，他能夠肯定以後再也不會有這樣的感覺——當馬車離那座他家族住了六百年的老房子越來越近時，他感覺到了老家的土地、天空和遠處盛開的紫色花朵的美麗以及一顆熱乎乎的心，為甚麼會有這樣的感覺呢？他上次是怎樣駕車離開那裏的，那時候不敢想它那些緊閉的房間和躺在四柱牀上的孩子。他有沒有可能發現孩子有了一丁點好轉，他看見孩子時不再害怕？那個夢多麼逼真啊——那個回應他的聲音多麼奇妙、多麼清晰啊，"在花園裏——在花園裏！"

"我要想辦法找到鑰匙，"他説。"我要想辦法打開門。我一定要——雖然我不知道為甚麼。"

他到達莊園後，以通常的儀式迎接他的傭人們注意到他的氣色好多了，他沒有回到他通常所住的那些與眾人隔絕、只有匹契爾伺候他的房間，而是進了書房，派人去叫梅洛太太。她激動、好奇、不安地趕來。

"柯林少爺怎麼樣，梅洛太太？"

"哦，先生，"梅洛太太答道，"他——他有點不一樣了。"

"更糟了？"他問道。

梅洛太太真的臉紅了。

"哦，你知道，先生，"她想要解釋，"克拉文醫生，保姆和我都弄不懂他是怎麼一回事。"

"為甚麼呢？"

"説實話，先生，柯林少爺可能會好轉，也可能會更糟。先生，他的胃口令人難以理解——他的舉動——"

"他是不是變得更——更怪了？"她的主人問道，焦慮地皺緊了眉頭。

"是的，先生。跟以前相比，他變得很怪。他通常甚麼都不吃，然後突然又狂吃一頓——然後又突然停下來，像以往一樣把飯菜全都送回去。也許你絕對不會知道，先生，他從來不讓人把他帶到屋外去。我們每次想要説服他讓我們用輪椅把他推出去，最後總要弄得他像片葉似的抖個不停。他會歇斯底里，克拉文醫生只好説，他不敢強迫他，因為負不了那個責任。哦，先生，就在他要死要活地鬧了一次之後不久，毫無先兆地，他突然又吵着每天都要由瑪麗小姐陪他出去，讓蘇珊·索爾比的兒子狄肯為他推輪椅。他對瑪麗和狄肯着了迷，狄肯把他那些溫順的動物帶來，而且，信不信由你，先生，他每次外出總要從早留到晚。”

“他的氣色怎麼樣？”這是他的另一個問題。

“要是他正常吃飯，先生，你可以認為他是在長肉——但是我們擔心他可能是虛腫。有時候，當他單獨跟瑪麗小姐在一起時，他會發出奇怪的笑聲。以前他可是從來都不笑的。要是你同意的話，克拉文醫生馬上就來看你。他這輩子都未曾這麼困惑。”

“柯林少爺這時候在哪裏？”克拉文先生問。

“在花園裏，先生。他老是在花園裏——雖然任何人都不准靠近那裏，怕他們看着他。”

克拉文先生幾乎沒聽見她最後的話。

“在花園裏，”他説，把梅洛太太打發走之後，他站在那裏一遍又一遍地重複着。“在花園裏！”

他費了很大力氣才使自己站在原地未動，等他覺得自己平靜下來之後，就走出了房間。他像瑪麗那樣，穿過了灌木叢裏的門，在月桂樹和噴水池之間往前走。在秋日艷麗的花壇的環繞中，噴水池不時噴着水。他走過草坪，轉進常春藤旁的長路。他走得不快，而是慢慢的，眼睛盯着小路。他感覺自己像是被拉回到了他摒棄已久的路上，他不知道是為甚麼。快要接近那裏時，他的腳步更慢了。儘管厚厚的常春藤覆蓋着，他還是知道那扇門在哪裏

——但是他不知道那把被埋掉的鑰匙到底在哪裏。

於是他停下來，靜靜地站着，打量着四周，但是幾乎就在他剛剛停下之後，他吃了一驚，屏息傾聽——問自己是不是在發夢。

常春藤厚厚地覆蓋着門，鑰匙被埋在灌木下面，在那孤寂的十年裏，沒人從那門口經過——然而花園裏面卻有聲音。那是奔跑的腳步聲，好像是在樹底下追逐，還有壓低了的嗓門聲——驚呼和歡叫。聽起來真像是孩子的笑聲，是孩子們難以抑制的笑聲，儘管他們盡力不想被人聽見，但時不時地——根據他們興奮的程度——會迸發出來。天哪，他這是做的甚麼夢啊——他到底聽到了甚麼？他是不是失去了理智，以為自己聽到了人類的耳朵不配聽到的聲音？當初那個遙遠而清晰的聲音難道就是指的這把聲音？

接着，難忘的時刻來臨了，這是個難以控制的時刻，那些聲音忘了克制自己。腳步越跑越快——接近了花園的門——傳來一個孩子快速有力的呼吸聲，一陣狂野而無法抑制的歡叫聲——牆上的門砰地打開，那層常春藤往後面蕩去，一個男孩從裏面全速穿了出來，沒有看見外面的人，幾乎一頭撞在了他的懷裏。

克拉文先生及時伸出手去，孩子才沒因為甚麼都不看，撞到了他身上而跌倒。當他把孩子推開一點要看着他，為他會在這裏而感到驚愕時，他實實在在地倒抽了一口涼氣。

這是個高大英俊的男孩。身上煥發着生氣，由於奔跑而讓臉上充滿血色。他把濃密的頭髮從額前掠開，抬起一雙好奇的灰色眼睛——一雙充滿着男孩子的笑意、四周有黑色睫毛的眼睛。就是這雙眼睛讓克拉文先生透不過氣來。

"誰——甚麼？誰！"他結結巴巴地說。

這是出乎柯林意料的——這也是在他計劃之外的。他從沒想到過這樣的見面。然而用能夠贏得賽跑比賽的速度衝出去與他見面，這也許更好。他把身體挺得筆直。瑪麗一直在隨他一起跑，她相信他是要讓自己看來比以往任何時候都高。

"爸爸，"他說，"我是柯林。你不敢相信吧。我自己都很難相信。我是柯林。"

像梅洛太太一樣，他不明白爸爸是甚麼意思。可是他爸爸卻匆匆地說：

"在花園裏！在花園裏！"

"是的，"柯林急忙接着說。"是花園做的——還有瑪麗和狄肯跟他的動物——以及魔力。誰也不知道。我們一直保守着秘密，就是要等你回來告訴你。我很好，我跑得比瑪麗快。我要做個運動員。"

他完全像個健康的孩子——他的臉上煥發着紅光，他的話連珠炮似的滾出來——這種難以置信的欣喜讓克拉文先生的心都顫抖了。

柯林伸出手去，扶住爸爸的手臂。

"你不高興嗎，爸爸？"他最後說。"你不高興嗎？我要永永遠遠活下去！"

克拉文先生把雙手搭在孩子的肩上，讓他站穩。他知道他一時間都不敢說話。

"帶我到花園裏去，孩子，"他終於開口說。"把這一切都告訴我。"

於是他們帶他進去。

花園裏好大一片秋日的金色、紫色、紫羅蘭色和耀眼的猩紅色，到處都是一簇簇緊挨在一起的晚開的百合——白色的或白色與深紅色相間的百合。他清楚地記得當年第一棵樹被種下的時候，到了每年的這個季節，它們就會綻放出最後的光輝。晚玫瑰攀爬、懸掛、叢生，陽光讓黃色的樹木色澤更加濃，令人覺得是站在一座金色拱頂的神殿裏。新來的人默默地站着，就像孩子們當初剛走進那片灰色中時一樣。他朝四處打量。

"我原來以為它會死的，"他説。

"瑪麗也是這麼以為的，"柯林説。"但它活過來了。"

然後他們坐在樹下——只有柯林除外，他要站着講述他的故事。

柯林用他那種孩子的方式把故事不停地倒出來，阿奇博爾德·克拉文心想，這是他聽到過的最奇妙的故事。秘密、魔力和野生動物，不可思議的半夜相會——春天的來臨——受傷的自尊引起的怒火令小酋長站立起來，當面呵斥老威瑟斯塔夫。奇怪的伴侶，裝假行動，小心守護的最大秘密。克拉文先生邊聽邊哈哈大笑，直到熱淚盈眶，有時候，雖然沒有笑，眼眶也湧起了眼淚。運動員、演講家、科學發現者，這些都集中在一個笑吟吟的、可愛的、健康的孩子身上。

"現在，"故事最後他宣佈説，"再也沒有必要保守這個秘密了。我敢説，他們要是看見我的話，準會嚇得發瘋——但我再也不坐輪椅了。我要跟你一起走回去，爸爸——走回屋裏去。"

本·威瑟斯塔夫是個盡忠職守的人，他的工作難得讓他離開花園，但是這次他藉口給廚房送蔬菜，梅洛太太邀他到傭人房去喝杯啤酒，所以他正好在場——如他希望的那樣——目睹了米塞爾斯威特莊園這一代發生的最有戲劇性的一幕。

一扇開向院子的窗同樣可以瞥見草坪。梅洛太太知道本・威瑟斯塔夫從花園裏來，心想他或許看見了他的主人，甚至碰巧看見了他與柯林少爺見面。

"你見到他們兩個了嗎，威瑟斯塔夫？"她問道。

本把啤酒杯從嘴邊拿開，用手背擦擦嘴唇。"噢，見到了，"他意味深長地說。

"兩個都見到了？"梅洛太太又問。

"都見到了，"本・威瑟斯塔夫答道。"謝謝你，太太，我還想來一杯。"

"他們在一起嗎？"梅洛太太說，激動中匆忙給他把酒杯斟滿。

"在一起，太太，"本・威瑟斯塔夫一口把第二杯酒喝掉一半。

"柯林少爺當時在哪裏？他看來怎麼樣？他們互相說了些甚麼？"

"我沒聽見，"本說，"我只是站在梯上朝着牆頭裏面看。但我可以告訴你，外面發生的一些事情你們在屋裏的人是不知道的。你們要發現的事情馬上就會發現。"

不到兩分鐘，他嚥下最後一口酒，並朝着窗莊重地揮舞着杯，從窗朝外看去，透過一片灌木，可以看見一小塊草坪。

"看那裏，"他說，"要是你好奇的話。看是誰穿過草地走過來了。"

梅洛太太一看，立刻舉起雙手，輕輕發出一聲尖叫，每個聽見這聲尖叫的男傭人和女傭人都衝到窗跟前朝外看，他們的眼珠差點要從眼眶裏掉出來。

　　米塞爾斯威特莊園的主人穿過草坪走過來，他的樣子是許多人從沒見過的。他的身邊是高高地昂着頭，眼睛裏充滿笑意，像約克郡的任何一個男孩子一樣健康、平穩地走着路的──柯林少爺。

　　　　　　　完